9. 1.

~ ESCAPE WITH ~

JENNY COLGAN

Jenny Colgan is the author of numerous bestselling novels, including *The Little Shop of Happy Ever After* and *Summer at Little Beach Street Bakery*, which are also published by Sphere. *Meet Me at the Cupcake Café* won the 2012 Melissa Nathan Award for Comedy Romance and was a *Sunday Times* top ten bestseller, as was *Welcome to Rosie Hopkins' Sweetshop of Dreams*, which won the RNA Romantic Novel of the Year Award 2013. Jenny lives in Scotland. She can be found on Twitter at @jennycolgan and on Instagram at @jennycolganbooks.

JENNY COLGAN

The Christmas Bookshop

SPHERE

SPHERE

First published in Great Britain in 2021 by Sphere
This paperback edition published by Sphere in 2022

3 5 7 9 10 8 6 4 2

Copyright © 2021 by Jenny Colgan

The moral right of the author has been asserted.

A CIP catalogue record for this book
is available from the British Library.

ISBN 978-0-7515-8422-6

Typeset in Caslon by M Rules
Printed and bound in Great Britain by
Clays Ltd, Elcograf, S.p.A.

Papers used by Sphere are from well-managed forests
and other responsible sources.

Sphere
An imprint of
Little, Brown Book Group
Carmelite House
50 Victoria Embankment
London EC4Y 0DZ

An Hachette UK Company
www.hachette.co.uk

www.littlebrown.co.uk

*To vaccine scientists, because, man, you saved us,
you brilliant, brilliant people. And the vaccinators too.
Thank you.*

'And oh, how sweet and pleasant it is to the truly spiritual eye to see several sorts of believers ...'

Quaker saying

Edinburgh

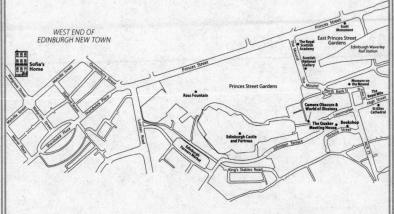

WEST END OF EDINBURGH NEW TOWN

Sofia's Home

Princes Street

Ross Fountain

Princes Street Gardens

Edinburgh Castle and Fortress

Scott Monument

East Princes Street Gardens

Edinburgh Waverley Rail Station

The Royal Scottish Academy

Scottish National Gallery

Museum on the Mound

Camera Obscura & World of Illusions

The Quaker Meeting House

Bookshop

St Giles Cathedral

Johnston Terrace

King's Stables Road

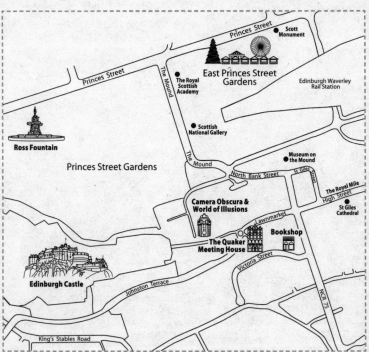

Princes Street

Scott Monument

Princes Street

The Mound

The Royal Scottish Academy

East Princes Street Gardens

Edinburgh Waverley Rail Station

Ross Fountain

Princes Street Gardens

Scottish National Gallery

The Mound

Museum on the Mound

North Bank Street

St Giles Street

The Royal Mile

High Street

Camera Obscura & World of Illusions

Lawnmarket

Bookshop

St Giles Cathedral

The Quaker Meeting House

Edinburgh Castle

Victoria Street

Johnston Terrace

NCR 75

King's Stables Road

Prologue

'But it's *August*!' said Carmen into the phone, putting down her book. 'August! It's almost sunny outside! I have sandals on! Ice cream vans patrol the land! I put sunblock on last week and almost needed it! How can I possibly get my head round what you're asking me?'

'I'm just saying,' her mother's soft voice came again, and Carmen sighed. They had the same tussle every year. 'It's just useful to know early, that's all. And of course Sofia . . .'

Carmen screwed up her face.

'Yes, she's popping out yet another sprog and overpopulating the world, blah blah blah, I know.'

'Carmen June Hogan. Be nice.'

'Come on, Mum. She's already got three. She's just being greedy. Anyway, I don't know what I might be doing at Christmas. I might be going away.'

'Who with?' Her mother sounded sceptical.

'I could meet someone between now and Christmas! And they could whisk me off to Barbados! Or LA!'

She could almost feel her mother smiling down the phone.

'So you're not coming home for Christmas because you'll be in LA.'

'I could be in LA.'

Carmen couldn't, she thought to herself, be the only person in the world who was both nearly thirty and who still turned into a stroppy teenager when confronted by her mother.

But it *was* only August. She just didn't want to think about the summer being over, or about another Christmas – sleeping in her old bedroom, which was full of ridiculous junk now that didn't belong to her: sewing machines and what-not. Reading all her old paperbacks on the shelf: the Follyfoot series, C. S. Lewis and *The Dark Is Rising*, seeing as it was Christmas.

Then it would be everyone making the hugest fuss of Sofia's noisy, bratty children and giving them so much stuff (which always had to be wooden and expensive) that they could barely tear the wrapping from one gift before they dived to the next.

With every passing year too, Sofia's gifts to the rest of the family got more and more lavish and expensive, making it more and more apparent who in the family was doing well – and who was still sleeping under her Spice Girls duvet and handing out discounted gifts from the shop she worked in.

Her mother ploughed on regardless.

'I mean, Sofia wants to show off the new house and won't want to travel ... I thought we'd all go to hers and I'd cook ... ?'

Sofia worked as a lawyer in Edinburgh, a hundred miles away from their dying industrial west-coast Scottish town, and was doing very nicely, thank you, with her handsome international lawyer husband and babies and Range Rovers, blah

blah blah. Carmen still worked in the department store she'd had a Saturday job in when she'd been at school. The store was shabby, and getting worse all the time. Literally nobody in the family ever brought this up, which made it worse.

As if sensing her thoughts, her mother's voice lowered. 'And how is Dounston's doing?'

Carmen understood, although she hated the tone.

'Well ... we'll be doing better by Christmas,' she said, and both of them desperately tried to believe it.

Carmen hung up without satisfactorily settling the question of Christmas – or rather, by refusing to commit, knowing full well her mother would go ahead and count her in anyway. And of course nothing else *would* come up and she would indeed be back there again, either at Sofia's new place – whatever it was like; for sure she would have the worst bed in the place – or under her old Spice Girls duvet on the twenty-fourth which made her feel lower than ever. She looked around the staff room.

Her best mate at the shop, Idra, had just come in and was eyeing up the floral mug which belonged to their supervisor, Mrs Marsh, that was never to be used on pain of death.

'Don't even think about it,' said Carmen.

'I am going to *pee* in it,' said Idra, incandescent. 'She's putting me back on fricking hats.'

Carmen groaned sympathetically. Hats were next to the door, the idea being that when you tumbled in out of the freezing cold from the rapidly emptying high street, the very first thing you would need was a hat.

3

Unfortunately for whoever was manning the till there, it meant gushing blasts of freezing air mixed with the petrifying ferocity of the air heater above making you sweat whatever you wore. Although these days, that door was opening less and less.

Carmen measured her days in books. She kept a paperback under the desk for quiet periods, when she had remade as many window displays as one could usefully do in one day, and dusted, polished, straightened and checked the samples. When she had first started working at Dounston's, they had always been so busy, and she'd kept her reading for the bus and lunch-time. Now, she could get through a novel every three days, and it kept getting faster. It was very, very worrying.

'She hates me the most,' said Carmen on the topic of Mrs Marsh, as she looked at the next week's rota. She had the most inconvenient possible combination of shifts – an early followed by a late followed by an early and a late on the same day – that somehow still left her short of full-time hours and therefore enough money to get through the month without squeezing everything and everyone and having absolutely no fun at all and taking home all her mum's leftovers on a Sunday night.

'She told me I looked like a tramp,' said Idra.

'What were you wearing?'

'I literally took off my cardigan. For, like, ten seconds.'

Carmen laughed, then fell silent as the person they were talking about glided noiselessly into the room. Decades of working on shop floors had taught Mrs Marsh to glide despite being a heavy woman, constantly on the lookout for miscreants, pilferers, time-wasters, malingerers and basically anyone who looked like they might actually be enjoying themselves shopping in a department store.

She was silent on her tiny feet – always clad in smart black

4

court shoes, however much they must pinch and contribute to the varicose veins spreading up her legs year on year like slow-growing ivy, just visible through the American Tan tights. Her midriff was solid and her large bosom was trussed into something from the Larger Madam section of the lingerie department which rather made her look like she only had one very wide breast which could also function as a shelf in a shop emergency.

Carmen and Idra agreed that Mrs Marsh's idea of perfection was a completely empty, perfectly clean and tidy store with absolutely no customers in it messing things up, letting their kids knock over glassware, dirtying the polished floors with their muddy shoes or disrespecting lift etiquette (Mrs Marsh remembered the days when the lifts had an attendant, and mentioned it often). Having nobody in the shop was just about the way Mrs Marsh liked it.

The awful thing was, as they had seen for the last few years, it looked like Mrs Marsh was finally getting her wish.

One by one, the other shops had moved away from their unimportant regional satellite town – BHS, Next, Marks and Spencer, WH Smith – and had all fallen like ninepins.

Dounston's, where generations of local brides had made their gift lists and chosen material for their wedding dresses, where mothers-to-be had bought their prams, where families had bought their china and sofas, their material, their white goods; Dounston's, which stocked school uniforms in August and fancy perfume at Christmas, and toys in the wonderful toy department that made children gasp every year as they came to queue for a photo and a small present from Santa in the grotto: Dounston's was widely predicted to be next on the high street casualty list.

It didn't seem possible to Carmen that something so solid, so intertwined with the life of the town and its citizens – with its stained-glass window depicting the ships the men built up the road on the Clyde, and its coffee shop selling French cakes and scones and disdaining the very concept of something as fancy as a latte – would ever shut its doors. It was the heart of the town.

But the town seemed finished. Dead. The high street was nothing but charity shops and mobility scooter hire shops and money-sending places and the occasional doomed enterprise by the council to sell local paintings or craft.

People wanted the town centre to work but not quite enough to pay for parking when the out-of-town retail park didn't charge you *and* was all shiny and had a Wagamama's.

People wanted the town centre to work, but not really enough to pay £17.99 for a bone china mug with a shepherdess on it when they could get something perfectly serviceable for under a fiver on Amazon. Or to traipse all the way into town for three metres of pink ribbon only to find there wasn't any pink ribbon in stock and they'd have to have burgundy even though they wanted pink and actually it would have taken two minutes to click on the precise shade of pink they wanted on that online store and get it delivered the following day.

Carmen got it. She was as guilty as anyone else at convenience shopping, even when she was in town every day. Plus who used napkin rings these days? How many scatter cushions could any sane human even buy in their lives? And bridesmaids didn't make their own dresses any more, from the big swathes of purple and pink satin (sateen if you were economising). They ordered them from overseas, from where they arrived, late and ill-fitting, and they would have to come in, red-faced, asking for

6

advice on adjustments and hemming and buying the odd spare zip at the very last minute.

But only three days after the Christmas chat, it happened. They were summoned. Idra loudly protesting that she should have poisoned that bloody mug, as Mrs Marsh, who must have been past retirement age – Idra reckoned she was ninety – was taking a certain pleasure in telling them they were all getting their jotters or, in her smart poshed-up elocution voice, 'sadly being made redundant'.

She looked around through her wide glasses with the pastel rims and patted her short, sprayed-down hair.

'*Some* of you, I'm sure, will get excellent references and find another job without any trouble at all,' she said, looking pointedly at her favourite: bloody suck-up Lavinia McGraw.

At this, Carmen and Idra glanced at each other and Carmen got that awful feeling when you know you're going to laugh at something incredibly inappropriate.

Because it was awful. It was devastating. A disaster. And she had seen it coming. Everyone had seen it coming. And she had done absolutely nothing about it. No point blaming Mrs Marsh now.

Chapter One

Sofia d'Angelo née Hogan eyed up the wreath on the shiny black front door, narrowed her eyes and adjusted it again, then stood back to admire the perfectly symmetrical effect.

She couldn't help it. As soon as she'd seen the house, she'd just known. She'd fallen in love with it right away. Okay, so the basement was a little damp. It was an old house. Love was love. Nobody was perfect. Although today, number 10 Walgrave Street looked as close to it as made no odds.

It sat in a terrace of varying heights, but was one of the smallest houses: four storeys in total if you included the basement. It was made of heavy grey sandstone, built in Georgian times at the very far end of the 'new' town of Edinburgh (which wasn't new at all) and it had five perfect twelve-paned windows, like a child's drawing, a filigree balcony outside the upper-storey windows, a line of smart stone steps leading up to the front door and black wrought-iron railings, currently sporting entwined thick vines of holly, lit up with tasteful warm yellow lights and sporting red tartan bows. It was like a house on a Christmas card, warm light seeping out from inside onto the freezing pavement, and a huge Christmas tree with the same warm lights and red bows on each floor.

Two Christmas trees! Sofia hugged herself with glee. They had come a long way from the little council flat on the other side of Scotland.

She'd booked her Christmas Ocado spot in September, and the children's thoughtful wooden gifts had been already wrapped in different paper, obviously, because Santa understood things like that; she had her party dress, although she generally swung by parties very quickly, and even more so being so pregnant. The nativity plays and carol concerts were locked into the calendar as well as the overpriced trip to the Christmas fair, and the special Lyceum Christmas show. And it was still only early November. They had only just taken down the tasteful Halloween wreath, the pumpkins, and the orange and black decorations around the doorway, and put away the large basket of sugar-free sweets.

Everything was going well in Sofia's world.

Except for Carmen of course.

Their mother had been on the phone. Her sister been three months living back at home without a hint of a job and every week her mother called and begged Sofia to find her something. These calls were getting increasingly desperate. There was no work where they lived, particularly not in retail. And Carmen was not helping herself.

When Sofia had been small, she had liked to line up her dollies and give them all small lectures about how to behave at tea. Everything in her world was ordered and neat. Then, when she was four, her mother had become pregnant. This period had involved a lot of people telling Sofia what a wonderful big sister she was going to make, which had pleased the small Sofia very much, particularly since she'd received a haul of excellent presents and the baby had got lots of boring old clothes. It had been a magnificent time. Being – even for one very small – a clever sort of person, she had immediately prepared to welcome Carmen as her friend, ally and camp follower in all things.

Unfortunately, the screwed-up red-faced screeching monster who appeared did not look remotely like the little sisters in Sofia's baby books. As she grew older, she didn't like dollies or playing tea or wearing new dresses. She didn't like dresses at all, in fact, and she hated school, which Sofia loved. From the moment she arrived, Carmen was a ball of fussiness. She fussed at going out or coming in or going upstairs or having a bath or getting her hair washed or going to swimming lessons or visiting people's houses, at getting in her buggy or getting out of her buggy.

Sofia could never make Carmen see why it was a lot easier just to be nice to people whether you felt like it or not, and let them smile and pat your head and give you a biscuit. It seemed very straightforward to Sofia. Carmen, on the other hand . . . she was a small pin poking into Sofia's momentary self-satisfaction. She frowned. Apparently, things were . . . looking tricky again, their mother had said. Which explained why Carmen had been a no-show at her daughter's birthday party and hadn't even bothered to send a card, or call, or let her know remotely what was going on with her life.

Well, there was no point in getting upset about it now. Sofia smoothed her brow; no Botox till after the baby. She'd worry about Carmen when she absolutely had to.

She took a last happy look at her darling house, and clip-clopped past the icy puddles on her way to work.

Chapter Two

'Sofia doesn't want me.'

'Nonsense,' lied her mother. 'You're just at different life stages, that's all. And you hurt her feelings about Pippa's party.'

'I hurt *her* feelings?' Carmen said. 'I'm sitting here, with nothing going on, living back in my bedroom having lost my job, but somehow precious Sofia's feelings are all that matter.'

'Darling. Please. Not even a birthday card?'

'She doesn't want me there. I'm just her weird little sister that everyone has to feel sorry for, still working in a shop which I'm not even doing any more, still not married and not all smug and pregnant like all her other snooty city friends.' Carmen couldn't help colouring.

'It's all right to be jealous,' said her mother, who then took on a haunted look as she realised she'd said exactly the wrong thing.

'I'm not jealous! Who wants to be neck deep in kids, stuck?' said Carmen. 'I just figured she'd not be that fussed. I figured she'd have better things to worry about than whether I came to a stupid birthday party.'

'Than her only sister being there for her own family?'

'But it's not my family!' said Carmen. 'And it's something every *ten minutes*. A wedding. A christening. A birthday party. A baby shower. Please give up all your precious free time, Carmen, and come and tell me how brilliant I am and how brilliant my life is and how brilliant my children are and by the way I want you to bring me really expensive gifts that you can't really afford and we'll go to restaurants you can't really afford and I'll make a massive deal out of paying for my poor sister. Ooh! Look at my gigantic house!'

Carmen folded her arms crossly. She really missed her little rented flat, but she was so skint. She had had some shifts here and there in coffee shops and bars, but the entire town was looking for work. Her parents being so lovely about everything wasn't helping. She knew what they were itching to say – that she had been a clever girl, she could easily have gone to college, got a trade or an occupation. But she had been headstrong, hadn't listened.

So she directed her frustration elsewhere.

'Plus you guys are up there worshipping at the grandchildren altar every five minutes, dropping everything. It's like this entire family is just the Sofia fan club. And the moment I didn't want to be in it, it was, like, *bad Carmen*.'

Her mother didn't say anything. There was some truth in what Carmen was saying: three children was a lot of parties and gifts and fuss. She wasn't even sure Carmen knew what age they all were. But plenty of women were doting aunts. She so wanted her girls to be close. She wanted everyone to be close: that's what family was.

'I think she really needs you now,' she said, not really thinking that at all.

'She doesn't,' said Carmen. 'She's got her "amazing nanny".' Sofia spoke about the amazing nanny in glowing terms Carmen was sure Sofia had never used about her. 'And Federico.'

'He's been away working all the time,' said her mum. 'She's about to have another baby. She's still working. Three kids is a lot, even with a nanny. And she has space. And she's said she can help you.'

'You are kidding, Mum!' was what Sofia had actually said when her mother had tried again. 'You are not going to dump the brat on me. I have three kids, plus Federico, another on the way, a huge case I can't leave and you want me to sort out Carmen as well?'

'Want something done, ask a busy person?' tried her mother hopefully. 'There's nothing left round here, Sofia, nothing. The town is finished.'

'I know,' said Sofia. 'It's buzzing here.'

'And your sister . . . I just hate to see her so sad.'

Sofia felt a twinge of guilt.

'She won't want to come. She thinks Edinburgh's just full of smug old boring posh prats in red trousers.'

'She . . . '

That was exactly what Carmen thought, and had said aloud, on several occasions.

'I just thought . . . ' her mum said. 'She pretends everything's fine, but it isn't really and it's killing us. She's not seeing anyone; she's not got a job . . . I'm so worried.'

14

'Why is Carmen my problem?'

'She isn't,' said her mother. 'She's everyone's problem. No, I don't mean that. But I just thought ... I thought she could get to know your kids.'

Sofia snorted.

'She doesn't even know their names!'

'She does!'

'She didn't even bother with Pippa's first communion. There was an empty space at the table at the reception.'

'I know,' said her mother. That had been a bad one.

'She texted me twenty-four hours later to say "Soz." *Soz.*'

'She doesn't know what it's like,' said her mother. 'Having children. When you think about them all the time. When they are so central to you. She doesn't get that at all.'

'I know,' said Sofia.

'When you worry and worry about them and if one of them is unhappy, you would do literally anything to make it better ... '

'You're laying it on with a trowel, Mum!'

Sofia's busy mind, though, was already turning.

'I mean, was she any good at her job? Really? Or just hanging about taking the piss like she did at school?'

'No, she was,' said her mum. 'Everyone got their bridal from her, back when you still did that and didn't order it off the internet.'

'Is she still dragging those scary men home?'

Her mother winced.

'It's been tough on her.'

'Remember the poet?'

'I do,' said her mother. 'The Sunday lunch where he declaimed a full sex sonnet in front of your father was quite something.'

They both laughed, then stopped because it was mean to laugh about Carmen. But sometimes she brought it on herself.

'Ugh,' said Sofia.

'Ooh,' said her mother. 'That means you have an idea ...'

Sofia thought furiously, and finally said, 'If she messes it up though ...'

'She'll be fine!' said their mother, crossing her fingers tightly.

Chapter Three

It was just a thought, Sofia reminded herself the following day. Not a commitment. Not a promise.

But Mr McCredie had been a client for so long, since before Sofia's time. If – and it was a big if – Carmen was a good shop assistant, well, this could be just the thing to stave off the worst, at least until they could find a buyer. And please her mother. And maybe even make Carmen a little grateful and pleased. So.

It would be one nice piece of news to impart, hopefully, on a day when she had very little good news to impart.

Most people who came into her office were pleased to see Sofia's bump, or at least offered good wishes or made a polite enquiry. Sofia's client that morning, Mr McCredie, was not most people. He seemed extremely uncomfortable that it even existed, averting his eyes from her middle.

She smiled more than usual and did her best not to mind:

Mr McCredie was eccentric, after all, and the news was so bad, it was probably best not to have gushing congratulations over the baby before having to tell him the worst.

'So?' He looked nervous and glanced at his very old, very large watch. He hated these meetings. Sofia wasn't overly fond of them either.

'Mr McCredie, I have done what you asked for but I have to tell you – and you should speak to your accountant too – but I'm afraid that's it. This is nearly the end. There's almost nothing left to sell.'

It was heartbreaking. A family fortune, a good name, a huge Highland estate which had brought in income for years.

But Mr McCredie had no interest in managing the estate, had let it go to rack and ruin, the huge house falling apart. He had no family, no siblings to take it on. He had the Edinburgh flat and the bookshop, but the latter was making absolutely no money and so he had sold more and more land, and spent more and more of his inheritance, his capital, just to live.

And now the country house was sold, and the money for that had been swallowed up by the capital gains tax and the land tax and everything else. Sofia had the unpleasant job of telling him that he had been bequeathed a fortune, and that he had run through it all – not by gambling or marrying or living an extravagant life, but simply by not paying attention.

Mr McCredie said something surprising.

'That's all right,' he said. 'All I care about is the shop.'

'Aha,' said Sofia. 'Yes. The shop. I'm afraid there's bad news about that too.'

Mr McCredie looked startled. He ran an ancient bookshop in an old part of town, that was more or less all Sofia knew. That, and the fact that it made absolutely no money.

'They're going to raise the rents,' she said. 'Haven't you heard?'

Mr McCredie shrugged. He was not, she knew, the best person at opening envelopes.

'It doesn't . . . it doesn't seem to make any money.'

For the first time, his face was genuinely worried.

'Well, it's . . . it's not about that. It's more . . . we sell old, rare books. Very specific. You can't just walk in and get the new Ian Fleming you know.'

Sofia decided not to tell him there hadn't been a new Ian Fleming in quite a while.

'I realise that,' she said.

'I've been building a collection – I have some of the finest architectural studies of the city in existence!'

'I know. It's just . . . if the shop can't pay its way, I don't know how it can be subsidised.'

'But it's . . . I've had it for such a long time. There have been bookshops on Victoria Street for two hundred years.'

Sofia nodded.

'I've asked around,' she said. 'You could sell it as a going concern.'

He blinked.

'Oh goodness. I really don't want to do that.'

Sofia winced.

'No, I mean, you can only sell it as a going concern. If it doesn't start making money, you're just going to lose it anyway, without getting any money for it.'

The old man blinked slowly.

'And the rents go up in the new year.'

'I don't understand what you're telling me.'

Sofia would never ever have mentioned it was because he

19

refused to read the many letters they had sent him on the subject. The reason it was at the last minute was not down to her. Sofia couldn't bear anything last minute.

'You have to show a profit,' she said. 'Over the next two months ideally – including Christmas, and before the rent hike. If you do that, you will probably find a buyer. If you keep losing money . . . you're going to lose everything.'

This time when he looked up his eyes were damp.

She sighed. The universe was conspiring with her bloody mother.

'By . . . by *Christmas*? I have to turn a profit by Christmas?'

'I think,' said Sofia, 'I think I know somebody who can help.'

Chapter Four

Everywhere in Edinburgh is uphill. This doesn't seem like it can possibly be true, but it is.

And possibly nowhere truer than Waverley Station, sunk at the very bottom of a drained loch, perched incongruously in the middle of a city, where other more sensible cities have rivers and bridges and appropriate things.

And in the dark freezing afternoon numbness of the grey station, full of whistles and the smell of coffee drifting across the terminal, a small, cross figure was hoisting a rucksack on her shoulders and staring upwards mutinously.

'Oh you don't have to get a cab, it's hardly any distance,' Sofia had texted, but it turned out if you had to walk uphill constantly and it was a howling gale it did feel like a big, gigantic, ginormous distance.

First off, from the top of the wind-strewn staircase leading from the station, the city rose around her, but Carmen barely noticed it for the thousands of tourists in front of her taking up all the space with their huge backpacks. She'd been to the city before of course, on school trips, or up to the festival, but she didn't know it well. As she shoved her way up, head down against the wind, the first thing she saw was a huge outdoor bar propped right in front of the station, with a live band and twinkly lights all around it.

Further on, leading into the darkening evening, was a winter funfair as far as the eye could see, as well as stalls selling sausages, mulled wine, hot chocolate and schnapps. Obviously they started early around here.

People were everywhere: little children, eyes wide, in their light-up trainers; teenagers laughing and shoving each other; young girls in sleeveless tops and short skirts, oblivious to the weather. Carmen noticed none of it, blindly following the map on her phone and trying not to get run over by what, to her shock when she glanced up, turned out to be a tram, dinging angrily at her.

They have trams? she thought, jumping back. Who knew?

She remembered once again her parents' strained looks of disappointment as her mother had let slip, as kindly as she was able, that her sister's law firm handled the affairs of someone who had a shop and was looking for some seasonal help.

'You let *Sofia* find me a *job*?' said Carmen, distraught.

She had been quite capable of looking for a job herself. Okay, she had also been doing quite a lot of doomscrolling and watching Netflix and reading all the *Anne of Green Gables* books again, because that was just self-care and she was grieving for the loss of the job and the life she'd had and why wasn't that okay?

'So Sofia knows best again?'

Her mother and father looked at one another.

'She's just trying to help,' said her mother.

'She's just *showing off*. What if I hate it?'

Carmen was aware she was being a brat, sitting at home, getting

22

her laundry done and her meals cooked and her father – her gentle father, who almost never reproached his girls – nonetheless looked up from over his crossword and raised his eyebrows.

Her voice cracked.

'I mean … you know this is a very hard time for me.'

She had applied for so many jobs, but without a degree or any qualifications, she wasn't having any luck at all, unless she either wanted to be an exotic dancer or a delivery driver. Carmen was not a hundred per cent sure which of these she'd be worse at.

She waited for her parents to spring to her defence as they always did, say she was going through a bad patch, that the shop closing obviously wasn't her fault, that she deserved a bit of down time to recover from the blow.

Neither of them said anything. Her father stared at the floor. Her mother looked miserable, but didn't open her mouth.

'You all think I'm being a brat,' said Carmen, devastated.

'No, *chica*,' said her mother. 'It's just … we just want to see you on your feet and … '

'You think I'm wasting my life.'

'No life is wasted,' said her father, but it had sounded an empty platitude in the tidy, tiny kitchen.

I will be nice. I will be grateful, Carmen said to herself as she finally pulled herself onto the correct street.

She'd been sent pictures of the house but Carmen had never really paid attention, just assuming it would be big and posh and stupid. She didn't expect it to be all of those things, but also heartbreakingly adorable.

Chapter Five

Sofia felt nervous and trepidatious answering the door. This was ridiculous, she told herself. It was her sister. They could be close. Other people were close to their sisters! She wished Federico was here and not in Hong Kong. He was good with Carmen – at teasing her and bringing out her fun side, and not prodding her sensitive spots, namely how she compared to Sofia and how skint she was. Still, at least Carmen would be slimmer than her for once. Sofia took a lot of care over her food and working out, while Carmen ate a lot of pizza and moaned that Sofia was 'lucky'.

And their mother, while being quietly thrilled, had pledged that she wasn't going to interfere or contact them. It was really for her own sanity: she couldn't handle them on the phone every five minutes complaining about the other one. She would miss her grandchildren – she doted on them – but maybe this would be the spur Carmen needed to get to know her own family.

She very much hoped so.

Like many mothers, Irene couldn't quite believe her children were adults. In her eyes, they were just little girls in grown-up dresses (or ripped jeans in Carmen's case). She remembered Sofia trying to get Carmen to behave for five minutes so they could get an ice cream, one holiday down in Ayr. The queue stretched out of the Italian ice cream shop as more and more people came away with their 99s and oysters while the little girl was getting more and more frantic despite Sofia trying to calm her down, until Carmen got so upset she had lashed out and knocked another child's ice cream over. It had been an entire catastrophe. Irene had bought the other child a new ice cream whereupon their sibling had started to kick off, then Irene said Carmen couldn't have one for yelling whereupon Sofia had stared at her own ice cream, and offered Carmen 'a lick . . . No, Mum, she's taking all of it! She's taking all of it!' and that had more or less been the end of their day out.

But they were sisters. Sisters always came through in the end, didn't they? It had been so hard, watching Sofia fly through school. Carmen had been such a little reader, but by the time she got to school she couldn't bear to be compared with her brilliant sibling, and fell further and further behind, almost, it felt, on purpose.

'Don't call them,' Rod, her husband, had said, reading her thoughts as usual. 'Let them get on with it. They'll sort it out.'

Irene had lifted her hands to show she wasn't already on the phone.

'All right, all right.'

'Hey!' said Sofia, flinging open the door with her widest smile.

Carmen, for once, was almost speechless.

'*Look*,' she said. 'Oh my God. Look at your house!'

Sofia smiled more naturally this time. She liked people loving the house as much as she did.

'Come inside; it's freezing,' she said.

'But I just want to . . . I mean, this is like something out of a storybook. God. Are you just, like, happy all the time?'

There was a wistful tone to Carmen's voice, but she genuinely meant it. It was like a doll's house come to life. She couldn't even be jealous; it was something so lovely and far out of reach. It would be like being jealous of Amal Clooney.

Sofia smiled.

'Come in, will you.'

The smart hallway had a cupboard for stowing away boots and coats, and Carmen started to unload, taking in the shiny parquet flooring which led to the huge opened out space of the kitchen, with glass right across the back wall, sliding out to the little square townhouse garden, which had a small football net set up on it. On the left was a door that led to a beautiful small sitting room, done out in trendy shades of black and grey. It was all gorgeous. Carmen was suddenly rather conscious of her grotty coat and mud-spattered jeans. She felt she was scruffing the place up just by being there.

'Tea?' she said, hoping Sofia might say, 'Oh what the hell, let's have wine.' Except – *durr* – she was pregnant of course. Boring.

She padded on her bare feet, following Sofia into the huge kitchen, only for her sister to raise her eyebrows in a query.

Unsure what she meant, Carmen paused. Then she glanced up the beautiful stairwell, with its metal banister railings topped with wood. Standing at the top was a child in a green velvet dress with the same determined set of face as her mother. She was pretty and tidy, with shiny hair combed back down her shoulders, a ballet class posture and a direct look.

'Oh hello ...' Carmen scrabbled. 'Phoebe?'

'I'm Pippa actually. Phoebe's still upstairs. Mummy, she should be here, shouldn't she? It's rude.'

Sofia nodded, as a little paper plane shot out past Pippa.

'HI!'

'Jack,' said Carmen with more certainty, as he was the only boy. He was about eight, with short hair that stuck up like a brush, a round cheerful face and freckles.

'Hihowareyou?' Jack called, heading for the small garden out the back before it got dark with a football under one arm.

'PHOEBE!' shouted the larger girl in a high-pitched shriek. Carmen still wasn't quite sure what to say as Pippa advanced down the stairs. She felt oddly judged as her niece looked her up and down.

'You missed my first communion,' she said accusingly. 'It was in November. *Daddy's* sister sent me this dress.'

'Oh,' said Carmen.

'Pippa, darling, don't—'

'I'm just saying. I'm in primary six, by the way. I like dancing and horses and I don't like K-pop so please don't give me any K-pop things.'

'Um, okay,' said Carmen.

'PHOEBE!'

'Please don't screech,' said Sofia. 'Tea?'

'I'll do it,' said Carmen, conscious that Sofia had a massive bump in front of her stomach and her mother had kept reminding her that she was there to *help* as she wasn't paying rent. They were still being a little stiff with each other.

'No, no, you catch up with the children,' said Sofia, filling the kettle. The kettle looked expensive, thought Carmen. How did you even buy an expensive kettle?

Pippa sat down.

'My favourite show on television is *Just Add Magic*, but we don't watch much television because Skylar says screen time is very bad for your eyes and also your soul.'

'Who's Skylar?'

'She's the nanny,' said Pippa just at the same moment as Sofia said, 'She's someone who helps us out.'

'Where is she?' said Carmen.

'Oh, she's a student so she's at a class now. You'll meet her . . . PHOEBE!'

There was the noise of stomping on the stairs and everyone looked up.

Another version of Sofia appeared, but this one was not glossy: instead, she had messy tangled hair. She was plump, her face looked sticky, and her lower lip stuck out so she appeared to be pouting.

'Were you asleep, darling?' asked Sofia, looking up.

'No,' said Phoebe in a grumpy voice.

'This is your aunt, Carmen.'

Phoebe regarded Carmen with an unimpressed gaze.

'I know she doesn't send birthday presents,' said Pippa, 'but you have to be nice to her. Kindness wins!'

Carmen winced. Phoebe was still staring at her. It was not a cheery look.

'Did you bring us anything?' said Phoebe finally.

It hadn't occurred to Carmen. She mentally filed through the contents of her bag and remembered a packet of Kettle Chips she'd been planning on sharing with Sofia over a bottle of wine that of course Sofia couldn't drink. Oh lord.

'PHOEBE,' said Pippa. 'That's rude. That's rude, isn't it, Mummy?'

Sofia waved her hand in a faintly disparaging manner.

'It is rude though.'

'Shut up!' said Phoebe.

Carmen felt the uncomfortable sensation of both sympathising with and faintly disliking quite a small child.

'Um,' she said, and opened her big bag which, filled with clothes just thrown in when she'd woken up late for her train, practically exploded all over the kitchen, by far the messiest thing in the house.

'Wow,' said Pippa.

Carmen retrieved the Kettle Chips with effort.

'Here you are,' she said, hurling them in the children's general direction. 'Share those?'

As if summoned by a whistle only he could hear, Jack came hurtling back into the kitchen at full steam.

'CRISPS!'

Phoebe was already tearing open the packet. 'Go away – they're for me!'

'No, they're to SHARE,' said Pippa, trying to look above it but desperately putting out her hands to scoop up the largest crisps.

'But I ASKED FIRST!'

'Ugh, these are PLAIN,' Jack announced, sputtering crumbs everywhere.

Sofia sat bolt upright, eyes wide.

'But it's nearly supper time!' she said. 'You can't have crisps, guys!'

They stared at her over the opened packet, mouths full of crumbs.

'But our AUNT is here.'

'What even is supper?' said Carmen. 'Do you mean "tea"?'

Sofia frowned as the door opened and in entered one of the shiniest people Carmen had ever seen.

Skylar – as Carmen deduced this must be – had long blonde hair, very good skin, a yoga-fit body and bright blue eyes. She walked in and stared at the burst suitcase lying on the floor and the children squabbling over the crisps as if she wasn't sure she'd come into the right house.

Sofia looked a little tense.

'Oh, hi, Skylar!' she said overbrightly. 'This is my sister, Carmen.'

Skylar did something that Carmen found astonishing: she held up a finger to tell Sofia – the great lawyer – to be quiet for a second.

'Hello, children?'

She had the kind of intonation that went up at the end.

Immediately they stopped squabbling over the crisps. Pippa stepped away.

'Namaste, Skylar,' she said quickly.

'Namaste,' mumbled the others, both reluctant to release their grip on the packet.

Skylar let out a beaming smile and turned to face Carmen.

'Hello!'

'Uh yeah, hi.'

She really was so pretty, it was hypnotising.

'It's just if we're going to be working together? Sofia doesn't normally let the children snack? On junk food? Just before we eat? It's really, really bad for them?'

'Um, we're not going to be working together?' said Carmen, realising as she did so that somehow she'd let her voice go up at the end of the phrase.

Sofia groaned and busied herself over the teapot.

'I mean, are we?' said Carmen, turning her face towards her sister.

'I thought ... a couple of nights a week Skylar has university classes ... maybe you could ... I mean, you don't have to of course, but maybe you could ... cook and do bedtime?'

The children looked at Carmen as if they were as doubtful about this as she was.

'But I'm going to be working too!'

'Sorry, could you just move that bag?' came Skylar's voice. 'Only I want to get the recyclables out so I can help preserve the earth? You know you can't recycle crisp packets?'

Carmen made the mistake of not zipping up the bag again, which meant, as she knelt down to pick it up, her washbag and knickers burst all over the floor.

'KNICKERS!' said Jack, bursting out laughing. Phoebe laughed too, while Pippa pursed her lips and looked disapproving. Sofia looked absolutely pained at all this horrible stuff going on in her Martin Moore kitchen. Face bright red, Carmen knelt down and started stuffing everything into the bag which now, of course, wouldn't zip up. It seemed to take an hour to remove her washbag – which was filthy, and she thought out of the corner of her eye she caught Skylar mouthing something – and a couple of jumpers, stick them under one arm, sit down on the bag and zip up the rest, all the while watched by three mouth-breathing, crumb-covered children.

'I'll show you where you're sleeping,' said Sofia, getting up from her chair with some difficulty. 'Actually, I should give you the tour.'

'I'll get the couscous going?' said Skylar. 'I hope you haven't all ruined your appetites?'

There was another staircase that went down instead of up.

Up contained a huge drawing room, a master suite with dressing room and bathroom, a pristine guest room, then up again under the eaves were the children's beautiful rooms in sailor prints and White Company fairy lights and bunting. Carmen smiled tightly at the tour as Sofia, slightly apologetically, then took her down to the basement.

'So I thought . . .'

Sofia was using the bright tone of voice Carmen recognised from childhood, from when she had to deliver disappointing news like she'd only got an A minus instead of her usual A plus, or Carmen couldn't keep that cat she'd found in the street as it belonged to somebody else.

' . . . you could sleep down here. It's got its own bathroom so you wouldn't have to share with the kids, and its own entrance so you can come and go as you like!'

She made it sound so appealing there had to be something wrong with it, and sure enough, as they passed through the beautiful light-filled folding-door paradise of the warm kitchen upstairs and descended into the basement, it became apparent.

There were three tiny rooms ahead of them, obviously once used by servants, and a bathroom with a shower but no tub.

Behind them was a large utility room full of all the rubbish most people had to fit into their real houses – ironing boards, washing machines, wellington boots, winter coats. No wonder their house could look tidy, thought Carmen crossly, when you could just throw all your stuff down the stairs.

'And you'll be next to Skylar so you two can get along!'

'As the hired help,' said Carmen.

Sofia sighed. She was doing her best, but it never seemed to work with Carmen.

'Look,' she said. 'It's just a couple of nights. Just to help me, that's all. Sometimes I get in late. And some mornings.'

'Well, I might get in late,' said Carmen. 'What is this job anyway? Mum just said retail.'

That was not remotely true, but Carmen hadn't really been listening. Also, Sofia hadn't been a hundred per cent open with her mother about how bad things were at the shop in case Carmen went off on one and refused to come.

'It's a bookshop,' said Sofia. 'One of my clients owns it. Mr McCredie. Needs someone to help him over Christmas.'

'Well, that sounds okay.'

'You like reading, don't you?'

Sofia had never been a bookworm like Carmen: she had studied hard and read textbooks, and now she liked interior design magazines, whereas Carmen followed her heart and read books wherever her interests took her; about space, history, romance, anything she felt like, alighting from one to the next like a butterfly.

Carmen shrugged.

'So,' said Sofia.

'Okay,' said Carmen. 'What is Skylar studying?'

'Something arty? Not sure.'

'She seems very . . . organised.'

Sofia was in no mood to discuss Skylar after a hit-and-miss trail of previous au pairs had spent their days crying with home-sickness, ransacking the fridge, smoking in their rooms, flirting with Federico and actually stealing.

'She's great,' she said. 'Please don't fall out with her. I really need her.'

Carmen was about to snap back that she didn't fall out with anyone, but thought better of it on the grounds of it not being strictly true.

'Okay,' she said. 'I'll be good.'

Sofia smiled.

'You don't *have* to be good,' she said, the way she'd done when they were both small and Carmen was in trouble again. 'You just have to look good to the grown-ups.'

Which was peace of sorts, and enough for their mother when Sofia called to tell her all about it, and which lasted slightly less than twenty-four hours.

Chapter Six

Well, thought Carmen the next morning, as she woke up in the strange quiet dingy room and looked around. Supper had been difficult: Phoebe had refused point-blank to eat the couscous and everyone had silently blamed Carmen after the whole crisps incident, then Sofia had encouraged Pippa to play her bassoon, which she had, loudly and uncharmingly, and encouraged Phoebe to sing, a suggestion which was met with as much enthusiasm as the couscous, while Jack repeatedly kicked the expensive Shaker kitchen table leg and Carmen had thought she would just go to bed early before she caused any more trouble.

And now she was starting work. At a new job. Cor.

Perhaps it would be all right. A lovely bookshop where people came to sit and read and it was quiet and she could drink tea and grab a copy of something good and sit quietly in the corner until somebody needed her.

That would be all right, wouldn't it? It would be nice. Bit of light dusting. It would be easier than haberdashery, with its wedding rush and bridal lace fretting. Books were hardly a big deal. Plus young Mr McCredie, as Sofia had called him, was apparently 'nice if a bit quiet'. That didn't sound too bad. He couldn't possibly be worse than Mrs Marsh, that was for sure. Carmen had wanted to ask how old he was exactly, but didn't want Sofia getting that simpering look she got when she got all excited about Carmen's love life and lied about how much she liked Carmen's boyfriends when it was obvious that anyone less than Federico, with his immaculate hair and manners and job and tailoring, she considered basic scum. The fact that occasionally Carmen had dated fairly basic scum didn't help either. Hey: there was a lot of scum about. That was just the law of averages.

She went up to breakfast – the two younger children were sitting at the table: Jack in a pair of little old-fashioned pyjamas with buttons, and Phoebe in a fussy nighty. Her hair stuck straight out and she wore a menacing expression that in someone slightly older would have inspired Carmen to bring them a coffee.

Carmen asked how to get to work and Sofia frowned and said you walked, that's how you got about the city; the buses only went to weird places and the tram only went to the airport and nowhere else at all.

'Nowhere else?' said Carmen, perturbed.

'Nowhere else *at all*.'

'Huh. What about a bicycle?'

'How good are you at riding bicycles up steps?' said Sofia.

'Can I borrow your car?' said Carmen, looking out at a bunch of leaves swirling down the street in a high wind.

'A car?' said Sofia. 'In central Edinburgh?' She sounded like Carmen had suggested getting to work on a dragon. 'They'll kill you.'

'Who?'

'The ... traffic wardens.' Sofia looked suddenly anxious, as if even saying their name might summon them. 'Don't risk it. I beg you.'

She turned away and went to the annoyingly spacious and well laid out cupboard under the stairs where she retrieved for Carmen a massive engulfing expensive padded parka.

'Try this.'

Carmen glanced down at her well-worn leather jacket.

'I'm okay.'

'I mean it. You'll freeze.'

'I'll be fine,' said Carmen, looking at Google Maps.

'Go up the steps here and then along and then down the steps there,' said Sofia. 'Or you could go round the castle and up the castle steps.'

'I don't want to go up *any* steps,' said Carmen. Sofia smiled nicely. 'Do you want me to make you a packed lunch?'

'No, thank you.'

Carmen would have loved a packed lunch but she wasn't going to give her eight-months-pregnant sister even more of a reason to get up and prove herself effortlessly more competent at everything.

'I'll find my way. Don't fuss! And I can make packed lunches!'

'Yes, please,' came a little voice by her side. 'I like Nutella sandwiches.'

Sofia gave a loud strangulated laugh before casting a worried glance at Skylar, who was cross-legged on the rug meditating quite obtrusively.

'Ha, as if we would ever have Nutella in the house.'

'I had it at a party once,' said Phoebe in a wistful tone as if describing a paradise lost. 'I will never forget it.'

Carmen wondered if buying them all enormous jars would do as Christmas presents.

'No, don't worry about it,' said Sofia. 'I do them all on Sunday nights and take them out of the freezer as we go.'

'What is it today?' said Phoebe.

'Hummus and radishes!' said Sofia. 'Isn't that amazing? I've made it into a happy face for you in your lunch box.'

'Radishes don't make anyone happy,' said Phoebe.

'I love radishes, Mummy!' said Pippa, appearing in the kitchen doorway. Somehow already in her blue school uniform and neat tartan kilt, she looked immaculate, ironed, put together, her shiny hair shimmering in a neat ponytail.

Sofia smiled at her.

'Well, good for you,' she said. 'Would you like some extra raisins?'

'Oh yes, please!'

'"Oh yes, please",' mimicked Phoebe. '"Oh please, please, I would like more STUPID RAISINS because I am STUPID PIPPA".'

Carmen headed for the door, just in time to hear Sofia admonishing Phoebe for her rudeness.

'And wish Auntie Carmen good luck on her first day in her new job.'

'Good luck, Auntie Carmen!' sang out Pippa.

Phoebe frowned.

'I hope the other people are nice to you,' she said in a tone of voice that made clear she didn't expect that ever to be necessarily the case.

'Thanks,' said Carmen, who was rather worried about that herself.

Sofia wasn't wrong about her up and down steps theory. She had insisted she take Princes Street. There was another way, but it involved upper streets and lower streets and, without wanting to be insulting, she said she wasn't sure Carmen was quite ready to take that in. Carmen had agreed with her.

So instead, she walked along the main road of the capital. One side was lined with the usual big city shops and brands, but on the other, ridiculously, was a set of formally laid out gardens with bandstands and fountains. These ended abruptly at the foot of a cliff which rose hundreds of feet in the air, an ancient grey castle perched on the top of it as if in a different realm altogether. This was a city in the lowering grey cloud, busy with its own affairs in the sky.

Running through the gardens, as if to make things even more ridiculous, ran several railway lines clogged with locomotives, like a giant's train set.

It was quite the oddest place Carmen had ever been to, and, even more weirdly, everyone she passed, heads down, most clad in pompom hats and parkas similar to Sofia's, (which Carmen, shivering in her leather jacket, now regretted passing up) didn't even seem to notice that half of their main shopping street had been ripped away and replaced with a fairy-tale.

She found the steps behind what appeared to be a huge Greek temple – Well of course, she thought – and, panting and realising how unfit she was, reached the top opposite a pitch-black version of Dracula's castle. There were yet more steps ahead.

You are *kidding*, said Carmen, almost out loud, and frowning at Google Maps.

Sure enough, the map directed her to a narrow set of steps that spiralled up and vanished into the gloom. She looked back and surveyed the city now spread out at her feet, the gardens neat, the streets heading back to the water in perfect rows, an occasional honk from the trains below, the endless drone of the bagpipes played all day for the tourists and the faint dinging of the trams, going nowhere. What a strange place this was.

Carmen sniffed, and marched on up through the dark tunnel of something absurdly called 'New College' and found, to her surprise, that it popped her out at the top of the Royal Mile.

The ancient thoroughfare that ran between the castle and all the way down to Holyrood Palace was full of shops selling anything and everything that could get some tartany nonsense stamped on it, but it was early in the morning and the tourists were not yet abroad.

Anyway, Carmen didn't notice the eye-level shops straight-away. As she emerged from the dark tunnel of the ancient steps, she could see only a three-sided courtyard and a towering structure with windows that seemed to funnel upwards.

How could they have built so high without lifts or modern technology? There was no car noise here, no trains, not even a bagpipe, just quiet footsteps passing by. And as she walked through the courtyard and stepped out onto the cobbles, polished beneath her feet, Carmen had the slightest sense of a spell, of a step in time. She wondered who else had stepped on them in their time: kings and queens, the poor and forgotten, uncounted for hundreds of years. She herself could be anyone: a dairy maid, a farmer's girl, a grand lady, stepping out into an unchanging Edinburgh world.

A lonely shaft of sunlight appeared and lit up an old black

and white building next door to the narrow passageway she had emerged from, and she watched it shine on the ancient panes of glass, so neatly and tidily divided, six on the bottom, six on the top.

Who lived here, she wondered, among this most ancient of roads, with stone watering troughs for horses still standing, and tiny narrow passageways and mysterious staircases disappearing hither and thither? And did you feel it every day, that it was magical?

Then a busker loudly set up with a drum and a penny whistle close by, and the spell was broken, and she realised the shop in the building was selling something called Ye Olde Tartan Fudge and she sighed. Work, after all, was still work, and she was running late.

She had one more set of steps to go, thankfully downwards, to take her onto Victoria Street.

As soon as she got there, she checked again: this was definitely the right place and she almost sent a message thanking Sofia. Because Victoria Street was about the most irritatingly pretty place she'd ever seen.

The street was a row of curved buildings underneath some kind of balcony arrangement – Edinburgh's notion of sticking streets on top of each other was incredibly peculiar, like the area called the New Town being really, really super old – and curved down towards a large open space at the bottom called the Grassmarket. This must be, Carmen realised, what Sofia meant by an upper and a lower section.

There were little shops lining the length of the street, each painted a different, cheerful colour – pink, green, blue. There was a hardware shop, a French restaurant, a magic shop with a wide array of herbs and broomsticks, expensive-looking shops for hunting and fishing and tweed, chichi little restaurants – and a bookshop.

It was green with a beautiful display of bicycling frogs towing books wrapped in Christmas paper. It was adorable and perfect and for a second Carmen genuinely felt quite excited.

Then she saw it was the wrong number, and in fact a books and antiques shop, not what she was looking for at all. The McCredie shop, it turned out, was two doors down.

This shop was also green, but in this case, a pale olive colour. And in fact, it didn't really look like a shop at all. The dusty window was crammed with maps, with folders and big old reference books but not in an enticing, imaginative way like the other bookshop. Instead they were simply piled up haphazardly against the glass, so it was impossible to read what they actually were.

The place looked less like a shop of any kind and more like a two-storey fire hazard. She checked her phone again. Yup. This was definitely the place. But what on earth could she do here? Who would ever even come here? She couldn't imagine any customer ever being enticed through its doors.

She frowned. Maybe it was one of these scams and actually fronted a massive drug-running business. Sofia wouldn't have put her up to that though. But otherwise how could anyone who ran a place like this afford to use Sofia's services? That made the most sense so far.

There were dead flies in the window and thick dust over many of the objects. Carmen thought briefly back to Mrs Marsh and what a heart attack it would have given her.

Taking a deep breath, she pushed the door, which tinged with an ancient bell, flattened down her hair and walked in.

Chapter Seven

Inside, the shop did not seem any less of a disaster area – or any more of a place where any sane human would want to spend their time or their money.

The main room, painted green to match the front, was lined with shelving in which books – mostly old – were jammed so tightly you couldn't pull any of them out.

The titles appeared to be filed willy-nilly. There was a large glass cabinet at the front on which sat an old-fashioned till, and on top of those were two or three old books displayed that clearly hadn't been touched – and Carmen had never heard of them – for a very long time. The rest of the cabinet was covered in an unruly sprinkle of invoices, paper, receipts, advertising flyers, empty envelopes and general detritus.

'Hello?' said Carmen loudly, but there was no reply.

There was a floating set of steps to the higher shelves, but that too was piled high with what looked like atlases; not just atlases but atlases Carmen wagered were too old to have half of the new names of countries in them. There was a section of books about Edinburgh itself, which had obviously been fingered and read by tourists so often they were in a dreadful state, and couldn't possibly be sold now. A spider's web in the corner of the window was pretty, but Carmen rather thought it did not give an ideal impression.

'Helloooooo?'

Still nothing. How on earth, thought Carmen, did this shop make a living? How?! How could it possibly support one person, never mind two?

A dilapidated metal circular display, presumably meant to be placed outside when the shop opened – although it was now ten past ten, so the shop really ought to be open already – contained a stack of creased, ancient and wildly inappropriate postcards. Did people really want to come to Edinburgh and send home a postcard with an engagement picture of Charles and Diana?

'Um ... Mr McCredie?'

She looked down at the floor; something seemed to be sticking to the sole of her foot, and she wasn't completely sure she wanted to know what it was. 'Mr McCredie?'

Finally she heard from the back – if this was the front of the shop, Carmen wasn't sure she wanted to know what the back looked like – a shuffling noise, as if someone, she thought, was trying to push their way through quite a lot of paper.

Peering in that direction, Carmen saw that the room narrowed and then, through an opening, vanished back into gloom; there was no telling how far back it went. From where she stood, it looked as if it burrowed straight into the heart of the ancient cliffside itself.

Just as she was thinking this, Mr McCredie appeared, blinking in the weak sunlight, as if he were a misdirected mole.

Carmen blinked herself – he was not, it turned out, remotely young. Quite the opposite.

He was portly, with surprisingly small feet and hands, which meant for a round man he moved with unexpected delicacy. He had bright pink cheeks and tufts of white hair, as well as a pair of glasses on his nose, another pair tucked into the pocket of his waistcoat and a third hanging out of his tweed jacket pocket. His eyes were tiny, blue and, at the moment, rather confused.

'I don't think we're open,' he said in a broad sweet accent that lengthened every word: *I do-ant think we-rrrrr oaaa-pen.*

'Well, you should be,' said Carmen, smiling. 'Hello! I'm Carmen! I'm your Christmas extra staff.'

Mr McCredie frowned and touched his hands to his glasses to make sure they were still there. They were.

'Oh yes?' he said. He frowned again.

'Sofia sent me. Your lawyer. You said you needed someone . . . '

Fear slightly gripped at Carmen's heart. She couldn't be blanked for a job again, she just couldn't. What would she do? She'd have to apply to be a wench at the Christmas market and it was freezing out there. This place was clearly a tip, but she was here now and obviously they were quite slack about hours and, well, she desperately needed to be out otherwise she was going to have to turn into Sofia's cleaner.

'Did I?' said Mr McCredie absently. Then he remembered. The whole horror of the meeting. And his face fell. He looked at the girl in front of him. She was short and rather pretty: dark hair and eyes and cheeks pink from being outside. Her mouth had a stern set to it and she had a curvy figure, rather old-fashioned-looking. Goodness. Was this the person who was going to save him from the awful fate of having to leave

46

his beloved books, his beloved city, retire to some terrible bungalow somewhere?

He looked around. 'You've worked in a shop before?'

'I have eight years' senior retail experience,' said Carmen proudly.

'In bookselling?'

'Um, haberdashery,' said Carmen.

Mr McCredie blinked. 'Buttons and what-not.'

'Buttons and what-not,' agreed Carmen.

'Well ...' He indicated the room with his hand. 'It's not exactly like selling buttons.'

'I can imagine.'

'Do you read?'

'Of course!' said Carmen indignantly. She decided not to mention how much she loved her e-reader. He didn't look like an e-reader kind of a person at all.

The door of the shop tinged, and a woman walked in. Mr McCredie looked at Carmen in a 'go on' kind of a way.

'Hello,' smiled Carmen.

The woman looked around, slightly discombobulated by the mess. Carmen couldn't blame her. But maybe this worked well here. Maybe it was an authentic gold mine of a place that people liked because it wasn't like other shops which had clean shelves and ... took credit cards. Hmm.

The woman was pushing a large pram, and there was nowhere for it to go without bumping into things.

'Let me take that for you,' Carmen said hastily, looking at the round bright baby, fresh as new minted coconut ice, sitting up and taking a keen interest in their surroundings.

'Oh, it's all right,' said the woman. 'I was looking for a copy of *The Jolly Christmas Postman*.'

Carmen smiled; it had been a favourite of hers, except she'd lost all the letters and Sofia, who never lost anything, had got cross with her.

'Of course,' she said. She couldn't imagine a bookshop at Christmas time that wouldn't have it. She smiled winningly at Mr McCredie, who frowned distractedly.

'I'm not sure ...' he said. 'Do you know what year it was published?'

The woman looked bemused.

'Um, no?' she said as if this was a very bizarre question to be asked, which it was.

'You file your books by year?' hissed Carmen, genuinely surprised.

'Um, sometimes,' said Mr McCredie.

Carmen quickly leafed through a box of children's books. There was an old hardback edition of *The Water Babies*, several lavishly illustrated lives of the saints and a very old picture book about a rabbit who had wings, carrying a lantern over a snowy waste.

'Oh my,' said the woman, as Carmen held it up. 'Is that Pookie?'

Carmen snuck a sideways glance at it.

'It is!' she said. '*Pookie Believes in Santa Claus*.'

'My granny had these,' said the woman wonderingly. 'I think she had this very one.'

The copy was red-bound, with gold picked out on the illustration. Although Carmen had never heard of it, there was something unutterably charming about the illustrations.

Carmen gently brought it forward; it smelled comforting, dry and warm and she opened it and held it up to the baby, who *ooooh*ed and pointed.

'Oh, it's lovely,' said the woman. 'I know what happens next ... show me the page Santa Claus arrives ...'

'Oh, I'll show you,' said Mr McCredie, taking it off them. 'I met the author, you know! She lived in Edinburgh. And married her publisher! Such a journey. So anyway, the publisher was originally William Collins, then they were bought out but the original artwork ...'

The baby in the pram clapped its hands with delight as Carmen smiled at her.

'You know,' said Carmen, interrupting her boss, which she normally wouldn't do, but she had immediately got the sense that they might be there all day, 'she's very much at an age where she might eat quite a lot of *The Jolly Christmas Postman*.'

'That's true,' said the woman. 'But I have to have this. I just have to. How much is it?'

The printed sum on the back read 2/6 which was absolutely no help to anyone, and Carmen looked at Mr McCredie, who shrugged and mentioned something called the Net Book Agreement and patently had absolutely no idea and seemed about to launch into quite a long book-based spiel again.

'Uh, seven pounds?' ventured Carmen and by the way the woman's face lit up, she instantly knew she'd made a terrible mistake. Oh well. Too late now.

'Where's the card-reader?' she hissed at Mr McCredie, who, it became immediately obvious, had no such thing.

'Um, we take cheques,' he said, prodded into action. The woman and Carmen looked at each other, Carmen giving an apologetic smile. Finally, after the woman handed over a ten-pound note, she managed to count out three pounds in small change from a battered grey tin underneath the till.

The bell rang as the woman manoeuvred the large pram out of the doorway.

'Oh,' said Mr McCredie. 'Because the really interesting thing about Pookie is he became a complete word-of-mouth success after the war. There were so many rabbits, you know, but this one had wings. I've filed him with all our rabbit books. Sub-species wings. Such a special title.'

Carmen looked at him.

'You don't separate children's books and adult books?'

He blinked, not really understanding.

'But books are for everyone,' he said. 'Who knows what you'll love? How dare you tell children what to read?'

Carmen rolled her eyes.

'Well, technically I agree with you,' she said. 'But . . . should we try selling a few first?'

He looked at her. 'Well, your sister tells me I have to let you do your thing.' He leaned forward. 'I'm sure you're going to be excellent. Right, I am off to do some reading. I'm so glad you're here to save the shop.'

'What?' said Carmen. 'What did you say?'

'Your sister says I'm going to lose the shop if it doesn't make any money, and I'll be out on the street. They're putting up the rent. If we don't make money over Christmas, the bank is going to take everything. But you're here to save the day.'

'*What?*'

'*What?!*' Carmen was still shouting as soon as she got back to Sofia's. Well, she wasn't quite shouting, but it was close.

'What were you thinking? It's closing down! You dumped me in some absolute piece of filthy crap – it's filthy, Sofia. It's awful. It's completely useless and this guy is going to be homeless unless I – what? – perform miracles?! He won't let me into the stockroom! Says it's his own system!'

'I thought you'd take it as a compliment,' said Sofia, who had hoped dearly that this might be the case without in any sense actually expecting it. 'Only you can turn it around.'

'I can't turn it around! It's an absolute ... It's a disgrace! You can't find anything and there's nothing recent and no money for stock and now it's going to get shut down and he'll end up on the street and I'll have *failed again*. Thanks a bunch.'

'I think there are better ways for us to manage our outdoor voices?' said Pippa in an officious tone, and Carmen managed to stop herself snapping at a child, but very much only just.

'I mean, what were you thinking? Fob off my useless sister in a pigsty for a month and get some free babysitting?'

'No! That's not what I meant at all!'

'I'll just head down to my cell, shall I? So you and Skylar can go to yoga?'

Sofia reflected that it would have been slightly more useful indeed if she hadn't been in full yoga kit, which cost way more than Carmen's normal day clothes.

'I thought you could save it,' said Sofia. 'I have faith in you.'

Carmen raised her hands in annoyance.

'You saw me as *useful* to a *client* for five seconds. You didn't think about me at all. Not once. And now I am going to destroy an old man's life while mine stays as *sucky as ever*. Thanks, sis.'

Chapter Eight

'Oh God, what am I going to do?' she WhatsApped Idra. 'I don't even know where to start.'

She had left the house without speaking to anyone the next morning. She worried she'd be too early to get in, but it appeared Mr McCredie didn't even bother to lock the door at night. Now, with a weak winter sunlight streaming through the filthy windows, she was looking at the piles of books with their mad filing system in despair. There was no sign of Mr McCredie at all. This job as a stopgap would have been, well, boring and pointless, but okay. The customer yesterday had turned out to be one of about five, most of whom walked around and left hastily; two of whom bought a single postcard each.

'I shouldn't care but he's a really old bloke and he's going to lose the lot.'

She was acutely jealous of Idra who had got a job in a restaurant and was absolutely loving being busy and pocketing tips for doing essentially the same job as she had before, only this time with ice cream. As Christmas grew closer, she was doing better and better, and could not believe she'd wasted so many years attempting to tell people that fascinators suited them. 'Fascinators don't suit *anyone*,' she'd pointed out more than once. 'They would make Gigi Hadid look ridiculous. It's a stick with nets! It costs £59.99. It's fuchsia! It doesn't keep your head warm or cold! It doesn't stay on very well! And, let me just remind you, it doesn't suit you.'

'Oh God. Can't you come home?'

'Back to Mum and Dad's house while they pretend that I'm not a total failure? Walk out on my pregnant sister?'

'Sucks to be you.'

'Thanks!'

She stared outside the window. There were hordes of people walking up and down the beautiful, curved street, rich-looking tourists with money and time to spend. She sighed and looked around. The whole thing would need ... I mean, God, what would she even do? She didn't know how to run a bookshop; she knew how to display ribbon nicely and how to cut velvet without losing an inch and how to convert metric to imperial and back again in her head in a heartbeat.

She picked up the nearest book. It was one of a set of Charles Dickens, a very old edition in properly bound leather. She sighed and leafed through all of them, wondering where she could find a cloth to wipe the dust off. She found *A Christmas Carol*, and put it, facing outwards, in the window. Then she WhatsApped Idra again.

'Got any restaurant jobs going? I have *no* idea what I'm doing.'

There was no reply. Then, half an hour later, her phone rang.

'Hey!'

'Hey yourself! I'm on my break.'

'I think this might be all break,' said Carmen, looking around. 'Hang on – does the restaurant need someone?'

'Sorry,' said Idra. 'They've got me.'

'Oh, yes.'

Carmen sighed.

'But I had an idea and it's hilarious.'

'You mean terrible.'

Idra giggled in a way that insinuated that was exactly what she meant.

'You're not the only person in the world who has moved to Edinburgh, you know.'

Carmen frowned. 'What do you mean?'

'My spies have it that someone has been spotted barging in and out of Jenner's –' Jenner's was the ancient department store that still graced Princes Street. '– sniffing loudly and complaining about dust on the banisters and footfall.'

'You are kidding,' said Carmen.

'None other,' said Idra. 'Apparently she's moved to live with her sister.'

'Like me! Oh my God, I'm Mrs Marsh! Oh God!' said Carmen. Then: 'Hang on. What happened to Mr Marsh?'

'Aha! It gets even more complex.'

'She killed him.'

'That was my first thought too,' said Idra. 'But it turns out, he never existed.'

'You're kidding.'

'Nope. She invented the Mrs to get more respect.'

'Oh God,' said Carmen. 'That's the saddest thing I've ever heard. Oh God. I'm going to turn into her.'

'Well, she does know a lot about running shops. You should hit her up for tips.'

'Haha, *no way*. Oh my God. Can you imagine? Christ. I'm not *that* desperate. Anyway. It's a big city. What are the chances of my bumping into her?'

The doorbell tinged and a broad shadow filled the room.

'Oh, you are kidding . . . ' said Carmen into the phone. 'Idra, I'm going to kill you.'

'Don't be daft: it'll help,' said Idra, not sounding remotely apologetic. 'Gotta go – there's a team of *really* hot lawyers in for a business lunch and I am going to get them extremely drunk and smile for tips and possibly marry at least two of them. Fa-la-la-la-la la-la la la!'

And she was gone.

Carmen looked up in the dusty room.

'I heard you were here,' said Mrs Marsh, folding her arms.

Don't be ridiculous, Carmen said to herself. There's nothing to be scared of. She can't sack you again.

She eyed Mrs Marsh back, feeling as if she'd been summoned by the headmistress.

'Okay. Do you want to buy a book?' She had seen Mrs Marsh read: Regency romances with passionate women on the arms of dukes and lords.

Mrs Marsh raised her eyebrows.

'So this is a *shop*?'

'What did you think it was?'

'Storage of some kind.'

'Well. It is a shop, and I'm very busy,' lied Carmen.

Mrs Marsh tutted loudly. Carmen rolled her eyes.

'This place is a disgrace. I mean, look at it.'

'Mrs Marsh, I don't think you work here?'

It struck Carmen as ridiculous that she didn't actually know Mrs Marsh's first name.

'Well, obviously,' said Mrs Marsh. 'Because if I did, it would be nothing like this.'

'Actually, I'm here to revamp it,' said Carmen proudly. 'I'm here to do a kind of consulting interior design exercise.'

She felt annoyed with herself for showing off, but she wasn't going to be talked down to by the malevolent ghost of her old boss, not here and not anywhere.

Mrs Marsh stepped forwards, ran her finger along a line of books for dust, and found plenty.

'So where are you going to start?' she said. 'Remember what I told you?'

Carmen felt annoyed. Mrs Marsh had various retail mantras she was always trying to instil in them, and she and Idra had made a point of completely ignoring them and sniggering up the back.

'What have I always told you?'

It was definitely something beginning with C. Crappy, cloudy and cluttered? Cheap, cheery and crud? Carmen frowned.

'Clean! Clear! Curated!' said Mrs Marsh, after waiting on a pause.

'Oh right,' said Carmen, feeling sulky.

Mrs Marsh caught her gaze suddenly.

'You know,' she said, and Carmen realised it cost her something to say it, 'it was the fashion and the white goods that did for Dounston's. Did you know that? Haberdashery was always profitable. Always.'

This ... it almost sounded like praise. Carmen frowned.

Mrs Marsh turned around slowly, like a battleship, and reached for the door.

'I don't know what I'm doing here,' said Carmen suddenly. 'I'm not quite sure where to start.'

Mrs Marsh whipped back round immediately.

'Well, get to know your stock for a start rather than standing around like a pudding. And for goodness' sake get something going on for Christmas. It's the beginning of November. Forty per cent, you know! Forty per cent of your year's sales to see you through happen in the next eight weeks! Did you listen to nothing I said?'

Carmen didn't answer that.

'Well. Better late than never. You get this place looking Christmassy. And get it *tidied up*. Fill it with Christmas ... things ... '

'Books.'

'Yes. And for goodness' sake, clean. I don't want to leave wrapped in filth. And neither does anyone else.' She gave Carmen a penetrating gaze. 'Are you up to it or not?'

And then she did leave, without a goodbye, without even waiting to hear the answer, leaving Carmen shaken and annoyed.

Presently, a group of tourists came past, and peered in the window. They weren't to know they were entirely audible through the thin glazing.

'Oh my God, look at that,' said a loud woman's voice. 'Do you think something new is going in there?'

'They should put a juice bar in,' said another voice. 'I mean, look at the crap in there.'

'Oh yes, all these bloody hills,' came another as they marched past. 'You get thirsty.'

'Oh, I don't know. If you ever want some really shit postcards ... '

'Shh,' said the first voice. 'They might hear you.'

'Well, I'll apologise the very next time I don't go there,' came the voice, fading away.

They're right, thought Carmen in despair. They're right. This is a stupid amount of work, like Mrs Marsh said. I'll never manage it. It's too much for me. I always fail. Sofia could probably do it in, like, ten minutes. But I'm not like her. It's just too much. I'll find something else. This is just a waste of time. It's stupid.

She'd explain to Mr McCredie. She wasn't any use as a skivvy in a shop with no customers, with a boss who didn't want it to be a shop at all as far as she could tell. This was just a waste of time. Anyway, he was one of those old posh Edinburgh people. He'd have money. He'd be all right, Sofia was probably just egging him on to make her feel bad as usual. There were thousands of restaurants in Edinburgh. If she left now, she could make the tour this afternoon, find a cool well-paid job like Idra. Everyone needed waiting staff this time of year. Sofia could solve her own damn problems.

'Mr McCredie,' she announced. There was no answer in the silent shop.

She listened. What was that? A tiny noise coming from somewhere. Oh God, what if they had mice? Of course they'd have mice. Paper-chomping mice, making delicious nests ... did mice eat paper and make nests? Probably. Edinburgh mice probably made seven-storey nests. Then made the entrance on floor three and a half.

She stepped forward quietly and tilted her head. It sounded like ... less like a mouse, perhaps a cat mewing? She stood stock-still. Then she realised. It was a person.

She frowned. It could be … well, Mr McCredie, as she had learned that morning, left the door open all night, so it could be anyone. It could be him. Or a homeless person or someone ill … or a burglar. Probably not a burglar. The cash till was sitting there, untouched.

Carmen took out her phone cautiously, just in case she had to dial 999. Then she took a step forwards, through the entrance at the back, and into the forbidden stacks. She couldn't see a light switch anywhere; her hands groped along the wall, but with no luck.

It was the oddest thing. The shop went on, deeper and deeper, narrower and narrower. But there started to be fewer and fewer books, but a pot plant here and there, and the strip lighting faded to be replaced by darkness, and then she noticed that the hard floor of the shop had turned softer. I wonder, is that a plank? she thought, stooping down to feel it with her hands. But instead of feeling the hard, smooth stone of the floor of the bookshop, she felt something extremely soft and gentle and warm to the touch, like fine old wood. This is very odd, she said to herself, and went on a step or two further.

The next moment, she saw that there was a light ahead of her – not a strip light in the ceiling where the stock room should be, but a soft glow, some way off. A moment later, she found that she was standing in the middle of a sitting room, with rugs under her feet and wallpaper on the walls.

She looked back over her shoulder and there, between the dark book stacks, she could still see the open doorway of the shop, and even catch a glimpse of the busy road outside.

Looking around the room, Carmen thought she had never been in a nicer place. It was a dry, clean room with a carpet on the floor and two little chairs and a table and a dresser and a mantelpiece over the fire, and above that a picture of an old man with a grey beard. In one corner there was a door which Carmen thought must lead to Mr McCredie's bedroom, and on one wall was a shelf-ful of books. And on the seat nearest the fire was Mr McCredie, crying as softly as he knew how.

'Goodness, Mr McCredie. Are you all right?'

As he looked up, the man's blue eyes filled with more tears and then they began trickling down his cheeks, and soon they were running off the end of his nose; at last he covered his face with his hands and began to howl.

'Mr McCredie! Mr McCredie!' said Carmen in great distress. 'Don't! Don't! What is the matter? Aren't you well? Do tell me what is wrong.' But the man continued sobbing as if his heart would break.

Carmen poured him a fresh cup of tea from the warmed pot she saw and placed it next to him. Finally, he straightened up.

'I'm ... I'm so sorry. I've been such a bad person.'

'What do you mean?'

'I've let the shop go to rack and ruin ... I've wasted my life, betrayed my family ...'

He looked up at the stern, grey-haired picture of his father and held up a letter.

Carmen looked at it.

'It's from the council,' he said.

'I know,' said Carmen. 'I know what it says. Sofia told me.'

Mr McCredie started to cry again.

'I know,' he said. 'But I didn't really believe it until now.'

'I'm sure it will be okay,' said Carmen. 'I'm sure it can be saved.'

'It's too late!'

'Nothing is ever too late,' said Carmen, hoping she believed that. 'Never!'

'But it's nearly Christmas.'

'Nonsense,' said Carmen. 'It's winter here for about nine months. It's never Christmas. I'm sure there is lots we can do. Also, forty per cent of business is done at Christmastime.'

'Do you think?'

'So I heard.' She looked around. 'Sorry, do you live here?'

'Upstairs mostly,' said Mr McCredie. 'This is where I come to read.'

'It's lovely,' said Carmen. 'Like a little cave.'

'I know but I've wasted so much time here when I should have—'

'It'll be fine,' said Carmen severely, trying to head off another flourish of tears. Oh, for goodness' sake. 'Everything is going to be fine.'

'But you're going to leave! I heard you talking to your friend.'

'Well, you shouldn't eavesdrop.'

He sniffed and nodded then looked up at her meekly.

'I'll stay till Christmas,' she said finally. 'And you need to let me do what I want and stop telling me not to go in the stacks or move anything.'

He swallowed.

'I'll try.'

Chapter Nine

'Are you going to take us on any outings or anything?' said Jack, bouncing his ball on the floor the next day, which happened to be a Sunday, meaning the shop was closed, even though Carmen thought closing the shop several Sundays before Christmas was a dumb idea.

'Like where?' said Carmen. The children had more or less given up on expecting much of her. She didn't seem at all impressed by Pippa's gold stars, she didn't care about football and she didn't seem to notice Phoebe at all. She wasn't like Federico's brother, their uncle Julio, who played in goal and held skipping ropes and tickled Phoebe even though she pretended to hate it and bought them two ice creams a day whenever he swung in. That was a fun uncle to have. Carmen, Pippa loudly told Skylar, was not a good auntie at all, and Skylar said very firmly not to forget that we always had to Be Kind? and Carmen didn't have a goal in life? And was very sad? Which would have been fine had Carmen not been just coming out of the shower

62

at the time, and had to dig her fingers into her hands to pretend she hadn't heard. She and Sofia were still not speaking which was very annoying as there was a delicious-smelling venison stew on the burner and Carmen was starving.

'Like what?' said Carmen shortly.

'Like the zoo?'

'Zoos are cruel,' said Carmen. 'It's just animals in prison.'

Jack sighed.

'Well, I'm just BORED.'

'You and me both, kid.'

She had a sudden thought.

'Can you clean?'

'What, like clean my room?'

'I'M NOT CLEANING MY ROOM,' said Phoebe, appearing as she did out of nowhere, the frowzy head crosspatch as ever. 'IT'S *MY* ROOM.'

'I don't mean your rooms,' said Carmen. They looked at her, still suspicious. 'Do you want to come with me and clean out the bookshop?'

'What's in it for us?'

'I can't get my new dress dirty,' said Pippa, fastidiously patting down the purple pinafore.

'Why not?' said Phoebe. 'It's horrible. You look like two plums stuck together.'

'Be kind, Phoebe,' said Pippa primly.

'Will I get a broom?' said Jack.

'Yup.'

'And a treat?'

'You drive a hard bargain.'

Skylar came in in her yoga kit again, blonde hair freshly washed and bouncing.

63

'Have a great day with the kids, yeah? Bye, guys! Don't forget: five portions! Namaste!'

She looked at Carmen and spoke in a low voice.

'Please don't just dump them in front of a screen? It's really unfair on Sofia because they just play up later, do you see?'

Carmen rolled her eyes.

'Oh, I have plans, don't worry.'

Sofia was sceptical about the whole thing. On the other hand, she reflected, Federico was in Hong Kong doing Hong Kong things, Skylar was out yoga-ing, so if Carmen took all three out she would have the entire house to herself. She could lie back, read a magazine, maybe break into one of those hampers a grateful client had sent over. She wouldn't have to umpire between what used to be three small people but now appeared to be four. It was, in fact, such an appealing concept that Carmen could have been taking them off to mine coal and she would put up only feeble resistance.

She still had to at least put up the bare minimum though. She wasn't one of those women who worked and were also desperate to get away from their children. No. She definitely wasn't.

'So if I have to stay and do this stupid job,' Carmen was saying.

'You want to use my children as slave labour?'

'You don't want them to learn how to clean?'

'Not particularly,' said Sofia.

'We have a cleaner,' said Pippa. 'It's what happens to you if you don't work hard at school and go to university.'

Carmen caught her breath. Sofia, who knew she should have dealt with this before, felt utterly ashamed of herself.

'Yes. Okay. Great. Take them.'

'But, Mummy!' objected Pippa.

'You'll want to put some old clothes on,' said Carmen directly to her.

'Yay,' said Phoebe.

They took the bus, even though it wasn't far, and Carmen was once again shocked by their amazement at the novelty factor of being on a bus.

'You never catch the bus?' she said and they shook their heads, then went upstairs, where Jack and Pippa nabbed the front seat. Phoebe looked all set to make a massive scene about not getting one, and Carmen let her while she stared at her phone, formidably ignoring all the tutting Edinburgh ladies sitting around them. In surprise, Phoebe calmed down faster than normal as they pootled up the Lothian Road, past the huge red sandstone Caledonian Hotel.

All the way up Victoria Street, the children *umm*ed and *awwww*ed, and Carmen realised that now the Christmas decorations were up – great shining silver stars making the pretty street even lovelier – the shops had really come into their own, each (everyone except for them was open on a Sunday, she also noticed) lovelier than the last: dark green and red Christmas trees inside and outside the expensive tweed shop; beautiful paper mobiles and lights in the lovelier bookshop; golden lamp-posts and fairy lights twirling around the magic shop;

great thick swathes of holly and ivy in the coffee shop where Carmen promised them milkshakes later. Even the hardware store had little trees lined up in a tidy row with little soldiers posted between them, she noticed as they went in to purchase a large brush, which Mr McCredie didn't seem to own but desperately needed.

'You're Mr McCredie's girl,' said the man in the store, his burgundy apron decorated with holly.

'Word gets around,' said Carmen.

'Oh yes, we're a family here,' he said. 'Well, we try to be. Mr McCredie, he's never been one for wanting to join in. We wish he would. You can't do this alone.' Then he lowered his voice. 'Do you think he'll be able to hold on?'

'I don't know,' said Carmen, and suddenly didn't want to disappoint anyone.

'I hope so.'

'Do your best, love.'

And he threw in a dustpan for free.

They were no good, that was true. They moaned and complained and said they were tired and their hands hurt and she, Carmen, was mean for making them work.

But somehow, gradually, the dust lifted, and the windows got polished – not terribly well – and they tuned the radio to a station that only played Christmas songs, and Carmen vanished at one point and did indeed bring back three of the largest milkshakes anyone had ever seen, which – as Sofia and Skylar had passed her a forbidden food list which included McDonald's, all fizzy drinks, sweets, sparkling water, fruit juice (bad for teeth apparently) – Carmen considered something of a triumph, at least till Phoebe jolted Pippa and spilt hers and there was a huge fight between the girls and a big mess on the floor.

But it was undeniable that, as they piled the books to the side, things were starting to look better. With everything stacked neatly and a path cleared, for starters, it at least looked like a shop, without maps piled willy-nilly to the sky, and the whining and complaining calmed down as they found more interesting books. Phoebe came up to Carmen.

'There's no Christmas books!' she said. 'It's meant to be Christmastime and there's no Christmas books. This is a stupid shop.'

Carmen was inclined to agree with her.

'Do you think we should have more Christmas things?'

'I think you should have nothing but Christmas things,' said Phoebe. 'Even if they're boring grown-up things.'

Carmen thought again of what Mrs Marsh had said. Well, maybe she had a point. And she didn't know how on earth to sell all this stuff – these old books – otherwise.

'Okay,' she said. 'Guys, every time you find a book that says "Christmas" on it, bring it to me.'

'What will you give us?' said Jack instantly.

'The satisfaction of doing a job well,' said Carmen, sticking her tongue out at him. 'Oh, all right. And a marshmallow.'

'We can't—' started Pippa, but was silenced with glares from the others.

'You should read Christmas books in the shop,' said Phoebe. 'Then everyone would come.'

'That's . . . actually not a bad idea,' said Carmen. 'Except I'm not very good at reading aloud.'

'Neither is Phoebe,' said Pippa in her disconcertingly adult tones. 'She needs special help at school.'

'I DO NOT!'

'She does.'

And Carmen dropped the story-time discussion straightaway, but she rather liked the idea nonetheless.

By the end of the afternoon (it was already growing dark at 3.30 p.m.) the shop was looking, if not gleaming, markedly better and tidier. They had taken Carmen's advice to drag out any Christmassy-looking titles incredibly seriously. And in fact, due to Mr McCredie's completely obscure filing system, to the left of rabbits and upwind of knights and just above shipping, they hit gold: an entire section of the stacks devoted to Christmas titles – ancient stories Carmen had never heard of, like *Jolly Jill Saves Christmas!*

It was like finding treasure. They wiped them all down carefully and put them in the front window with a flourish. Coming out to examine their handiwork, it still looked – well, lame, frankly, compared with the other glorious lit-up beacons up and down the street.

But it looked like a shop.

When they arrived home, the feeling of solidarity with the tired, grubby children didn't last terribly long. Sofia tried to be gracious and say thank you but patently couldn't really hide her disapproval at the state of them and she found herself making lots of remarks about bassoon practice and homework and caught herself at it. Oh God, when had she turned into such a nag? She had frittered her afternoon away: social media, then fallen asleep on the sofa, waking up groggy and with a headache she couldn't take anything for. This point of pregnancy was just so exhausting and the amount of time Skylar seemed to need for 'personal self-care', lectures, yoga, massage therapy, having her aura read was increasing all the time. She did need Carmen. Even if they were absolutely mucky.

Chapter Ten

Carmen tried to tell herself the city was only so lovely because it was filled with annoying rich people who wore red trousers and had surnames as first names and were all snotty show-offs like Sofia.

But it wore you down, the magic. Even now, only in November, when night fell so early it felt like every street was beating back the dark every way it knew how: early trees appearing in windows, glowing gold, in the smart New Town apartments and the big bay windows of the West End terraces; lights garlanding every road and stretching across the wide bank of George Street, with its expensive shops and bars wreathed in holly and lights; the pillars of the huge Dome restaurant swathed in metres of foliage and lights sparkling and twinkling; the Ivy restaurant transforming its doorway into the cupboard doors of Narnia which took you into a snowy scene. Up on the Royal Mile was a cathedral built entirely from light which you could stroll through and hear the carol singers. From every tiny coffee shop in every nook and cranny came enchanting smells of gingerbread and cinnamon, and over the Christmas market, with its the smell of mulled wine hanging in the air. At the top of the mound, which Carmen passed every day, was the tallest Christmas tree she had ever seen, and a huge rainbow of lights. It didn't matter how low you thought you were, thought Carmen. It was still pretty nice.

Mr McCredie was looking at her gingerbread latte with some consternation.

'What . . . ? I'm not quite sure I understand.'

'It's coffee that tastes of gingerbread. You should try it: it's delicious.'

He frowned.

'I don't think I would like that.'

Fastidiously, he stirred the slice of lemon in his tea in a dainty cup and saucer with a willow pattern and a tiny handle.

'No,' smiled Carmen. 'Maybe you wouldn't.' She looked around. 'But I have to say, your filing system came up trumps. Look! Everything about Christmas!'

Mr McCredie frowned.

'So you're saying we only sell books about Christmas?'

'I think it has potential,' said Carmen bravely.

They looked at each other. Carmen wished he wasn't putting quite so much faith in her.

The shop had started to look like a shop, but it still wasn't getting many people through the doors. Carmen dusted and attempted to look cheerful over the following week, but people would still ask her for the new Jack Reacher or Richard Osman and she'd have to look apologetic, or they'd ask for something incredibly esoteric and difficult, and Mr McCredie would suddenly appear at the desk from his nook and contentedly spend hours discussing with the person (generally a man) their area of interest and what they'd read around the same subject which, although it often would not end in a sale, clearly made Mr McCredie very happy.

One morning, a long shadow fell across the floor. It couldn't be that late already, thought Carmen, looking up from where she was practising her wrapping, which was still terrible. It was just an idea, in an idle moment, that they could offer gift-wrapping. Unfortunately, if it took ten thousand hours to become an expert, she thought, she had probably done it already with gift-wrapping, but she still wasn't very good at it, even though – crucially – she was only wrapping flat square things. She was slightly regretting her suggested innovation.

One of the tallest men Carmen had ever seen slouched through the door, with a couple of boxes at his feet. He looked at her, bemused.

'Hello?' said Carmen.

'Um. Hello. Where's young Mr McCredie?'

'He's busy ... reading.'

The very tall man frowned.

'Well, yes.'

Carmen expected the man to start browsing, but instead he folded his arms and just stood there, leading Carmen to the ridiculous but inescapable conclusion that he wouldn't buy a book from a woman. He wasn't an older man either, although in his cords, tweed shirt, worn muddy-coloured jumper, cap and waxed jacket, he certainly looked like one.

'Can I get him for you?'

He looked at her.

'You're allowed in the stacks?'

Carmen beamed.

'Apparently so.'

'Goodness. What next: the metric system?'

He glanced out at the street where he had left the Land Rover with its hazards on, a call known to attract the most implacable enemy of all Edinburgh drivers: the traffic warden. He peered down the road, enjoying a clear line of sight. Nothing yet, but they had the habit of popping up stealthily out of nowhere.

Mr McCredie appeared from the stacks eventually, brushing crumbs from his jumper and feeling for his spectacles.

'Ramsay!' he said joyfully. He peered out of the window. 'Oh for goodness' sake, won't you just pay for parking?'

Ramsay sniffed. 'Never! Those robdogs.'

'Well, we'd better be quick. How's the family?'

'Good, good.'

'How many is it now?'

'Five . . . Well, it's going to be six actually.'

Ramsay went rather pink with pride.

Carmen couldn't help it. 'You have six children?'

'Well . . . five and a bit.'

Carmen blinked.

'Doesn't your wife mind?'

'Well, she isn't my wife yet and it's mostly her idea so . . .'

Ramsay's voice trailed off, but there was a twitch in the corner of his mouth as there always when he thought of Zoe.

'Cor,' said Carmen. 'I hope you have a big house.'

Mr McCredie laughed.

'Oh, there's plenty of room up Ramsay's way.'

'So you have a huge house but not enough cash to pay for parking?'

'It's not the money!' said Ramsay. 'It's the sport.'

'What have you got for me?' said Mr McCredie.

'Hang on, you're a sales rep?' said Carmen.

They both nodded as if this were obvious. Carmen had assumed they were friends (which they were). Mrs Marsh treated all sales reps as if they were dangerous criminals.

Ramsay's face lit up. 'Wait till you see what I've got for you today!'

'What? Don't tell me: an *Up on the Rooftops*?'

'You are joking, aren't you? We'd all be in the Bahamas right now.'

Nonetheless he heaved the two heavy boxes up onto the old desk and, curious despite herself, Carmen inched closer.

'Oh, this is Carmen,' said young Mr McCredie finally. 'She's helping me out over the holidays.'

'Nice to meet you,' said Ramsay. 'You have ... '

He indicated something, and Carmen, who had been rather cross with him not dealing with her as the person in charge of the shop, put her hand up to her head. Somehow she had managed to stick a red bow on the side of her neck.

'Oh!' she said, ripping it off crossly.

'I thought it was a feature,' said young Mr McCredie. 'You know. Seasonal.'

'A bow stuck on my neck? You thought this was part of my shop modernisation?'

'Um ... '

As a distraction, Ramsay opened the box carefully. There were a lot of big old dusty hardbacks, which Mr McCredie looked at reverently before he gently handled each one.

'What's this?' said Carmen, picking up one on 'the Sublime in Landscape Architecture, 1759–1805'.

'Illustrated plates,' said Ramsay.

'Ooh,' said Mr McCredie.

'No!' said Carmen. 'We don't have a market for that.'

'But it's beautiful,' said Ramsay, and Mr McCredie nodded his head emphatically.

'But who is going to buy it?' said Carmen. 'Sublime fans?'

Mr McCredie looked at her stubbornly, his hand on the old binding.

'What else have you got?' said Carmen, giving Ramsay a narrow look.

Beneath the pile of random books was a full set of identical heavy green hardbacks. Carmen pulled out the top one.

It was beautiful. Bound in a dark green, there was a coloured plate of a snow queen, recessed on the front. When you opened the cover, there was a fine layer of tissue paper which rustled gently and, once turned over, there was an image of the queen in front of her icy castle. The books, though clearly rather old, were perfect; they had never been open.

'Well,' said Mr McCredie reverently.

Carmen found herself desperate to put out a hand to touch another one. 'These are lovely. Hans Christian Andersen?'

Ramsay nodded. The endpapers were marbled and there were full colour plates throughout the stories, as well as regular line drawings and a silk placeholding ribbon.

'This is treasure, Ramsay,' said Mr McCredie. 'Where on earth did you find it?'

'A lot of digging at an estate sale,' said Ramsay in his deep rumble. 'Looks like a younger son venture gone rather wrong, don't you think, and covered up?'

'Well, quite,' said McCredie. 'They must have cost more to produce than they could ever have brought in. Those posh boys and their book enterprises.'

Ramsay and Mr McCredie shared a conspiratorial glance at that, and both started to laugh.

'Would have been in copyright then too,' said Ramsay, shaking his head.

'Well,' said McCredie. 'You clever thing.' Then he pulled himself up, and turned to Carmen, who had her arms folded.

'Um . . . what do you think, my dear?'

She looked at the books again.

'Yes. Christmas, cold, winter, beautiful . . . yes. These will do. We'll take these. None of the others.'

Mr McCredie winced and looked pained, but Ramsay wasn't remotely fussed.

'They're lovely,' said Carmen, handling them once more. The colour internal illustrations were each covered with the lightest, most delicate sheets of tissue paper. 'I can't imagine who wouldn't want one.'

'Traumatised children?' mused Ramsay. 'When we read the boys *The Snow Queen*, Patrick put all our glasses in the bin in case he broke one and got a bit in his eye. Hari helped.'

'Oh, all your children,' said Mr McCredie affectionately, at which point Carmen inserted herself and asked about prices, and bickered back and forth with him in a way Mr McCredie found frightfully vulgar and embarrassing and Ramsay rather enjoyed, until they finally shook hands. This set Ramsay grinning cheerfully until he saw a familiar peaked hat skulking up the steps of a shop close by and knew fine well what that skulking was in aid of and charged out of the shop brandishing his keys.

The old Land Rover took off in a cough of black smoke as the peaked cap stamped crossly past the window, the machine at the ready.

'Yes!' said Mr McCredie.

'What?' said Carmen. 'He's stealing parking!'

'He's doing business,' said Mr McCredie. 'Paying for parking would kill his profit margin.'

'Is that what he does?'

'Well, technically he's a laird. But poor as a church mouse with a property to keep up, and land, and about a thousand children, only some of them his own.'

'Don't make me feel guilty for changing your buying methods,' said Carmen. 'Because I shan't.'

And they worked together, setting out the beautiful new editions. They piled them irresistibly near the door whereupon, to Carmen's delight, they started to sell straightaway – not to children, but to adults, drawn in by their own childhood memories, and the beauty of a thing.

Every time the bell dinged, Mr McCredie would glance up in wonder and surprise, and Carmen would smile secretly to herself and make sure the lovely books were somewhere adults could pick them up and admire them.

Marbled endpapers, Mr McCredie observed, meant nothing to children. But they meant a lot to those who loved colour and beauty and stories that would never end. And Carmen made sure to put lots of children's books next to them, so the adults would buy a fancy gift for themselves and then often something not quite so precious for the children. Carmen also emailed Ramsay and told him she could sell as many Christmas books as he could unearth, and he sent her a jolly thumbs up and started on a mission for her.

Flushed by her own success, Carmen was feeling unstoppable.

'Maybe I should do a story time next,' she said. Mr McCredie raised his eyebrows.

'Do I have to be there?' he said. 'It's just ... there would be rather a *lot* of children.'

She noticed how anxious he got when sticky fingers approached his beloved first editions.

'Quite the opposite,' she said. 'You'll need a rest from manning the till so much. I order you to stay in the back sitting room while I do it.'

He smiled at her, and Carmen had the oddest sensation that this might just work.

One morning, the bell tinged just as Carmen was wondering why young Mr McCredie didn't turn some more of his books out with their covers facing customers – it seemed a reasonably obvious retail thing to do, but then things seemed to work differently here.

She got down from the stepladder and smiled brightly, waiting for the inevitable, 'Is young Mr McCredie not about?'

This could be said in a variety of different ways, Carmen had learned, and in this man's case – he was thin, with a knobbly red face, wearing a long greasy-looking overcoat and clutching a much-used plastic bag stuffed with papers – it was said furtively, and for the first time, she saw a sigh of relief when she said, 'No, it's just me.'

'Well then,' he said, arriving at the glass-topped desk, pushing aside several copies of *Christmas with the Savages*

Carmen was cheerfully planning to recommend to today's customers.

'Doesn't look very Christmassy, your shop,' he said.

'I know,' said Carmen, who was thinking the same thing, but she couldn't spend the shop's money as they didn't have any and it wouldn't help to get them further on the red side. Maybe she should ask Sofia, although she baulked at the idea.

Although things were going better at the shop, relations between the sisters were still frosty, and their mother was refusing to be drawn in and had declared herself Switzerland. Sofia complained to Federico every night, which was first thing in the morning in Hong Kong so he was rarely at his best. Plus, he just liked to hear her voice, loved the rattle of the children in and out: Jack barking short answers to questions about how things were going; Pippa on the other hand elaborating on exactly who had misbehaved at school that day and why and how the boys hadn't listened to Mrs Bakran, and had got into trouble; and Phoebe, more often than not, simply breathing snottily down the phone. He liked it all, just let it wash over, soothed by familiar noises. Which actually rather fired Sofia up, thinking he was agreeing with her, when he was just generally soothed by thoughts of home. He was a good man, Federico, but like many others he was guilty of letting his wife handle the domestics, despite the fact that she'd been to law school and graduated higher than he had.

Carmen was using the bottom door to get in and out of the house. The most contact she had with her sister's family was on the nights Skylar was out, when she would sit on the sofa and let the kids fight while looking at social media on her phone and sending rude messages to Idra she really couldn't let the children see.

She thought this was probably quite a nice break for the kids from being prodded to practise their instruments/do their homework/read an improving book every second of the day. Sofia didn't agree. They communicated in stiff texts.

Carmen was reflecting on this sad state of affairs when the man in the shop snorted.

'Now,' he said. 'Has Mr McCredie mentioned me?'

'Who are you?' said Carmen.

'Ha! Aha. Very good. Well. Just as well. I'm Justin Feeney.' He looked at her face. 'Well. Um. Okay, right. Mr McCredie told me to come in because I have the perfect book for your shop!'

He held up a packet of poorly stapled together pieces of foolscap. On the front of it was a rather badly sketched picture of a fish. Added in pen was a Santa hat. The title of the work was clearly *The Fish*, but the word 'Christmas' had been inserted in between 'The' and 'Fish'.

'*The Christmas Fish*?' said Carmen slowly.

'Yes! It's supporting independent publishing,' said Justin proudly. 'I do them myself.'

'Okay,' said Carmen. 'What's it about?'

'It's about a man's struggle against a fish,' said Justin. 'He has to fight and overcome the slippery fish in a titanic struggle between man and fish. The fish is a metaphor.'

'For Christmas?'

'No. For women.'

'Oh,' said Carmen. 'Where does Christmas come into it?'

Justin frowned.

'Actually I'm not sure you'd really understand it out of context. But I think Mr McCredie definitely wants to take some to sell. They're only ten pounds each, wholesale.'

'I think I'd have to ask him,' said Carmen.

'But you work here, don't you?'

'Yes,' said Carmen, then lied. 'I'd definitely have to run it past him.'

Justin frowned, and Carmen was sure she saw him mouth 'fish' to himself.

'You can leave one if you like,' she said, looking up happily as another customer entered, 'so we could take a look at it . . . '

'To steal my idea? Not likely,' said Justin, grabbing his plastic bag and heading out again. 'You'll be sorry.'

Still, thought Carmen. It proved her 'Christmas only' push was working if people were desperate to get their books into the shop. And he was irritatingly right about the decorations issue.

Carmen watched him go, stalking off down towards the Grassmarket, clutching his plastic bag close, and felt sorry for him.

Or, she would have felt sorry for him if, over the course of the next four days, every time the old-fashioned black phone rang startlingly loudly, making her leap in the air, it would be somebody with a badly disguised Edinburgh accent asking if they had any books in about fish as that was the kind of thing they liked to read at Christmas. And as Mr McCredie had told her on strictest terms that next time he came in she had to buy one and give Justin ten pounds from the petty cash, because that was the correct thing to do at Christmas, she found herself feeling rather told off.

As was familiar to most people in Edinburgh, you weren't just front-facing staff; you were tour guides and historians too, and Carmen was having trouble, not being a native, although she had figured out the answers to 'Where's the castle?' ('Up the steps on the left'), 'OMG, WHAT'S THAT NOISE?' (the daily one o'clock cannon designed, Carmen was reasonably sure, simply to startle people into having heart attacks and thus cut down on tourist numbers) and 'Where's the café J.K. Rowling wrote Harry Potter?' (Carmen rotated her favourite coffee shops on this list, reasoning everybody deserved a shot).

So when the door tinged on a morning that had her staring longingly at the fireplace and wishing there weren't rules against having an open fire in an old room filled to the brim with paper, and a rangy figure bounced in, looking exactly like a student, she steadied herself.

He had a battered rucksack slung over his back, a burgundy hoodie over a Breton shirt over a long-sleeved shirt – i.e. he appeared to be wearing everything he owned, a common response from people who had arrived quite recently.

He was tall, with light brown skin, dark hair in a top knot and green eyes; striking enough that Carmen felt a faint sadness that she was about to be directing him to the youth hostel down the other end of the Grassmarket, and that many of the shop's customers were generally closer in age to Mr McCredie than to herself.

'Hello?' she said cheerfully.

'Hello,' he said. His voice was deep, with a very faint accent and Carmen picked up the well-used desk map in anticipation.

'I was wondering if you had a copy of *The Physiology of Tree Soil.*'

Carmen looked at him and was about to call for Mr McCredie

when she realised Mr McCredie would instantly corner him and talk his ears off.

'I'm sure we could order it for you?' she said. 'Are you a student?'

He smiled.

'Do I look like a student?'

'You could not look more like a student if you had one of those raggedy scarfs and were trying to split a coffee four ways.'

He laughed.

'You don't like students?'

Carmen shrugged. Sofia's elegant friends who had occasionally come to visit, or showed up to her hen night, her wedding, her christenings, all her simply fabulous parties in a variety of increasingly fancy apartments seemed callow and entitled, bristling with confidence and money. And always, at the back of her mind, her father saying, when she announced she was done with school and was off to work in Dounston's, 'But you're such a *clever* girl.' She had always been jealous of students. She covered it up by treating them with a bit of disdain. She could have been one too. It just hadn't worked out like that.

'I have a huge chip on my shoulder,' she said eventually.

He smiled.

'Well then, you will be pleased to know that although I have been a student for a very long time, I am now a lecturer.'

'Who dresses like a student.'

'You're more confrontational than most people I've just met who work in a bookshop.'

'Chip! Shoulder! What do you lecture in? *Trees?*' Carmen giggled.

'Um yes,' he said. 'I'm a dendrologist.'

'A *what?*'

'Tree person,' he said hurriedly. 'Trees. I'm a student of trees.'

'Oh,' she said. Then she thought about it. 'You'd have liked our book about sublime landscapes.'

'I would like that!' he said.

'Ah. We don't have it.'

'And the other one . . . ?'

'Okay, well, let me order it for you,' she said. There wasn't a computer in the shop, and she had to call the wholesalers on her phone – really embarrassing – so she kept a book for orders. As she wrote down the details, he picked up a book near the till. It was an illustrated edition of *A Christmas Carol* Ramsay had sent over on – kindly – a sale or return basis, with paintings by Arthur Rackham.

'Wow,' he breathed.

'I know,' said Carmen. 'Isn't it awesome?'

'I love his woods . . . his trees.'

'I suppose you would.'

He grinned.

'I suppose I would too.'

'Would you like it?' said Carmen. He lifted his hands off instantly.

'Oh. No. I'm . . . thank you. It's all right.'

But his eyes still followed it regretfully.

'Sure. Can I take your number?'

He looked at her. His eyes were very green indeed, she noticed. How unusual. She wondered where he was from.

'Um.' He seemed awkward.

'For the order,' she said briskly, annoyed with herself because she knew she was colouring. 'So we can tell you when it's in . . .'

'Of course, of course. Sorry,' he said. 'Oke.'

'Okay?' she said.

'No, I mean, Oke. That's my name. O-K-E. Well, it's short for . . .'

He stopped himself.

'What?' said Carmen.

'It really doesn't matter,' he said.

'Ooh,' said Carmen. 'Okehampton?'

'Um, I don't know what that is.'

'Ocarina? Hang on, *I* don't know what that is.'

They smiled at each other, but he remained tight-lipped and so Carmen wrote 'Oke' down alongside a number that started +55.

'I don't think we can phone that,' she said, looking at the manual dial telephone on the desk. 'I'm not sure it does international calls. Where is it, Mars?'

'Brazil . . . but I've ordered the book?' he said, looking slightly confused. 'Of course I'll come back for it.'

Carmen, a veteran of many years of retail, smiled slightly tightly at him.

'If you say so. If you're absolutely not going to disappear to Brazil.'

There was a bounce to his walk as he headed towards the door. He was definitely a student, thought Carmen. If he was lecturing as a real job, he wouldn't be hanging out at 11 a.m. anyway.

Just as she was thinking this he turned around.

'Do I get my student discount?' he asked, and she felt bad for mocking him when he was almost certainly incredibly poor.

'Of course,' she said quickly, even though she had gone from age seventeen to age twenty-five completely furious that a student discount even existed for those gilded souls swanning around drinking coffee and talking and doing not very much while grafters like herself were on fifty hours a week. She didn't even know what the discount might be. Well, she'd work that out as it went.

He grinned again.

'Cool. Bye!'

Chapter Eleven

Carmen mounted the stairs from the basement. There was a chicken curry on that smelled absolutely divine, and Carmen looked at the little family for a moment, sitting up nicely, eating what appeared to be vegetables. She felt a pang. Was that what she wanted? Was she just jealous?

Then Pippa made a remark about Phoebe having food on her face in response to which Phoebe kicked Pippa hard under the table.

'Why do you do that, Phoebe?' Sofia asked, dark eyes wide with concern. 'I feel you could be happier if you didn't feel the need to be so disruptive. Do we need to have a family conference?'

'Perhaps she's feeling undervalued, Mummy,' said Pippa complacently. 'Phoebe, do you feel you're not listened to?'

Phoebe furrowed her brow and made a growling noise.

'It's all right to feel frustrated,' went on Sofia. 'Just let it out.'

At this, Phoebe kicked the laid-back Jack so sharply he cried aloud.

'Well, maybe we don't let our feelings out *quite* like that, Phoebe,' said Sofia, and a sullen silence descended.

'Um, hi?' said Carmen.

Sofia would have got up if she wasn't so encumbered, she was so pleased Carmen wasn't hiding in her room.

'Join us,' she said.

'Okay,' said Carmen. 'Uh, I wanted to ask you ... please can I have some of your Christmas decorations for the shop? Have you got any you didn't use?'

Sofia blushed, ladling curry onto a plate for Carmen and sprinkling it with almonds. It smelled heavenly.

'Ah,' she said. 'Well, the thing is ... ' She hated confessing this as she liked people thinking that she did everything herself, and that things came easily to her. 'I rent the decorations.'

'You what?' said Carmen, who hadn't the faintest idea that was even a thing.

'Someone comes and puts them up and takes them down again.'

Carmen was absolutely speechless.

'That's why you're not allowed to touch the Christmas trees,' said Phoebe, nodding and carefully moving all the bits of carrot away from the chicken. She had to eat them, but she could put it off to the last possible moment. The house might fall down or something and she'd regret eating the carrots first.

Carmen blinked.

'Okay,' she said. She hadn't even realised that people who weren't celebrities could do this kind of thing.

'So how is everything?' said Sofia, trying to change the subject.

'Mr McCredie is nice ... Well, he's odd. What's his background?'

'Well,' said Sofia, 'I can't discuss my clients' personal business.

88

But as for what everyone knows, the McCredies are quite a well-known family in Edinburgh, go back a long way. He's young Mr McCredie but I think his dad was young Mr McCredie too. It's very confusing. His grandfather was rather famous – he was on the Scottish polar expedition, you know.'

'The what?'

'The expedition to the South Pole.'

'With Captain Scott? That one?'

'No! The Scottish polar expedition. 1902 or something. They did some exploring, didn't get to the South Pole but they found a new bit of land and set up a weather station that was quite useful. They were very famous at the time, but nobody died on the expedition, so people don't remember it now.'

'Even so, that's amazing.'

'It is.'

'Goodness,' said Carmen. 'Young Mr McCredie doesn't look like the outdoor type.'

'No, he isn't, not at all. So then the other young Mr McCredie ...'

'That's not the South Pole one?'

'Goodness no. That's young Mr McCredie's father.'

'But he's not still alive?'

'Oh no. He was a great war hero, decorated and what-not. Then I think their son came as a surprise.'

'Why?'

'Well, the whole family was known for its derring-do – lots of brothers in the military and so on. Lots and lots of boys.' She paused. 'All dead now. I have the archive in the office; it's quite fascinating. But Mr McCredie was an only child, born just after the war, only interested in books really. Didn't do anything that was expected of him.'

'Is he married?'

'Never married.'

'Gay?'

'I don't know. I don't think so.'

'Hmm,' said Carmen. 'Is he nice? Do you like him?'

Sofia nodded. 'He's a little ... distracted. But yes. Very kind, I think. I wouldn't ... I wouldn't have sent you to work for someone horrible, Carmen.'

'No,' said Carmen. 'Just the only person in this town skinter than me.'

'You need to MAKE THE SHOP LIKE CHRISTMAS,' interrupted Phoebe, chased inevitably by Pippa saying, 'Don't interrupt.' 'And DO STORIES.'

'I am going to do a story time!' said Carmen. 'Tell your friends.'

'She doesn't have any friends,' said Pippa, widening her eyes. 'I am so sad for her, aren't you?'

'No,' said Carmen. 'Other children are total idiots, everyone knows that. Total buggers.'

And while Sofia internally gasped, Phoebe, for the first time, betrayed a hint of a smile.

Chapter Twelve

Carmen gave the shop a critical eye the next morning. The problem was, everywhere else was so lovely. Victoria Street itself had hung sparkling silver stars down the middle. All along the street she could see decorations and lovely windows and shop proprietors chatting with one another while helping each other hang garlands, and wondered why Mr McCredie didn't get involved.

She marched up to Mr McCredie, who was sitting by his fireplace in the nook, poring over accounts in his half-moon spectacles and looking unpromising. She startled him of course, but he went to pour her a cup of tea. She was beginning to not mind it with lemon in it. She had got nowhere trying to convince him to try a gingerbread latte though.

'Do you have any Christmas decorations?' she said. 'I think we should put some up. Everyone else has absolutely loads.'

'Doing things everyone else does has never been my speciality,' said Mr McCredie.

'I bet,' said Carmen. 'But do you have any?'

He led her through the door she had assumed led to his bedroom, but it didn't: there was, in fact, a flight of stairs.

'Edinburgh architects must just have been off their faces the entire time,' said Carmen.

'I think building vertically in a vertical city makes perfect sense,' said Mr McCredie. 'Look at Amsterdam.'

At the top of the staircase, Carmen gasped as the door opened into a huge drawing room.

It was above ground – absurdly, an entire storey above ground; nothing made sense – and it looked out onto the other side of the block onto the Royal Mile itself.

Two windows faced the front and two the back, but they weren't in grand proportion like Sofia's house; instead they were small and higgledy-piggledy. The room itself, however, was large, with high ceilings and a vast fireplace against the left-hand wall. There was a grand piano in the corner covered in a pink fringed cloth, with pictures in silver frames lining it. The rug was faded, with an old design of pink roses, covering the wooden floor. Old sofas of elegant design, with curled wooden arms, were put out tidily. A candelabra swung from the ceiling, and old paintings lined the walls. It was a beautiful room, although it felt like it belonged to an earlier age. Mind you, so did this city, Carmen was beginning to learn. It was beautiful, but somehow strange; out of time, like those houses people leave behind or board up, which remain untouched for sixty years.

There was nothing new in the room at all. There was a radio but no television; there were books of course, but no magazines; a clock, but no computer or even a charger. Nothing that looked like the normal detritus of modern life. Even the photographs were all terribly old: black and white and in dusty frames. Nothing from Mr McCredie's own life. He was there as a child; he was not there after that.

'Wow,' said Carmen, looking for something to say. 'Well. This is lovely. And you have a secret tunnel to the office. That is pretty cool.'

'Is it?' said Mr McCredie, looking around. 'It was my parents' home really. I never quite ... found a way to move on.'

Once again, Carmen got the sense of sadness coming from him, chiming completely with the room, full of unwound clocks. Not anger, like you found in some men, not bitterness. Just sadness, like a child who has had a treat taken away and doesn't quite know what to do with themselves.

'Good house for parties,' said Carmen, meaning it. Through another door to the side was a small kitchen and another set of stairs, but here was big enough for a ballroom.

'Oh, there used to be ... yes. There used to be parties in here,' said Mr McCredie, his eyes growing misty. 'My mother loved a party. We'd have a band; there'd be music and dancing ...'

'An amazing place to grow up.'

'You'd think,' he said shortly. 'Oh yes ... I had everything, I suppose.'

Carmen looked at the pictures on the piano. His mother had been very beautiful: long dark hair, strong brows, a strong chin and a little mouth like his. His father was rather fierce-looking, with a big mop of hair and quite a beard. He was actually very attractive, Carmen thought.

'Was your granddad really an explorer?' she said before she realised what she was saying.

He blinked, but then obviously assumed that most people in Edinburgh would know his family. Sofia had said they were well known, thought Carmen, relieved that she hadn't dropped herself in it.

'Well, he went on the Graham Land expedition,' said Mr McCredie, showing her an old photograph of lots of men grinning cheerfully below the decks of a ship, wine bottles open. 'He was really just a boy then though.'

'That's amazing,' said Carmen genuinely. 'Explorers in the family! I didn't even realise it was a job. Were you never tempted to head for the snowy wastes?'

Mr McCredie looked down. 'Oh, yes. But I'm not sure I'm the type.' He frowned. 'Where *are* those medals? I'm sure he got given one once.'

'It must be worth a lot, surely,' said Carmen.

He looked at her.

'I doubt it,' he said. 'Nobody cares about these things these days. Unless you were on the expeditions where people died.'

At which Carmen wondered then why it was that he had absolutely no idea where they were, and nobody who would care for them after he'd gone.

'Well, I'm here to fetch your Christmas decorations,' she reminded him. 'If they're in the attic, I can probably scout for the medals at the same time.'

Mr McCredie had picked up one of the pictures of his mother, a studio shot from the 1940s, as she looked on at a three-quarter angle, past the frame, her lovely brows and high cheekbones outlining her face.

'She's gorgeous,' said Carmen, but he didn't answer her.

The loft was at the top of the next flight of stairs, up from a landing with several large doors off it – this house was huge. An old ladder racketed down as Mr McCredie pulled the string. He frowned.

'I don't know when I was last up here.'

'You don't get the decorations down every Christmas?'

'I never get them down at all.'

Carmen frowned at this, then, armed with her phone torch, ascended into the unknown.

Chapter Thirteen

Carmen could straighten up once she got into the attic. There were little windows poking out, and from the back window there was a superb view over the top of the Grassmarket out towards the hills beyond, which she stared at for quite a while. It was also completely freezing up there though. A bit of insulation wouldn't have gone amiss.

The attic was full: old boxes, suitcases with initials stamped on, tea chests and old frames. There were skis so ancient they had leather bindings on them and were made of wood. Carmen blinked and wondered if they had traversed the Antarctic. It was kind of amazing. No sign of any medals though. She wondered if Mr McCredie had perhaps sold them years ago and simply forgotten.

Carmen was getting dusty, but she didn't mind that. Mr McCredie was bouncing rather awkwardly on his small toes down below.

'Be careful up there.'

Carmen poked her head through the hole. 'Doesn't anyone in your family ever throw anything away?'

Mr McCredie blinked.

'Why would one?'

'I don't know,' said Carmen, thinking of the rucksack that constituted most of her worldly possessions, for once with a certain amount of fondness. 'Doesn't it ever weigh you down?'

Mr McCredie looked up from his chintzy pink drawing room, with the china, the pictures in their silver frames, the old piano desperately needing tuning, the embroidered footrests and ornate poker set.

'I don't know,' he said, his little eyes peering over his spectacles. 'It's the only home I've ever known.'

Carmen smiled. Maybe if her parents had expensive antiques rather than odd liquors brought back from Spain and a large Virgin Mary marked 'A GIFT FROM LOURDES' that used to light up with fibre optics which she and Sofia had loved but hadn't worked in years, then maybe she might have felt the same way.

But then, it didn't look like he was enjoying it at all.

'There is SO MUCH STUFF up here,' she hollered.

Packing case after packing case of books, spooky old teddy bears and hockey sticks, rugby boots and an entire set of dishes in an elaborate box. Carmen frowned at the latter – surely it would be useful somewhere, for something. But Sofia had trendy mismatched earthenware in deep turquoise and blue that either came from Morocco or was strongly pretending that it did. What could she possibly do with a dozen dainty floral saucers?

She saw something that looked like tinsel coming out of an old box, and in her haste to get over to it, banged her leg hard on a low table she hadn't noticed.

'Bloody bloody buggering hell!' she yelped.

'Are you all right?' came the tremulous faraway voice.

'Yes,' said Carmen, not loud enough for him to hear. 'That's the noise I make when everything is going incredibly well.'

She bit her lip and rubbed her leg. That was going to bruise – bugger. She looked at what she'd tripped over, and her mouth dropped open.

In front of her, covered in dust, was an old train set with little fields and trees and stations, working signals, porters on the tiny platforms and criss-crossing rails. It was huge and complicated and beautiful.

'Wow! Is this your train set?'

'Oh yes!' said Mr McCredie. Suddenly his voice had perked right up, and he got quite excited.

'I haven't seen it in years. Can you bring it down?'

'Why don't you just . . . ?'

Carmen stopped herself before she suggested that he sell it. It wouldn't be any use and she would turn into Sofia, telling everyone else what was best for them.

'Okay,' she said.

There were also Christmas decorations right next to it, she saw.

She made Mr McCredie cover up his old, very expensive Persian rug with dust sheets as a starting manoeuvre before she brought down the two boxes of Christmas decorations and – carefully and in pieces – the train set.

As he blew off the dust, his eyes widened and Carmen could see him for the boy he must have been: bespectacled, and full of enthusiasm for the little electric locomotives. There was even snow on the fir trees, and little metal figures of a railway porter and a mailman putting large brown sacks of mail onto a goods carriage proudly marked Royal Mail.

'Does it still work?' said Carmen. Mr McCredie looked all ready to start re-laying track.

'Don't set it up here,' said Carmen suddenly. 'If I move the window display ... oh yes! We could put it in the window.'

'We're not selling my train set.'

'We're not! It's just to attract children in. And surround it with books about Christmas and trains. And Christmas trains.' Carmen frowned. 'Let me order quite a lot of *The Polar Express*. I have a hunch this is going to work.'

Mr McCredie looked at her.

'Well, I suppose ... I have no reason to doubt you so far.'

This felt so good to Carmen that she beamed at him. They carefully carried all the boxes of the train set to the front of the shop whereupon Carmen ordered the books and served customers and Mr McCredie had an undeniably happy two hours setting up the track and the buildings and the trees and even the hill tunnel before the station in perfect order, armed with a damp cloth as Carmen sternly gave him dusting instructions. It was an enjoyable morning for both of them.

Nothing was doing when they clicked the switch on the track, but Carmen dashed down to the friendly hardware store man, returning with an entirely new plug, some bits of wire and odds and ends that the nice gentleman assured her would be just the ticket, and an invitation to the magic shop's party. She mentioned it to Mr McCredie who winced and said, 'Oh. Bronagh's. We'd better go, or she'll put a spell on us.'

'You should go,' said Carmen. 'It feels like this entire street all really support each other.'

Mr McCredie shrugged.

'Oh,' he said, fiddling with the mechanism. 'I'm not really one for joining in.'

'Well, tough luck,' said Carmen. 'Because I said yes for the both of us.'

They held their breath as Mr McCredie replaced the plug, which had been round and brown and made of Bakelite, and amazingly the little trains took off, lights on at their fronts, trundling round the track against one another.

Not only this but the signal lights worked too, lifting and lowering as the trains grew near.

They stood watching it, completely entranced.

'We need smoke pellets,' said Mr McCredie, who looked nearly tearful at his childhood toy come back to life.

'How . . . Is that how they make smoke?' Carmen crouched. There were even tiny plastic figurines in the passenger carriages: women reading newspapers in little hats; men in suits with trilbies and broad shoulders.

There was something slightly sinister in the thought that they had been up there, trapped in their carriages for forty years, stuck in an eternal waiting room. But of course that was fanciful nonsense.

'Of course.'

'You know, I could get cheap lights too, from Poundworld,' mused Carmen. 'And put them in the trees for Christmas. And some cotton wool for more snow.'

'*Poundworld*,' frowned Mr McCredie. 'What on earth is that?'

'I'm taking you,' said Carmen. Then she reconsidered. 'No. You might have a heart attack. But just give me a bit of petty cash and trust me.'

'I can't believe we have . . . a "window display".'

'How . . . ?' said Carmen. 'How on earth are you a shopkeeper?'

'I prefer "custodian",' said Mr McCredie, but he was too distracted by the little trains.

Carmen went back into the main house and through the rest of the old Christmas decorations, discarding the crumbling and irretrievable, but there was a surprising amount of good-quality little gold-coloured candlesticks, a beautiful ceramic nativity set, some brass angels and, loveliest and strangest of all, a doll's house which looked not unlike Sofia's house, with its steps up, and with perfect little rugs and beds and the dearest patterned arm chairs, blankets and curtains, but instead of little people inside were little dressed toy mice, perfect in every way, with fur and whiskers and little bright beady eyes, wearing waistcoats and spectacles, aprons and bustles. Carmen had to suppress something in her that would very much have wanted it for herself.

Then followed a rather jolly afternoon of splashing out on artificial snow and tiny strands of lights at the happy, busy Poundworld. As Carmen worked on both windows – trains on one side, doll's house on the other – more and more people stopped by to see what they were doing, and several popped in and bought books.

Finally, at around 4 p.m., everything was ready, and Carmen stood back. She flicked the switch and suddenly, at last, the shop was alive: the lights of the train and the stations and the little lamp-post that came with the house glowed golden and beautiful, as did the working fairy lights that she had hung in the tiny windows of the house itself. And the little train, now with a tiny holly wreath round its front engine, tootled on towards the tunnel before the station, and at last, on the busy thoroughfare that is Victoria Street at Christmastime – at last, there was a crowd outside their shop.

Carmen put up a sign – 'Children's Story Time: 4 p.m. on Wednesday' and for once was happy as she locked up the shop (she had decided to take over the keys, given Mr McCredie's rather lackadaisical approach).

'Goodnight,' she said.

Mr McCredie shook his head.

'What? Oh,' he said, mumbling slightly.

'What?' asked Carmen.

'Well. I have always loved my books. But . . . I don't think I have ever enjoyed being a shopkeeper before.'

Which sent Carmen home in such a good mood that it made it even odder that that night she had the dream.

That night, bundled in the single bed at the bottom of her sister's house. Carmen had the oddest dream. She was on a train.

It was an old-fashioned sort of train, with compartments rather than everyone sitting in the open, and she was sitting on a long seat, covered in a dusty, carpet-like material, with straps above and a mesh luggage rack.

Outside the old window, which was also covered in mesh for some reason, she could catch a glimpse of the snowy woods the train was hastening through, with a clickety-clack on wooden rails that felt oddly comforting.

She realised suddenly that she wasn't alone in the carriage and looked up sharply. A woman wearing a pink hat so close to her head it appeared to be moulded on looked up too and smiled sweetly. She was wearing pink lipstick and reading a book called *Up on the Rooftops*.

'Tell him,' she said pleasantly, but as she spoke Carmen knew they were growing closer and closer to a tunnel, even as the snow fell more and more thickly and the train sped up and the woman opened her mouth wider so she could speak above the shrill sound of the whistle blowing as the tunnel got closer and closer and the noise got louder and louder and the woman's mouth got wider and wider and she was saying something, screaming something, but they crashed into the tunnel, and Carmen jolted and woke up, completely confused and unable to recognise where she was, frozen. It was pitch-black outside, but according to her phone it was after 7 a.m.

She sat up in bed, keeping the duvet pulled around her.

Oddly, she wasn't terrified. It hadn't felt exactly like a nightmare, or that the train was going to crash or the tunnel was going to swallow her: she had been frightened, but not terrified. And she felt sad, somehow, a deep sadness down inside her somewhere that she hadn't understood whatever it was that the woman was trying to tell her.

Chapter Fourteen

The dream faded from her like brushed-off sand as she headed to the bathroom, already aware of Skylar's performative *ohmmmm*ing morning meditation coming from next door, and by the time she had unpacked the book for the Brazilian student – it was huge, very heavy, dense with diagrams and not a single line was comprehensible to Carmen in any way – and saw the pleasingly large turn-out for the story time, she'd practically forgotten it altogether.

It was Sofia's doing of course – she'd got on the mums' WhatsApp group, an extraordinary source of power in Edinburgh society, so the little shop was heaving with buggies and small children looking expectant and absolutely delighted at the train set. Rather too delighted in fact: Mr McCredie was hopping from foot to little foot, looking anxious.

'Don't touch,' said Carmen hopefully, then: 'And there are candy canes for after!'

'Yayyy!' went the children.

The mothers made extremely dubious faces.

'But it's all right: I've brought enough satsumas for every-one,' said Sofia with a smile which made Carmen slightly want to stab her.

She sat down on a little stool, wishing she wasn't quite so much on view, held up the beautiful glowing picture of a little girl who was wearing very few clothes in the snow – in contrast to the children, who had so many layers of arctic-ready Puffa jackets on none of them could raise their arms above their head – and they *ooh*ed and *aah*ed agreeably. Carmen began:

> *Most terribly cold it was; it snowed, and was nearly quite dark, and evening – the last evening of the year. In this cold and darkness there went along the street a poor little girl, bareheaded, and with naked feet ...*

She was gratified at the widening eyes and the children edging in closer to hear.

'NAKED FEET?' said one of the boys.

'It just means bare feet,' said Carmen, as some snigger-ing started.

'Yes, please be quiet,' said Pippa, and for once Carmen was pleased at the girl's ability to give everyone a solid telling-off, as she certainly couldn't have done it – all these blonde women were making her feel slightly intimidated as it was.

She carefully led the children through the lighting of the matches – the amazing goose, the wonderful Christmas tree, the angelic grandmother. After the student's fascination, she had dug out a Rackham edition – the child haunted, the Christmas tree a glistening, extraordinary apparition – and the children paid rapt attention.

105

But in the corner, at the cold hour of dawn, sat the poor girl, with rosy cheeks and with a smiling mouth, leaning against the wall – frozen to death on the last evening of the old year. Stiff and stark sat the child there with her matches, of which one bundle had been burnt. 'She wanted to warm herself,' people said.

There was a silence in the shop.

'What?' said Phoebe. 'You are kidding me.'

'Where is the girl gone?' said one of the boys.

Pippa's face was full of dismay.

'Could you read to the end please, Auntie Carmen?' she said in her usual polite way, but there was a trembling edge to her voice.

'She DIES?' burst out Phoebe, tears already threatening

'Oh goodness, she *does* die,' said one of the blonde women. 'I had completely forgotten that.' Then, more quietly: 'Shit.'

'I didn't . . . I don't know this story,' said one of the other mothers. 'It doesn't sound remotely appropriate.'

'It's the greatest children's writer of all time,' said Carmen, then cursed her quick tongue.

'So . . . she really does die? In bare feet in the snow in a corner all by herself with no mummy or daddy?' whispered a tiny girl Carmen hadn't noticed before, whose eyes were now bigger than her entire face.

'Well . . . I mean, she does get to go with her grandmother?' said Carmen hopefully.

'Her DEAD GRANDMOTHER? That definitely means she's dead then,' said the same boy who had had something to say about naked feet. At this, the girl brimmed over uncontrollably and, as is often the case, it proved rather infectious,

106

until there was a clutch of sobbing infants at Carmen's feet, mothers tutting at her and she suddenly wished that she too had conveniently frozen to death in a corner the previous evening.

'Well!' she said, glancing quickly through the rest of the book. Her eye alighted on *The Snow Queen* but as soon as she picked it up and read a line about shards of ice entering people's eyeballs, she decided that on balance discretion was the better part of valour.

'Thank you all *so* much for coming.'

'BUT! SHE'S! *DEAD!*'

'I think on balance,' said Carmen desperately, 'I'm going to give the candy canes to your mothers and they can decide what to do with them.'

This earned her several looks of sharp enmity from the other parents, of which Sofia was acutely aware but Carmen was not.

'Aha!' said Sofia. 'Here's another page! I just found it! Where she wakes up and she was only sleeping.'

'Let's see the picture,' said the boy.

'There's no picture,' shouted Phoebe, who was nearest. 'She's dead. She's really, really dead!'

Another storm of sobbing commenced.

'I'll take one of those candy canes,' said one mother desperately, backing out of the shop.

'Yes, me too,' said another, pulling the little boy away until eventually it was just Sofia and Carmen left in the shop.

'Well. You had a shot,' said Sofia in a voice that was a lot more patronising than she'd intended. Carmen eyed her.

'I'm sure you can tell Mum and you'll all have a good laugh,' she said, straightening up. 'God, why can I never get anything right?'

107

'That's not true,' protested Sofia. 'I mean it!'

Behind her, it turned out that the shop wasn't quite empty. The little girl with the huge eyes was still there.

'That was a very sad story,' she whispered to Carmen.

'I know,' said Carmen. 'I forgot stories all have to be happy and jolly these days.'

The little girl shook her head.

'I liked it,' she said, still whispering.

'We'll take it,' said the well-heeled-looking mother. 'That's a beautiful edition, in wonderful nick too. Children's books today are so terribly anodyne, don't you think? Love yourself love yourself be kind blah blah love yourself. I think we can get a little beyond that, don't you, Leone?'

And tiny Leone smiled and took the book after Carmen carefully wrapped it up in paper and held it tight to her breast, as if she both loved it and was slightly scared of it, which were not, after all, the worst emotions to feel about a book.

'Thank you,' she whispered.

'You know,' said the mother, as she turned around, Leone ahead so she could peel round the corner and gaze at the train set with those huge eyes of hers. 'That's the first time she's spoken in public since she started school. Thank you.'

And the bell tinged, and Carmen watched them leave, just as the very lanky studenty man came in. He frowned at Sofia's tear-stained children.

'There are also a lot of crying children in the street,' he said, looking bemused.

'It was a sad Christmas story.'

He looked puzzled.

'I thought Christmas stories were happy.'

'So did I,' said Sofia quietly, trying to haul the children away, even though Jack would have happily sat for several hours watching the train set.

'*The Little Match Girl*,' said Carmen. He shook his head. 'You don't know it?'

He smiled.

'I don't . . . I don't really know any Christmas stories.'

'What, at all?'

She frowned at him.

'I don't celebrate Christmas.'

'Oh! Sorry,' said Carmen.

'No need,' he said. 'From where I'm standing, it looks like a full-time job.'

Phoebe had stopped sobbing, her head whipping around.

'You don't celebrate CHRISTMAS?' she said loudly. Sofia grabbed her hand.

'Lots of people don't celebrate Christmas, darling, don't you remember? You learned it at school. Which has *lots* of people from different backgrounds. So there's Eid and Hanukkah . . . '

But Phoebe wasn't listening. She marched up to Oke.

'My friend has Hanukkah AND Christmas,' she said. 'I don't think that's fair AT ALL.'

Oke smiled.

'Well, I don't celebrate Hanukkah either, so don't worry.'

Her face screwed up.

'Well, what do you celebrate?'

'We don't.'

At this all the children's mouths fell open.

'No Christmas?'

'No Eid?'

'What about on your birthday?' This was from Jack.

Oke shook his head.

'You don't celebrate YOUR BIRTHDAY?'

'Don't you know when it is?'

He smiled.

'Yes, I do. But we don't celebrate.'

'That is SO SAD,' said Phoebe, her face starting to twist again. Oke knelt down on his haunches so he was at her level.

'Not for me,' he said. 'I'm a Quaker. We try to live with ...' His hand batted around as if looking for the right expression. '... a kind of ... gentle grace. Every day. So that we don't have to make a fuss or make ourselves excited.'

'Because you're always happy like it's Christmas?' said Phoebe disbelievingly.

'Well, I wouldn't know,' said Oke. 'But yeah. Maybe we just try and average it out throughout the year.'

Jack and Pippa both looked thoughtful.

'That sounds RUBBISH,' said Phoebe and Sofia made her apologetic face as she bundled her away. 'Well, it does! No presents! No Christmas cake! No chipolatas! NO BIRTHDAYS!'

She was still complaining as the bell tinged on their way out.

'I have never met those children before in my life,' said Carmen hastily.

'Bye, Auntie Carmen!' hollered Pippa, clearly on purpose. Carmen decided the best thing to do was just stare straight ahead.

Oke smiled.

'Uh ... my book?'

'Oh. Yeah.'

Carmen ducked under the counter and lugged out the huge book.

She smiled.

'You'd think they'd put a Christmas tree on it.'

'Would you?' said Oke, but he was joking.

The book was staggeringly expensive. She felt terrible even letting him buy it when clearly he should be spending his money on a good winter coat and a pair of gloves – the air was Baltic. She felt sorry for him.

'Thank you,' he said, and he opened an old leather wallet and counted out the cash carefully.

'Oh. And I forgot, the discount is ... uh ... twenty per cent,' said Carmen, pulling it from the top of her head.

His eyebrows raised.

'That's very generous.'

'We're a very nice shop,' said Carmen. 'And not prejudiced about non-Christmassers *at all*.' She frowned. 'I didn't know there were Quakers in Brazil.'

'You've been Quaker-hunting in Brazil?!'

She laughed. 'No. Sorry.'

He smiled too. 'It's true. There aren't very many of us. But there are a few. Thank you for not being prejudiced about non-Christmassers.'

He looked around at the ridiculous amount of decorations.

'Well, do feel free to tell your pro-Christmas friends!' said Carmen.

'I will,' he said, nodding his head politely and dinging his way out of the shop.

Chapter Fifteen

A few days later, Carmen received an extremely surprising phone call just as she was looking round the shop with a distinct sense of satisfaction.

She had come in early and the lights of Victoria Street were still glimmering in the early morning darkness and, among the glitz and sparkle of the other shops, for once theirs stood proud too, the train trundling around. She was adding little figures every day just for fun, a cow here or there, and today she had a plan to put Santa next to the chimney on the top of the little station.

And a new box of books had arrived wrapped in polystyrene which normally she would have complained about vociferously, for the waste of it. But maybe, today, she was going to crumble it into pieces and let it tumble like snow . . .

She was thinking happily about this – as well as thoroughly enjoying a warm mince pie she'd bought from the coffee shop down the road, which normally she would have felt a bit guilty about but there was no doubt about it, all this endless marching up and down but mostly up Edinburgh hills, as well as Sofia's meticulously balanced meals, was having a rather positive effect on her waistline, which meant there was room for a mince pie now and then, and they made the shop smell so nice – so she answered the rotary telephone cheerfully: 'Good morning! McCredie's bookshop!'

A very confident English voice said hello back and asked to speak to the manager and Carmen without blinking once said she would be absolutely fine.

'Well,' said the voice. 'You know Blair Pfenning is coming up to Edinburgh on a publicity tour?'

Carmen had not known this but she was more than aware of who Blair Pfenning was: the huge bestselling writer who wrote about the power of the spirit to create love. Or possibly the power of love to create spirit. Carmen wasn't a hundred per cent sure on all the details because her first love was fiction, but she knew he was always on morning TV laughing with Phil and Holly on the sofa, and had very white teeth.

'Um, so?' she said.

'He's looking for somewhere picturesque to shoot a piece for BBC Scotland,' said the voice. 'And one of the staff up there brought her daughter in for a reading and suggested using you as a backdrop. Do you think it might be possible?'

Mr McCredie had appeared and was listening in. Carmen looked at him and he shook his head fiercely.

Carmen thought about it. They'd once used Dounston's as a backdrop for a glitzy period piece as the shop had a beautiful wooden staircase over a stained-glass window which looked wonderful as long as you didn't film any of the patchy torn carpet beneath their feet, and covered up the peeling 'NO

EXIT' signs. It had been exciting for about five minutes, then the reality of having about a thousand people in shorts traipsing about with miles of wire and cables and shouting into walkie-talkies and pushing past actual real shoppers and telling everyone to be quiet all the time, over and over again, had actually turned out to be a total and complete pain in the arse.

'I'm not sure—' began Mr McCredie. She shushed him.

'Well,' she said. 'You know this is an incredibly busy time of the year to disrupt the shop like this.'

'We understand,' said the voice.

Carmen blinked. This could be very, very good for them.

'We'll need him to do a signing,' she said.

The voice on the other end paused. 'Well, we'd have to see about that.'

'Our Christmas decorations are very beautiful,' said Carmen. 'And of course we'd have a lovely display of the books to go on camera.'

'On *camera*,' Mr McCredie was moaning in agony. She gave him one of her looks, then quickly leafed through the catalogue on her desk.

Feeling the Christmas Spirit of Love sprang out at her: it was one of his. There was a picture of Blair, white teeth gleaming, looking worked-out in a red jumper and a hat, sitting next to a huge Christmas tree surrounded by cheery multicultural children. Carmen wasn't sure it was necessarily a good look. He looked a little bit like a sperm donor.

The woman sniffed. 'He can give you half an hour.'

'How long do you want the shop for?'

'Oh, it won't be long.'

'That means hours,' said Carmen. 'I want forty-five minutes for signing.'

114

'He's going to be tired, coming in transatlantic.'

'Maybe he can draw on some of that festive spirit and positive energy,' said Carmen.

The woman on the other end of the phone laughed. 'Okay. He's all yours. Get the turn-out though, won't you? I don't want it to be two crazy ladies and a dog.'

'Yes!' said Carmen, after she'd put down the phone. '*Ching ching ching!*'

'Oh lord,' said Mr McCredie. 'And that was very rude about two crazy ladies and a dog.'

'We are going to turn a profit if it kills me,' said Carmen. 'Although judging by the look of this book, it will be a zillion crazy ladies and absolutely no self-respecting dogs.'

It was amazing, once she started putting it about on social media, how many huge Blair Pfenning fans there were.

'Seriously?' she said when Sofia mentioned she might just be able to swing by from the office.

'Have you seen his teeth?' said Sofia. 'So straight!'

'I thought you only read *Interiors* magazine and the *Edinburgh Law Review*.'

'No!' said Sofia. 'I read! Self-help can be very useful.'

She gave her sister a meaningful look.

'Really?' said Carmen. 'As useful as Rainbow Rowell? Or Douglas Adams? I doubt it.'

Sofia, though she was clearly excited, turned to Carmen seriously. This could be just the thing to put some get up and go into her sister.

'And his advice, you know. Find something true to your spirit and your soul and do it every day.'

Carmen frowned.

'What, make packed lunches?'

'No,' said Sofia. 'Find your centring bliss.'

Carmen's glance went to the wine fridge.

'Not like that. Anyway. I think he's super.'

'I think he sounds up himself,' said Carmen, looking at him online where there were lots of pictures of him showing off his horses.

'"Being with my horses is the only place I can feel truly free",' she read. 'See. All his friends are horses. He obviously doesn't have much conversation.'

'Maybe he's rich and lonely,' said Sofia.

Carmen sniffed. 'Yeah, that's what young, fit, super-rich guys with all their hair are. Suffering from a terrible lack of company.'

'Well, you should wash *your* hair just in case.'

Pippa marched in with her bassoon.

'I'm going to be leading the school show!' she announced. 'Mrs McGillicuddy said so!'

'Oh darling, that's wonderful!' said Sofia while Pippa smiled defiantly at Carmen, as if it were a victory over her too for not having praised her enough. It had not escaped Pippa that Carmen often seemed to be siding with Phoebe, and that would not do. Not at all.

'Congratulations,' said Carmen, without offering to listen to it. She assumed there'd be enough of Sofia's children doing enforced showing-off between now and the big day.

'I think you should get Phoebe to audition, Mummy,' said Pippa, as if they were two friends the same age. 'Don't you think it would be good for her confidence?'

116

Sofia looked unsure.

'Oh darling, you know what happened last year.'

'What happened last year?' said Carmen.

'Oh, it was so awful. She froze in front of the entire school!' said Pippa with much relish. 'It was just so embarrassing. People talked about it for months. POOR Phoebe,' she added with a long sigh. 'Poor, poor Phoebe.'

Frowning, Sofia took out oatcakes and soya milk for snacks.

'Why am I poor Phoebe?' said Phoebe, trailing in, her scarf rucked off her shoulders, one of her plaits falling undone and what looked like paint down her jumper.

'I was just saying what a wonderful singer you were,' said Pippa. 'And how it would be nice to get a chance to hear you sing this year.'

Phoebe turned a dull shade of pink and shuffled towards the fridge.

'Yes, we never hear you sing these days,' said Sofia, adding 'Wash your hands' without thinking about it.

Phoebe made a non-committal noise and then a disgusted face as she looked at the oatcakes.

'I hate those things,' she said. 'Can't we just have biscuits?'

'Not if you want to be healthy,' said Pippa. 'I think they're yummy, Mummy.'

Didn't Sofia realise she was being played? thought Carmen. Maybe she was just too tired and pregnant to notice. Jack swooped in without saying anything, grabbed a handful of the oatcakes, crammed them in his mouth and carried on out to the garden to hit a ball against the wall.

'I'm sure Auntie Carmen would like to hear you sing,' went on the inexorable Pippa.

'I don't mind,' said Carmen. 'You can sing or not sing, I don't care. Nobody sings worse than me anyway.'

'I know,' said Phoebe. 'I've heard you in the shower.'

'I know!' said Carmen. 'And that's with the *good* acoustics.'

They grinned at each other. Pippa immediately took out her bassoon and started on an extremely loud rendition of 'Once in Royal David's City', all ninety-five verses.

'You got Blair Pfenning!' said Sofia in a tone that she thought was proud and encouraging but Carmen thought was patronising and irritatingly astonished.

'Just wear a bit of lipstick!' she added, as Carmen headed downstairs. 'That's all I'm saying.'

Chapter Sixteen

Carmen couldn't believe it. At 9.30 in the morning, in the freezing cold, snaking all the way down Victoria Street and into the Grassmarket, there was a queue! A queue, to get into *their* shop! This was completely unprecedented.

It was almost entirely women, with a few men staring at their phones and not looking up or around, possibly in case anybody recognised them. The women were dressed up in tweed coats and smart scarves, boots clopping across the cobbled road. Carmen's mobile phone went off after she'd wandered up the Grassmarket to get the good coffee. The little café was done out beautifully for the holiday season in a Nordic snowflake theme, with little paper snowflakes tumbling from the rooftops, and every cappuccino coming with a little flake on the side. Carmen treated Mr McCredie to a cappuccino, but she accidentally ate the flake before she made it all the way up the hill.

'Hi, yeah, we're in the hotel?' said a busy-sounding publicist. 'Are you ready to go?'

'Um, no,' said Carmen, swallowing the last piece of flake. 'I haven't opened up yet.'

There was a disappointed sighing noise.

'Only our schedule's really tight?'

'I get that,' said Carmen. 'We're on it. Come when you like.'

A camera crew were stamping their feet around the entrance and already setting up; Carmen knew enough to aim straight for the person with the clipboard.

'We have to do the filming first,' she tried to explain to the queue. 'It's going to be a bit of a wait . . . if you want to go away and come back again?'

The faces turned towards her were steely. Nobody was going away and coming back again.

'I'm afraid I can't let you in till we're done?'

The wind whistled through the stairwells; up the hill and over the top of the terrace. Clouds scudded overhead, occasionally letting in a flash of light, but mostly reminding you that daylight had not arrived before 8.30 a.m. and would be leaving promptly at 3.30 p.m. and not really showing its face much in between so if there was ever an opportunity to be somewhere nice and cosy inside, nature couldn't give you much more of a clue than to do it now.

Still, the feisty women were in no mood to desist, so Carmen smiled apologetically at them and made her way indoors, even as she could feel the daggers shot at her back.

The camera people did mysterious things with lights and trailing cables and tried not to drop more books on the ground than was strictly necessary under the circumstances. The woman with the clipboard smiled and talked into a walkie-talkie, and told them to turn off the train set. Carmen reminded Mr McCredie that they were bringing the superstar in through the back door, i.e. the alleyway close that led into his house, and he smiled weakly then promptly forgot all about it again.

Finally, the shop was looking as lovely as it could. The TV people had brought along a lot of extra holly garlands and had hung them on the shelf with little sparkly fairy lights which, while they looked very pretty, Carmen had to admit would be absolutely useless for anyone actually attempting to browse or buy a book on the shelves. The people trying to peek in the window were politely shooed away and everything was cued up and at 10.45 a.m. 'He's on the move!' was heard over the walkie-talkie, and Carmen scampered up to the back alleyway to escort the great man through the McCredie home and in through the stacks.

The young publicist was slim, blonde and as pretty as a model, and she grinned broadly as she bustled forwards.

'Well, isn't *this* charming,' she said. 'Come on, Blair, it's just over here.'

A tall man behind her shuffled slightly. He didn't look at all like the snooty uber-confident man of his publicity. He was wearing owlish glasses, his hair looked rumpled and his mouth was pulled shut so you couldn't see his bright teeth at all.

He sighed.

'It won't be long,' said the girl in an encouraging manner, as if explaining things to a small child. There was another long sigh.

'Okay,' he said.

'Are you ready?' said the girl. She beamed a bright smile. 'I'm Emily, by the way. Nice to meet you all! And this is Blair.'

Blair raised a weary hand. Was he terribly hungover? Carmen wondered. Although that wouldn't go with his reputation of *positive self-happy self.*

'Okay, Blair,' said Emily, as the TV crew stepped forwards

121

and introduced themselves one by one. A woman carrying a large bag approached.

'Hair and make-up?' she said. 'I've cleared a space.'

She had but it was right behind the till and in the way of everything which, coupled with the cables, meant that Carmen couldn't do much more than stand and watch. Mr McCredie had darted away like a mole when he'd seen everything and everyone there – again. Carmen pondered once again that if seeing a lot of people in your shop was worrying, no wonder your retail career hadn't flourished.

However, she took people back and showed them how to get coffee and tried to avoid the gaze of the angry shoppers waiting in the cold, sticky-beaking through the window. She needn't have worried: a small feisty-looking woman who was, she realised, the director, marched outside and yelled at them to get out of the way or it would take all day, and meekly, the queue retreated, to the faint annoyance of the magic shop but the clear delight of the coffee shop, who immediately started offering queue delivery.

'Okay, quiet on set, everyone,' shouted the director finally, and Carmen edged forwards so she could have a look.

It was absurd. As if a different person had materialised. The grumpy-looking sleepy person slouching in half an hour before was nowhere to be seen.

In front of Carmen now, standing by the silenced train set and a rapidly erected Christmas tree, was a shiny, glowing, somehow much bigger person. He had flicked brown hair, bright gleaming eyes and incredibly bright teeth which he was flashing as if he was enjoying the happiest moment of his life. The director demanded silence, and the cameras started rolling. The red-headed presenter introduced him in tones of awed reverence, and he made a broad 'aw shucks' face.

'Hi there,' he was saying in a confident accent pitched precisely somewhere between British and American. 'I am just so happy to be here in Edinburgh, one of the most beautiful cities in the world.'

The red-headed presenter giggled.

'Well, it's *so* lovely to have you here. Can you tell us a little about your new book?'

'Of course, Caroline.'

He leaned forwards and seemed to look the presenter – or the camera – straight in the eye.

'It's about if you ever feel you're just not good enough – that your Christmas will never be quite perfect enough – if you don't think you'll choose thoughtful gifts or that your family won't be thrilled to see you or that the turkey will be dry ... '

He gave a broad, shining smile, filled with compassion and joy.

'I just want to tell you that you are good enough. You are absolutely good enough. You are loved. And everything is going to be okay.'

He smiled beatifically again. Carmen screwed up her face.

'Isn't he *amazing*?' said Emily, who was standing next to Carmen, watching him slavishly.

'Is this it?' said Carmen. 'Does he have something to say that isn't just "everything is going to be okay"?'

'I know,' went on the relentlessly cheerful voice, 'that it doesn't sound much, just saying, "everything is going to be okay". But you know what. Sometimes, it's enough. And I just want to tell you that you – *you* – are enough.'

Carmen could have had a few things to tell him about how that didn't exactly fly after they had shut all the old employment opportunities in her old home town and thrown half the decent people of working age on the dole with no way out and the other half, like her, had had to move away altogether, but she managed to restrain herself.

'Even if you – what's the phrase? – "burn the tatties",' he said with a silly Scottish accent to show he knew it wasn't very good.

'Well, that's terrific,' said the presenter, looking rather pink – he was very close to her. 'It's so lovely to see you here.'

'Well – Blair! Is there a more Scottish name?' he went on. 'It's the most wonderful land of my forefathers and I can't wait to meet as many Scottish people as I can. I'd say I hope they're all as pretty as you, but I wouldn't dream of saying something like that these days so I will say I hope they are all as pretty as Dean the cameraman.'

There was appreciative laughter among the crew.

'And I'm going to be down at the sick kids' hospital this afternoon signing copies of *Your Child's Calm Wellness in Five Minutes a Day*, so I'm looking forward to meeting people there too.'

'Thanks for giving up your time like this.'

'Are you kidding? It's an honour. And seriously, you are all so lucky to live in the heart of such an amazing place. I feel inspired here, I really do.'

'Well, we're happy to have you. And now back to the studio . . .'

Blair Pfenning stayed frozen in place as the cameras switched off and Emily jumped forward and directed him to the signing table.

'Can we get them in please?' she said, as the camera operators were dismantling cameras and sound men were taking fuzzy things off mikes. She bustled to the doorway and started bringing people in two at a time, all of them hopeful and expectant, clutching copies of Blair's books, most of which looked worn and well-loved.

And he was distantly charming with everyone; didn't rush, took his time, made sure he was spelling people's names correctly and complimenting hats and brooches. He submitted merrily to photographs, flashing that brilliant grin, putting arms nearly round the women but not touching them and, when someone started to tell him a problem, passing them on to Emily to take their details but promising that someone from his office would get back to them.

Finally, by noon, every adoring person had been swept from the shop, every last piece of cabling had been removed, the spare decorations had been packed away, every single book was sold so the cashbox was overflowing and the shop was temporarily quiet.

It was like watching the air go out of a balloon. He seemed to almost shrivel in front of Carmen's eyes. The smile and the teeth vanished; his body slumped. He took off the Harris tweed jacket with the elbow patches and pulled on a grey hoodie Emily had stretched out for him, zipping it up to his chin and putting on his glasses. He laid his head down on the counter.

'We done?'

'Four local radio stations, two national, children's hospital, BBC again.'

'We just did them.'

'This is the whole of the BBC. That was just local.'

A tearful noise came from under the hoodie.

'Oh, for fuck's sake.'

'Let me get you a coffee.'

There was no answer from the large figure now prone upon the case.

'Um,' said Carmen. 'We are, believe me, so appreciative.'

She really and truly was. They had taken money continuously; the old till had tinged and rung and the stack of Blair Pfenning books had dwindled to nothing. She had never known anything like it, not even during one of the periodic bursts of craft sales in haberdashery that followed Kirstie Allsopp appearing on television.

'But would you mind if I got into the till?'

He glanced up at her, his eyes hollow.

'Whatever,' he said.

Emily had left to get coffee, and they were alone in the shop.

'Are you all right?' said Carmen wonderingly.

'Don't I look all right?'

'You did two minutes ago,' said Carmen. 'Now you're lying down in a shop.'

'Uh, jet lag?'

'I've had jet lag,' said Carmen. 'I could still lift my own head.'

He sighed.

'Well, bully for you.' He looked up at her suddenly. 'Is there anywhere really cosy and lovely to eat around here?'

'There are loads of places to eat around here,' said Carmen. 'I'm sure Emily will know them.'

His face fell.

'I've spent thirty-five hours with Emily and I have another four days to go.'

Carmen raised her eyebrows.

'Professionally,' he mumbled into his hoodie. 'Please. Could we go? Could you take me? Before she gets back.'

'Um, I can't really shut the shop.'

'Fuck off,' came the voice. 'I just trebled your week's takings and you know it.'

'Yes but—'

'Say I forced you into it.'

'Well, I would have to,' said Carmen. 'Seeing as you're trying to force me into it.'

He glanced up then.

'Do you want me to go full Charming Blair?'

'Not particularly.'

'I will, you know. I've got low blood sugar and if I don't get out pretty soon I'm going to throw a tantrum. So let's try this first.'

She narrowed her eyes at him as he threw himself upright, pulled down the hoodie and shook back his hair. He leaned into her and stared right into her eyes.

'It would be good and nourishing for the soul, underappreciated bookshop girl, if you were to let me take you out for lunch and add a little lustre to this grey miserable day and of course . . .' He grinned the grin. 'It would be beyond my honour and pleasure to escort you and treat you.'

'Is that supposed to be charming?'

'It is fucking charming! Six million copies' worth of charming!'

'I think it's creepy.'

'It's creepy, yes, okay, whatever. Please. Come on. Aren't you hungry? I haven't eaten for twenty hours.'

'Why not?'

'Calendar shoot.'

Carmen laughed aloud.

'Seriously?'

'I know,' said Blair. 'Oh well.'

He zipped his hoodie up again and gradually let himself drip back onto the table.

'Hang on – is the only way I can get you off my cash register going to lunch?'

'Uh-huh,' came the muffled voice.

'Oh, here comes Emily.'

Emily was clip-clopping up the road with a cardboard case full of coffee cups.

'Oh no! I'm trapped! Please don't let me do local radio.'

'I love local radio!'

'Who cares? Come on, take me out the back way. Come on. Now. Let's rush.'

He gave her a sarcastic flash of that ridiculous grin. Emily was getting closer, poring over her phone.

'Oh God, she's going to tell me to do something extra. And I need some Dutch courage before the hospital. Come. Come. *Please!*'

He looked up at her then, and his brown eyes were yearning and sincere rather than attempting to be soulful.

'Oh God,' said Carmen.

At that point, looking bemused, Mr McCredie bumbled into view. 'Ah, Carmen . . .'

'Lunch break!' shouted Blair. 'We're just off for lunch break.' He bounced up from his prone position. 'I'll bring her back in an hour . . . ish.'

'A *lunch break*?' said Mr McCredie, as if he'd said, 'A swim in an aquarium?'

As he never left the shop himself, Carmen had drawn the conclusion that he couldn't imagine a reason why anybody would ever want to.

That sealed it. She stepped forwards and looked up at Blair.

way everyone is so pleased to see you all the time or the way everyone is super-nice to you?'

Even now, someone at another table had spotted him and was looking happy and poking their dining companions to mention it.

Blair threw his hands in the air.

'It's all bullshit ... darling,' he said, looking like he was about to remember her name, then not doing that. 'You know that.'

'I do not know that,' said Carmen, who had £39 in her current account and had only ever met one other famous person, a very old sexist comedian who had come to open the ill-fated new computer department (nobody knew how they worked and they kept getting nicked) and had been drunk out his mind at 11 a.m. and kept pinching people's bums. Idra had reckoned she got more attention out of showing the bruise to people than she would have done from suing him.

'It's all fake,' said Blair.

'Is the money fake?'

'No,' he admitted.

'Are the books fake? They do read like it's just some ...'

Carmen stopped herself and figured there was a reason it wasn't generally recommended to drink at lunchtime.

'Some what?' said Blair, looking dismayed.

'Nothing. Some words?' tried Carmen.

'I mean, people really believe in these books,' said Blair. 'They really help people.'

'Of course they do,' said Carmen quickly.

'Not you though? Don't you need help?'

'I do need help actually,' said Carmen, about to tell him a bit about her life, but he was carrying on.

'. . . I mean, I just feel I do what I do and it really works for people, so I just should be happy for that, right?'

'Uh, sure?'

'But I hate it. All the travelling. All the people. All the fake glad-handing. It's not real. None of it's real. You're real . . . '

'Carmen,' said Carmen helpfully.

He was giving her the look again.

'I mean, so many towns. So many fans. And then people like you who say my books are just some . . . what were you going to say?'

'I wasn't going to say anything,' said Carmen stoically.

'Well, I like your honesty,' he said. 'You're refreshing.'

He leaned forwards awkwardly.

'Do you . . . do you think I'm a fraud?'

Carmen took another sip of the delicious Champagne and decided she might as well be honest as she was hardly going to be invited out for lunch with an author again.

'I think everyone's a fraud,' she said.

Blair blinked.

'What do you mean?'

'Everyone's just faking it. Look at the prime minister. Faking it. Look at people who are in charge of things. Faking it faking it faking it. Of course you're faking it. I'm faking it. I don't know how to run a bookshop. Not the faintest clue. Mr McCredie doesn't either. Faking it is just another word for being a grown-up. So.'

'So,' said Blair sadly. 'I'm nothing special.'

'My sister isn't faking it,' said Carmen suddenly. The thought had only just occurred to her. 'She's genuinely really good at stuff. Christ. No wonder she's exhausted all the time.'

'Your sister sounds amazing.'

132

Carmen thought about it. 'Well, I suppose so,' she said. 'I'd never tell her though. Everyone else does all the bloody time.'

'She needs one of my books.'

'Oh, she thinks you're awesome too.'

'Oh, that's nice,' said Blair, who wasn't particularly interested in Sofia really. 'But honestly, I have absolutely no idea what I'm doing sometimes.'

'Well, that makes you and everyone else.'

'Dang,' he said. 'I thought I'd be a bit more special than that.'

'So does everybody else.'

'Ow!' said Blair. 'You are being very hurtful.'

'Don't you have, like, nine therapists to help you with this?'

'Are you kidding? Therapists all have my books in their office. Sorry, does that sound conceited?' He looked up, hollow-eyed. 'Because . . . sometimes I'm a bit worried that everything I do . . . it's all . . . I mean, some of it's a bit contradictory.'

Carmen looked at him, surprised.

'I mean. Smile at the dawn? What does that even mean? Find your own happiness? Well, what if your happiness is . . . I don't know . . . kicking dogs? Do what you love. Unless you're a paedophile. I mean, it's . . . I think people get unhappy trying to do what makes them happy. Don't tell my publisher.'

'I Wish it Could Be Christmas Every Day' came on the in-house stereo.

'Like that,' he said. 'Christmas every day would be hell. It would be torture; it would be awful. But maybe that's what I'm telling people to aim for.'

'Well, the pay *is* good . . . ' ventured Carmen.

'Do you know?' he said. 'Do you know what they did with my teeth?'

'Painted them with Dulux?' said Carmen cheerfully.

He frowned at her as if he wasn't entirely sure she'd made a joke.

'Worse,' he said. 'They're veneers.'

'I know,' said Carmen. 'Like Simon Cowell. Big scary shiny gnashers.'

'Do you know how they make veneers?'

'Do they stick a horse's teeth on top of your own teeth then cover them in Tipp-Ex?'

'Kind of,' said Blair. 'But first they have to file down your own teeth.'

Carmen blinked. She hadn't known this.

'What do you mean?'

'They take off your own teeth. File them down to little nubs so they can stick other teeth on over the top.'

'You're telling me your teeth are tiny pointed fangs?'

Blair nodded. 'I did that to myself.'

'You filed off your own teeth?' Suddenly Carmen wasn't hungry. Even looking at the china plates made her feel sick. 'That's ... that's barbaric.'

'Isn't it?' said Blair. 'And for what? So I get more TV appearances and more adulation and money?'

'When you put it like that ...' said Carmen, but she still wasn't interested in her food. 'Did it hurt?'

'Yes.'

'What were your teeth like before?'

'*Fine*,' said Blair sadly. 'I wouldn't mind, but people keep coming up and telling me their terrible problems like I can help and all I can think about are my sore teeth.'

'Your books *have* helped loads of people,' said Carmen. 'Otherwise people wouldn't buy them.'

'People buy things in the hope that it will make them feel

134

better,' said Blair. 'It gives you a momentary boost, just buying it, but not for long. It's just a stupid dopamine hit whereby I tell you things are going to be *great* and you fantasise that they are and you feel better. Then you go back to your shit normality and it's all shit again and guess what, you're not living the life you imagine, you're living the life that got dumped in your lap when your parent got sick or your partner became a drunk or your children are disappointing. So you think you'll make yourself better and you buy another book. That's my *entire business plan*.' He frowned. 'I don't normally talk like this. Jet lag.'

'And Champagne.'

'Oh yeah. And you're a good listener.'

Carmen didn't want to say that she hadn't really been able to get a word in edgeways, so she just smiled.

'Well, stop doing it then,' she said.

'If I stop doing it, Emily loses her job,' he said, looking at her then – not in his 'hey, let me grasp your hand and do full eye contact' way, but quite straightforwardly. 'So do half the publishing team at my office, who by the way when they're not publishing any old rubbish by me are publishing really good books that nobody reads.'

He sighed.

'I can't do that. I just can't.'

He glanced at his watch.

'And soon I have to go to a children's hospital.'

'So you'd skip the interviews but not the children's hospital?'

He rolled his eyes.

'I'm a cynic, sweetie, not a monster.'

She smiled at him, feeling surprisingly slightly sympathetic.

'Can't you write a book about being authentic?' she said. 'Then you could be authentic.'

'I did!' he said despairingly. 'It sold millions – you really have never heard of me, have you?'

'I totally almost have,' protested Carmen.

'It was called *Live Your Happy Authentic Life for a Better, More Confident You.*'

'But you didn't try it on yourself.'

'I'm trying it right now,' he said. 'I think I might be a bit of a drag.'

'You're all right,' said Carmen.

'Thank you,' he said. 'Could I possibly ask you to forget all of this and not sell it to a newspaper?'

'How much for?' said Carmen, then when he looked stricken she had to laugh at his appalled expression.

'I'm kidding,' she said. 'You idiot. But do you just unburden yourself on any random stranger that walks past?'

He gave his card to the waiter.

'You're not random . . . '

'Carmen,' she supplied again.

He glanced at his watch, ignoring his buzzing phone.

'You know I have a little time before the hospital.'

She looked at him.

'And my room is just upstairs.'

She sat bolt upright, and almost burst out laughing.

'Is this you living your authentic life?'

He shrugged.

'Um . . . a bit.'

'Ha. Well, well done, I suppose.'

'You mean that?' He got up and grabbed his jacket.

'No, I mean, well done you for being authentic. I'm patently not coming upstairs with you.'

'Okay!' he said, somewhat insultingly. 'No harm done.' He

asked the waiter to call him a cab, something Carmen hadn't realised you could actually do.

'Nice meeting you . . . ' he said, back to the low tones he had had before.

' . . . Carmen.'

'Carmen.'

She got up to leave, shaking her head.

'Thanks for lunch.'

But he was on the phone, and not even looking at her.

Chapter Eighteen

Sofia slumped in her chair, exhausted. She was putting off maternity leave as late as possible – she absolutely hated looking as if she couldn't handle anything or wasn't in complete control, and frankly walking from her office to the maternity wing was the kind of person she would like to be. Federico was unsure about this but had learned long ago not to get in his wife's way. So she managed to keep a fairly good display at the office but by the time she crawled home she was fit for nothing.

Skylar was going out again, and Carmen was supposedly making dinner (while moaning about having to do it), which only involved her heating up a pie she'd bought and opening some tins of beans, which Sofia was too exhausted to complain about and anyway, she secretly thought smelled quite nice.

She'd been hoping for a quick nap but had just heard some surprising news which made her lift her head up.

'You turned down *Blair Pfenning*?'

Then she felt bad for sounding so surprised. Thankfully Carmen, normally so incredibly touchy, let it go for once. Maybe it was because she was being allowed to eat pastry.

'Oh, he would have stuck it into a postbox if it was handy,' said Carmen, who was in fact still a little tipsy from the Champagne.

'Are you absolutely sure this happened?' Sofia said. 'He wasn't . . . you know, just saying thank you?'

'Yeah, you're right, what could someone half-decent possibly see in me?' said Carmen.

Ah, there it was.

'That's not what I meant!'

'That's exactly what you meant!'

'Please, Carmen . . .'

Carmen went back to stirring the beans. She was wondering whether or not she slightly regretted it herself. It would have been a funny story to tell, and it had been a while.

'I mean, it would have been a funny story,' said Sofia, in a conciliatory tone, as if she was reading Carmen's thoughts.

'Or he might have fallen in love with me and whisked me off on an exciting world tour!'

'Well,' said Sofia. 'I am very glad that isn't happening. Because . . . it looks like you're doing very well with the shop.'

Carmen looked up. Was Sofia trying to be a goody-two-shoes or did she mean it? As she did so, it struck her how utterly exhausted Sofia looked. Even with money and help . . . it couldn't be easy. She put on the kettle to make her some tea.

'Did he take your number?'

'He did not,' said Carmen. 'Which pretty much settles it for the falling madly in love with me thing . . .'

'You could message him! He's on Instagram.'

'I don't want to! He's weird.'

'But very handsome and rich.'

'He has teeth filed to tiny points,' said Carmen. 'And anyway, his publicist has my number *if* he wanted it, *which* he doesn't.'

She couldn't help glancing at her phone regardless. Sofia saw that and hid a smile. There was nothing of course.

Jack charged in.

'Mummy! Mummy! They said it's going to snow!'

'Who said that, Jacky?'

'*Newsround*.'

'There's still *Newsround*?' said Carmen. 'Cor. Most boring show ever.'

'No,' said Pippa. 'It tells you what's happening in the world. We watch it at school.'

'You get it at school?'

They all nodded.

'You get telly at school? How is that fair?'

'Supper doesn't smell very NUTRITIOUS,' countered Pippa.

'Well, that's because it's tea, not supper,' said Carmen. Phoebe entered the kitchen, trailing as always, and scowling as always.

'It's pie,' said Carmen. 'You'll like it, won't you, Phoebs?'

Phoebe looked upset although Carmen had no idea why.

'I don't think so,' she sniffed.

'Good, good.'

'Bring some here,' said Sofia. 'I am *starved*.'

'BUT IS IT GOING TO SNOW?' said Jack loudly. Sometimes being the only boy in the house was quite tricky.

'I don't know, darling,' said his mother, tousling his hair and glancing out the back window, but it was pitch-black, only the lights of other houses dimly visible above the back wall.

'Oh, Mr McCredie thinks it is,' said Carmen. 'He said tonight will be bad and tomorrow will be beyond imagining.'

Phoebe frowned.

'I can imagine a lot of things.'

'Well, imagine lots of snow and it might happen!'

It wasn't the boom that woke Carmen up. It was a pair of feet more or less in her face in the narrow bed.

'WHAAA—?' she said, starting awake in a panic, then realising through her foggy brain that if it was a murderous rapist, they were very much going about it in completely the wrong way. She had been on the train again, the tiny dusty train, the woman in her hat, the tunnel coming closer, closer . . .

She glanced at the toes wriggling frantically two centimetres from her nose.

'Phoebe? Is that you?'

Under the blankets came a tiny *eep*.

'What on earth is the matter?'

The little body was shaking.

'At least turn the right way up.'

There it was then: a boom, and the little body went rigid. Carmen leaned out and switched on her bedside lamp which did almost nothing except make the rest of the dark room even darker. There was something odd about the light, something soft about the noise, but the boom . . .

'What was that?'

Slowly, like trying to tempt an animal out of its burrow,

Carmen stroked Phoebe's back and gradually persuaded the child to turn the right way up.

'You'll suffocate down there,' she said, as Phoebe's stubborn black eyes and shock of messy hair finally emerged over the tip of the duvet. Phoebe didn't smile. She was whispering.

'It's the . . . thundersnow!' she imparted.

'Oh, of course it is! said Carmen. 'Amazing!' She frowned. 'I thought you'd have gone to Skylar.'

Phoebe shook her head.

'Skylar says "sleep heen" is very important.'

'Sleep heen?'

'Yes. Never disturb someone's sleep. It is very important. To be CLEAN.'

'Sleep *hygiene*?' said Carmen waking up slowly.

'Oh yes. Anyway. It's scary.'

'Oh no, I'm sure it's not,' said Carmen, swinging out of bed and wincing. She wished she knew why Sofia thought keeping your bedrooms warm was common. The polished wood beneath her feet was like ice.

'Don't go!'

'Come on, I'll just take a look . . . '

Phoebe pushed herself back under the duvet, hunched over with her head over her knees. Carmen vowed that she was going to overcome her lifelong hatred of slippers – she had an unnatural aversion to sheepskin – otherwise she was going to get chilblains.

You couldn't see anything from down here in the basement, but the world outside was in a deadly hush, the window absolutely freezing to the touch, and Carmen felt a rush of excitement.

'Come on,' she said. It was just before 5 a.m. Phoebe shook

her head severely. 'Just . . . come and have a look. A quick one. How about we bring the duvet with us?'

Phoebe looked worried so, in the end, Carmen half picked up the trembling girl along with the duvet and took them both up the stairs to the kitchen, which still had vestigial warmth from dinner, and the back window that looked over the little garden.

Snowflakes danced and swirled against the pane, so dense it was as if the house was surrounded by a thick moving blanket. Thunder shook the house, which made Phoebe jump, but Carmen just hugged her closer with the duvet around them both. It was oddly comforting to feel the little warm body close to her, willingly coming in for a cuddle.

The silence was unusual; they were in the middle of a city, just off a busy thoroughfare. Normally there were ambulances screaming, bin lorries beeping as they backed up, taxis honking and late night party groups laughing and squealing.

Now, here it was as if they were the only people in the universe as the dancing silent huge flakes of snow whirled in their intricate patterns; so common and so very, very extraordinary.

'Oh!' said Phoebe.

Some footsteps skittered along the flagstones behind them. As soon as Jack realised they had a duvet with them, he nodded and dashed back upstairs quietly, coming down with his own, covered in tasteful embroidered wooden cars, rather than the Hibernian Football Club logos his little heart desired above all else.

Silently, he moved next to Phoebe and instead of pushing and shoving him with her sharp elbows like she normally would, she budged up to make space for him to press his elbows on the cold window sill and stare up into the sky, so dizzy with flakes

143

you couldn't tell if you were looking up or down; it made your brain turn somersaults.

Jack, normally such a jumping bean, was stock-still in awe at it, pointing occasionally with Phoebe as the shed became completely engulfed, or a flash of lightning suddenly showed them their faces reflected in the window glass and they all jumped. To Carmen's immense relief, Phoebe started to laugh when they realised they'd been scared by their own faces.

There was another step behind them, and Carmen glanced behind her. Pippa was there too, about to announce herself and presumably tell everyone to get back to bed or she'd tell Mummy. Carmen, however, raised her finger to her mouth, then beckoned her forwards; there was enough space between the two duvets for her to snuggle between her siblings, and to Carmen's surprise she managed to do so with the minimum of fuss.

The silence, the warmth of the small bodies, the astonishing display of the snow – all affected Carmen deeply as they looked out, awestruck, into the garden, transformed into a mysterious grotto of wonder.

Finally, Jack's voice piped up.

'Can we go out and play in it?'

'At five o'clock in the morning in your pyjamas?' said Carmen. 'Your mother would have my guts for garters.'

There was general disappointment.

'You can if you're ready before school later though,' said Carmen. 'Get your wellies out . . . Actually,' she added, as there came another boom, 'I wouldn't be the least bit surprised if they cancelled school.'

At this, there was a sharp intake of breath from all of them.

'I'll miss my bassoon lesson,' said Pippa worriedly.

144

'I wanted a snowball fight,' said Jack.

'CLOSING THE SCHOOL,' said Phoebe in the dreamy voice of one upon whom unimaginable riches have been bestowed.

'Well, we'll see,' said Carmen hurriedly. 'Now, back to bed.'

But nobody was remotely capable of going back to bed: Phoebe protested that she was too scared to go by herself, and would have to sleep in Carmen's bed; Jack said if they went to bed he was just going to go out by himself; and Pippa sniffed and tutted like an old woman on the bus.

Carmen, so unused to her nieces and nephew, for once hit on the right solution: making everyone hot chocolate – the Aga was still warm, and they huddled around it as she ransacked the cupboard for something that might pass as hot and a treat.

She finally found an untouched bag of very posh hot chocolate in a Valvona & Crolla hamper which must have arrived as a client gift. Carmen looked at the children and they looked back at her wonderingly as if, on this night-time trip of marvels, they couldn't possibly be realising their wildest dreams. Carmen figured out how to put on the hob and whisked up the milky frothy foam – it was dark chocolate, *durr*, the worst kind, so she added plenty of milk and sugar to make it palatable – and filled up their little stripy mugs with their names painted on them, and they sat around the table, talking about their plans for their snow day – the biggest snowman! Getting the neighbours in a snowball fight! Tobogganing!

And then, well, there was an entire Christmas hamper right there, and it wasn't fair not to let them try the crystallised ginger – 'yum' according to the girls, 'DISGUSTING' according to Jack – and have one of the little hand-wrapped chocolates and smell the tea and okay then, just a Florentine,

145

until the midnight feast was finished, and little heads began to droop, and Carmen shooed them upstairs together, making Pippa promise to supervise extra tooth-brushing, and only the dirty cups in the dishwasher later that morning betrayed that the little gang had been there at all – that and the unexpected kiss from Phoebe that was so fleeting Carmen wasn't sure if it too had been a dream.

Chapter Nineteen

'What the hell is *thundersnow*?'

Carmen squinted at her phone and the text message from a number she didn't recognise. She frowned.

'Who's this?'

'It's Blair. Blair Pfenning. Blair who took you out to lunch? That Blair? You know? Yesterday?'

Carmen found her heart jumping. Goodness. Well. This was a surprise. She had trained herself not to expect it. And also, he was a knob. But ...

Maybe he couldn't stop thinking about her. I mean, she had thought he was a bit jumped up but still, it had been ... it had been such a lovely treat. At a moment when she didn't have a lot of treats, when she had had a tough old time of it, and she certainly didn't have a lot of people taking her out to lunch, especially not Champagne and dragon phlegm lunches.

In his cosy hotel room with underfloor heating, Blair Pfenning stared at the contact list the publicist had left behind, with several precautions to make sure he could get his own plane, and how much she'd miss him but she had a major thriller writer flying in to London and ... and he'd waved a hand magnanimously and announced that he wasn't a baby even though he was secretly furious and feeling very annoyed. He needed a full-time assistant to follow him around; he was far too important to get to the airport by himself.

'I've booked the cab for nine,' she'd said. 'It's a black cab, so it can get through the traffic faster.'

'Fine,' he'd said shortly, and quickly put all his clothes through the hotel's express laundry service so he'd at least feel he was getting his money's worth.

Then of course she'd flounced off back to London on the train – and he was now completely stranded with a cancelled flight, which she couldn't help him with as her train had run into snow just south of Newcastle and appeared to be stuck till the Army could get to it.

Blair had been curt in his sympathies.

She had, however, left the contact sheet with him. He'd thrown it in the bin, but then bent down and retrieved it. Surely someone could sort him out.

'Oh yeah. Hi.'

He sniffed. She should be thrilled to hear from him. People normally were.

'Thundersnow?'

'It's a stormy meteorological event ...'

148

'No, I know what it is. It's what's cancelled my bloody flight to LA.'

Carmen looked at the message. She had absolutely no idea what he wanted from her. Did he think she knew some special way to fly him out of Edinburgh to LA? Or was he just bored? Was he flirting with her?

She had of course googled him the previous evening, in her bedroom, well away from Sofia's prying eyes. Divorced. She had a look at his ex-wife. She was an extraordinary-looking supermodel with a slightly tight bitter look around her mouth, although to be fair that was when she was simultaneously being asked by the *Daily Mail* whether she regretted divorcing Blair when his book *How Divorce Can Make You Happier Than Ever!* had just sold its three millionth copy.

That morning, when she'd finally woken again, tired but somehow refreshed, she'd gone to the front door, accompanied by the yawning children. The dark hadn't quite left the sky and the snow was still falling in spirals – more gently now – but there were pink streaks across the rooftops between the gaps. It was gorgeous. And now this.

Clutching her phone, she went upstairs for breakfast.

School was indeed cancelled, much to Sofia's disgust, even as Jack and Phoebe were yelling with joy and dashed to pull their wellies on over their pyjamas. Skylar was trying to get them to eat their soaked oats. It wasn't very good of her, she knew, but she felt a slight satisfaction in the children listening to her, and as soon as Phoebe started to talk about last night, the other two shushed her immediately.

'Whatever happened to my Valvona and Crolla hamper?' Sofia was complaining, looking in a cupboard. 'I was going to donate it to the homeless.'

Skylar looked sternly at the children.

'There wouldn't be any stealing, would there?'

Carmen and the children exchanged glances – the children's faces were terrified.

'Because you know we've talked about things that are kind? And unkind?'

'I took it,' said Carmen instantly. 'I'll get you another one. Or two maybe.'

'You ate an entire hamper? By yourself?'

'Yes, I did.'

'All the crystallised ginger?'

'I love crystallised ginger.'

'You ate an entire box of crystallised ginger? Between yesterday and today. After most of a pie and a can of beans?'

'Chill out, sis,' said Carmen. Nothing could dent her good mood today.

'That can really mess with your stomach pH?' said Skylar. 'I mean any amount of sugar is poisonous, but that sounds lethal?'

'Well, if I die you can say I told you so,' said Carmen, winking at the children and deciding to keep her exciting Blair news until Sofia wasn't being annoying. Plus she wouldn't put it past Skylar to have some dig about how someone texting her would give her brain cancer?

The house had quietened by the time she had to go to work; the children had joined their friends in St Mary's Cathedral Gardens down the road, the vicar cheerily promising to judge a snowman competition. She opened the front door.

In the first shining moment, she saw the whole strange-familiar world, glistening white. The roof of the terrace opposite was mounded into square towers of snow, and beyond them all the walls and houses and churches were buried, merged into one great flat expanse, unbroken white to the horizon's brim. Carmen drew in a long, happy breath, silently rejoicing.

And now her phone was dinging.

'Babe, I'm stuck! Didn't you know what I meant? There's no flights out!'

'Could be worse,' typed Carmen. 'You could be stuck in somewhere that *isn't* one of the most beautiful cities in the entire world, freshly blanketed in snow.'

'Ugh,' came back. 'And I only have suede shoes.'

'Can't your glamorous sidekick go buy you some wellingtons?'

'She left last night, left me to catch a ducking plane on my own. Which now isn't going.

'Ducking autocorrect.'

'It's okay. I get what you mean.'

Carmen stifled a smile. Aha. What a big baby he was.

She walked along Princes Street to get the full effect of the capital under snow.

The castle looked like a dream, like something from *Game of Thrones*, the road lined with people trying to catch the pink clouds floating behind it on camera, even as the snow still danced in front of her face and flakes landed on her coat. Underneath, the snow was powdery and soft, not yet iced over and brown, or hideous slushy puddles.

She stuck her phone back in her pocket – it was too cold, taking off her gloves to type every time – and dodged the photographers.

The mound steps were slippery, the road nearly as bad, but she did not regret taking the long way round as she more or less climbed her way up and over the top of the Lawnmarket, watching people move about in awe, and children racing each other for the exceptional pleasure of breaking the pristine ice of a puddle; a few optimistic sleds were already clustering in Princes Street Gardens.

By the time she got to the shop, she was pink in the face and Blair Pfenning was waiting outside for her.

'Are you going to open the shop?' he said, looking rather disgruntled.

'It's snow, not a volcanic eruption.'

'It's *thundersnow*.'

'If you didn't think I was opening up, what are you doing here?'

He shrugged.

'I thought Mr McCredie might like to discuss book sales.'

Carmen laughed as she put the key in the lock, and Blair thought how fresh she looked; young with a red scarf and hat that suited her marvellously.

'Well, I can't really see that happening,' said Carmen. 'I think he thinks books being exchanged for money is on a fundamental level really quite vulgar.'

Blair looked around. The shop was warm and cosy now Carmen had showed Mr McCredie you could programme a thermostat, and also that they had a thermostat. She busied herself grabbing her duster, while Blair frowned.

'I'd love a coffee,' he said.

She gave him a side-eye.

'Kettle's on the fridge through the back,' she said.

'What? After I sold enough books to keep this shop going for months?!'

Carmen glanced at the poster of his face which was still on the opposite wall and gave it a look.

'I'm busy!'

'You are,' said Blair. 'I need boots. Look at my shoes. It's a disaster.'

'You are so spoiled! And I am very busy.'

He looked up and down the street. Cars couldn't get along it without slipping, and the snow was only just being shovelled away from the doorways. There wasn't a soul in sight.

'You bloody aren't.'

'I have to shovel snow,' said Carmen.

'Aha!' said a voice emerging from the gloom.

To Carmen's complete astonishment, it was young Mr McCredie, dressed head to foot in the most peculiar outfit she'd ever seen. On his feet he wore long pointed shoes which seemed to be made of some kind of hide. His trousers were oilskin, ancient and patched, and he had a heavy tweed jacket over a jumper with another hide skin over the top, and a big furry hood.

'Ooh, lovely *finneskos*!' said Blair.

'Thank you,' said Mr McCredie, beaming broadly and showing off his bizarre shoes. 'Best reindeer fur.'

'Splendid!'

'Wait a second,' said Carmen. 'You're wearing *reindeer*?'

'Technically right now I'm more reindeer than human,' said Mr McCredie.

'You're like the most evil Santa Claus ever.'

'This jacket,' he said, 'went to the South Pole. Almost,' he added. 'Fortunately,' he also added, mostly to himself.

'Wow,' said Carmen. 'Shouldn't it be in a museum?'

'Oh yes, eventually,' said Mr McCredie. 'Plenty of wear in it still though.'

Carmen looked at him. There was no doubt that he looked as happy as she'd seen him, lifting his ancient shovel.

'Hey, have you got another pair of those?' she said, staring at the ridiculous pointed boots. 'Blair needs some.'

'Well, I . . .'

'No, it's all right,' said Blair hastily. Whether they worked or not, he most certainly was not putting hundred-year-old reindeer boots on. You never knew when you might get papped.

'Carmen was just taking me to buy wellingtons.'

'Was I?'

'After all, you can hardly open up yet.'

But Mr McCredie just waved them off and started shovelling snow.

'Be careful,' said Carmen.

'You saying a McCredie can't handle themselves in snow?' he said back to her and she smiled at him properly.

'Okay,' she said. 'I'll bring back hot chocolate this time.'

'I don't know why you're insisting on rotting my teeth at this age.'

Because, Carmen thought to herself, somebody needs to spoil you. And I don't know why, but it seems to have to be me.

Blair picked his way carefully down the street as Carmen slid, laughing.

'Oh, come on,' she said. 'Isn't it lovely?'

He sighed.

'Would you mind just calling the airline for me?'

'What? Yes, I would. Why?'

'Oh, I don't understand the accents, do I? You'd be much better than me. Go on.'

'No!'

'I'll take you somewhere lovely.'

'LA?'

'If you like.'

He smiled his very white teeth at her.

'Don't forget I'm afraid of your teeth,' warned Carmen.

'Oh yeah, fuck it, I forgot.' His face fell. 'Oh God, Carmen, I'm really lazy and useless and I like getting other people to do stuff for me – is that any better?'

'Does it still end up with me on hold for an hour to an airline?'

'Let's eat somewhere really, *really* nice.'

They had landed at the bottom of Victoria Street, where there was a little shop in blue with a beautiful window decoration of robins and holly and lots of expensive country-style clothes, Burberry and Harris tweeds.

'They must do wellies,' said Carmen. 'I wonder if they're open?'

There was someone inside. Goodness, thought Carmen. Did everyone on Victoria Street live inside their shops at night like little dormice?

'Hello! Are you open?'

The door was flung open by a large red-faced man.

'You're asking if a shop selling kit for INCLEMENT WEATHER is shut in INCLEMENT WEATHER?' boomed the man. He had the same kind of voice as Mr McCredie: technically Edinburgh but sounding not completely unlike a posh English person. 'COME IN!'

'Thanks,' said Carmen. 'I'm from McCredie's?'

He frowned at her.

'He's HIRED someone? He's SELLING THINGS?'

'He's trying to,' said Carmen.

'Hi, I'm Blair Pfenning?' said Blair, giving it the full teeth. The man ignored him. 'Well, blow me down.'

'He's out there now, clearing the snow.'

'He's OUT?'

The bluster left the man.

'Well. Goodness, young lady. I don't know what you've done but that seems rather impressive.'

'I haven't done anything,' said Carmen.

'We've all got that rent rise, you know. Well. We will all be so very pleased he's making a go of it.'

Once again, Carmen reflected on what a community the street was, and wondered why Mr McCredie wasn't a part of it.

'My feet are not getting notably drier,' observed Blair.

The man shook his head. 'Bad business there.'

'With Mr McCredie? Why? How?'

The big man turned and went back into his shop.

'I'm Crawford,' he said back over his shoulder. 'Crawford Finnieston.'

'Got any wellingtons, Crawford?' said Blair.

'So, hang on, what bad business?'

Crawford blinked rheumy blue eyes.

'He hasn't told you?'

'No!' said Carmen.

Blair found a shelf full of green wellingtons.

'What is it?' asked Carmen.

Crawford shrugged. 'Oh, I won't tell tales out of school, young lady. Nothing, nothing, just town gossip.'

Carmen looked around. It was an extraordinary shop: flowered wallpaper, antique dressers and mirrors, as well as stuffed animals – not for sale, it appeared, just there because Crawford liked them – and bodywarmers and hunting clothes.

'This is the poshest shop I've ever been in,' said Carmen.

156

'I can well believe that,' said Crawford. Then, slightly more gently: 'Where did you work before?'

She told him.

'Ah, a sad day,' he said. 'I knew it well. Although rather good for me. The little girls of the west coast have to come get their jodhpurs from me these days.'

'I like these,' said Blair, pointing at a large pair of waders hanging up.

'They're for fishing,' said Crawford.

'Well, surely they'll work in the snow too?'

Crawford and Carmen shared a look.

'No' here,' said Crawford, bringing up the wellies.

'They're £300!' said Carmen before she could help herself.

'I'm going to bill the publishers,' said Blair airily. 'They're the ones who left me in this mess.'

'They sent the thundersnow?'

He tried on a pair with a tartan fold-over at the top, and looked at himself in the mirror, obviously liking what he saw.

Crawford nodded. 'Although . . . ' he said.

'I know,' said Blair. And in a twinkling of an eye he was in a changing room, trying on a pair of navy cords with a tweed shirt, a mustard waistcoat and a wildly expensive waxed overcoat. He'd texted the number of the airline to Carmen, but she was studiously ignoring it.

'Ta-dah!' he said, emerging as a full country gentleman. Carmen burst out laughing, but the smile faded as she saw the disappointment on his face.

Actually, he looked rather nice, if ready for a costume party. The waistcoat suited him wonderfully, showing off his broad shoulders; the cords balanced his slim bottom half.

'Do you have a personal trainer?' said Carmen.

'Who doesn't?'

Carmen rolled her eyes.

'What time are we going to kill some foxes?'

'Want to try the flat cap, sir?'

'No,' said Carmen. 'I think that's far enough. You don't want to go full Nigel Farage.'

'I *don't*,' said Blair with a shiver. He looked at himself in the mirror.

'This isn't me at all,' he said. 'Am I wrong to like it?'

'I like it,' said Carmen.

'Really?'

'Really.'

'Well, all right then.'

The bill was absolutely eye-popping, but Blair didn't bat an eyelid, just tossed a gold credit card over the counter.

He marched out in his expensive wellingtons and shiny new clothes, admiring himself repeatedly in the windows as they passed. A few more people were blindly feeling their way through the snow, including a woman who, when she realised who she was walking past, tripped up in shock.

'Madam,' said Blair, back to his charming best, helping her up.

'Blair Pfenning!' she managed. 'I . . . I love you!'

'Well, how nice,' he said smoothly, carrying on moving even as she fumbled for her camera with frozen hands.

'Goodness,' said Carmen. 'Does that happen a lot?'

'Not nearly enough,' said Blair. 'For example, some people just leave me stranded in a strange city without a flight out.'

'Hot chocolate,' said Carmen firmly, steering them into the little café at the bottom of the hill, its windows all steamed up. They ordered two for staying in, while Blair stabbed buttons on his phone and made large sighs.

'Oh, for *goodness*' sake,' said Carmen, as they sat down by the window, watching the lovely street taper up into the snowy horizon, the cut-out white snowflakes fluttering prettily above their heads, the scent of cinnamon heavy on the air. It was ridiculously adorable, particularly without being thronged with its usual thousands of tourists. Although, thought Carmen with her business head on, it would be quite nice if they came back *fairly* quickly.

'Give me one of your marshmallows,' she said, having finished her own.

'No!' said Blair, pouting. 'Why should I?'

'Because if you give me one of your marshmallows, I'll sort out your flights for you.'

His grin was back, although he hastily damped it down. '*Really?*'

She took his phone and pulled up the airline's website. Sure enough, with his booking reference and the airline being well aware of the thundersnow situation, it took her about six minutes to complete the transaction.

'Put me in a window seat,' he said quickly. Then he came over to sit next to her. 'It is business, isn't it?'

'Yes,' said Carmen. Goodness. Flying off to sunny LA in business class. That would be something.

He sighed.

'Honestly. You'd think they'd bump me up to first for all this inconvenience.'

She looked at him, shaking her head.

'Yes, all the terrible hot chocolate and shopping-based inconvenience.'

She handed back the phone while he busied himself with making sure he had the right seat.

159

'I mean, 1A is obviously ideal,' he was saying, 'but it looks like someone else has it and frankly you'd rather be in, like, row *six* than with someone next to you who wants to talk to you. Worse if they've read your books.'

The sweet waitress, her hair in plaits, came forwards timidly.

'Excuse me, are you Blair Pfenning?'

'Yes, hi?'

She beamed.

'Hot chocolates are on the house!' she said.

'Oh well, that's *fantastic*,' said a man who'd just spent four figures on a new outfit. Then, sotto voce to Carmen: 'We should have ordered extra marshmallows.' He turned his beam on the waitress. 'Would you like a photo?'

Blair was being super-charming and Carmen was trying to be snooty about it. Although, if she was strictly honest with herself, it was actually quite exciting being next to a famous person when everyone was incredibly nice to you all the time and brought you free hot chocolate and they chatted idly to you about where exactly you should sit when travelling business class to Los Angeles, as if that were something she could feasibly have an interest in.

Also, there was something rather sweet about him, dressed in his new Edinburgh clobber, proud as a peacock. She was more used to her boyfriends turning up in trackie bottoms with stains on them of unmentionable provenance. She wished Sofia could see her now. Not that she could ask for a selfie – that would be so annoying, and make her exactly the same as the waitress. Whereas anyone seeing them . . . together . . . sitting together . . . might think they were boyfriend and girlfriend. Although that would be absurd: he was awful.

But people didn't think that, she thought to herself. Everyone

160

else reckoned he was amazing, people who didn't know him. Look how lovely he'd been to the woman in the street, and the waitress. They would think she was lucky.

She refused to let herself pursue that thought as the door opened with a howling jet of wind and a tall figure, not at all well-dressed against the weather, bundled in, blowing on their hands, standing politely behind where Carmen and Blair were sitting, waiting to be called forward.

'I mean, if you're going to go to LA, you kind of have to go in style?' Blair was saying, still looking at the airline's website.

'Oh, I totally agree,' Carmen said. 'Definitely. Goodness, who doesn't think that?'

'Hi, Oke!' said the waitress to the person who'd just come in.

Carmen stiffened, then glanced behind her.

'Oh hi,' she said. She was annoyed with herself for being caught out in a boast she didn't really mean, which was absurd as it wasn't like she knew Oke; he was just a customer who came in her shop.

Oke smiled. 'Isn't it amazing?!' he said, gesturing outside. 'So beautiful.'

'You don't look dressed for it,' said Blair, and Oke's face fell.

'Well. No. No. I suppose not.'

And Carmen felt even more embarrassed; he was wearing a T-shirt, a long-sleeved shirt, a jumper and a jacket over the top of that and he still looked absolutely freezing. It must be warm in Brazil, she thought.

'There's a shop up the road will sort you out.'

Oke blinked.

'Thanks, man.'

'Your tea,' said the waitress, and passed a small cup over to Oke, who looked pleased to put his hands round it to warm

161

them, and paid with a five-pound note. He received very little change back.

Carmen watched it happen in disbelief. He'd been short-changed.

'I'm sorry,' she said, unable to help herself. Her voice went wobbly and unreliable. 'I don't think you've given this man all his change?'

It felt like the shop had gone silent. Everyone was looking at her.

The waitress blushed bright pink at being addressed by the person she had indeed assumed to be Blair Pfenning's girlfriend, and had been wondering what exactly this totally normal-looking person had that she didn't have, and actually it had been making her think even better of lovely Blair for stooping to go out with someone that just looked like anybody, that wasn't in expensive clothes or super-thin or anything. It just showed what an amazing, super guy he was deep down inside, like Pierce Brosnan, and made her love him more than ever.

'Um, sorry?' she said, flushing from pink to bright red, her eyes darting to the till.

'Well, you gave him a cup of tea and didn't give him any change.'

Oke looked at her with amused eyes, and Carmen wondered with a horrible icy chill if she had perhaps got it wrong.

'Yes, it's a suspended cup?' said the girl, looking terrified.

'What's that?'

'It's ... um ... when you buy a cup of tea or coffee along with your normal stuff for someone, like a homeless person, who can't afford one. Then any time someone can come in and ask for one?'

Carmen felt horribly embarrassed, as if the entire shop was

162

still staring at her, as indeed it was. Oke wasn't saying anything at all, just staring at the ground, at his wet trainers, in huge contrast to Blair's shiny wellingtons.

Blair looked up suddenly.

'Well, that's an awesome idea,' he said, completely surprising Carmen, and flashing his toothy grin to the shop. 'Here, I want ten suspended hot chocolates.'

At this all the focus turned to him, and there was practically applause. Blair beamed his shiny smile again and flashed his gold bank card once more. Oke, normally so chatty, took his tea, smiled briefly at Carmen and left.

'Wait!'

She felt terrible, absolutely awful. Both at accusing the shop girl – God, could she ever drink their lovely hot chocolate again? – but worse, she had accused Oke of being a rube, of not knowing what he was doing.

She caught up with him in the snowy street, the sound of everything muffled, no cars passing.

'Oke!'

He turned round. She had forgotten to put her coat on and was shivering.

'Look at you,' he said. 'You're dressed worse than I am.'

He immediately went to take off his jacket and give it to her.

'No, I don't need it ... I'm so sorry,' said Carmen.

'I don't know why you're apologising to me,' said Oke.

'Because I made it look as if you didn't know what you were doing. Sorry.'

He shrugged.

'Okay. Have you apologised to Dahlia?'

'Who's ... ? Oh. The waitress.'

He nodded.

'You slightly accused her of stealing?'

'Oh *God*,' said Carmen. 'I always do this. I just dive straight in and speak and get myself into so much trouble.'

Oke smiled.

'Have you ever thought about *not* doing that?'

'All the time,' she said, looking up at him. The snowflakes were settling on his hair. 'But usually it's exactly five seconds after I just said the thing that got me into trouble.'

He looked serious.

'Well. Okay. You're cold; are you sure you won't take my coat?'

'Don't be ridiculous – you aren't wearing enough as it is.'

'Well, I'm glad you care,' he said.

'Did they not tell you in Brazil it was going to be cold here? Are Quakers not allowed Christmas, birthdays and *weather*?'

He laughed. She glanced over her shoulder into the shop. Blair was staring at his phone and frowning and sneaking looks at her.

'I should go,' she said. 'Um, what are you up to?'

'I am going to the Quaker house. They have a meeting there, and a homeless drive.'

'Cor. You really are very Quakery.'

'I'm not really,' he said. 'Well, apart from the Christmas thing. Loads of Quakers celebrate that. We just never got the habit. But sometimes it is ... comforting. In a foreign land. To sit among brethren, doing familiar things. You don't have to believe all of it. And it is good to sit among silence sometimes.'

'I can see that,' said Carmen. She frowned and remembered something she'd read somewhere. 'Hang on. Is it true that Quakers can't lie?'

'Yes,' said Oke. 'Although that may be a lie.'

164

He saw her face.

'I am joking of course. Then I am going to visit my favourite tree.'

'You have a favourite tree?!'

He nodded and she was about to ask more when the coffee shop door banged behind her.

'You abandoned me!' said Blair. 'All those people, just looking at me. It's a security issue you know.'

'Is it though?' said Carmen, sceptical.

Oke looked at both of them. Blair looked him up and down, then turned the full beam of his attention onto Carmen.

'You must be freezing,' said Blair, performatively taking off his new expensive jacket and covering her shoulders with it. 'Come on. Let's go have fun. And also, can you phone the airline for me again? My seat change hasn't come through. *Nothing* works. Christ, it's awful.'

'Nice to see you,' said Oke and Carmen smiled, glad he wasn't annoyed. He turned up the steps towards the Quaker meeting house as Blair was about to take her back to the café.

She excused herself, and dashed back in.

'I'm so sorry,' she said to Dahlia, who rather stiffly said it was fine and not to mention it. But she added that she wasn't really in the business of overcharging people and Carmen said she knew that and left a huge tip which actually then felt like she'd made everything slightly worse. She screwed up her face and headed back up the hill to the bookshop, which now had its pavements perfectly swept and a rather jolly-looking Mr McCredie standing outside in his reindeer kit. A woman was walking along very, very slowly with a bundled-up toddler who had so many clothes on he looked like a bouncy rubber ball.

165

'Mummy! Mummy! Man! LOOK! SANTA!' he shouted, his high voice loud in the silent street. His eyes were wide as he regarded Mr McCredie as one would a vision from the past, and Mr McCredie smiled broadly and bowed to the child, and the snow kept falling.

Chapter Twenty

'Just come back to my hotel room. Finish the booking,' Blair had urged.

'*Blair*,' she said. 'Am I seriously the only woman you know in Edinburgh?'

'Yes. So?' he reflected. 'Well, that girl in the coffee shop was cute.'

'Go get her then.'

'Oh no, it's too boring to meet new people and pretend to be nice to them. Come on. You're right here and my hotel room is only . . . well, up like nineteen flights of steps.'

'No no no no no. Get out of here: I have to sell some books.'

Carmen shook him off – he looked genuinely startled by this – and went back to work.

And sure enough, as more and more people ventured out to take a look at the beautiful landscape and make snowmen in the Grassmarket and throw snowballs at the traffic wardens which was very bad and something obviously you should never ever do, the shop got busier and busier.

In a way, Carmen was wondering to herself, in the past she had certainly hopped into bed with people far less attractive and attentive than Blair, then laughed herself stupid about it with Idra later. Her sister was turning her into a prude, she decided. Also, to be entirely fair, it wasn't as if Blair was giving her even the faintest of empty promises about how much he wanted to see her again or how special he thought she was.

'Bye then,' said Blair sulkily, standing in the snow.

She smiled.

'Bye,' she said. Then she added truthfully: 'It was very nice to meet you.'

Blair snorted.

'It cost me ten hot chocolates. Hmm. Maybe I should go see that girl. I bet she's feeling very grateful.'

'You are a massive sex case. Get out of here.'

'I'm just being authentic to my true feelings,' he said. 'Come on. Please. I need fun. My LA schedule is full of meetings.'

'You're telling me that going to LA to live in luxury and get ferried about isn't fun?'

'Well, you had your chance,' he said, and Carmen laughed and tried not to feel disappointed as his brand-new shiny mackintosh disappeared into the white sweep of Victoria Street, and was swallowed up by the tourists.

Chapter Twenty-one

Sofia sat down at the kitchen table and let out a big sigh. Every day got tougher. Federico kept offering to cut his trip short and come home but she hated to look like she wasn't coping or be treated like some weakling. Also, deep down, she knew it was her who'd wanted a fourth baby – he would have been perfectly happy with two. She knew Carmen thought she was just showing off, which was incredibly hurtful. But it made her feel like she had to shoulder the burden herself.

Though, if she was being honest, it wasn't nearly as bad having Carmen here as she'd feared. Work was tiring, but home was not too bad.

'Let me make you an herbal tea?' said Skylar, not pronouncing the 'h' as if specifically to annoy Carmen.

'Oh, would you?' said Sofia.

'Sure thing? And I'm just off to my lecture!'

'You're a student, aren't you?' said Carmen, coming in from

work, pink-faced from the cold and happy at another day's solid takings, despite their slow start.

'Uh-huh!'

'You don't know a PhD student there? Called Oke?'

'Oke what?'

'How many Okes are there?'

'You mean Oke Benezet?'

'I expect so.'

'Oh yes! Everyone knows Oke. He circulates the departments, gives lectures on trees in literature, trees in art. Massive tree guy, right? Looks a bit like a tree.'

'What do you mean?'

'Tall, thin, hair bun like leaves at the top ... name spelled like a tree, pronounced like a Chardonnay?'

'Oh yeah,' said Carmen, who hadn't thought of that. 'How funny.'

'How do *you* know him?'

There was something in Skylar's tone that Carmen couldn't put her finger on, but she disliked it.

'He's a customer. I thought he was just a student.'

'Post-doctoral research fellow?' Once again Skylar's voice tipped into that register that implied Carmen was a total moron. 'That means he has his PhD already – so he's entitled to be called doctor – and he's working in the field. So he's lecturing too.'

'Thanks, prof.'

'I'm not a professor,' said Skylar, wrinkling her lovely brow. 'That comes after being a lecturer then—'

'I'm only kidding,' said Carmen hastily, as Skylar set down Sofia's tea, adding a nutritional ball of something or other that looked uncannily like something you should be putting out for birds this time of year.

'Enjoy your lecture. What's it on?'

'A history of homeopathy?'

'Oh,' said Carmen. 'So, like "water through the ages"?'

Skylar smiled pityingly at her. 'Sure, if that makes it simpler for you.'

And she swept out, her blonde hair bouncing behind her.

The oddest thing happened then. Sofia looked at Carmen and Carmen looked at Sofia, and suddenly all their antipathy melted away, and in the warm kitchen, with even more snow softly falling outside in the dark, they both started to laugh.

'It's not just me, right? She is being mean to me?'

'You started it!' said Sofia. 'And stop it. Good help is really hard to find and she's awesome with the children.'

'Well, let's hope they don't get sick with something and she wants to treat them with watery water.'

'It's good to have her,' said Sofia firmly. 'It makes us all eat better, live better ... '

'Oh my God, I am surrounded by life improvement experts! It's doing my head in! I quite like my completely unsuccessful life,' said Carmen, glancing at her phone.

'Why are you looking at your phone?'

'No reason.'

'You're obsessed. Who are you talking to?'

'Nobody.'

Completely betraying her, the phone pinged. Carmen could not hide her grin.

'Who is it?!' said Sofia, even though she appeared to be semi-prone with her eyes shut.

'What? Nothing!'

Carmen snatched up the phone.

'I'M SO BORED.'

'READ A BOOK,' she texted back.

'You keep smiling every time you look at your phone! I know that look!'

'I do not!'

'Carmmennnnn. I remember this from when you were a teenager.'

'Which wasn't *that* long ago,' pointed out Carmen quickly.

Sofia sighed.

'And all the boys were texting you. I was jealous.'

Carmen put the phone down, dumbstruck.

'You were not! *Everyone* was jealous of you.'

Sofia shrugged. She knew this to an extent of course. But even so.

'Well, you seemed to be having so much fun.'

'And getting into so much trouble! While you were going out with Duncan MacInlay, like proper going steady. He was super-handsome! And I was stuck waiting for some loser to text. Or not, which was more usual. Can I have some wine?'

'No,' said Sofia. 'If I can't have any, you can't either.'

'But your teas all taste like watered-down shampoo! And you have a fully stocked wine fridge! For showing off.'

'It's not for showing off,' said Sofia. 'It's waiting for me as soon as I get this space hopper out of me and then I'm going to drink the entire thing.'

'Have you had a bad day?' said Carmen.

'I'm just tired.'

'Okay, well, I'm going to pour myself a glass of wine and let you sip it. Anyway, you couldn't possibly harm that baby in there – look at the size of it! It's going to come out driving a car.'

'At least that would be speedy,' said Sofia. 'And no: Skylar says the science isn't settled on alcohol and babies.'

'I shall water it down. Then it will be homeopathic wine.'

Sofia laughed and waved her away.

'Skylar isn't the boss of you.'

'Oh, thank God, she is,' said Sofia. There came a caterwauling from the next room.

'See, she's only been away five minutes.'

'I'll get them,' said Carmen. Sofia did her best not to betray what an amazing turn-up it was that Carmen was actively volunteering to be with the children.

'Could you give them something to watch? Something improving, please. They could do without being traumatised again.'

'I said I was sorry,' said Carmen, going into the front room to fiddle with their incomprehensible TV remote.

She stopped in the doorway, turned back and looked at the huge, completely out-of-proportion shape of her sister. Without her or any of the children in there, it was like Sofia just let her face slump completely. She was practically asleep.

'What?' she said in a tired voice, opening her eyes again.

'Oh nothing,' said Carmen. 'I was just going to ask you if you're *sure* you want another one?'

Sofia made a shooing motion at her and Carmen fled the kitchen.

'Okay,' said Carmen in the den, looking in some confusion at the vast array of television options that confronted her. 'What services have you got?'

It looked like all of them, which was odd, because Sofia was so against the children watching more than about nine seconds of TV a day. This must just be what rich people do, thought Carmen. You just take everything whether you're going to use it or not. She thought of Blair and his new jacket and ridiculously overpriced wellingtons.

'Ooh,' she said, firing up the Disney channel. 'They've got *Muppet Christmas Carol*! You must have seen that!'

'Actually it's "puppets"?' said Pippa.

'Not these ones,' said Carmen. 'They're Magnificent Puppets. So. Muppets. Seriously, have you really never heard of the Muppets?'

'We've watched all of David Attenborough,' said Pippa.

'Okay. Well. There's lots of animals in this,' said Carmen. 'Mostly chickens though, I seem to remember.'

Phoebe crept forwards with interest to the trailer, which showed lots of frogs and pigs dancing.

'Ooh,' she said in delight.

'I'm just putting something with animals on,' hollered Carmen through to the kitchen. Sofia made an acquiescent noise.

After setting up the file, Carmen went back into the kitchen.

'What do you mean, you were jealous of me always getting texts from boys?' she said, glancing at her phone.

'It was non-stop! *Beep beep beep!* For Carmen!'

'But you had a gorgeous handsome boyfriend who adored you! That's all I ever wanted.'

'I was seventeen! said Sofia. 'I should have been dashing about, having mad affairs with everyone and being scandalous! Duncan was boring as shit!'

'But you went out with him for years!'

'God and it felt like it.'

'You looked so lovely at prom.'

174

'I know,' said Sofia. 'I hadn't eaten in three days. I nearly fainted.'

It was the oddest thing. Possibly the physically overloaded condition of Sofia and the new-found bounciness of Carmen was levelling the playing field. Or perhaps they were both tired of the enmity, the competition. Or perhaps, Carmen thought, it was like that World War One Christmas truce, because it was snowy.

'I couldn't believe how beautiful you looked in the front room,' she said now truthfully. 'You looked like you were going to an amazing fancy ball.'

'All I did was dance with boring Duncan to Daniel bloody Bedingfield songs. God, it was boring. Not like your prom.'

'Could we not talk about my prom?'

'Oh, come on, it was *hilarious*!'

'You did not think so at the time! You looked just as disapproving as Mum and Dad! And Mrs Leckie! Oh God.'

'You climbed up on the roof of the school rollicking drunk and threw tangerines at people.'

'Only terrible people. And it wasn't my idea.'

They both laughed.

'Okay then. Tell me about the mystery texter.'

They both stared at the phone.

'So Duncan MacInlay really is dull?' mused Carmen. 'I mean, is he free now?'

'You're getting off the point.'

'I'm just saying, he was hot.'

'You're very welcome to him,' said Sofia. 'He's working at a car showroom in Musselburgh. He sends me updates every time they get a new Ford in.'

'Not even, like, a Tesla showroom?'

'Not even, like, a Tesla showroom.'

'The thing is . . .'

Of course Carmen wanted to tell Sofia that Blair was texting her. She wanted to tell everyone, to shout it from the rooftops. Well, almost everyone, she thought. She hadn't introduced him to Oke when they'd all been in the café. Almost as if he could see through Blair as well as she could.

Anyway. This was silly: she'd be swanking, one, and also it wasn't like he was actually chatting her up. She was literally the only person he knew when he was trapped in the city. It was tech support, if anything.

But he was now sending her funny little pictures of his new wellingtons, and cute messages and, well, it gave her a little warm feeling inside. That was all. The attention was nice.

'It's nothing,' she said. 'Just a work thing.'

'Is it Mr McCredie?' said Sofia. 'I didn't even know he had a phone.'

'Your client/lawyer confidentiality is *rubbish*,' said Carmen. 'And no, I don't think he does.'

'So who can it . . . ?'

She sat bolt upright, her huge breasts bouncing off the top of her bump.

'That's like a party trick,' observed Carmen.

'It's not that writer?'

Carmen couldn't help it. She pursed her lips.

'No way. *No way*. You're being texted by Blair Pfenning. You're not. You're *not*.'

'Oh, it's just work stuff,' said Carmen, her face completely giving her away.

'No, it isn't!' said Sofia. 'His talk was yesterday!' She pulled out her phone.

'What are you doing?'

'I'm looking on *Mail Online* to see if you're mentioned.'

'Don't be ridiculous. They cancelled his flight and he had no suitable clothing: I was just helping him out, that's all. With flights and stuff. His publicist got stuck on the way back to London.'

Sofia looked at her.

'That doesn't explain why you smile every time your phone buzzes.'

'I do not!' insisted Carmen, trying to hide a smile. It buzzed again.

'I AM NOT STAYING AT THE PREMIER TAVERN,' it said. 'THIS IS CRUEL AND UNUSUAL. PLEASE RESCUE ME OR I SHALL COMMIT A CRIME AND GET THROWN IN JAIL ON PURPOSE AS IT PROBABLY HAS BETTER AMENITIES.'

'His posh hotel was booked,' said Carmen. 'Because nobody can get out of the city. There isn't a hotel room anywhere. The airline offered to put him up in this wee place and he isn't happy about it.'

Sofia was still scrolling.

'You know he's divorced but he's not officially seeing anyone,' she said. 'Ooh, his ex-wife seems bitter.'

'Stop doing that.'

Suddenly Sofia didn't seem so tired any more. She looked up suddenly.

'Invite him over.'

'What?!'

'Invite him here! We'll have dinner; he can sleep in the guest room.'

'What? Why can't I sleep in the guest room?'

Sofia looked awkward.

'We thought you'd be comfier down there . . .'

Carmen frowned.

'You did not,' she said. 'You wanted me out the way in case I was a pain in the arse.'

Sofia pursed her lips. In the silence, a text beeped again. There was another silence. Then finally Sofia cracked.

'Okay, okay, I'm sorry. What does it say?!'

'*You're my only hope*,' said Carmen. 'He's a doof.'

'He sounds cute,' said Sofia.

'He does it on purpose,' said Carmen, but the idea of Blair Pfenning in the house ... because of her ... she couldn't help it: just for bragging rights, because nobody ever asked her to prom ... She took another sip of her wine.

'Well, he is all by himself,' she said.

'*Ooh!*' said Sofia, clapping her hands. 'God, I wish I wasn't so damned massive.'

'Because you're going to leave Federico and all your children for a man who writes stupid books?'

'No!' said Sofia. 'He's on television as well.'

'Want to come over?' Carmen texted.

'Where do you live? Is it up a mountain and you share it with nine ginger-haired heroin addicts who are going to beat me up for having an English accent?'

'Fine, don't.'

'No, okay, give me the address.'

'Too late. You missed your chance.'

'Do you know what's on the room service menu?'

'Nope.'

'NOTHING! THERE ISN'T ANY ROOM SERVICE! THIS IS TORTURE! PLEASE SAVE ME!'

'Is he coming?' said Sofia. 'Only I'll crack out the smoked salmon and blinis and Champagne ...'

178

Carmen sat up.

'Seriously?'

'Yeah, it's for Christmas but you bringing a very hot man home is Christmas by anyone's standards, so why not? I have caviar too.'

'You do not.'

'Client gift. Unless you ate it as well last night.'

'Oh my God. he's going to love it here. Ridiculously over-priced fishy weirdo food is exactly what he likes.'

Carmen looked at her phone thoughtfully. Actual Champagne? Twice in a week? She smiled at her sister.

'This is how you get all these great jobs and stuff, isn't it? Just bulldoze people into it.'

'If I have to,' said Sofia, levering herself up. 'Right, get the good glasses. And don't drop any.'

Chapter Twenty-two

He did, Carmen thought, look very, very well, the snowflakes settling on his dark locks, which she realised for the first time were rather too long. Maybe he thought it gave him a distracted, scholarly air, she thought.

He was still wearing the new jacket and the tweedy waistcoat, and it suited him. And he was carrying a bottle of Champagne. Smoothie.

Of course Sofia had instantly ordered her into a dress and to put on some make-up. She had refused the dress – how obvious could you be? – but had relented to some eyeliner and lipstick.

It's not a date, she kept telling herself. This isn't a date. It's just a set of circumstances.

On the other hand, it was a lot closer to a date than she had had in a long time.

Sofia, somehow miraculously restored by the prospect of fancy company, hoofed upstairs, but of course the guest bedroom was already in perfect condition. Carmen followed her in – she hadn't even been *in* here on the whistle-stop tour of the house. It was a gorgeous room overlooking the garden, with an immaculate hotel-style en suite with underfloor heating, a brass bed with white linen and an old-fashioned patchwork quilt. A few recent hardback novels had been placed on the bedside table, several of which Carmen wanted to read and none of which she could afford. She snaffled two on the way out while Sofia refreshed a water carafe and put on the small bedside lamps.

'*What?*' said Carmen. 'Seriously, why am I not sleeping here?'

'Well, we thought you'd like your privacy – our room is right next door.'

'Yes, but your room is the size of an aircraft hangar.'

It was. It took up the entire side of the house and had two bathrooms and a dressing room. It was bigger than the entire flat Carmen had rented back home, and that had had four people living in it.

'Anyway, play your cards right and you might be.'

'Are you *pimping* me to Blair Pfenning?'

'I'm just saying, he's, like, I mean, he is really, really rich.'

'You are!'

The bell rang and they looked at each other and grinned.

'You get it,' said Sofia.

'Can I pretend it's my house?'

'No.'

'Can I pretend I live here all the time and that's nor-mally my room?'

'If you want to share it with him, sure.'

'*You super pimp!*'

And that was how he found her, still giggling merrily, a little flushed from the wine and indubitably happy to see him, which

181

was just how he liked it, and for a fleeting second he wished he'd brought some mistletoe. On the other hand, the bottle of Veuve Clicquot seemed to make up for it.

'I was expecting some complete slum!' he said, taking off the spanking-new brogues he had nipped back in for the previous afternoon. He thought this *Monarch of the Glen* look might be his new thing and was wishing there was a MacPfenning tartan. 'You work in a shop!'

'I much prefer it when you do that fake charm thing you do with people you don't know,' grumbled Carmen, stepping back.

But still, she couldn't help being proud of the haven her sister had made with the sweet smell of the expensive scented candles and the warmth and tasteful modern paintings – real, actual paintings with paint on – on the dark blue walls.

'Well,' he said.

Sofia descended the stairs as gracefully as any eight-months pregnant person can, i.e. not very. But her smile was lovely.

'Hello,' she said. 'Welcome, Blair.'

'Look at your beautiful house!' he said, gallantly, flashing the teeth. 'It is *so* kind of you to have me for dinner; I really can't believe you're letting me impose in this way.'

'Too much! Too much!' hissed Carmen.

'Shut up!' Blair whispered back. Sofia observed them both with some amusement.

'Come, let me show you round,' she said, but just as she did so there came the most ear-piercing scream.

They all jumped as Phoebe came barrelling out of the front room, closely followed by Jack, who was trying to look like someone who was not running for his life in terror but merely concerned for his sister.

Phoebe was in floods of utterly helpless tears and turned from Carmen to Sofia.

'What on earth is it?' said Sofia.

The TV noise from next door abruptly came to a halt and Pippa marched to the door, her small face furious, her little mouth pursed.

'THAT,' she exclaimed, 'is FAR too frightening for children.'

'What have you been watching?' said Sofia immediately.

'Oh yes, I put on *Cannibal Drill Killers*,' said Carmen, stung. 'It's the Muppets! The Muppets aren't scary!'

Instantly Phoebe burst into tears again, getting louder, and Jack and Pippa started immediately shouting that yes in fact they were VERY, VERY SCARY, and Phoebe carried on moaning and crying and gulping for breath. Blair was standing there, looking as if he didn't know what on earth to do with himself, as indeed he did not.

'For goodness' sake,' said Sofia. 'I asked you if it was suitable and you said it was animals.'

'Puppet animals!' said Carmen. As a group, they tried to head through into the TV room to see, impeded by Phoebe who, whimpering, grabbed their hands and refused to let them through. Jack eventually pushed open the doorway into the dark room, where Pippa had freeze-framed the screen onto a huge hooded ghostly figure holding out a skeletal finger. In the dark room, on the ridiculously gigantic six-foot screen, it looked incredibly frightening. Phoebe immediately let out a piercing scream again and Sofia shouted, 'Switch it off, Jack!' but he gave her a horrified look and mutely shook his head. Pippa was trembling but said in a wobbly voice, 'I'll do it, Mummy.'

'Oh, for goodness' sake,' said Carmen, uncurling Phoebe's fingers and entering the dark room to switch it off, furious at how embarrassed she was at the commotion. 'It's *A Christmas Carol*. It's great literature.'

'That's an adult book,' said Sofia disapprovingly.

'NOT! WHEN! THERE! ARE! MUPPETS! IN! IT!'

She struggled to find the right button on the remote, mistakenly turning on a crashing movie channel which had the Rock blowing something up which was absurdly loud through their super-expensive sound system and provoked another scream from Phoebe.

'Oh, for *God's* sake,' she hissed to herself, stabbing at the remote.

'I could come back,' lied Blair, whose evening had taken a slightly more domestic turn than he'd planned.

At that moment, the door shot open, and looking lithe and blonde and completely unfazed, Skylar entered, beaming.

'Skylar!' said Pippa. 'Skylar! Phoebe got scared at a monster on the television.'

'Oh, dear me,' said Skylar.

And she entered the little sitting room, took the remote from Carmen, turned off the TV and switched on the little lamps, making the room cosy and warm, then turned around and beamed at everyone. Carmen saw there were still snowflakes resting on her hair.

'Oh, don't worry, everyone, I'll fix it?'

And then she caught sight of Blair and was struck dumb. Carmen, standing to the side, felt dumpy and square and completely invisible next to the pink-cheeked fresh sheer youthfulness of Skylar.

'Hello!'

'Well, hello,' said Blair, going full teeth.

'I'm Skylar!'

'What a lovely name.'

'Sorry, are you Blair Pfenning? I've read all your books! I really, really loved *Find Your Love Light and Let It Shine*.'

Slightly irritated with herself, Carmen remembered she had meant to take a look at at least one of Blair's books at the shop but had been utterly engrossed in *A Christmas Murder* instead and hadn't got around to it, apart from looking at his jacket photograph of course.

'Did it help you?' said Blair in his special soothing voice. Meanwhile, Phoebe was still pointing at the now-off television in horror.

'I'm sorry,' said Carmen, crouching down. 'There is a scary ghost thing.'

'AND! TINY TIM IS DEAD!' came a cross voice behind them. Pippa was folding her arms, still not happy.

'He's not dead.'

'There's an empty chair and the pig is crying!'

'Also why are some of them frogs and some of them pigs?' said Jack earnestly. 'Is that what happens if your mother is a pig and your father is a frog?'

'Yes,' said Carmen wearily. 'All the girls will be pigs and all the boys will be frogs.'

'Come, let's get you a drink,' said Skylar to Blair. 'Ooh, you brought Champagne! So naughty drinking on a school night.'

'It gets happier in the end,' Carmen was saying to the children as Skylar led Blair to the kitchen. 'It's fine! It all ends up fine.'

'But Tiny Tim is dead and they're in a graveyard,' explained Pippa.

'With a MONSTER,' wobbled Phoebe.

'It's all lovely and happy at the end, I promise,' said Carmen desperately.

185

'You're developing quite the knack for terrifying children,' said Sofia over her shoulder, following Skylar and Blair through to the kitchen, where the delicious aroma of lasagne, as well as the freshly heated blinis, made everything seem amazing. Carmen stood up to follow them.

'Auntie Carmen,' said Pippa, 'I think it would be the best thing if you came to watch the end of the film with us.'

'What?' said Carmen.

'So Phoebe isn't tramat-at-ised.'

'I'm not traumata-taised!' came a wailing voice.

Carmen sighed.

'Maybe I'll just grab a glass of Champagne to take—'

'No – now!'

'So,' she could hear Skylar saying, as they sat round the comfortable kitchen table, 'I try and follow a very spiritual path myself? But I'm always doubting myself, you know? I just wondered if you could give me any advice.'

Carmen would have snorted, seeing as she didn't think Skylar had doubted herself for a second in her life, plus she could see Blair settling back with the look on his face of a man who absolutely just adored being asked for advice, and inwardly sighed.

A little paw grabbed hers and she looked down at the wide brown eyes of Phoebe's, so like hers.

'Are you sure the baby frog doesn't die?' came the little voice.

'I absolutely promise,' said Carmen, and grabbed Phoebe and sat down with the little one on her lap, and Pippa and Jack on either side.

In fact, though, she had forgotten how good and serious Michael Caine was in it and how funny Gonzo and the rat were, and she laughed in an over-the-top way every time the rat fell over to show Phoebe it was all right and there was nothing to be scared of.

And then, as the look of fear came over Scrooge's eyes and he decided to change his terrible ways – how the screen erupted with songs and skating and penguins for some reason, and every Muppet danced for joy.

And Phoebe leaned closer and closer to the screen till Carmen had to haul her back, as the entire parade sang a song around the houses, got to the house of the frog and the pig – Carmen could feel the worried intake of breath in the little body – flung open the door with his gigantic turkey, and there was Tiny Tim, hopping about on his little froggie legs, and Phoebe cheered and just about exploded with joy, and all four of them laughed and gathered together and, when Carmen intoned 'God bless us, every one!' along with the film, they stared at her in disbelief that she knew it.

'It's a very famous story,' she said. 'Lots of different ways to tell it. You're going to love them all.'

'I want to watch it again,' pronounced Phoebe. 'Right now.'

'We're not allowed too much television,' said Pippa. 'It's bad for your chi.'

'It's Christmas,' protested Carmen, pointing to the smart advent calendar where Pippa had, with great ceremony, thrown back a door that very morning. There was no chocolate in the calendar. 'I think it will be okay.'

'Yayyy!'

187

Finally getting back in the kitchen, Carmen found the mood was sombre.

'Because the thing with me is,' Skylar was saying sincerely, her blue eyes saucer-round, 'that people really underestimate me? Because they don't think I look like an academic person? And I have to put up with that kind of discrimination, like every day.'

'Yes, I see how that must be terrible for you,' Blair was saying in a voice that sounded suspiciously like he was trying to pretend to be a doctor on television.

Carmen shot Sofia a 'what the fuck?' look. Her sister just looked a bit disappointed. Oh well.

'They're watching the film again,' said Carmen to Sofia.

'The film that terrified the hell out of them?'

'No, no, they'll be fine with it now.'

And sure enough, faint voices could be heard attempting to sing along with the animals in perfect happiness and harmony.

Sofia looked surprised. 'Do you think?'

'I don't think any screen time is safe for children usually, don't you agree, Blair?' said Skylar, looking up at him.

'You can go do constructive play with them now if you like,' said Carmen.

'Actually, it's my night off – that's when I normally go to extra lectures at the university,' said Skylar. 'Oh, I saw Oke. He says hi.' She leaned flirtatiously over to Blair. 'He's a special friend of Carmen's.'

'Is this the guy who gets cheated in coffee shops?'

Skylar laughed as if this was hilarious, even though she couldn't possibly have known what they were talking about.

'So yeah, it's all right for the boys to be students,' she said. 'But when it's me – they barely take my questions.'

Blair fixed her with that sincere look of his.

'I'm here to tell you,' he said, teeth glinting, 'that everything is going to be okay.'

'Wow,' said Skylar, seemingly on the verge of tears. 'Wow. I can't tell you how good it is to hear someone say that?'

'Oh darling, I'm sorry,' whispered Sofia as Carmen cleared up the kitchen after dinner, having necked a lot of Champagne and wine to catch up, and Blair and Skylar stayed deep in conversation at the table, Skylar laughing dramatically every five minutes and tossing her long blonde hair over her shoulder more than seemed strictly necessary.

'I didn't actually like him!' said Carmen fiercely. 'It was you who wanted him to come over.'

'I know,' said Sofia. 'I'm sorry though.'

'I don't want him to stay.'

'No,' said Sofia. 'Totally.'

'I should have known,' said Carmen.

'You shouldn't,' said Sofia sharply. 'He's clearly a rat fink.'

'Well, I don't think you get handsome, rich *and* nice. Mind you, you did.'

'Yeah,' said Sofia. 'And I've seen him for fifteen minutes in the last month. Stop putting the pots in the dishwasher like that: they'll never clean.' She turned towards the table with a vast yawn. 'Well, I think I'll head for bed. Goodnight, Blair. It was lovely to meet you.'

Blair didn't look very keen to go but Carmen also made a big show of looking at her watch.

'Yup, time for bed,' she shouted through to the children. She smiled insincerely at Blair. 'So good to see you.'

He finally took the hint and put his coat on and, after rather a lot of hand-pressing, took his leave of Skylar.

'Fuck me,' he said at the door. 'That was an excellent hand with the Champagne-pouring.'

'It's because Sofia can't drink it,' said Carmen. 'She's just urging it on everyone else in a kind of agonised yearning. Also, she wants to wake up tomorrow and feel absolutely brilliant and laugh at everyone else who feels terrible.'

Even as she said it, she realised, as the cold air hit her, that she was actually quite drunk. Skylar had made a massive point about drinking a huge glass of water between each tiny sip of Champagne, so Carmen had steadfastly refused to drink water, childishly, and she was feeling it now. She swayed a little and rested against the door frame, still so cross that he had spent the night chatting to somebody else.

'God,' said Blair suddenly. 'Come on. Come back to my shit hotel room. Let's just have fun. My flight is leaving at 6 a.m. Come on. Let's go and be *really* badly behaved.'

'Fuck off,' she said. 'You just spent the entire night talking to Skylar!'

'She's a fan!' he said, genuinely surprised. 'Come on, you know I can't disappoint my public. But I want to be my real self with you.'

There was no doubt she was tempted. He looked so handsome in the light from the old-fashioned street lanterns, wolfish, as the snowflakes settled in his hair and on his expensive coat; a handsome man, when she hadn't as much as kissed anyone in months . . .

He smiled at her and for the first time she thought, That's

your real smile. He didn't show all his teeth, just the incisors, so it was almost more of a wolfish snarl. And yet far more attractive than his real one.

'Isn't this the point where you say, "Everything will be all right, I promise"?'

'Oh no, fuck that,' he said, suddenly sliding a cold hand round her waist. She gasped.

'Everything will be very, very bad. Very.'

He leaned forward and she smelled his expensive aftershave and, underneath it, something more raw. Suddenly, despite herself, she felt a tug of want; a tug of wanting to throw all her cares to the wind. She had been so *good*, working so hard, getting on with Sofia, trying so hard . . . couldn't she just have this?

'Carmen?' Sofia's voice came from inside the house.

Carmen and Blair looked at one another, caught on the doorstep.

'Shut the door – it's freezing!'

Blair looked at her meaningfully.

'Come on then.'

'Carmen!'

Carmen blinked. The taxi he'd booked turned into the silent street, its light glowing a warm yellow. A black cab, a hotel room . . . she pushed herself unconsciously a little closer against him. His hand slid further around her waist, possessively, confidently, and she tilted her head slowly upwards, her lips getting closer and closer towards his, when—

SLAP!

The huge mound of snow went straight down the back of their coats, down the back of her thin jumper, all over her hair. It was freezing, wet and stung her.

'What?!'

And there was only the sound of giggling on the wind – Carmen looked up. To her surprise, Phoebe's window was open and she and Jack could just be glimpsed, giggling, scraping snow off their window ledge.

'You were kissing!' shouted Phoebe.

'THAT'S DISGUSTING!'

'We were not!' said Carmen, shocked but finding it funny too.

'Bloody brats,' said Blair, straightening up. 'This is cashmere!'

'Um, so, goodnight,' said Carmen, the cold snow bringing her back to reality. 'Go to bed, you monkeys, or NO MORE MUPPETS!'

The giggling immediately ceased and the window slammed down.

He looked at her, confused.

'You're not coming? Seriously?'

'Am I getting into a cab with a man they've never met before in front of my tiny niece and nephew?' said Carmen. 'No.'

'Oh, for fuck's sake,' said Blair. He turned and headed for the cab.

'Bye then,' said Carmen.

She only got a grunt in return.

Carmen went and lay down on Sofia's bed, banging her head into the many differently shaped tidy pillows Sofia mystifyingly took off and replaced on the bed every single night and morning.

'You could have gone,' said Sofia rubbing in face cream. 'You don't have to be in love with him, do you?'

Carmen gave her a look.

'What?'

'You never cease to surprise me,' said Carmen, finally drinking a pint of water, barely stopping, gasping at how cold it was.

'I know, but how long has it been?'

'He called the children brats!'

'They were being absolutely fucking brats!' said Sofia. Then she burst out laughing. 'Oh my God, I can't believe I just said that. Oh my God.'

'Did you drink some of that Champagne on the sly?'

'I very much did not do that,' said Sofia, laughing. She looked at Carmen with uncharacteristic softness. 'I think it's having you here.'

'What, not getting laid and packing the dishwasher wrong?'

'Something along those lines,' she said. 'I think you're good for me, Carmen.'

Carmen looked up, surprised.

'Thanks,' she mumbled, finding it hard to look Sofia in the eye. Then she paused. 'I'm having a good time too.'

'Even with me being a dishwasher fiend?'

'Yes,' said Carmen. 'And the children aren't brats. They're wonderful.'

There was a very quiet noise from downstairs. The sisters looked at each other.

'It couldn't be,' said Carmen, quicker off the mark.

'What? *What?*' said Sofia. But Carmen was already heading up to the big windows looking over the street. Sure enough, the cab had circled round and come back – and there was Skylar, her long blonde hair tipping down her back, dashing up and hopping in.

'Come on – it's funny,' Sofia was saying.

'I know,' said Carmen. 'But it's just been so *long*. And I liked ...'

'What?' said Sofia.

'No, it's stupid.'

'What?'

'Well. I ... I liked the idea. I mean, everyone is so sorted and well off and has nice houses and I'm completely stuck. It was ... it was fun. The idea of it. Going to fancy places and being treated well.'

'Being treated well by people who aren't him.'

'Yeah yeah yeah, I know, I know. It's all right for you, sleeping *upstairs*.'

'Do you want to sleep in the spare room?'

'No, thank you,' said Carmen carefully. 'I already stained the downstairs sink with hair dye.'

Sofia heaved herself up with a sigh.

'Need a hand?'

'No, I'm okay, thanks.'

'She'd better be back in the morning,' said Carmen, slugging more water. 'I'm not getting up for the kids.'

'And I won't be able to,' agreed Sofia.

194

Chapter Twenty-three

It was actually worse than that. Skylar was back by the time Carmen got up, feeding the children porridge and natural honey at the table and looking as fresh as a daisy.

'Morning,' she trilled. 'Oh, Carmen, thank you *so* much for introducing me to your friend Blair! He's just amazing.'

'Carmen was kissing him!' offered Phoebe.

'I was not!' said Carmen. 'They are completely mistaken.'

'Oh, it's okay,' said Skylar. 'I know.'

She smiled beatifically.

'He said he might stop back in Edinburgh on his way back from LA! He's heading to Amsterdam and said he has to stop somewhere! Then he might take me with him.'

Carmen couldn't help it. That stung. Not because of Blair, he was an idiot. But . . . but . . . It was a little more than sleeping in your sister's basement and having a temp job.

'Well, that's nice,' she said, trying to sound pleased for Skylar and not making a particularly good job of it. 'Why is there never any blooming white bread in this house?'

'Because it's poison?' said Skylar. 'Anyway. Blair was saying he feels he has a real mission? To travel, even though it's not wonderful for the environment – he plants ten trees every time he goes anywhere, isn't that amazing?'

Amazing bollocks he does, Carmen thought.

'. . . and he says it's just so important to spread a model of positivity throughout the world, don't you agree, children?'

'Through kissing?' said Phoebe.

'Well, no,' said Skylar. 'Although, kindness is always good.'

'Were you *very* kind to him?' said Carmen, not caring that she'd promised Sofia not to upset Skylar. And it didn't even matter; it bounced off.

'Oh, I had such a wonderful night,' she said. 'What a great day! Come on, everyone! Shall we do our sun salutations before school?'

'There isn't any sun,' Phoebe pointed out, looking sad as Carmen departed for work.

The snow wasn't so magical today. It was slushy and getting tired-looking. There were puddles everywhere which were tricky to avoid if, like Carmen, you were staring fiercely at your phone and feeling thick with regrets.

You'd have been feeling worse if you'd slept with him, she kept telling herself. Dating someone she didn't actually like . . . Although that cold hand firm on her back . . . No.

The magic shop several doors down from Mr McCredie's

was bustling that day, and Carmen paused to glance in. A large woman with very long orange hair popped her head out.

'HELLO!' she boomed. 'You're young Mr McCredie's girl, aren't you?'

Carmen nodded.

'Quite the difference you're making up there. Now I've told him, but he never listens. You *must* come to our party on Thursday!'

'Of course – you're having a party.'

'Of course. All the shops on this street have one. Except for yours of course. You should change that.'

Carmen wasn't remotely in the mood for any type of party but promised faithfully to look in and bring the copy of *The Winter Almanac* to Bronagh, the magic shop's proprietor. It had been sitting on the front desk for a month.

'We have a book you ordered.'

Blair was on a plane, she told herself. It was a really long flight to LA, with a change in Amsterdam so you had to go the wrong way before you went the right way. Not that she'd checked (she'd checked).

Anyway, what was he going to say? 'Oh, I made a terrible mistake sleeping with someone else *after* you turned me down when it was my total right to do so?'

He's a bad man, Carmen told herself for the millionth time.

Her phone rang and she grabbed it. It was Idra.

'Hey!' said Idra. 'What's up?'

'Um,' said Carmen, reluctant to explain. But actually it turned out that Idra calling and saying 'what's up' was a way to tell her *her* news, which was all amazing, as it happened. Someone had come in to eat lunch there every day and she hadn't thought anything of it, then on about the fifth day he'd begged her to go out with him as otherwise he was going to get unbelievably fat and then he really wouldn't have a chance with her and she had laughed and agreed – nobody ever asked you out in the hats and accessories department – and he turned out to be super-lovely and some kind of software engineer who made a fortune and was taking her away skiing after Christmas!

'You've never been skiing,' said Carmen.

'I know,' said Idra. 'I am going to lie and say I have an injury from other skiing and have to sit on the sun deck and drink mulled wine all day.'

'They have a sun deck?' said Carmen. 'This doesn't sound like Glenshee.'

'Italy!' said Idra smugly.

Carmen went quiet. Oh goodness.

'Wow,' she said.

'Tell me you are really, really super-jealous,' said Idra.

'I will do that.'

'See! Now we've left stupid old Dounston's, all sorts of amazing things are going to happen. You're in Edinburgh, full of rich blokes and Harvey Nicks and fun! It's all there, Carmen. Go grab it!'

The morning was busy in the shop and every second person who looked local appeared to be going to Bronagh's party, many of them buying her books as gifts, the more abstruse the better.

'Do you have ...?' said one rather vampiric skinny young man. He leaned over the counter. 'A *secret* section? For forbidden books?'

'Sure,' said Carmen. 'Seeing as this is a fourteenth-century monastery built on a hellmouth.'

'Ahem,' said Mr McCredie, who was signing for a delivery.

'Sorry,' said Carmen, ashamed of her bad mood. 'I shouldn't have said that. Sorry. No. I mean . . . Sorry.'

The skinny young man picked up his book on poisons and left silently.

'I am really sorry about that,' said Carmen. 'My stupid mouth.'

'Oh no,' said Mr McCredie. 'I just didn't want you to tell him about the forbidden section.'

'What?'

But he had already disappeared into the back.

Carmen's mood was no better, even as she handed over the delivery Mr McCredie had been signing for to a customer.

'You're absolutely sure it's nine copies?' She had never sold nine copies of anything.

'Yes, it's for my Christmas book group! We're going to meet and discuss the Christmas book for five minutes, then drink mulled wine and eat mince pies until we are sick!'

The woman, who was dressed almost entirely in plum, looked delighted at the prospect.

'*Actually* sick?' said Carmen.

'One year, yes. So. Nice and short, is it?'

Carmen happily gathered up their entire pile of *Night Watch*, a clutch of funny and heartfelt stories about working in a hospital at Christmas time.

'It is,' she said. 'But it's *really funny*.'

'Well, that's good,' said the woman in plum. 'Although frankly, it barely matters. Nobody will remember a thing about it.'

She paid and swept out of the shop, seemingly looking forward to her terrifying night full of vomit, and Carmen tried to distract herself by looking at the accounts.

They were undoubtedly improving. The big old beautiful editions – particularly of children's books – and the big girls' annuals of Christmas activities were selling like hot cakes. And a huge box of hardback copies of Noel Streatfeild's *White Boots* from 1951 was steadily moving, except for one Carmen had held back for herself and was avidly reading in a corner, following the plight of poor Harriet and nasty Lalla.

The Box of Delights worked well positioned next to the train, and for *The Night Before Christmas*, of course it could only be the little mouse house. She had turned it round so the front door, with the steps leading out, could be seen, then she'd gone online and bought tiny light-up Christmas trees and little model gas street lights, and lit every room behind its windows, one Christmas tree shining through and another one outside.

Children knelt down in awe in front of it, mouths open, ignoring the puddles soaking through their trousers. Carmen had actually got slightly obsessed with it and started moving the mice about, making them do different things. When she found herself up at 10 p.m., making a tin foil lake with paper clip ice skates, she did start to wonder if she was going too far, but the next day the little skating mice drew a crowd to rival the train set, and they sold endless copies of both *The Night Before Christmas* and a book Carmen had never seen before, which was more or less the same except instead of nothing stirring around the house, there was something stirring and that something stirring was a mouse, who then proceeded to attempt to get the better of Father Christmas, although they ended up friends.

To distract herself further, she took a picture of her latest mouse creation – today she had covered one mouse in cotton wool to make a snow mouse – and was just putting it on Instagram when Oke walked in.

'A regular customer,' said Carmen, smiling at him.

'I live upstairs,' he said.

'Oh! I didn't know that.'

'That big building up the steps? It's a student residence. The one you walk up and over every day.'

'Is it?! I had no idea. Is it full of people with lots of spare time in the day?'

'You were never a student.'

'I wasn't.'

Even all these years on, it was still a sore point. She had ploughed her exams, staying out all night, laughing her head off, pretending like she didn't care. There didn't seem much point, when Sofia got nothing but As and was studying law, for goodness' sake. What was she going to do? Her parents had begged and pleaded, but she already had a Saturday job in the department store, and loads of friends there. It didn't make any sense, she'd argued, to get into loads of debt when she could just start earning. Her parents had put a brave face on it, but she'd known that yet again she'd broken their hearts, whereas Sofia was off conquering the world – her year abroad in America had probably been the worst. Their mother had kept badgering Carmen to go visit, hoping it would kindle something in Carmen – and then Carmen had gone, and couldn't have felt more out of place with the cool, multicultural, international, incredibly smart crowd Sofia hung out with, making friends all over the world, visiting luxury homes and at home anywhere.

'That could still be you,' said her mother when she'd got back, jet-lagged and dreading the next long day's shift of standing in the shop, being shouted at by Mrs Marsh, who would be dusting and talking about netting, waiting to retire.

'It can't,' Carmen had said grimly. It couldn't. She couldn't fit in with them and their travel and their knowledge, and their immediate acceptance of Sofia as one of them.

'Sorry,' said Oke kindly. 'You look lost in thought. I didn't mean to hit a sore spot.'

Carmen felt raw all over that morning; completely exposed and vulnerable.

'You didn't,' said Carmen. She blinked. 'I ... I would have liked to have gone ... I think. But at the time, I ... I thought I couldn't keep up. I failed my exams.'

'On purpose?'

'No! ... Maybe,' she said. 'If I didn't try, then ... I suppose I had an excuse for failing.'

Oke nodded. 'I can understand that.'

There was a pause.

'This is the bit where you tell me all the best people didn't go to university, and the University of Life is brilliant, and everything is going to be absolutely fine,' said Carmen.

'Where I am from,' said Oke, 'there aren't as many good options for people without an education, so no. I would never say that. But look at the good you are doing with your life.'

'I don't know if I'm doing much good,' said Carmen.

'I think your mice are making people happy in the world. They make me happy!'

'I don't think that counts: I like doing them.'

'It counts. Anyway. I need to order another book and I need to say thank you for the discount and the way I would like to thank you is with this!'

He brandished something at her.

'What's that?'

It was a tourist flyer for Camera Obscura, with a two-for-one offer, valid on a weekday morning, which it still was, for about forty minutes.

'Camera Obscura?' said Carmen, frowning. 'I've heard of it. It's a touristy thing, isn't it? What even is it?'

'It's how they used to draw things before photographs! It's amazing.'

'Isn't it for children?'

He rolled his eyes.

'And the young at heart.'

'But what actually *is* it?'

'It's a hole in the roof!'

Carmen frowned.

'You want to go see a hole in a roof?'

'It changed the world!'

'How?'

'Because! You had perspective and straight lines and could draw and trace things and get precision into art and work and, well, it's just very, very cool. It's over 2,500 years old. Don't you think that's quite cool?'

'That striped building by the castle?'

'Now you're being dense on purpose. The technique.'

Carmen picked up the leaflet. It was covered in wacky light shows.

'Why is it covered in wacky light shows?'

'That's just to get the kids in,' he said. 'But they have the original at the top. I think it's worth seeing.'

'The original box with a hole?' Carmen frowned. 'But we can still go see the wacky light show, right?'

'If you like.'

Well, it was better than mooching about trying to work out what the time difference was between LA and Edinburgh. Carmen traipsed back through the stacks.

'Is this a lunch hour again?' said Mr McCredie, but his face wasn't quite as low as it normally was.

'Possibly . . . Are you reading *White Boots*?'

'Possibly. Don't worry: I'll hold the fort.'

Carmen smiled.

'Do you remember how to work the new card machine?'

'You wave it,' said Mr McCredie. 'And magic beams come out of people's magic devices.'

'Their telephones.'

He snorted.

'That's not a telephone,' he said. 'It's a magic wand hellbent on destroying the world. But you call it what you want. Magic waves, blah blah blah.'

'Good,' said Carmen. 'Ooh, and upsell.'

'Up*what*?'

'Upsell. So we'll wrap things for a quid. Ask them if they want it wrapped, then wrap it with the paper under the desk and charge them an extra pound.'

Mr McCredie blinked in sheer misery.

'That is the single most vulgar thing I've ever heard of!'

'Is it?' said Carmen. 'Good for you, but every little helps. Anyway, who wraps your gifts?'

Mr McCredie looked down.

'I ... I don't ... I don't really ...'

Carmen swept in to save him.

'You don't have to give gifts,' she said quickly. 'You're too busy giving books away all the time.'

He smiled hollowly, grateful.

Carmen still looked pensive as she joined Oke on the pavement outside the shop, her breath showing in front of her. The lights strung up between the lamp-post and the great silver snow-flakes dancing in the twinkling light all the way down Victoria Street never failed to make her smile.

'You'd think,' she said, without even realising what she was saying, 'people couldn't possibly be unhappy somewhere so beautiful.'

Oke gave her a look.

'I thought you were unhappy,' he said.

'I never said that,' said Carmen.

Oke stopped and looked puzzled.

'No,' he said. 'I apologise. You did not say it.'

'But you thought I was?'

He held up the half-price voucher and pretended to study it.

'No.'

'You don't have anyone else to share that with?' said Carmen, wondering.

He blinked.

'Yes. But most of them are busy.'

His accent was so faint, just a slight 'th' sound on the 's' of busy. She liked it.

'I was busy.'

'That's true.'

She glanced at him.

'Do you always literally have to tell the truth? Always?'

'It's just a habit,' said Oke, looking a bit awkward.

'Should I ask you how many people you asked before ...?'

'So – fortunately it is just here and there's no queue, look!'

'Hence the voucher,' said Carmen.

Why, she found herself thinking, did she always have to settle for the last-minute invitations? Why couldn't anyone ask her out on a proper date, give her time to get dressed up, get excited about things? Why wasn't she anyone's first choice? She thought of Idra, choosing ski clothes, and tried not to look petulant.

'Don't be sad!' said Oke as they entered. 'Look. They have those flashing lights that you like.'

She stuck her tongue out at him, and decided to at least try and enjoy herself.

The Camera Obscura was in a beautiful, ancient narrow building at the top of the Lawnmarket, right next to the castle's huge courtyard. You entered through a narrow door and filed up narrow ancient steps, diving in and out of different rooms.

Despite herself, it was fun. The sideshow exhibits were funny: forced perspective rooms that made them look big or tiny; a rather pretty light tunnel; a hall of mirrors.

This was just ... going to see some lights. In her lunch hour.

She laughed in the mirror maze, where lights shimmered and changed and it was impossible to tell how big it was: an infinity of mirrors, perhaps, in the ancient house, reflecting back and back. Once they got separated you could see glimpses of the other person, but not precisely tell where they were.

The last people in front of them had carried on up the steps, and there was nobody behind them – it was very quiet – and suddenly Carmen realised in the dark sputtering maze she didn't know where Oke was at all. She pressed herself against the side of a mirror. When she let out an involuntary giggle, it echoed throughout the space eerily. She glanced around, her heart beating faster. She could just see a flicker of his old coat, reflected over and over, but she couldn't see where he was.

'Where are you?' she said, her voice bouncing off a thousand panes of glass.

'You will have to find me ... me ... me.'

She spun around, sure that he was right there behind her, but there was nothing, just a flicker of a coat against the mirror, replicated into infinity in two glasses facing one another.

She stepped to the side, concentrating very hard on listening over the sounds of her breathing and her rapid heart. There was something just on the left ... She leaped there and gasped as she saw a satsuma bouncing off a side mirror and onto the floor.

'You ... (you you you) Did you just throw a satsuma at me (me me)?'

'It distracted you,' said the voice, and she stole past the satsuma and towards anything, any tiny spot of light darting here and there, but he was absolutely nowhere to be found as she ran around columns of mirrors, the lights changing colour, disorientating her as she came face to face with herself and an empty nothingness again and again and again, and she nearly collided with the walls as she went faster and faster, running out of breath. It wasn't possible.

'You've left the room!' she called out eventually. All she heard in response was a chuckle that seemed to come from everywhere and nowhere at once. Increasingly desperate, she spun around; where *was* he? And again, nothing. Crossly she hit at the wall, and made a clanging noise, then leaned against it, quite out of breath and a little spooked.

Suddenly she felt two hands across her eyes and spun around, till she was in his arms. The room went oddly still, and she was conscious of his tall presence above her, how close she was to another man for the second time in a very short space of time, who, it felt to her in that moment, was taking her for granted.

She jumped back in shock.

'What are you *doing*?' she said.

His face was absolutely stricken and he jerked his hands upright.

'I am so sorry! I am so, so sorry! I shouldn't have touched you! I'm so sorry!'

He looked scalded. Carmen's anger faded almost immediately. It wasn't his fault, was it, that she was feeling cross and undervalued and jealous?

'You just gave me a fright, that's all,' she said.

'You should have kicked me!' said Oke. 'I am so, so sorry.'

'Okay, stop apologising.'

Rather stiffly, they both went on further upstairs. They found themselves inside a large turret with doors either side leading out onto a narrow turreted balcony. Once more, there was nobody there, and outside it became clear why: the sky was bright blue but the air was utterly freezing cold.

Carmen forgot to be cross. Right there, straight up was the castle, bold and terrifying as it must have been, designed all those years ago to strike fear into anyone considering attacking the city. It was strange, she was so used to looking at it as abstract, symbolic, just something colouring the background of this extraordinary place. Carmen found herself leaning away from it, so overwhelming did it appear.

But everything from the turret seemed extraordinary, leaning in over her, bamboozling her sense of perspective. A church, its steeple almost bending over her. Absurdly high ancient buildings around courtyards and squares.

To her right, the higgledy-piggledy Royal Mile, descending past St Giles and all the secret closes and passageways, dropping to Holyrood, out of sight below so you felt you could almost fall into it.

And from the front, a vertiginous drop down to the water, the cliff, then the railway tracks, then the green of Princes Street Gardens and the straight neat lines of the New Town beyond and further across the water to the Kingdom of Fife.

She stood still, even in the freezing sunlight, just staring, awestruck.

Oke approached her quite cautiously.

'What do you think?' he said.

Carmen swallowed once then spoke.

'I didn't ... I've never really seen the New Town like this before. It's laid out ... like it was designed.'

'It was designed!' said Oke.

'Was it?' said Carmen, annoyed that she felt stupid. He realised his mistake at once.

'Oh sorry.'

'No, tell me,' she said, trying not to be prickly. 'I do want to know.' And she did.

'Well ... Edinburgh was the first designed city in the world. The birth of the Enlightenment. The whole idea that we could plan our futures for ourselves; that we were not dependent on the whims of God, that we could conquer our animal natures, find our place in the world. That from this higgledy-piggledy ...'

He swept his arm around the show – the jammed-together old

houses on the up-and-down cobbled streets of the old town.
'. . . thrown-together world, you could have beauty, order, fresh air. The New Town is philosophy made stone. It is a promise from the past to the future: that better times are coming. That entropy can be overcome. Well. For a while.'

'But all the fun happens in the Old Town,' said Carmen, naturally contrary as ever.

'Well, yes, of course,' said Oke, smiling. 'Agents of chaos. Humans need that too.'

'I'm an agent of chaos,' said Carmen glumly. Oke looked at her curiously. 'What?'

'Nothing,' he said. 'I just wondered for a moment if you were.'

'You really know how to make a woman feel good.'

'Who said that's a bad thing?'

'Every teacher I ever met.'

'Until now,' said Oke.

Then he cleared his throat and looked out over the horizon. And on this bright hard heavenly northern day, more Russian weather than Scottish, it was there, plain as day: the castle built to impose and threaten, and the jumble of rooms in the Old Town – she thought of Mr McCredie's wobbly illogical house – piled here and there, often with whole families living in single rooms, surviving for hundreds of years. And ahead, the orderly roads running down to the water, beautiful wide pavements, beautiful houses and stunning gardens in the squares.

'Those gardens are private though,' said Carmen.

Oke nodded.

'Oh, it's built on dirty money,' he said. 'You can't get away from that. But what is terrible about it doesn't mean it isn't beautiful.'

He turned her around.

'And over there – you can't see it; it's past the city – but over there is my favourite tree in all the world, and part of the reason I came here. It's called the Ormiston Yew.'

'How can you have a favourite tree?' said Carmen. 'Doesn't it make all the other trees jealous?'

The guide beckoned them back in and, hands cold, they wandered into the little observatory room. The guide started to explain clearly how the Camera Obscura worked – the little hole, the lens – but Carmen didn't really listen, so transfixed was she by the view on the large round table: the city, just as she had seen it laid out in front of her. It looked like a picture, but the traffic moved and the traffic lights changed. She was watching the world on a table.

'Oh my *goodness*!'

The guide smiled, obviously never tired of people's reactions. 'Oke, look at this!'

They pored over it, making cars drive over their fingers, zooming in through the clear air to boats on the water, to the great clock on the Balmoral Hotel, forever set four minutes fast to chivvy the late traveller. It was as if you could tumble straight into the whole wonderful world of the city, see all its secrets, go behind any door.

'This is . . . so amazing.'

Carmen felt as they watched it that odd feeling of peace she'd felt while making the little mouse decorations, or the old days of choosing the right lace for the right wedding dress back in haberdashery. It felt like flow; time vanished, and she forgot all about the previous evening. They were both surprised when another group, a school party, interrupted them, their noisy chatter and shouting showing they had also had a rather exciting time in the mirror maze, a fact borne out by the teacher's slightly weary expression.

They took their chance to leave; Carmen had, once again, rather outweighed what might be expected of a lunch hour under normal circumstances.

At the door, they parted.

'I have a lecture,' said Oke.

'Ooh, what are you learning today, super-swot?'

He frowned.

'I'm *giving* a lecture,' he clarified.

'Oh yes, I remember!' said Carmen. 'Well! Get you.'

He smiled and, without touching her in any way, turned to leave.

'Thank you,' said Carmen finally as they clattered back down the narrow stairway. 'Thank you for taking me there. I really enjoyed it.'

He grinned.

'I want to see everything before I go.'

'Where? Where are you going?' she said suddenly.

'I don't know ... It was a term placement but they've asked me to stay on for a bit.'

Carmen suddenly found she was interested in the answer.

'And are you going to?'

He shrugged.

'Not sure yet.'

'So you might just be disappearing at Christmas?'

Carmen was surprised to find that she rather minded. It had been nice to meet a friend.

'I don't know – when is that?' he said, but he smiled to show her he was teasing.

Carmen smiled back.

'Okay,' she said.

Oke raised his eyebrows. That was not, if he was being honest, which he always was, the response he had hoped for. He liked the passionate dark-haired girl. He liked her a lot. But she had . . . well. Normally Oke did well with girls. But this one . . . He remembered the man in the very expensive clothing she'd been with in the Grassmarket. She didn't look like the kind of woman who was very interested in how much money a man made, but who could tell? He didn't know Scottish women at all.

'Thanks again,' she said, gingerly stepping out onto the slushy pavement.

'You're welcome,' he said, and disappeared into the throng, his distinctive gait making his hair visible in the crowd as she watched him bounce up the hill of the Lawnmarket in the direction of the tidy orderly university, and Carmen scrambled down the icy steps and back into the higgledy-piggledy disordered world of the bookshop.

Chapter Twenty-four

The following few days remained trying. Sofia had ordered a gingerbread kit for Carmen to do as a family project on her babysitting night. It had not been a success.

Phoebe had licked her bits of the kit together, and eaten all the Smarties decorations as Pippa, who was doing her own carefully, harangued her. Jack had looked at it, said, 'What's the point of this?' which Carmen had found very difficult to give a good reason for, before he added, 'Can you just do it and tell Mummy I did?', then Phoebe collapsed in floods of tears when she couldn't get anything to stick and Carmen, who was not remotely crafty, didn't do a much better job, and when Sofia came down from her nap, she almost cried because in fact the sections were meant to stack on top of each other and make a perfect replica of their own house and the kit had cost a solid fortune and, apart from Pippa's layer, it all looked like a dog's dinner and Sofia ended up staying up till 2 a.m. redoing everything and was teary and exhausted and hormonal which

Carmen felt was not her fault and they had both attempted to pull their mother round to their point of view.

On the other hand, it looked sensational.

It had been a chilly morning. And now Carmen, while grateful for the custom – rather sweetly, she'd bumped into Crawford, who had bought three beautiful books on winter birds for his window display, and added a note explaining where to buy them and they'd had lots of queries – was not feeling at her best.

'Because,' she was saying, 'a place where you borrow books is called a library. And in fact twenty metres away across the road is the National Library of Scotland. And in there they have every book ever written! And you can have any one you want!'

The old woman, who was Mrs MacGeoghan, was still looking belligerent.

'But I want to read this one.'

'You can,' said Carmen. 'But I'm afraid you have to buy it.'

She could hear Mr McCredie rustling about in the back, getting nearer to the shopfront which wasn't ideal as he would probably let the lady take it if she promised to bring it back, and they weren't out of the woods yet, money-wise. Sofia had told her if they made a profit and paid a few of their debtors by the new year, it could go up for sale as a going concern. What Carmen would do then, they didn't discuss. Idra had mentioned restaurant jobs going and her mum had said there were community initiatives happening. She'd find something.

'But I'm a pensioner,' the old woman continued.

'I realise that,' said Carmen. 'That's why I absolutely would suggest a library. They are wonderful, amazing places. But this isn't one.'

'Well, that's just ... evil capitalism!' said the old lady who was, Carmen couldn't help but notice, wearing the same incredibly expensive brand of wellingtons Blair had bought.

Although the day hadn't been all bad, she reflected. Before she left the house that morning, amid the usual school hubbub, Phoebe had sidled up to her and pressed something warm into her hand.

'Uh, thanks?' Carmen had said, glancing down and realising to her horror that Phoebe had given her a piece of warm cheese.

'It's for the mices,' Phoebe had whispered. 'At the shop.'

'Oh,' said Carmen. 'But you know, they're not real.'

'In the DAY they're not real,' whispered Phoebe. Her gaze strayed towards the room with the television in it. They'd watched *The Muppet Christmas Carol* every single second they'd been allowed to.

She leaned up on tiptoe, casting a sharp gaze around the room first in case Pippa was listening in.

'I think at night they come alive,' she whispered. 'And that's when they'll need cheese.'

'We certainly will get alive mice if I put down that cheese,' said Carmen. 'But they won't be wearing bonnets.'

She looked at Phoebe's disappointed face.

'But it's a brilliant idea,' she said. 'I bet we could make some cheese to add to the house. Not real cheese, but maybe . . . what looks a bit like cheese?'

They both frowned and looked for a moment extremely similar, although they didn't realise it. Phoebe grinned suddenly.

'My sponge!'

'You're a genius!'

'I hate my sponge,' she said.

'What are you two whispering about?' said Skylar suspiciously. 'Have you done your thankfulness this morning, Phoebe?'

'I'm doing it right now?' said Phoebe defiantly. 'I'm being thankful for my sponge.'

'That's right,' said Skylar, beaming. 'Cleanliness is so good for the soul, don't you think, Carmen?'

She served up a dish of gloopy oats which had been soaked overnight.

'Come on, everyone.'

'Actually,' said Carmen, thinking of the tray of warmed croissants the coffee shop normally had ready about now. 'I'm going to eat on the way. But it looks great. Bye, everyone.'

Sofia, tearful and exhausted as she was, was at least finally on maternity leave. It wasn't technically due to start for another week – two weeks before the baby was due – but she'd got stuck in a lift and everyone agreed it was for the best, being unusually cautious even by lawyer standards. She had been furious about it, but eventually capitulated. Carmen had looked up, and said in a conciliatory tone, 'Sofe, are you going to have the baby today?'

'I'm going to admire my gingerbread house,' Sofia had responded.

They all regarded it. It *was* rather cool now it had been entirely dismantled and done again properly.

'But if you can't eat it WHAT IS THE POINT?' Jack still moaned.

'Jack,' said Carmen in a warning tone, and he piped down immediately. Sofia looked at Carmen suspiciously. What she didn't know was that Carmen had been back to Poundworld and bought three advent calendars with chocolates in them and the children had been stashing them under their mattresses.

'I am going to lie down and read magazines today,' said Sofia from the depths of the big sofa.

'Actually, I was thinking about this really great pregnancy yoga app we should try out together?' said Skylar.

'I think I am too tired for school and will stay on the sofa with Mummy to keep her company,' said Phoebe.

'No, you won't, Phoebe,' said Pippa straightaway. 'Mummy won't want you to do that.'

'You want me on the sofa, don't you, Mummy?' started up Phoebe, and Carmen had happily escaped into the still chilly air, the snow still thick on the ground, shaking her dream of trains and tunnels from her head.

Back to the present, Mrs McGeoghan was a regular, and something of a pest, and she was now dealing with Carmen's refusal to turn the bookshop into a lending library by standing at the side of the bookshelves and reading the entire book in full view of other customers. Carmen was doing her best not to acknowledge it, but couldn't help keeping an eye on her. If she folded over a corner, she was going to go for her. Or licked her fingers when she turned over a page.

'Then I'm going to do her,' she whispered to Mr McCredie.

'Now, now,' said Mr McCredie. 'She doesn't mean any harm.'

'She absolutely does mean loads of harm! If by harm you mean taking money away from you and food out of our mouths and ruining our books and cluttering up the shop!'

'But look,' said Mr McCredie, as the door tinged. 'My dearest girl, you have brought so many people in. So many.'

Carmen was incredibly gratified by this statement when he stopped talking and gripped the bench he was leaning against.

A tall group of people, fair-haired, had stepped in. They were well-dressed and expensive-looking, clearly European tourists, a combination Carmen had already learned that, while not quite as excellent a prospect as American tourists, nonetheless remained a very good opportunity, so she pushed forward the lovely tartan copy of *A Scottish Festivities* recipe and decorating book right under their noses: many people liked to recreate Hogmanay and black bun and ceilidhs and other Scottish treats at home for themselves once they had left their holiday behind, and this was the perfect book for them to do it with.

'Hello,' said the women at the front of the group. She was blonde and friendly-looking; prosperous and with the look of someone who was almost certainly the backbone of any local charity committee she sat on. 'Excuse me?' The voice was northern European – German? Dutch? She smiled, but also looked a little anxious. 'We were looking for the McCredie family?'

'Well, you've come to the right place,' said Carmen, turning round to where Mr McCredie was – but he had vanished.

With a quick side glance at Mrs McGeoghan, Carmen shot off through the stacks.

'Mr McCredie!'

She came upon him practically cowering in his armchair, the complete opposite to the emboldened man he'd been that week, sweeping the snow from the pavement in his *finneskos*.

'Mr McCredie, there's someone here who wants a word.'

'I don't want to see them.'

'Do you know them?'

His face paled, and he shook his head.

'I don't . . . I don't think so.'

'So what's . . . what's the matter? They're not creditors, are they?'

He shook his head.

'I don't ... I just ... '

'Can I deal with them for you?'

'No, I don't ... Thanks ... No, please just say I'm unavailable.'

Carmen put her hand on his shoulder.

'Are you sure you're okay?'

He looked terribly pale in the dim light.

'Yes. Please just ... '

He flapped his hands uselessly in the direction of the shop.

Carmen returned, looking warily at the family.

'We are so sorry,' said the woman. 'I did not mean to disturb you. We found some very old letters that came from here, that was all.'

And she left a card reading Gretl Koonings, with a +49 code on it.

Chapter Twenty-five

As if nothing had happened, shortly before 5.30 p.m., Mr McCredie appeared, dressed in a perfect tweed suit – very old, of course – and a polka-dotted bow tie. His glasses were rimmed with gold and he had smartly polished shoes on and it was very clear that the visitors were not to be discussed.

'Mr McCredie! Look at you all dolled up,' said Carmen, cashing up.

'It's Bronagh's party.' He frowned. 'You told her we were coming. It doesn't pay to get on the wrong side of a witch, in my experience. Especially not in this city.'

'Oh God, the witch. I wonder if she would like some spell books?' Carmen looked down at her denim skirt and stripy top. 'I completely forgot about it – I'm not dressed for a party at all.'

On the chime of 5.30 p.m., there was a sudden hush outside – Carmen tilted her head, about to lock the door – when a pure sound filled the freezing air. It was clear as a little bell and took Carmen a moment to realise that outside someone was singing.

'Oh good, good: she's invited the St Giles boys,' said Mr McCredie, referring to the cathedral twenty metres up the road, as more pure tenor voices joined in until a chorus was singing 'In the Bleak Midwinter'.

Mr McCredie had offered Carmen his arm on the slippery pavement. Looking up and down the street, the groups of browsers and shoppers and tourists had all stopped too, many of them starting to film, or put money into the boys' bright red collection bucket for Waverley Care.

It seemed to Carmen as if time had stopped, with the light snowflakes in the sky, the traffic muffled and faded, the tourists and their chatter and multilingual shouting and calling frozen in place, all entranced by the singing of children under a cold sky. They locked the shop and went two doors down. It made her feel cold and hot and lonely and happy and sad all at once; she felt a yearning, but she didn't know what for.

'Come, come,' beckoned Bronagh as she saw them both. She was holding up goblets of what looked rather sinister drinks – they were steaming – but on closer examination turned out to be mulled wine.

'Is that what you're wearing to a Christmas party?' said Bronagh, looking disappointed, even after Carmen handed over a beautifully wrapped copy of *The Winter Almanac*.

'I know; it's lame. I'm sorry,' said Carmen.

'Don't worry,' said Bronagh, vanishing inside and reemerging with a swirling purple velvet cloak. 'It's one of mine. Put it on.'

Carmen looked at it ruefully for a second, then, figuring she might as well go with the spirit of things, twirled it round her shoulders and took another gulp of the warming wine.

Inside was a huge collection of all sorts of people: other shop staff, Edinburgh regulars, a group of women playing mystical folk music in the corner, some people dressed as fairies, various suited and booted gentlemen-about-town – many with waistcoats. Carmen looked at the latter; she couldn't help herself. He was in LA anyway. Who cares? He'd probably thrown the wellingtons away.

He was a less pressing concern by the time Carmen had drunk her second cup of the mulled wine – which tasted nothing like the watery Ribena you got down at the Christmas fair; rather more like something perfumed and spiced, a mysterious concoction that warmed you right through from head to foot.

She passed lightly through the party, enjoying the interestingly attired guests, who clearly all knew each other – some parts of Edinburgh, she suspected, were as interrelated as a village. The shop was just as idiosyncratic as their own: stuffed birds hung from the ceiling; there was a broomstick assortment; and antlers lined the walls. Also along the walls were ingredients and spell books, jewellery in different birthstones and with many different crystals on display, dream catchers, soul stones and all. Carmen eyed everything narrowly. Mind you, she thought, if you would ever believe witches existed, it would be down in the depths of Edinburgh, in its dark closes and hidden corners, where they burned women on the Grassmarket, right outside.

There was an apothecary table behind the cash desk; there were capes and pestles and mortars and a locked glass cabinet, high up, with a warning sign, very small, saying 'these ingredients are for play only'.

'Hmm,' thought Carmen to herself, smiling. Well, it was probably harmless. She turned round to go see how Mr McCredie was getting on when she saw Bronagh standing right in front of her.

'Lovely shop,' said Carmen hastily. 'Isn't it gorgeous?'

'You think it's nonsense, I can tell,' said Bronagh, who looked like she could be slightly more frightening than her short stature and rosy cheeks would suggest. In fact, she had a touch of the Mrs Marsh about her.

'It's lovely,' said Carmen, pointing to a large collection of light green glass baubles, glinting in the light. The shop itself was decorated for Christmas in heavy wreaths everywhere from a tree Carmen didn't recognise.

'What is it?' said Carmen. 'It's beautiful.'

'Hawthorn,' said Bronagh. 'Keeps the spirits out. Except the ones I invite in.'

She smiled, but it was still a little unnerving as the fairies in the corner giggled and the odd hypnotic music kept playing; the choirboys outside had all gone home for their teas.

'Well, happy Christmas,' said Carmen. Bronagh frowned again.

'It isn't Christmas, my dear! It's midwinter! It's Saturnalia.'

'Okay,' said Carmen.

'Those bloody Christians. Came along and hijacked everything. It's all just marketing, you know. Coke marketed Santa Claus. Bloody Christians marketed midwinter.'

'Um . . . ' said Carmen.

'They took the ancient festivals and pretended it was about some . . . "baby".'

Bronagh shook her head.

'Bloody money men ruin everything. Happy solstice!'

They chinked goblets.

'We are halfway out of the dark,' she said. 'Of course, in my line of work that's not always a good thing.' She looked at Carmen. 'You are my guest,' she said. 'You must have a gift.'

'Oh, please, no, don't worry,' said Carmen.

'No, no, no I insist.'

She took a large bunch of keys from a buried pocket in her velvet gown and reached up to a little glass box.

She looked straight at Carmen.

'Ooh,' she said. 'How interesting with you. A man problem ... ?'

'Yes, well, that's hardly difficult to guess,' said Carmen. 'Seeing as I'm here on my own looking completely miserable.'

This was getting really embarrassing. She was grateful to Bronagh, she really was, but now she really wanted to be ... where? She thought about it. In fact, completely to her surprise, she wouldn't mind being in the house, on the big cosy sofa, watching *The Muppet Christmas Carol* again with Phoebe curled up under her arm, and Pippa making sarcastic remarks about it and Jack pretending to shoot people on the screen with a banana (no guns were allowed in the house of course, not even Nerf guns).

Huh. What a strange thought.

'No,' said Bronagh, giving her that dark intense gaze again. 'No. I think that's all fine.'

Carmen laughed. 'It is so very much not fine, I can assure you.'

'No, it's rather closer to home. It's family. A sister?'

'What?' said Carmen, but just as she did so, she heard someone say her name. Waving cheerily across the room, his top knot bobbing above everyone else, was Oke.

'Hello!' said Carmen, eager to get out of the conversation. She was going to head over to him, but he pushed his way through the crowd.

'Bronagh! Thank you so much for the invitation.'

'You know each other?'

'Happy solstice, Sister Witch,' said Oke courteously.

225

'Happy solstice, Brother Quaker,' said Bronagh, nodding her head.

'I like the cloak,' said Oke in his deep voice. The purple set off Carmen's dark hair, even though she immediately giggled and would have renounced it had Bronagh not been standing there doing Fierce Witch Face. He noticed, though, the flush that spread across her face, and the slight twitch she made to the cape as she turned around.

'I brought more!' came a voice behind Oke, and Dahlia, the girl from the coffee shop, appeared with two more goblets.

'This is so delicious, Bronagh,' she said, her face flushed. 'We should serve it in the coffee shop.'

'You'd get shut down by the procurator fiscal,' said Bronagh, patting her arm. 'And we need you.'

The girl smiled, then caught sight of Carmen for the first time and turned pinker. She blushed easily, obviously.

Carmen froze to the spot and looked at them both.

Oke read her look immediately and wanted to explain but couldn't think of a way around it. He knew Dahlia had a crush on him – he taught enough undergraduates to recognise the signs – and she had obviously known he'd been invited to the party along with everyone else from the Quaker meeting house, and had hovered in the freezing cold waiting for him to walk past so they could 'accidentally' arrive together. Now Carmen would think he was even more of a creep than she did already, sneaking up on her in the hall of mirrors, which he deeply regretted, and, that having crashed and burned, having moved straight on to the next girl who worked in a shop in the same street.

This was more or less exactly what Carmen was think-ing. Well. At least she knew it really had just been about the voucher. She sniffed and tried to look dignified, which is quite tricky when you're wearing a purple velvet cloak.

'Cor, you were with Blair Pfenning weren't you?! Is he here?' said Dahlia.

'He's in LA,' said Carmen, bullishly sounding as if she knew his schedule. It was a ridiculous piece of showing off – who exactly was she trying to impress?

Oke relaxed. Right. So she was seeing that other guy. Okay. Fine. Not that he was terribly interested in Dahlia but he'd hated upsetting Carmen. But he was being ridiculous to think that she was thinking about him at all. The people who dated the Blairs of this world and those who dated the Okes very rarely interacted. He told himself very strongly to pack away those feelings.

'Dahlia,' said Bronagh, 'come here, I have a present for you.'

'Wow!' said Dahlia happily, for whom this was turning into an excellent evening. Oke nodded to Carmen, then followed her too, naturally curious. Carmen hugged her glass like she didn't care and looked around the party. As well as the alternative-looking crowd, it was also full of your typically successful-looking Edinburgh women: glossy, perfectly dressed, slender and well-off. She was half-surprised not to see Sofia among them; she would fit in right away, which wasn't exactly what you would expect from a dark little occult shop at the bottom of Victoria Street.

'Who are all these women?' she whispered to Mr McCredie, who was in deep conversation with a very short man with a very long beard all the way down his front and gold-rimmed spectacles.

Mr McCredie gave a sideways look around the room. 'Oh, those are those glossy working mother types, always perfect,

227

never a hair out of place. Bronagh told me about them. She says they're *all* witches. No other way you could conceivably "have it all" apparently.'

He went back to his conversation while Carmen frowned. This was all too strange for words. Although if it were true, it would explain a lot.

Suddenly a large figure loomed in front of her, teetering on tiny shoes.

'Miss Hogan,' she said, and Carmen flinched. It couldn't be. It was. Mrs Marsh stood there, a burgundy dress stretched across that formidable singular bosom.

Carmen's first thought was 'I *knew* she was a witch' followed by an irresistible urge to call Idra.

'Mrs Marsh,' she said. 'I didn't realise you were one of the coven.'

Mrs Marsh sniffed.

'This nonsense. Not at all. I work for the university settlement office at the bottom of the street. Showing Victoria Street solidarity.'

Carmen gave a meaningful look to Mr McCredie, which he caught. 'Wow,' she said. 'It looks like this entire street gets involved even when they don't want to.'

Mr McCredie blinked and came over, and Carmen had to introduce him, much as she was terrified of her old scary boss infecting her new lovely one. Mr McCredie, a gentleman as ever, immediately bore Mrs Marsh off for a drink.

Carmen took off the purple cloak – rather reluctantly, as it was warm and had a nice way of bouncing as she walked – and headed for the exit. She suddenly wasn't in the mood, watching everyone else in the world having a good time.

The street outside was quieter now, but people were still on their way to the bars and restaurants of the understreets; the nightclubs would get noisier as the night went on.

'Here,' said Bronagh, materialising at her side before she left to take the cloak.

'Thanks for the invite,' said Carmen. 'It was good to get Mr McCredie out.'

'Oh, that poor man,' said Bronagh. 'Bad blood. Does nobody any good.'

'What do you mean?'

'Oh, don't mind me. Don't forget this.'

She gave her a tiny glass bottle with a clear fluid in it.

'Just dab it on your doorstep,' she said.

'Is this a love potion?'

'Oh goodness no, you don't need that,' said Bronagh. 'No. It's for the bond that holds two sisters; one of the strongest things on earth. Forged in steel, hard as iron, easy to burn, never to break. Goodspeed home.'

'Actually, we've been getting on all … Thank you,' said Carmen, seeing Bronagh's face. 'And happy solstice.'

She pulled out her phone, pushing past the Christmas revellers and curling over against the cold wind as she waited to cross Lothian Road, passing happy people on outings pouring into the theatres and concert halls and cinemas that lined it, piling up treats for Christmas, small children gazing in awe at the lights, girls in sparkly dresses, boys clutching bags of Maltesers, enjoying the thrill of being out after dark.

She walked into the shelter of the great red Caledonian hotel, with its black cabs lining up and where elegant ladies in long dresses and men in kilts were disgorging, obviously for some fancy party. She looked at the beautiful women, thinking about Mr McCredie's theory that they had to all be witches, and shook her head. Then she thought about Oke and Dahlia and found herself oddly sad. He was just ... well. He was different to the people she normally met. Mind you, since she'd moved to Edinburgh, everybody was.

She found herself almost unconsciously scrolling down back through her text messages with Blair, even though she knew it was unwise.

She counted back. It was 9 a.m. in LA. He would be in a meeting. She told herself not to send him a message.

Then she thought, Oh hell, what was there to lose?

And she typed, 'Don't tell me, your new hotel room is also a living hell.'

She squeezed her eyes shut, then sent it and put her phone in her pocket out of sight, almost daring herself not to look at it again.

She crossed over Queensferry Street and down Alva Street to the beautifully lit, perfect little house. All the houses on the surrounding streets were beautiful too, and many had matching trees in their windows, all with warm glowing yellow lights as if there'd been a New Town community memo. There probably had been. Even so, Carmen's tired heart lifted to see it. It was such a pretty house and even though Skylar was inside, so were the little people, and, to her own surprise, she knew she would be so happy to see them.

Just as she was looking for her key, her phone buzzed. She jumped like she'd been electrified. It couldn't be. But ... but ...

Slowly, like Charlie Bucket unwrapping his chocolate bar in the snow, she withdrew the phone from her pocket.

'Hell, darling, pure hell.'

There was a picture attached of palm trees waving above a stunning blue ocean, the sun bright in the sky, tanned figures visible running in the surf.

Carmen couldn't stop grinning, all the way in, taking off her shoes, putting them away TIDILY, as Pippa liked to remind her, unwinding her scarf and hanging up her coat.

Sofia had gone up to bed; Skylar was in the kitchen, trying to teach the children a song about coriander. For once, Carmen felt rather warm towards her. After all, she was just trying to do her best. It wasn't her fault that Blair had got in touch with *her*.

'Hi, Skylar!'

Skylar looked up and sniffed loudly. 'Oh my God, have you been drinking?' she said. 'You can smell it all the way over here. Really, drinking is just like totally going to destroy your liver. Makes you look older too, right, kids?'

The children looked at her.

'Yes, I think so,' said Pippa decisively.

'Hi, kids,' said Carmen, but even that couldn't bring her down too much. 'Guess where I was? A *witches'* party!'

Phoebe instantly looked worried.

'Are you a witch?'

'Well, I was at their party,' said Carmen, showing her a selfie she'd taken of herself in the big purple cloak.

'Don't get frightened,' warned Pippa.

'I am NOT FRIGHTENED,' said Phoebe, grabbing at Carmen's phone.

'Great, thanks?' said Skylar.

'I was only dressing up and pretending,' said Carmen hastily. 'I'm not an actual one. And neither was anybody else.'

'But witches are for Halloween,' said Phoebe.

'I know. Isn't it great?'

'I hate Halloween.'

'She does,' confirmed Pippa. 'She cried all the way round, then she threw up all her sweets.'

'I didn't throw up ALL my sweets,' said Phoebe.

'I know,' said Pippa. 'Then you started eating again even though we told you not to.'

Phoebe hit out at Pippa, who grimaced.

'Use your words, Phoebe,' said Skylar, shooting daggers at Carmen.

Carmen sat down on the other side of the furious little girl.

'You know what this proves?' she said. 'It just proves you have an amazing imagination.'

Phoebe screwed up her face doubtfully.

'It's true. Imagining things and being worried, being able to create something out of your mind that is so frightening you actually frighten yourself – that's an amazing thing to be able to do. You know, loads of people don't feel things like that – fear, or sadness or worry. They don't feel things like that at all.'

'That's right,' said Skylar. 'If you follow good life practices, you can eliminate all of those things.' She smiled beatifically. 'And reach a plane of higher content.'

Carmen frowned.

'That's not what I mean at all,' she said. 'If you get frightened sometimes, or very sad, and you let it out – well, it means you'll get the flipside too. Joy and happiness and excitement. The full range. End to end. It's just life.'

The little girl looked at her.

'Yes, with meditation and yoga you can smooth out the rough edges,' added Skylar quickly.

Carmen couldn't help it. She turned on her.

'Why?'

'What do you mean why?' said Skylar. 'Because it makes life better.'

'Does it?'

Skylar tossed her long glossy hair behind her back.

'What, you think it's better your way?' she said, a sneer crossing her lovely face. The children looked worried then at the bad feeling, and Carmen turned to leave, her heart beating fast.

'Don't know,' said Carmen as she got up to leave the room and she wouldn't have done it if she hadn't been tired and jealous, and had a tendency to shoot her mouth off when she was disappointed, and she was to deeply, deeply regret it very, very soon.

'Oh, by the way, Blair says hi,' she said.

'Really?' said Skylar sweetly. 'Because I was just speaking to him, and he didn't mention you at all. Bye!'

Chapter Twenty-six

The dream came again, creeping up on her: the train, the woman, the tunnel, the scream.

She sat bolt upright in bed, waiting for her breathing to calm down. There was no possibility of sleep now.

Miserably, she grabbed her phone, even though she knew it wasn't good for her. Ugh – Skylar was so pretty and perfect and smug all the fricking time – and she couldn't even moan to Sofia about it. In fact, if it came to it she wasn't sure Sofia wouldn't pick Skylar over her any day of the week.

But she didn't want to leave, didn't want go home. She liked her job, she realised. She was good at it. The shop was doing well and it looked beautiful. And she liked the children. Very much. But what else did she have? After Christmas, when everything would disappear?

She clasped her phone like it was a teddy bear or a security blanket. At least Blair provided a little excitement, she thought.

'Put your T-shirt on or you'll burn,' she typed.

'I'm naturally tanned,' was his response.

She smiled to herself.

'You massive liar. I bet you have your own tent and everything.'

'Why are you the only person in the world that doesn't think I'm amazing? Everyone in LA thinks I am FABULOUS.'

'😷😷😷🐻'

'Well, they do.'

'Well, they don't. It's just Hollywood BS.'

'How on EARTH would you know that? Have you ever even left that tiny place you live in?'

'You mean one of the great and ancient beautiful cities in the whole of history? Or do you mean Billericay, where you're from?'

'You read my book!'

'Durr no. Just the blurb.'

'Send me a pic. I'm lonely.'

She took a picture of the teddy bear one of the kids had left at the end of the bed. It was wearing a nurse's uniform.

'Saucy.'

'Thanks.'

'You should probably shave.'

'Sexist.'

'It wasn't the bear bum I had in mind.'

Carmen smiled, hugged her phone closer in her cold hands.

'Go on, send me a real pic.'

Carmen frowned to herself. No. This definitely – No. She thought about it. Angling, good lighting. No.

'I think you've got the wrong room,' she typed.

'😳'

'Go on . . .'

She took the bottom off the nurse's uniform of the bear, sent a picture of the bear's arse, turned off her phone and, to her own surprise, fell asleep.

Chapter Twenty-seven

She was super-nice that weekend in case Sofia suspected she'd fallen out with Skylar.

'I should take the kids on a Christmas trip, don't you think?' she said when the children were still upstairs.

'Ooh, that's a good idea,' said Sofia. 'There's a lovely illuminated walk through the botanical gardens and they can learn all about the plants.'

'I was thinking of maybe Edinburgh's Christmas—'

The entire room froze. Even the radio, which was playing Mariah Carey, seemed to fade away into quiet. Sofia and Skylar exchanged appalled glances.

Edinburgh's Christmas was the huge fair that took over the whole of Princes Street Gardens in the centre of the city, as well as St Andrew's Square, George Street, Castle Street ... it seemed to get its tentacles everywhere. Locals complained vociferously that it was too loud, too big, too expensive, too popular. What they meant, Carmen suspected (she rather liked seeing the lights flashing and smelling the popcorn and candyfloss and hearing the screams when she came home from work), was *too vulgar*.

For a moment, there was nothing, and Sofia and Skylar breathed a sigh of relief. Then, there were pounding footsteps on the stairs.

'Amazing,' said Sofia. 'They never hear me screaming my lungs out when it's time to put their shoes on.'

'ARE WE GOING TO EDINBURGH'S CHRISTMAS?!'

Jack looked cheery and excited; Phoebe suspicious, as if this was clearly a trick that couldn't possibly be happening. Pippa was a couple of steps behind them, pretending she was above all this and was only down to supervise.

Sofia rolled her eyes.

'You've done it now,' she said.

'I've done what now?' said Carmen.

'Please, Auntie Carmen! Please! Please take us! Will you take us?'

'How much money do you have?' said Sofia.

'What, me?' said Carmen, stung. 'Enough.'

Sofia shook her head. 'No, you don't.'

'We'll pay! From our pocket money!'

The children were painfully begging now. Jack looked as if he might be about to throw himself writhing on the floor.

'PLEASE just take me,' said Phoebe desperately. 'Skylar's going to make me drink THAT STUFF.'

Skylar was making green juice and she smiled beatifically. 'Because I want what's best for you.'

'You should drink it, Phoebe,' said Pippa. 'It's very, very good for you.'

'Please,' said Phoebe.

'But she can't go if I can't go!' said Jack hotly. 'How would that be fair? That wouldn't be fair!'

Pippa sniffed.

'Well, obviously I think it's bad too, Mummy, but if they're going to go I should probably go and make sure Phoebe doesn't do any rides that are too scary for her.'

'They're not too scary for me!'

'And that she doesn't have too much candyfloss.'

'They have candyfloss?!' said Jack.

'That stuff will kill you,' said Skylar quickly.

'It won't!' said Carmen. 'Seriously, sis, how bad is it?'

'I'll send Skylar to pick you up at five.'

'WE CAN GO?!'

The children's eyes were wide.

'For a little bit, seeing as your aunt is volunteering.'

'Then you have your school concert rehearsal,' said Skylar.

There was a collective groan.

'Not much point in Phoebe going then,' said Jack, sniggering. Phoebe would have kicked him but was worried Carmen might change her mind if she did.

It was loud. Very loud. There was screaming music, all different, on each ride, and every mulled wine stall and the many bars had live music. There were also doughnut stalls and candyfloss and fudge and everything was quite terrifying. Phoebe point-blank refused to go on the little train, which Carmen had rather liked the look of, because it was for babies, so Carmen ended up accompanying her on some terrifying thing that started off quite tame, then spun them round perpendicular to the ground, Phoebe pale white with fright, tears streaking down her cheeks. She had a full-blown meltdown when Carmen stalled at the rifle range (everything was indeed extortionately expensive) and there was a massive cacophonous row over who was making the Ferris wheel compartment wobble.

Which was a shame, as up there, next to the great dark Scott Monument, slowly lifting higher and higher, Carmen felt her own heart lift. The city, dark and exciting, full of light and people and movement, spread out at their feet with the lights of the fair, the great lit-up Christmas tree on the mount ahead, the twinkling stars, closer up here, the biting cold air and the feeling of Christmas right around the corner – two weeks to go now, as the children informed her daily, counting down every second.

It *was* exciting. That was until Phoebe dropped a glove through the narrow railings and almost went after it, causing Carmen to yell at her, something she had never ever done, and causing Phoebe in turn to have another fit which, once back on the ground, Carmen tried to assuage with extraordinarily expensive hot chocolates which cost extra for whipped cream and marshmallows. Then Phoebe spilled hers and insisted that Jack had done it, and finally Carmen began to see Sofia's point.

'Come on,' she chivvied them. 'Let's go to the Christmas tree maze!'

She cleaned Phoebe up carefully.

'You'll be fine. Take my glove.'

Phoebe did so, sniffing valiantly and wiping her nose on it. It really was bitingly cold; Carmen stuffed her hand quickly back in her pocket and took a large restorative swig of the extremely pricey mulled wine she'd set down on a wall.

'Come on then! Let's go! Everyone take my hand or grab my coat or something.'

'NO WAY!' said Jack, who had seen a friend of his in the crush and was nodding to him, *mano a mano* style.

'Okay. Well, don't get lost.'

'I think actually getting lost is what you're meant to do in a maze,' pointed out Pippa.

'You're right,' smiled Carmen. 'Gold star to you.'

Oke was on his way up – he had to fight through the Christmas fair every day to make it up the steps of the Mound to his student halls – when he saw her.

She was bent down, fitting a glove on one child, trying to snatch another to stop him running off and laughing with a third. Her cheeks were pink, her eyes bright. He sighed. She looked quite lovely. 'Come ONNNN, Auntie Carmen,' was the anguished cry he now heard from the smallest one. She stood up, rolling her eyes, but with a willing smile that was beautiful to him.

'Hello,' he said, and she whirled round, shocked.

'Oh,' she said, not expecting to see him there. 'Hello. How are you? Why are you here? There are almost no trees at all.'

'It's on my way home.'

'Of course.'

She looked up to the beautiful student buildings, grey stone above the city.

'I thought you'd gone full Christmas for a minute there.'

'AUNTIE CARMEN, COME ON!'

The children had burst into the maze.

Carmen looked at Oke.

He looked tall and relaxed in the cold grey light, a wrist of simple grey beads the only jewellery he wore; he didn't even wear a watch. He had found from somewhere a large old jumper – a charity shop, maybe – but it was good quality and suited him. He had also somehow managed to lay his hands on a long scarf that came down past his waist.

He stood out, she thought, from the people streaming around him; drew glances, particularly from the women, for his tall rangy figure, his face so thoughtful as he took in the crowds thronging in brightly coloured padded jackets, everyone in bobble hats, happy faces and excited children racing everywhere. Behind the little train, the great cliff face of Edinburgh buildings rose in front of him. To his left was a great spinning swing that went high in the air, up to the height of the Scott Monument, and every thirty seconds or so it would spin and the screaming would start, regular as clockwork, then it would descend again. The lights of the fairground attractions flashed behind him.

'Do you want to come in the tree maze?' said Carmen, displaying the tickets. 'If it's not . . . forbidden or something.'

He smiled.

'It is not forbidden. In fact, it's practically research.'

Inside the Christmas tree maze was rather lovely. The sounds and lights of the rest of the huge fair had faded away. The children had grabbed the small cards they had to stamp to win a prize and vanished down the long rows of dark Christmas trees, sprinkled with snow and hung with lights.

'So tell me about firs,' said Carmen.

He smiled.

'The Romans put them up. For Saturnalia. In mid-December.'

'Before Christmas.'

'Before Christmas, yes. A lot of things change over the years.'

'Cor,' said Carmen. 'Bronagh is right about a lot of stuff.'

'They predate dinosaurs.'

'*Really?* Wow. How long do they live?'

He shrugged. 'Five hundred years, average. Up to a thousand.'

Carmen looked at him.

'And we chop them down and put them in pots.'

She shook her head.

'AUNTIE CARMEN! Phoebe took my card!' Jack was thundering.

'I didn't! It got stuck!' Phoebe's voice could be heard, but she couldn't be seen. 'AND NOW I AM LOST!'

Carmen settled Jack down.

'Could you go find her? And then stamp her card too?'

'But why? She always fusses.'

'Because she is very small and you are extremely smart,' said Carmen.

Jack pondered this for a second.

'Really?' he said finally. Then he glanced up at Oke.

'Hi there,' he said, with no curiosity whatsoever.

'Hey, man,' said Oke. 'I have sisters too.'

They passed a look of mutual understanding, and finally Jack nodded and dashed back into the maze ahead of them.

'Phoebs! Keep yelling and I'll find you.'

In response, Phoebe made a high-pitched yowling noise not unlike a cat's, or a fire alarm.

'Nice boy,' said Oke.

'He is!' said Carmen. 'They're great.'

She looked at him as they walked on, the maze seemingly endless, their paths possibly in circles.

'How did you get so into trees?'

He shrugged. 'I always . . . I just always found it so amazing. That you would plant seeds and they would grow – where I live there are a lot of trees. They talk to each other.'

'What?' said Carmen suspiciously as they dodged a large party of drunk teenagers who were hollering at each other. 'What do they say? "Nice leaves"?'

'Sometimes, yes. They warn each other about diseases.'

'That can't be true.'

'Sure is. They share water. They can even divert water to one another if they have too much in supply.'

'Do they *really*?'

'Yes,' said Oke. 'Trees are astonishing communicators.'

'When they rustle?'

'It's more like a kind of bubbly noise. If they're thirsty. Like trying to get the last bits out of a straw.'

'Why isn't everyone absolutely freaking out about this?' said Carmen.

'Well, dendrologists are. For years, it was considered absolutely ridiculous to think it. Then studies came along and proved it.'

'Bloody hell.'

She looked at the trees looming above them in the maze.

'Oh goodness,' she said. 'Does that mean we shouldn't be cutting them down to make Christmas trees? Do they *scream*?'

He diverted her attention.

'Uh, would you like some of the pink sticky stuff? It seems popular.'

He pointed out of the front gate to a candyfloss stall.

'It comes on a stick!' said Carmen.

'Okay.'

Fortunately at that moment Pippa arrived and informed them she had filled in her entire card, collected her prize of a small chocolate bar and could they leave now as Skylar was picking them up and wouldn't be able to stop because of Scary Traffic Men.

'Okay,' said Carmen. A massive leaving tantrum was narrowly avoided when Jack came round the corner with Phoebe and two small bars of chocolate and Carmen couldn't avoid feeling slightly smug delivering the children perfectly on time to the agreed meeting place beneath the huge Bank of Scotland.

'Oh good, chocolate in the car?' said Skylar immediately. 'Yeah, that's great for everyone?'

Then she saw Oke behind Carmen and her entire face changed.

'Dr Oke!' she beamed. 'Wow! How amazing to see you? I, like, just loved your lecture on the symbolism of the birch in art?'

'Um, thanks,' said Oke modestly.

'Well, let's get you all going,' she said. 'I'm sure you're all going to be so brilliant in the concert?'

Phoebe's face fell immediately.

'Well, bye then,' said Carmen.

'Thank you, Auntie Carmen,' pronounced Pippa and for once the other two echoed her uncomplainingly.

'Thank you, Auntie Carmen!'

Somehow, without discussing it, Carmen and Oke walked on and came to a quieter section of the fair, away from the screaming. There were little wooden huts selling bits and pieces.

'I should shop for them,' said Carmen. 'The thing is my sister likes them to have lovely wooden toys.'

Indeed, the sweet little German stall they were standing in front of had wooden pull-along cars, bees, little aeroplanes. They were rather adorable.

'But I think they would probably like something plastic that buzzes and makes a lot of noise. But that would annoy my sister.'

He smiled. 'I am not sure it's the worst thing not to have to think about gifts.'

'But you don't have anyone in your family who would like one of these?'

She held up an adorable model plane.

He smiled. 'My sisters both have sons. But no, I am not sure it would be wise. Not at Christmas.'

'Well, what about something sent with love from a loving uncle very far away that just happened to arrive at about the right time? Would that be the worst thing?'

He looked. There was a little pull-along train too, with carriages. It was adorable.

'Well . . . ' he said.

'I'm doing three for two,' said the pleasant German man who was manning the stall. There was a wooden star too, which Oke couldn't help thinking would look very pretty in his sister's house.

'Well . . . ' He was weakening.

'Go on! It's the law! It's Christmas! Spending money on stuff! It's a very important cultural tradition when you visit new lands. It can just be this once.'

He smiled at Carmen then, and took out his wallet and bought eight little trains and three stars.

'*Wow!*' said Carmen. 'God, I'm sorry. I didn't realise they had so many children.'

A woman Carmen thought looked familiar stepped forwards from behind the little hut and spoke to the stallholder in German. Then she turned to them.

'You have bought so much! Here, please accept this with our compliments.'

She handed Oke a vintage car, which he took with thanks and immediately gave to Carmen.

'Ooh,' said Carmen. 'I can put it in the window of the shop with a mouse in it!'

Oke smiled as the woman leaned forward.

'Yes! You work in the shop,' she said, and Carmen recognised her as the woman who'd come in looking for Mr McCredie. 'Did you give him my card? He has not called me.'

She had quite a direct way of speaking.

'Um, yes I did,' said Carmen. 'I'm sorry. He didn't ... Can I ask what it's about?'

'We were clearing out an attic and discovered some letters. The return address is ... well, it is there. I should like to speak to him. Very much.'

She said something to the man in rapid German, and he looked startled, then carried on wrapping the toys.

'We are here until Christmas and then – *pouf* – we are gone. So. Please. If he does not want to phone, we are here. Every day. Wait.'

She turned back into the little hut and brought out another tiny little shape, exquisitely carved in wrought wood. It was a circle, quartered by a cross, smooth and timeless.

'Please give him this. For his tree. With our warmest wishes.'

'Thank you,' said Carmen, surprised, and, laden with bags, they retreated from the noise and cacophony of the fair. She explained the situation to Oke.

'What do you think it is?' said Oke.

'Goodness! I don't know,' said Carmen. 'I can't imagine Mr McCredie having any dark secret love children or anything like that. I think he's barely left the house he was born in his whole life. He likes books more than people. I'll tell him. Do you like trees more than people?'

'Some,' said Oke. 'You know where you are with a tree. Except for elms. They're bastards.'

'How?' Carmen was startled to hear him swear.

'Oh, try anything and they just die on you. Hi, elm, how you doing? … SPLAT!'

He mimed the tree falling over and she giggled.

'You look like a tree. You've chosen the right profession.'

'Because of my twig-like arms and legs? I know,' he said, undaunted. 'People say that all the time.'

'Well, better than … being a cactus specialist.'

'That's true.'

'Or a bonsai.'

He grinned.

'Ooh, bonsai are a whole other thing.'

They had wandered off the main drag and up the steps of the National Gallery. The screaming was still ringing in their ears.

'Well, I did all the consumerism, and I saw somebody throw up outside the waltzers,' said Oke. 'Will that do?'

Carmen nodded, although suddenly she was reluctant to leave him. There was something incredibly ... easy about being in his presence. But perhaps he had to get back to Dahlia. He started heading towards the steps.

'Would you like to come see a bit more Christmas? I think I'm getting the hang of it,' he said.

Chapter Twenty-eight

She couldn't match his loping stride as he cut through the crowds bustling around little wooden stalls selling carved fairies, fudge, candyfloss, teddy bears, mulled wine and hot chocolate, and she tried her best not to look as if she was absolutely out of breath as they climbed the steep steps of the Mound.

Oke turned at the very top to survey the bright lights of the market below, laid in front of them like a carpet, glittering and beautiful, with less shouting and fewer small children looking as though they were going to be sick.

'It's just people trying to be happy,' she said.

'I understand that,' said Oke. 'I'm just not sure it's the best way to go about it.'

'What do you think happiness is?' she asked him.

'A by-product,' he answered immediately, 'of being useful.'

She looked at him.

'What?' she said. 'What do you mean?'

He looked back at her, surprised.

'Well,' he said, 'if you do good work and are useful, that makes you happy.'

'What about going on holiday? That's not useful.'

'If you have been working hard all year and you deserve some time off, that is happiness. If your family is rich and your life feels like you're on holiday, I do not think that makes people very happy.'

Carmen thought unavoidably of Blair talking about 'I Wish it Could Be Christmas Every Day' and complaining about his hotel room.

'You're not very cheery,' said Carmen. 'Okay then, what about cuddling a puppy?'

'If you are going to raise that puppy and be there for them every second to care for their needs and look after them, then of course, that is happiness. But it's also work.'

'I thought you might be going to say hot chocolate,' said Carmen, rather regretful that they had passed the stalls a moment later.

'Would you like a hot chocolate?'

'I don't know. I think I do and I like the smell and then I have one and it's too much and I spill some and I feel sick.'

He smiled.

'Stick to being useful. The shop makes you happy?'

Don't be stupid it's a job, Carmen was about to say. Then she remembered yesterday, when a very small child had come in, clutching some fairly sticky coins in their hand, and had marched forwards, closely watched by their father, and asked loudly for a copy of *The Dark Is Rising*, and Carmen had said did they want it wrapped up and they shook their head very firmly because it was obvious they were planning on reading it the very second they left the shop, and Carmen had understood and counted out the child's change very carefully and told them to enjoy it.

'Hmmm,' she said.

'Ssh!' He suddenly hushed her as they stole up the steps past the large church building. 'Can you hear?'

If she strained her ears she just about could.

'They're rehearsing. For the big fancy concert at the castle nobody can get tickets for. But why would you need tickets?'

He looked at her, smiling. 'Come with me.'

There was a little side door off the steps that you wouldn't notice if you weren't specifically looking for it. Glancing up and down to make sure there was nobody there – though not many people wandered this close as it looked like it led somewhere private – he slipped open the plain black door.

Inside it was pitch-dark and he hushed her as she giggled. They found themselves in some kind of backstage passageway. It felt more like a theatre than a church: it was the assembly hall of the Church of Scotland.

The sound had now become very loud, but somehow quiet at the same time. It didn't sound like a choir. It sounded like one, multi-throated being, muffled in the dark passageway with cloths hanging down the walls.

'Wha-at can I give him, poor as I am . . . ?'

They crept round to where a tiny chink of light appeared in the wall and they could peer through the gap.

There were choirboys in red and white soutanes, and older men singing in black. There was a smaller section of women to the side, dressed like waitresses in black skirts and white shirts. The men were definitely more glamorous, thought Carmen.

The choirmaster wore black spectacles and his hair was grey and curly. He was concentrating ferociously on a huge book

251

in front of him on which lines of music notation were densely printed, and occasionally gesturing in one direction or another, or pointing at the pianist in the corner, or looking up for reasons Carmen didn't quite understand.

As she was looking at everything, Oke, she noticed as her eyes adjusted, wasn't doing any of this. He was standing, leaning against the wall, his eyes closed. He opened them when he realised she was watching him and, to Carmen's surprise, brought a flask out of his backpack.

It was full of hot chocolate.

'Don't have too much,' he whispered. 'You might spill it or feel sick.'

She was so surprised, she grinned widely.

'Wow,' she whispered, dampening down a voice inside her that wondered if Dahlia had made it.

'Ssh,' he said. 'I want to hear the music. And the conductor has bat hearing.'

They settled down on the opposite side of the passageway, widening the chink in the curtain imperceptibly so they could also see.

But you didn't have to see really. The area was vast and round – and freezing – and the sound swelled up from the ground and filled the air and passageway and all the spaces in between.

Carmen didn't normally go to concerts which weren't pop concerts, and had always assumed they would be a bit boring. But when she heard the men's voices swelling in the deep dark – the cry of good King Wenceslas' *'Mark my footsteps, good my page'* answering the page's lament, *'Sire, the night is darker now and the wind grows stronger'* – she felt the hairs on her arms go up.

The reason the conductor was looking skywards, she realised with a start that made Oke giggle, came at the climax of 'Hark the Herald Angels Sing' when – *BOOM* – a huge pipe organ burst into melody, crashing from the heavens itself.

And finally, it was the last carol, and the voices went so, so quiet and pure Carmen had to strain to hear the 'Scots Nativity' – *balloo*, *lamby*, *balloo*, *ballay* – the gentle words mothers had crooned to babies for hundreds of years, each baby special, each one the promise of love renewed.

Tears unexpectedly ran down her cheeks, even as she saw the conductor glance at his watch, and the choristers lift up their cassocks to reveal trainers and odd socks and perfectly normal people beneath the otherworldly sound they made. It was odd to connect old, grey-haired men and small, chubby, freckled boys with the grandeur and the glory of everything they had just heard as they slipped away and the choirmaster droned on about not being late to rehearsals and would the altos stop chewing.

'Oh my goodness,' Carmen said, as the freezing air hit them back out on the street. 'Goodness. That was lovely.'

She looked at him severely.

'But it made me very happy and it wasn't remotely useful. *And* it celebrated Christmas.'

Oke shrugged.

'Perhaps a little worship is useful?' he said.

Carmen's face fell. Oh no. Was he some kind of God-botherer, trying to recruit her?

'I had you pegged as a scientist with a bit of cultural Quakering on the side,' she grumbled.

'I am,' he said.

'But you definitely believe in God?'

He shrugged good-naturedly.

'Ask any physicist. *Something* is looking at us.'

Carmen didn't understand this but she pressed on.

'But do you believe ... in the Bible and the baby Jesus and stuff? And ooh, I am asking you and I know you can't lie, ha!'

He blinked.

'Well,' he said. 'I think if anyone were to believe in something more than themselves, if you were to believe in something, I would say it is not unreasonable to think that when you touch a baby's face you are touching the face of God. Have you ever seen a baby in an old people's home? They are worshipped. They become divine.'

'Hmm,' said Carmen.

'So I can see the appeal. But I do not have a true church, no. I was raised a very strict Quaker, in a place that has very few Quakers so ... we all stuck together. But no.'

Carmen smiled.

'You're a faker Quaker?'

'Yeah yeah yeah.'

His voice grew wistful for a moment.

'Although often I find in music ...'

'There is, like, divine stuff?'

'Well, that is as good a word as any,' he said, and they continued on in silence.

'You're a very strange person,' said Carmen.

'All God's creatures are strange,' said Oke, but he was teasing her, she knew.

The cold was biting now. Oke indicated a courtyard to their right at the top of the steps that led up to the Royal Mile.

'This is where I stay,' he said.

'I know,' said Carmen.

She smiled, and suddenly found herself moving closer towards him. There was nobody else in the dark alleyway. He looked at his hands, reluctant to make an advance, but she found his hand herself, in gloves too thin for the weather, and took it and put it between hers. His green eyes locked onto hers. The freezing night fell still, silence all around. She moved towards him again under the freezing Edinburgh sky, under the grey tenement walls, hundreds of years of history on all sides, in a world as old as time; she leaned towards him ...

Suddenly, footsteps hastened by, followed by a loud sobbing noise. They both glanced up.

It was Dahlia, staring at Oke, her face dissolving in tears.

'Oh goodness,' said Oke. 'Are you all right?'

He went to move after her, and Carmen would have done too, not sure what was going on, when her phone blared out, the noise bouncing off the old grey stone walls, an interloper, a thing that did not belong.

Oke turned and looked back towards her as Dahlia stopped in the close leading to the street, leaning her head against the wall as if inviting Oke to comfort her. Carmen felt a lump in her throat as she waved him on, looking at her phone in case the call was from Sofia.

The number was private. She pressed 'okay'.

'This *fucking* hotel room,' said Blair. 'It's too big. Too fucking big. I'm coming home, gorgeous. Via that freezing cold town you live in!'

She turned round to say something to Oke, once she'd finished the conversation as quickly as she could, but he was patting Dahlia on the back as she spoke to him. Oh my God. Oh my goodness, were they ...? She hadn't asked. She hadn't asked if they were together, even after she'd seen them at the party. That was her fault. She'd let herself get swept away in the moment, and the music. He'd probably taken Dahlia down there before already – that's how he knew the music was even happening.

As he turned round again to look at her, she kept the phone to her ear even though there was no one on the line any more.

'Great,' she said loudly, lashing out as she watched Oke and Dahlia's heads close together. 'See you, *Blair*.'

And she hung up, even as Oke was looking at her, his face hurt and confused, and stalked off, back the way she came.

Chapter Twenty-nine

The shouting crowds of the fair felt irritating now as Carmen pushed her way through them, her head a mess.

Blair was ridiculous. Of course he was. But he was ... She felt underneath all the nonsense he was funny and cynical and she couldn't help finding him attractive. Oke was attractive – of course he was – but Blair was a man of the world, had been everywhere, had met everyone, was *famous* – and was still texting her. She couldn't deny it was flattering and appealing and she remembered his cold hand on her waist ...

Oke was nice. Definitely nice. But he was seeing someone else anyway; he was just making a habit of acquiring shop girls as he went on.

Oh, but she had liked him. She had liked him a lot. But he belonged to someone else. Story of her life.

But Blair ... he had what everyone else had round here. Money and a career and he knew what he was doing and where his life was heading. Okay, he was a doof but ... God, it would be nice to have a bit of that. When everyone else in the world (she was still getting very jolly messages from Idra) seemed to have their shit together but poor old Carmen. It was all right to want that, wasn't it?

Carmen sighed. Christmas was getting to her, she could tell. There was something about the magical pull of this town, the swirl of snowflakes that was sending her – *argh* – *completely* mad. She had nearly kissed a near-total stranger.

Mind you.

Her phone kept buzzing.

She allowed herself, just for a moment, to imagine what it would be like: the sun streaming through the hotel bedroom window, the crisp white sheets, the fruit plate. She wasn't exactly sure what a fruit plate was but it sounded like something she should probably order.

What would it be like being Blair's girlfriend? Well, he lived in London, but he went to LA for work, and maybe the sun would stream over her face and she'd be in his arms and he'd ask her what she felt like doing that day – pool first, or a walk hand in hand on the beach? Or possibly rollerblading? She frowned as she crossed the road towards the lights at the Caledonian Hotel. She didn't actually want to go rollerblading at all. This fantasy had got completely out of hand.

'Hey babe, how's it going? Are you in the shower?'

'There's a snow shower,' she texted back. 'Not sure that's the same thing.'

'Hey, give me your email. I got something for you.'

Carmen did so, and couldn't help a bit of her thinking, Goodness, what if it was plane tickets for the next time he went to LA?

The email finally came through.

She looked around the busy shop as her phone pinged. Although, funnily enough, if a month ago she would have said that the only thing she wanted was a famous handsome rich man to whisk her off somewhere sunny, now, as she looked round, she found herself thinking, well, she couldn't leave the shop in the lurch this close to Christmas. At that moment, Mr McCredie was trying to help a woman who wanted several expensive guides to Edinburgh gift-wrapped and had managed to stick a piece of Sellotape to his whiskers. She went over to help, waiting and wondering what the email was going to be.

At first, it didn't make any sense; it was an attachment.

'You do stories in the shop, right? For kids?'

Carmen's heart sank a little; there was only one way he could have known this and it wasn't from her.

'I'm going to do a kids' Christmas book for next Christmas. Get some decent artist in, takes me five minutes, big picture of me on the front, sorted. Money for nothing.'

She finished. He wanted her to read it out to the children at story time, and for there to be a video of his book in a proper shop to pitch for the publishers.

'Show the kids loving it. Brilliant.'

It was called *The Mindful Christmas*. Carmen frowned.

'Am also pitching it tomorrow for a film series, so get back to me ASAP. Nobody will be interested in January.'

Her heart dropped. Oh for goodness' sake, Blair. Couldn't he have pretended for five solid minutes that it was her he wanted, and not something that would only benefit him? She'd gone to bed listening to the children babble about their amazing day down the phone to their father, thinking, Well, stupid Oke might have another girlfriend but hey – a *super-famous guy likes me* so at least there was that.

But of course there wasn't.

Carmen sighed.

Although, she supposed, it might help, of course. Push them over the line. Get lots more punters in, generate a bit of publicity. Every little helped.

She messaged Sofia, asking her to announce it on that terrifying mothers' grapevine she had, and sighed. Maybe it would be a huge success and he'd give interviews announcing, 'Oh, I couldn't have done it without my Carmen.'

Maybe.

After lunch, the very tall posh book rep, Ramsay, came in.

'Hello!' he said, smiling at Carmen, who was still deep in thought and had been too scared to ask Skylar if she'd heard from Blair the previous evening. 'Wow, I can't believe the difference you've made to this place!' He glanced back. Outside were two small boys, gripped in fascination by the train set.

'Sorry,' he said. 'Inset day. I had to bring them – baby Hugh is teething and Zoe is up to her eyeballs. They've been an absolute pain in the neck all the way down if that helps.'

'That's okay; bring them in.'

'Are you sure? I'll try and not get them to turn the place into a nightmare . . .'

'It's okay,' said Carmen. 'I'm used to kids. Actually, there are lots coming in at about three for a story time.'

'Oh, cool. Hey, look. I dug this out in a house clearance in Kinross – isn't it beautiful?'

And he showed her a series of hardback editions of the *Winter Tales of the Faeries* series, stunningly illustrated with bookplates.

'I've never even heard of these.'

'Legends from the deep north,' said Ramsay. 'To be shared over a yule log, I should think.'

Carmen picked one up entitled *The Shining Star*, which had the most beautiful raised engraving of a shepherd and a lamb on the leather-bound cover.

'Oh, this is gorgeous.'

'Thought you'd like it,' said Ramsay, looking around. 'Are you going to skin me again for it? Wow, it's getting more Christmassy in here every day.'

He beckoned the two boys forward and they stomped in, dinging the bell loudly. The slightly smaller one gasped in awe. The other, who was dressed in a shirt and tie for some reason, looked around in quite a calculating manner.

Mr McCredie materialised beside Carmen.

'Ramsay,' he said, wreathed in smiles. 'What have you been foraging for us today?' He looked down. 'And is this . . . it isn't . . . is this *Patrick*?'

'Well, of course I am Patrick,' said the boy.

Mr McCredie looked at Ramsay.

'You brought him here once when he was a baby! And I have scarcely seen him since.'

'I know,' said Ramsay. 'Things got a little hectic.'

He smiled.

'Ramsay fell in love with the nanny,' Mr McCredie helpfully supplied to Carmen.

Carmen smiled.

'Good money-saving technique.'

To his credit, Ramsay laughed.

'You'd think,' he said. 'Still skint though.'

'Hello, excuse me?' said Patrick on his tippy-toes at the countertop. 'I have some questions about the train set. It is quite a lot of questions. Hari, say hello. Sometimes he forgets to say hello unless I tell him but he is really quite clever. When I help him.'

Hari was a beautiful child, with messy straight black hair and olive skin, and he smiled cheerfully.

'Hiya,' he said in a surprisingly deep voice, his accent much thicker than Patrick's. 'Ah like your train set, ken.'

'Well,' said Carmen. 'I'm going to be doing a story in a little while – would you like to stay for it?'

Hari looked immediately interested; Patrick less so.

'I can read for myself perfectly well,' he announced. 'I AM nearly seven.'

'All right, Jacob Rees-Mogg,' said Carmen, before remembering she was being nice to children these days – everyone's children. But Ramsay just laughed.

'Patrick, what did we talk about showing off?'

'Being able to read is NOT SHOWING OFF!'

And he opened his backpack and pulled out a large paperback.

'What *is* he reading?' asked Carmen.

'Uh, *Teach Your Child to Read*,' said Ramsay.

There was a momentary silence.

'Aye, gies the story,' said Hari, just as the gaggle of children for story time started to arrive after school.

To her amazement, given not just the short notice but also the debacle which had happened last time, she had another good crowd of children. The girls were neat and tidy in their little kilts; the boys were wearing shorts even in the freezing cold, their bright red and blue socks – depending on their schools – lagging at half-mast.

'Is this story going to be frightening?' said Phoebe straight off the bat as they arranged themselves at the front.

'Sssh!' said another child.

'No, I CAN talk actually: that's MY AUNT.'

Carmen found herself overwhelmingly proud and happy at this.

'Hello, children,' she said. She glanced around, noticing a few familiar faces. There were actually more than there had been before.

'I, like, totally cried SO MUCH,' one girl of about eight was solemnly telling her friend. 'It was AMAZING.'

Carmen had briefly glanced at the sheaf of papers she'd printed out at home from Blair's email when Skylar sidled in, holding up her phone.

'I'm just going to video it?' she said. 'I was going to livestream it, but he's busy with meetings all day?'

Carmen froze inside. She realised now that this was exactly why she hadn't mentioned it. Because he wasn't asking her because she was special or because he couldn't wait to see her. He was asking because he knew she'd do it, and he knew Skylar would do it too.

And she felt absurd, and tiny and incredibly foolish, and as if Sofia would never do anything like this, and the world's biggest idiot.

'So, hi?' Skylar was talking into her own phone in front of all the children. 'This is, like, the most exciting thing ever? We're going to get a sneak preview of the *very first ever* children's book by Blair Pfenning? It's like a world exclusive? It's not even going to be out for a whole year! I know, like, *aahhh*, OMG, right!'

Carmen looked up in confusion.

'Okay, off you go!' said Skylar, still training the camera on herself, with Carmen just visible behind her. 'This is going to be so amazing, guys.'

Frowning slightly, nervous and wishing she'd done more than give the book a cursory glance, Carmen opened the first page.

'Now. *This is a story about a bear who learns to love himself. At Christmas. And his name was Jimmy, the Sad Christmas Bear.*'

The children eyed her suspiciously.

'Why do bears have to love themselves?' piped up a small voice. It turned out to be Ramsay's boy Patrick, even though he was ostentatiously not sitting with the others, and poring over a book about the history of Hornby with Mr McCredie. He frowned.

'They don't need to love anything! They just need to take in enough calories to last the winter.'

Carmen cleared her throat.

'*He was often unhappy and he didn't know why.*'

'Was it because he was a bear?'

'I'd love to be a bear,' said another small voice. 'GGGRRRRRR.'

'*Some days just felt low and grey, not sunny and blue.*'

'Bears can't see colour!'

Carmen looked at Ramsay, who held up his hands.

'Patrick, I need some help in the stockroom,' Ramsay said.

Patrick carefully clambered down from the stool he was on, which was rather too high for him.

'I'll need Hari to come too.'

But Hari, who'd been read to since he was little, wasn't going anywhere, so Patrick marched off behind Ramsay, complaining loudly as Carmen attempted to get back to the story:

'Please tell me, Mr Fox, why I am so sad?'
'It is because you need a friend! Like me, the Fox!'
And the Bear and the Fox held hands and went into the woods.

Carmen frowned.

'Then they met Mr Snake,' she continued.

'Is this *The Gruffalo*?' came a voice.

'Ooh, is there a gruffalo?' came several interested voices.

'Why am I so sad, Mr Snake?'
Mr Snake uncurled his body.
'Because you should do some breathing and yoga.'

There was a lot of confusion about this meeting between a bear, a fox and a snake and who would eat who first.

'So they all did some breathing and yoga,' read Carmen.

'Snakes are *very* good at yoga,' nodded Skylar.

'CHOMP!' shouted the children.

'I have MUNCHED YOU UP, PESKY SNAKE!' said one.

'NO, YOU HAVE NOT, BEAR: I WILL KILL YOU WITH MY LIGHT SABRE!'

'Okay, guys, settle down. *And then Mr Bear, Mr Fox and Mr Snake met Mr Frog.'*

'Why are all these animals boys?' Phoebe wanted to know.

'That's a very good question,' agreed Carmen, to a disapproving sniff from Skylar, who was still taping.

> '*Now we will all think about the beautiful woods and the beautiful sky and the beautiful rivers full of fish,*' *said the frog.*
> '*And we will not be unhappy any more.*'

'Because they eat all the fish?'

'Sssh,' said a parent.

'*And they thought about the beautiful woods and the beautiful sky and the beautiful rivers and how they were all friends and then they had a big Christmas party and lived happily ever after with the most important gift of all – loving themselves,*' Carmen concluded.

A ring of faces stared back at her.

'All the animals love each other?'

'Yes. Well. I think they're friends. And they love themselves.'

'And he doesn't get any real presents?'

'But he gets the gift of love,' said Carmen.

There was quite a lot of arm-folding going on down on the floor.

'And bears have no concept of co-operation with other species!' came a distant voice from behind the stacks.

'Well, wasn't that was just *wonderful,*' said Skylar, beaming into the camera. She turned it on the children, managing not to get Carmen in shot at all. 'Wasn't that lovely? Amazing new story by Blair: *Jimmy the Sad Christmas Bear.* Let's have a round of applause.'

There was a muted round of applause from the children, not replicated by the mothers who had secretly hoped Blair would be there.

'Excuse me, bookshop lady?' came a small voice. It was a

little girl with the long pigtails who'd been there before. 'I think I liked better the one where there was a little girl? And she died? And that was the end of the story.'

'But it was sad about the bear? And then he played with the other animals and they were all friends?' Skylar interjected.

'Meh,' said the girl. 'We have a lot of those stories at school.'

'Was it actually about anti-bullying?' said another one. 'All the stories are normally.'

'AND KINDNESS,' added a third.

'Well, kindness is good, isn't it?' said Carmen.

'Sometimes,' said Phoebe. 'People say "be kind" when they just mean "shut up".'

The other girls nodded vehemently.

'Well, okay,' said Carmen. 'Thanks for coming.'

'See you next week!' they all said cheerily, putting on their mittens, leaving Carmen slightly wrong-footed that this was apparently now part of their social calendars.

'So Zoe's coming down tomorrow, bringing the teens for a bit of Edinburgh's Christmas,' Ramsay was saying to Mr McCredie. Carmen made a face.

'Don't you start,' said Ramsay. 'Do you think we could possibly just leave them to it?'

'There's a lot of screaming and some vomit,' said Carmen.

'Well, perfect: teens love that,' said Ramsay. 'Anyway, we were wondering: are you doing a Christmas party?'

There was a silence. Carmen looked at Mr McCredie, who looked perturbed.

'Why not?' said Carmen. 'Think how many ...'

'... people in the shop, yes, yes,' said Mr McCredie. 'She has changed me, Ramsay.'

'I think she has too,' said Ramsay, his eyes twinkling.

'Well ... I suppose we could,' said Mr McCredie. 'Gosh. Well. Yes. We'd better. I have some burgundy down in the cellar that we could probably crack, seeing as we're on course to make profit for the first time in ... ahem ... some years.'

Ramsay grinned.

'You have a *cellar*?' said Carmen in disbelief. 'How? This building makes no sense.'

She glanced out of the window and saw that Bronagh was passing, her bright red hair piled high on her head, wearing a cloak and carrying a large archway of hawthorn.

'Bronagh,' said Carmen, slipping outside. 'If I said we're having a party, like, tomorrow would you be able to witch it round everyone who needs invited?'

'Of course,' said Bronagh. 'Although sometimes what you need and what you want aren't—'

'Great, thank you, that is so kind of you.'

Carmen still felt a little sad and foolish, imagining that Blair, a man she didn't even like, would like her. And the man she did like liked somebody else. It was particularly hard as she couldn't go somewhere quiet and just sulk about it. The shop was busy, Ramsay and Mr McCredie having decided to just try a soupçon of the burgundy to see how it went down, the streets were mobbed, and of course 'home' was Sofia's house, where Skylar was, uploading video to her boyfriend, Blair. Carmen's phone hadn't buzzed all afternoon. She was miserable. And stupid.

She marched home, where Sofia was chatting to Federico over the phone. Everything, as usual, was clean and tidy and warm and perfect, and it put Carmen in a worse mood than ever. The children had dispersed.

'Hey,' said Sofia, after she had finished her conversation with Federico. 'Don't make me get up off the sofa. How was Blair's book—?'

Carmen dissolved into tears.

'Oh God, that bad?' said Sofia, struggling to sit up. Carmen explained everything.

'Oh God,' said Sofia. 'So hang on – you don't even like Blair and it sounds like he's been a total a-hole, so why do you care if Skylar's dating him?'

Carmen shrugged. 'Because I ...' She sniffed and looked around at the gorgeous kitchen. 'I just wanted something cool. Something ... impressive. I mean, you have everything and I just ...'

'What, you would date an a-hole because I have a nice kitchen?'

Carmen shrugged.

'It's everyone. Skylar's getting some stupid degree in fricking water. You're super-successful. Idra's going skiing!'

Sofia didn't quite understand the significance of this last piece of information, but wisely kept mouth closed.

'I thought maybe a cool rich boyfriend ... would make me feel I was going places. Instead of stuck. In my sister's base-ment. In a temp job.'

Sofia bristled a bit. Then she made a terrible mistake. She was trying to explain why Blair would have been a bad match

269

for Carmen, and then her plan was to follow that up with how brilliantly she'd done in the shop and how it looked like they'd be able to put the business on the market in the new year, provide a nice retirement for Mr McCredie and how that was amazing, and she'd have loads for her CV now.

Unfortunately, she never got that far.

'Oh, let Skylar have that stupid Blair,' she began. 'She's much more . . .'

She regretted it instantly.

'Much more what?' said Carmen furiously, standing up. 'Pretty? Better than me?'

'*No!* That's not what I meant at all. Just that stupid blonde look, you know.'

'You just meant she's better-looking than me?'

'Oh Carmen! How can I get out of this conversation?'

'By saying the truth: you never believed for a second that someone good-looking and famous could possibly like me in a million years.' Carmen was so upset. 'You just assume I would try and take him off Skylar; never that she would try and take him off me, even though that was totally what she did.'

Sofia squeezed her eyes shut.

'I don't like her,' went on Carmen. 'She's mean.'

'She's not mean! She's very . . . useful. She's good for me. She's good for the children. Gives them good ways of living their lives.'

'Instead of what I do, you mean?'

Sofia lost her rag, which she did very rarely. Carmen was stunned into silence.

'That's not what I said! God, Carmen. You insist on taking every single phrase out of my mouth and wringing it for the *worst possible* angle. You're like judge, jury and executioner of me. And Mum. It's like we can never say a single word that isn't secretly dissing Carmen because that's literally all we have on our minds, every hour of the day and night. Carmen Carmen Carmen. Everyone be careful. Don't upset Carmen because she doesn't have a job! Don't upset Carmen because she doesn't have a boyfriend! I *swear* Mum didn't want me to have another baby because you don't have one yet.'

'She would never say that.'

'She basically implied it.'

'Well, how come? How come you get *everything*?' said Carmen, stung.

'What don't you have?' said Sofia. 'You're young, you're fun, everyone likes hanging out with you. You're creative – look what you've done in the shop. You've got famous guys chatting to you, you've got some lanky student hanging around. And yet you act like the world is so unfair just because you couldn't be arsed to pass any exams at school and frankly it gets *very boring*, okay? Here's the answer. I work my arse off. Federico works his arse off. I am exhausted *all the time*. I need Skylar, despite you being jealous of her, because she also works her arse off being a student and a nanny and frankly I need that for the children so they don't end up ... '

Her voice trailed off. Sofia never lost it. She bottled it up, she worked it out, she kept calm, she was professional, she was appropriate.

Carmen stared at her.

'... so they don't end up like me,' she croaked, her breath gone.

'No. That's not what I was going to say.'

'Yes, it was,' said Carmen. 'Yes, it was.'

Sofia stared at her.

271

'Well, you've got it out now,' said Carmen. 'So. Good to know, I suppose.'

'That's not what I meant *at all*!' shouted Sofia, but Carmen had already turned and slammed out of the beautifully painted, decorated old door, and without even saying goodbye to the children.

Chapter Thirty

The night was utterly freezing, and Carmen didn't have the faintest clue where to go. The air was cold; the streets were full. She couldn't believe that only twenty-four hours ago she had been so happy and full of excitement, playing with the children at the fair, then listening to that heavenly music. Now ... oh God. She could only imagine Sofia being on the phone to their mother immediately, getting her side of the story in, the pair of them agreeing with each other, saying, oh well, wasn't Carmen just like that. Oh God and then Skylar would get back and they could sit up gossiping – how did Sofia even know about Oke anyway? If it wasn't for Skylar yammering on all the time ...

Her fury kept her warm all the way up the street and into the Grassmarket. The bars and restaurants were overflowing, flooded with people laughing, hugging, pulling off coats, revelling in the Christmas spirit on this starry night, happy and full of goodwill towards men. Well, she bloody wasn't. God.

There was a light still on in the bookshop. Frankly, she

had no idea where to go. She knew Sofia would be anxious to smooth everything over if she went back and that made her angrier than she could say. She marched up Victoria Street and, sure enough, Ramsay and Mr McCredie were indeed killing what looked like their second bottle of burgundy, while the boys pored over a huge illustrated atlas, eating fish and chips and almost certainly getting greasy fingerprints on an expensive piece of stock, but for a moment Carmen was just relieved to see some people she wasn't related to.

'Hey,' she said. 'Have you got another glass for that wine?'

'Problems at home?' said Ramsay. 'Because let me tell you, nobody is more qualified to discuss domestic issues than the two of us.'

There was a pause, then both men burst out into hearty laughter.

In fact, there was massive comfort in being with the pair of them, Carmen found. Mr McCredie told stories of Antarctic derring-do, and how best to play croquet with an Adélie penguin; Ramsay spoke about how all the money AirBnB-ing one of the wings of the house had brought in had been spent on pyjamas to stop the children tearing around the house wearing more or less nothing. A couple of glasses of wine down, Carmen discovered that she was feeling much more relaxed even though her phone kept pinging every couple of seconds. She focused on utterly ignoring it.

'So, what's up with you?' asked Ramsay eventually. 'Are all men bastards?'

'The jury,' said Carmen heavily, 'is *out*.'

'Remember,' said Ramsay, who had some form in this area, 'men are *rubbish*. They are *rubbish* at going after women they like.'

'I agree,' said Mr McCredie, who had absolutely no form in this area.

'I know, but he thinks . . . '

'He doesn't know what he thinks,' said Ramsay confidently. 'Even if you think you have made things *very clear* to him, you could make them more clear.'

'It's not that . . . dreadful popinjay, is it?' said Mr McCredie, who didn't speak a lot, but saw everything. 'The charlatan writer.'

'No. Kind of. Well. It was for a bit but . . . no. Definitely not,' said Carmen. 'He's a dendrologist . . . that means—'

'Tree chap,' said Ramsay and Mr McCredie at once.

'Oh my God, you are *such nerds*,' said Carmen, laughing for the first time.

'The tall boy!' said Mr McCredie. 'Oh yes. Absolutely. I quite approve.'

Carmen smiled. 'Well, that's something, I suppose.'

'Is he an academic?' frowned Ramsay. 'I'm just saying. It would be nice for *someone* round here to have some money.'

'I know, I know.'

'But you like him?'

Carmen nodded. 'But he's seeing someone else. And he thinks I'm seeing someone else. It's just a stupid mess.'

Ramsay shook his head.

'Oh, you never know. One thing about dendrologists: very, very patient.'

Carmen smiled.

'It that true?'

Her phone rang for the ninth time in a row. Sofia. She pressed it reluctantly.

'Yes?'

All she could hear was slightly damp breathing down the line. Then, finally:

' . . . Auntie Carmen?'

'Phoebe? Is that you?'

'Mummy lent me her phone.'

Carmen was annoyed at Sofia's obvious emotional manipulation. On the other hand, she couldn't deny its efficacy.

'Uh-huh.'

'Are you coming home soon? I want you to say goodnight to me. And tell me a story. Not the one about the bear and the snake though. That one is rubbish.'

'It *is* rubbish,' said Carmen. 'It *sucks.*'

'IT SUCKS.'

'Okay, don't say that too loud.'

She sighed.

'Yes, I will be home.'

'It's very hard to storm out properly when there are children,' she said, hanging up the phone.

Ramsay smiled.

'It's very hard to do anything when there are children,' he said. 'You sound like a good aunt though.'

'Yeah, yeah,' said Carmen, getting up. 'Well. At least there's that.'

She didn't speak to Sofia when she got in, just went and saw the children in their rooms. Pippa was looking disapproving.

'You made Mummy sad,' she said.

Carmen screwed up her face.

'I know,' she said. 'Sometimes sisters fall out.'

Pippa nodded sadly.

'You got cross like Phoebe does.'

Carmen bit her lip.

'Well, I'm sure we'll get over it.'

'You should probably say sorry,' said Pippa.

'Everyone should,' said Carmen, beating a hasty retreat.

She popped in to see Phoebe.

'Pippa says I should say sorry,' she whispered.

'I NEVER SAY SORRY,' came the figure under the blankets. Carmen smiled for the first time that evening. Then:

'I'm glad you came back. Are you going to stay with us for ever?'

Carmen blinked, kissed her, but could not answer.

Sofia was waiting in the hallway, feeling awful, but Carmen kept her distance unhappily.

'I finish at Mr McCredie's after Christmas,' she said shortly. 'Mum says they're opening up a new bunch of cafés and stuff in the old buildings. Farmers' markets, that kind of thing. I'll go try my luck there.'

Sofia nodded numbly.

'I ... Okay,' she said. 'But you know I didn't mean it.'

'No, I know you did,' said Carmen. 'And that's far, far worse.'

Chapter Thirty-one

Carmen threw herself into work the following Monday, both with the huge line of customers, and getting things ready for the party. Mr McCredie did not appear until late morning but proved rather good at getting glasses and wine out and inviting customers willy-nilly. Carmen was surprised at him.

'What are you doing?' he said when he saw her still wrapping for people in the middle of the day. 'I thought you took that thing called a "lunch break" these days.'

'We're busy!' said Carmen. 'I have a lot on!'

'Well, I was going to ask you if you wanted to come with me.'

'Where?'

'There's a lunchtime lecture series I thought you might like. Mrs Marsh told me all about it. Ramsay said he'd mind the shop.'

Carmen eyed him carefully.

'Is it about the Antarctic?'

He shook his head.

'It's about the Ormiston Yew.'

'The what?'

'. . . a very famous tree.'

'Oh. Oh no. No.'

'I'm your boss,' said Mr McCredie.

'Oh my God, you *have* been speaking to Mrs Marsh.'

'She's formidable,' he said.

'You say that like it's a good thing!'

'Come come, you've been working too hard. You need a break.'

And he swept her out, completely surprised.

Slightly overawed and out of breath from marching down the bridges to George Square, Carmen approached the lecture theatre behind a briskly walking Mr McCredie. This was the very heart of the university, full of students marching past, confidently shouting out to one another, popping in and out of buildings.

She slipped towards the lecture theatre, expecting them at any moment to be stopped or challenged, but nobody even glanced at them.

The room was completely full. She scooched up next to a girl who didn't look best pleased to have Carmen obscuring her view. When she looked up, she realised that everyone else had laptops and iPads open, or notepads. A big sign on the board said 'THE ORMISTON YEW' and a slide of a tree that looked the size of a small town. Oke was in the middle of talking, gesticulating at the slide.

'So, here it is, the Ormiston Yew ...

'This layering yew was old when Mary Queen of Scots was born, mentioned in the earl's documents as providing shelter in 1473, when the yew was already old.

'Beneath this tree George Wishart and John Knox preached, beginning the reformation that swept this land, that led to the university itself as a seat of learning.

'There is a reason its exact location is kept quiet – and once again I apologise for not taking you on a field trip ...' There was a ripple of laughter. '... but if you take the 131 one of these days, stop before the humpbacked bridge, double back, cross the bypass and find the lane that says "private" on it ... follow that for long enough, take the left fork ... well.' He smiled.

'Is it there?' asked a voice.

'I couldn't possibly comment,' said Oke, smiling again. The huge yew tree in the picture looked like a forest above his head. Surely it wasn't just one tree? Carmen thought, looking up.

And then she looked back at him, at the lectern, standing tall, not bouncing for once, but steady in front of his audience, in control, completely engaged. He seemed a completely different proposition from the jaunty boy in the scruffy clothes.

He went on to talk about the yew in art, as a symbol – Carmen didn't understand everything, but he made so much clear, speaking about its use in archery; the myth that Pontius Pilate was born under one; how they were the most common tree found in churchyards, and that in fact people would have gathered there to celebrate druidic ceremonies. Churches were built on the site of yews, not the other way around. She thought of Bronagh and smiled. She would like this. Then she realised, glancing around, that Bronagh was there. The woman waved heartily across the crowded room and Carmen couldn't help smiling a little.

'Could you make a dendrogram?' someone was asking from the back.

'Well, that's a little reductive,' said Oke, still smiling. 'There's no need for an indicative diagram when the yew itself can show us in real time everything she needs to tell us . . .'

And he clicked onto a very confusing slide which Carmen didn't have the faintest hope of understanding.

But it was his clear desire to explain, to let the light in to what he was doing which was striking; he took the students seriously but explained patiently.

Mr McCredie was watching her carefully, wondering if she'd spotted it. That Blair – dazzling, silly Blair – was a child, and that Oke, who dressed like a teenager, was in fact a man. He did not speak much, Mr McCredie, but he didn't miss much either, and he had grown very fond of his charge, as he rather thought of her. He didn't want her head turned by nonsense, and he thought a lot of the serious, clever Oke.

Carmen had a miserable certainty that she had missed her chance. Blair, for all his fine clothes with his petulant selfishness, was a child. Was absolutely a child, sitting there, performing platitudes for adoring people listening to him, laughing at his lack of belief in it, revelling in his own cynicism.

Whereas this – whatever a dendrogram was – *this* was real. This existed in the world; was tough, difficult work to under-stand. She had been topsy-turvy this entire time. She had let herself get completely carried away by Blair's superficial glitter, even as she'd told herself she hadn't.

She thought again of his hands closing over her eyes in the

mirror maze, and the jump for breath, the sudden rippling excitement.

The lecture had finished, she noticed, while she had been lost in another world, still staring at him, as the disgruntled woman to her right was trying to get past her.

'Excuse me?' she said quite abruptly, and Carmen stood, ready to go – amazed at herself – but ready to go and find Oke, find him and tell him that ... well, that it had taken him talking about some stupid yew tree to make her realise – she really liked him. And nobody else, even if he was seeing someone.

She glanced at her watch as Mr McCredie walked out ahead of her.

Oke was surrounded by students jostling for his attention and was dealing calmly and patiently with each one, listening and taking them seriously.

He wasn't grinning with big white teeth, flattering people with empty promises to get them to do what he wanted. She flashed back again to his hand on her face; the feel of him in the narrow staircases. Oh goodness.

Just as she stepped out, he suddenly looked up and caught her eye over the heads of the students clustering around him. He stopped talking, startled, and just stared at her.

In the next second, Bronagh had grabbed his arm.

'You're coming to the party later?' she said to him, loud enough for Carmen to hear. 'In the bookshop?'

He looked puzzled, then nodded. Bronagh gave Carmen a big thumbs up, and Carmen had the sudden unsettling feeling that the whole of Victoria Street was somehow in on some conspiracy.

Then, as another student approached him, she glanced at her watch and fled.

Carmen spent the rest of the day completely flustered. She had brought her one and only party dress with her, and she carefully lined her eyes and put on lipstick in the pink floral bathroom on Mr McCredie's first floor. There was an ancient glass jar full of cotton wool balls. It made her sad to wonder how old they were. Anyway. It didn't matter, she told herself fiercely. Oke was with Dahlia. He'd probably bring her. She couldn't think about it.

Ramsay had the boys with him again, and a very pretty woman called Zoe who was shorter than him by about a foot and a half. They looked biologically unlikely, but she was carrying a very long baby in a sling. The baby's legs in cosy dungarees came down to her knees.

'Hi, I'm Zoe,' she introduced herself. 'I run a bookshop up in the Highlands. Well, I say "shop" … it's more of a van. Wow, isn't this place just lovely? And so *warm*! I *love* it!' She smiled. 'Keeping a van warm in the Highlands in the wintertime is quite the challenge.'

'It's lovely to meet you,' said Carmen. 'I like your boys.'

'Yes, we brought the teenagers here too but they're too excited to be off to the Christmas fair.'

'I heard – hope you gave them each about a hundred quid.'

'Don't start me,' said Zoe, tickling the baby's gigantic feet.

'I like your huge baby,' said Carmen.

'Thank you,' Zoe grinned. 'Except we called him Hugh. And he *is* huge. So that was patently a terrible mistake; I should have thought it through. Maybe we'll have a really tiny girl next.'

'You can call her Tina,' said Carmen encouragingly.

Patrick was crouched down, studying the train set in consternation.

'Mr McCredie.' He marched up to where the old man, wearing a smart bow tie for the occasion, was setting out beautiful crystal glasses that were giving Carmen conniptions in case somebody broke one. 'I need to talk to you about the third carriage from the back. It's jumping.'

Mr McCredie wiped his glasses.

'Well, it's old, Patrick. Old things don't always work so well.'

'No,' said Patrick. 'It's absolutely not working properly. I need to pick it up.'

'Patrick, don't touch the train set,' warned Ramsay, trying to hold back Hari, who was ready to pick up anything if Patrick wanted it.

Carmen looked over to see what was happening. The little boy was pointing at a carriage that suddenly looked oddly familiar to her. She blinked.

'She wants me to,' said Patrick. 'Carmen knows.'

Carmen froze suddenly and turned around.

'Who wants you to, Patrick?' she said.

'Oh, you know,' said Patrick carelessly.

'Which carriage exactly?' she found herself asking, her brain twisting.

It couldn't possibly be. She was tired and confused and very, very nervous.

'That one.'

It had been there all along. Right before her. No. This wasn't possible.

Mr McCredie bent carefully over the track with Patrick.

'What do you mean?' he said.

'Watch that carriage. It isn't running properly.'

Carmen had her heart in her throat. Turning away from Zoe, she came closer to the track and knelt down as it rattled on its way. Along with Patrick and Mr McCredie, she followed the little carriage with the moulded plastic figures inside – why had it never occurred to her before? Why not? Because it seemed so obvious now: that of course the train in her dream was the train in the shop.

And the carriage – now passing by the little station – had three little figures in it: two men and a woman in an old-fashioned hat. It was the same woman.

'It's that one,' Patrick said. 'Watch it as it gets to the tunnel.'

And as it rattled towards the little mountain tunnel, Carmen found her heart beating dangerously fast, and that she was holding her breath. The woman – her mouth opening – desperately trying to tell her something . . . it wasn't possible.

Just before the little train entered the tunnel, they all saw it. The carriage made a little jump, nearly coming off its tracks, recovering just in time as it disappeared, then trundled out the other side.

'It's mis . . . misa . . . misalingilated,' said Patrick.

'Do you mean misaligned?' said Mr McCredie.

'I do exactly mean that,' said Patrick.

Neither of them was paying any attention to Carmen, who was still staring at the little carriage in fear.

Mr McCredie shut the train set off from running, and very, very carefully picked the carriage up, unbolting it from the other carriages.

'There's something weighing it down,' he said. 'It's dragging everything else off.'

He looked underneath the wheels, but couldn't see anything. Then he pushed up his spectacles.

'I think there is something in here,' he said. 'Between the wheel arch and the carriage floor.'

'May I see?' said Patrick. 'I have very small fingers which are really very useful.'

Mr McCredie passed the carriage over to Patrick but he didn't have much more luck. Whatever it was, it was just out of reach.

'Hang on,' said Carmen suddenly. She rummaged in her big handbag and for once came up trumps with a stray set of tweezers. 'Let me see.'

They handed it over, somewhat dubiously, as she carefully pulled something out that was tucked just behind the wheel arch.

It was a very old, faded photograph, soft around the edges, black and white, folded up.

Mr McCredie started suddenly and gripped the side of the desk.

'Are you all right?' said Carmen.

'I think ... ' he said weakly. 'I think I'd better go and sit down ... '

Carmen – and Patrick – followed him through the stacks to his little fireplace.

'Ooh, I like this very much!' said Patrick approvingly.

'Patrick,' said Carmen. 'I wouldn't normally ask you but could you go back and see your mum and dad for a minute?'

Patrick opened his mouth to say a lot of very important things he needed to tell Carmen about his mum and dad, but when he saw the look on her face, he promptly shut it again and went off without a word. Carmen had grabbed a glass of wine as she went and handed it to the old man, who sat heavily in his chair, and then slowly, and with trembling hands, unfolded the little photograph.

Back out front, the party was heating up nicely. Ramsay had taken over pouring drinks for everyone – his arms were so long it was useful to pass things over people's heads – and Zoe, unable to stop herself from her normal day job, was more or less just selling books if people wanted them, and Bronagh was there with her group of gorgeously attired mystical friends. The man who sold his fish books was there, as were the ladies from the Drunken Book Group. The hardware manager had brought them a new shovel; the man from the clothing shop was wearing an extremely daring pair of red trousers and a dashing cravat. The mums from the story readings were all there, enjoying the wine and planning on making very speedy in-law-based gift choices at some point. There were some cheerful backpackers who had wandered in and were frankly astonished in this expensive city that someone was giving them a free anything; Mrs Marsh could be seen up and down the shop running her finger along shelves out of habit; Mrs McGeoghan was curled up in her usual corner, carrying on with *Our Mutual Friend* perfectly happily – only 370 more pages to go, so she would likely be done by Eastertime – and there was a contingent of traffic wardens Carmen had invited on the pretext of being charitable at Christmastime (and distracting them while everyone parked). The carol singers were also back, having been well primed for the Victoria Street parties and doing very well.

And Skylar and Blair.

Skylar had been looking forward to this all day – showing up once and for all with the hot man of the moment on her arm before she took off to London (hopefully) for the Christmas break where she hoped he would take her to lots of places which might want her to set up a mindfulness class for people; rich connected people were always looking for more yoga. And of course he was terribly handsome and charming. That was very important. They didn't really talk much about things Skylar liked to talk about, which was mostly Skylar, but surely he'd realise how fascinating she was in time and how many men wanted to be with her and come round to worshipping her like they did.

She looked absolutely her loveliest, all in soft pinks with the most adorable pompom hat – fake fur *obviously* – on her blonde curls, her cheeks lightly pink from the cold snow, and Blair had given her the most blazing smile when she'd arrived promptly to pick him up from the airport.

'Hey, babe,' he'd said. 'Right, let's go dazzle them, yeah? You look great. Totally.'

Skylar had arranged her face in an empathic look as the doorbell tinged and they entered the shop. And undeniably, with Blair being there, his celebrity was like throwing glitter over the crowd. Everyone was pleased to see him and started smiling; the noise level in the room went up with a jolly frisson; the large group of mums started sidling towards him, brandishing books they wanted signed, and he put on his toothy grin and started being charming for everyone. Skylar joined in.

'Where's Carmen?' he said out of the corner of his mouth. 'Where is she?'

Skylar shrugged.

'Probably scrubbing out some extra toy mice for the windows,' she said. '*Bless.*'

Blair was still looking around, not listening.

'She should really read *Live the Life You Love*,' said Skylar. 'There's an exercise in, like, Chapter Fourteen ...'

'She's fine how she is,' growled Blair. He grabbed a glass of wine off a tray – didn't hand one to Skylar – and then turned round full beam to an excited flushed-looking woman who had decided to buy six of his books for all her relatives (after the television broadcast had gone out, they had such a steady stream of customers he practically had his own corner), and took out the Sharpie he carried in his jacket pocket. Skylar stood by him proudly as he signed, keeping a hand on his jacketed elbow, and giving the woman a very quick burst of side-eye when she asked for a selfie. Just in case.

Carmen was very concerned, partly because she couldn't quite square what the odd little boy had said about her own dreams – surely it was just a coincidence. Because she was in the shop all day, looking at the train. Of course it had got into her subconscious.

But of course mostly because Mr McCredie was sitting by the fireside, photo in his shaking hand, eyes wet.

'What is it?' said Carmen. 'Please. Please tell me.'

Without answering, he simply handed over the photo.

Carmen stared at it for a long time. It was soft, creased with age, a small photo, about two-by-one inches, a black and white head and shoulders of a young man, fair and square-jawed, his hair Brylcreemed back in an old-fashioned style.

Carmen looked at the picture, then looked at Mr McCredie – his light hair and pointed chin. She looked at the picture again, then turned it over.

In faded blue fountain pen was written just one word –
Erich – and the date, 1944.

Carmen looked back at Mr McCredie.

'Do you know when I was born?' he said.

She shook her head.

'1945.'

'This is your dad?'

He tilted his head, and suddenly the nose and the profile
were unmistakable.

'So the Arctic explorers . . . ?'

He shook his head.

'Old Mr McCredie raised me.'

Carmen blinked.

'Is that what you call your dad?'

'Well, he was there. He loved my mother. They didn't have
any other children. I think . . . I think they probably couldn't.
He . . . maybe couldn't.'

'But who was Erich?'

'Have you heard of Cultybraggan?'

Carmen shook her head.

'It was the wartime internment camp. In Perthshire. Comrie.
Where my mother's from.'

Carmen thought of the beautiful, sophisticated woman in the
photographs from a few weeks ago.

'She volunteered nursing services during the war . . . ' He
shrugged. 'I suppose . . . it's hardly fair to think your mother
has to be a saint . . . '

'So, hang on . . . '

'I don't know anything about him,' said Mr McCredie stiffly.
'Except he was a German. My dad was a German POW.'

Carmen's heart overflowed with pity.

'And you knew?'

'Oh, my relatives had a lot to say about it. The McCredie side were quite a loud and vocal people.'

'From when you were small?'

'There were always whispers. The boys at school got hold of it. Christ.'

'My God,' said Carmen. 'That's ... that's ...'

'It was a boarding school.'

'In Edinburgh?'

'Yes.'

'Your parents, who lived in Edinburgh, sent you to boarding school in Edinburgh?'

'I think ... I think there was a limit as to how long my father could have me around. I didn't get a lot less blond.'

Carmen leaned over and patted him on the sleeve.

'Oh God, that must have been so hard.'

He nodded.

'Why didn't you ... why didn't you move? Get away?'

'To do what? Stupid useless bloody son of a ...'

He couldn't even say it.

'My mother never got over it. The shame. Everyone knew. Everyone. Bad blood. That's what they said.'

Carmen remembered Bronagh mentioning it. Goodness. Everyone did know. This was why. This was why he hid himself away.

'I don't understand: why did you stay in the city?'

'It's still my city. I love it,' said Mr McCredie defiantly. 'My entire family had been stupid bloody explorers. I wasn't going to do that just to impress my father. Who by the way could never have been impressed with anything I ever did.'

'And ... Erich?'

291

He shrugged. 'I don't ... I don't care. I don't even know his surname.'

Suddenly Carmen thought of something.

'I ... You know the people who came in the shop? The German people?'

He looked at her.

'I don't want to see them.'

'But ... they said they have letters. They have something! You have to see it.'

He shrugged.

'I don't care. I don't want to know. This whole thing – it ruined my life. My entire life.'

Carmen thought of the confused little boy, sent off to a cold dorm while his parents were only down the road.

'But they seem so nice ... It was a long time ago, Mr McCredie. Everyone would understand. Things are ... things are so different.'

'Not if he was tossing your grandparents onto trains it isn't.'

'Do you know what he did?'

He shook his head.

'No, but I can have a reasonable belief it was nothing good.'

'I mean these people ... They might be relations.'

He shrugged.

'It can't help me.'

She looked again at the creased photo. He was still holding it.

'Have you seen that picture before?'

He nodded.

'My mother ... my mother kept it in her wallet.'

'Fuck,' said Carmen, unable to help herself.

'Sorley – that was my dad – was a ... he was a difficult man. Very famous family. Used to getting his own way. Thought my

292

mother would be a pretty country girl he could dominate and make lots of breeding stock on.'

He half-smiled.

'He got more than he bargained for there.'

'But they stayed together?'

'Everyone stayed together. That's how it worked.'

'But she kept that picture. Did you find it?'

He smiled.

'I was trying to steal money. For sweets. It was after they got rid of rationing. I was so excited. I wanted to buy so much chocolate . . . but I found that.'

'What did she say?'

'She wanted to talk about it,' he said. 'Oh God. I did not want to hear it.'

'She couldn't have told anyone.'

'She never did. People made up their own stories anyway. Next time I checked her wallet, the picture had gone. And my train set was packed away in the attic.'

Carmen nodded.

'She must have loved him. To risk all that.'

He sighed.

'My mother was just about the most unhappy woman I ever met in my life.'

'But, Mr McCredie,' said Carmen urgently. She could hear the noise of the party, rising higher. 'Look what you have here. You have your beautiful shop. Your lovely house. And out there – there are so many friends. So many people who care about you.'

'That's all you,' said Mr McCredie. 'It's you that's made this shop busy again.'

'Yes, because my dumb sister Sofia – she cared about you so

much she got me up to work for you. And she's only your *lawyer*. People care.'

Mr McCredie wiped his eyes.

'Have a think about meeting the German people?' said Carmen. 'They're here at the Christmas market, at least for another week or so.'

He swallowed hard.

'Time heals a lot of things,' said Carmen.

Mr McCredie didn't say anything.

'And now,' said Carmen, 'I need you to come and say a few words otherwise everyone is going to go and spend all their money at the magic shop again. Bronagh will just put a spell on them.'

Already bored with Blair doing his glad-handing routine with the women getting their books signed – it was nice that they were giving her envious glances, but really it was terribly repetitive and nobody talked to her at all – Skylar turned round, looking at the rest of the party. The bell rang and the tall figure of the lecturer sloped in, wearing a fresh white shirt which was so new it probably still had pins in it. Skylar bounced over to him with her broadest smile.

'Dr Oke!'

He blinked.

'Oh yeah, hi,' he said, faintly recognising her. 'Is Carmen here?'

This was the second time Skylar had heard this tonight and she wasn't thrilled. 'Oh, she should be around somewhere,' she said. 'Now, I really particularly enjoyed the beetle section . . .'

'Thanks,' said Oke, but he was miles away. He met a lot of women, but he didn't give himself away easily. He couldn't; his values wouldn't let him, and he travelled so much, it often was not fair.

But . . . He remembered her running around the fair with the children, laughing her head off, her dark hair flowing in the wind. He hadn't been able to stop thinking about her. Nothing could be less practical, of course. But he had been asked, if he liked, to extend his teaching another term; he was wildly popular with his students.

Skylar eyed him up shrewdly. God, Carmen was just man-crazy, it was pathetic. First flinging herself at Blair – she, on the other hand, understood Blair on a spiritual level, which Carmen was obviously completely incapable of. And now this doctor was looking for her, when Carmen was barely educated and worked in a shop. It was ridiculous. She should do him a favour.

'Yes, poor Carmen,' she said, grabbing back his attention.

'Why, what's wrong with her?'

'Oh,' said Skylar, putting on her most pitying face and letting her rosebud lips turn down regretfully. 'She got a teensy-weensy crush on my boyfriend.' She stroked Blair's arm, who ignored her. 'Well, quite a big crush actually! I can't really blame her. But it's been tough on her. She's just been after him so desperately for ages . . . I think she thinks she is actually going out with him.'

'Really?' said Oke, frowning and confused.

'Oh yes, she's been desperate. He tried to turn her down politely but she wasn't having any of it. *Anyway*.' Skylar made her eyes go wide. 'I really, really hope she's okay.'

Just as she said this, the curtain to the stockroom opened and Carmen emerged with Mr McCredie; she was slightly pushing him forward, and a loud cheer went round the room for him, perhaps brought on by the alcohol and general cheer of a jolly Christmas party, as well as much natural affection for Mr McCredie and some relief that his shop was still standing.

He wasn't expecting it, and went quite pink, Carmen smiling broadly as she looked at him.

Then her attention was caught as, right in front of her, Blair looked up from where he was signing for someone else, met her eye and stuck his tongue straight out at her.

It was so unexpected a gesture that Carmen started and instantly blushed; it was entirely surprising he was here, bigger and cheekier than ever. He kept eye contact.

She didn't even see Oke, who was standing behind Blair and therefore had not seen the face he made; neither did Skylar.

But Oke did see the pink flush in her cheeks, the surprise and, he thought, the happiness when she saw Blair was there. He'd known enough girls get crushes on him in his own sphere to know what they looked like.

And now he was on the other end. The utter, soul-destroying disappointment.

Of course he'd seen them having coffee, but he hadn't . . . I mean, she'd come to Camera Obscura. It hadn't been a date. Not then. But he remembered her face in the church, listening to the music.

Before Carmen had even had a chance to tear her gaze away from Blair and guide Mr McCredie to the front of the shop where he could give a speech, Oke had turned around and quietly exited the shop, already in his head writing the email where he turned down another term's teaching. No. Enough.

He was far from home and had his head turned, that was all. It was snowing again. This country was freezing. He should go home to São Paolo; his family missed him. See his sisters. Take the presents, even. See his nieces and nephews grow. Catalogue his new samples. Work.

There was lots to do. He turned just at the foot of the steps. The bookshop was glowing golden and silver, full of happy people chatting and celebrating the time of year. The lights overhead on the Christmas stars that were hung all the way up the street, as if it wasn't already pretty enough, twinkled and glowed. It was like being inside a Christmas card.

But he did not celebrate Christmas. Quietly and, for Oke, slowly, he loped up the steps, home towards the halls of residence towering high above.

Chapter Thirty-two

'Babe! Tell me you've been misbehaving!'

Blair grabbed Carmen just after Mr McCredie gave a lovely speech where he thanked everyone for their neighbourly support up and down the street, and the biggest round of applause was kept for the new windows and displays – 'all done, of course, by Carmen Hogan' – which made her very happy and blush all at once. She wished suddenly that Sofia could have come, even if her bump would barely fit in the door, then felt angry again when Mr McCredie thanked Sofia too, and she remembered that this entire thing had been Sofia's idea, that she had been right all along. And where was Oke? She couldn't see him anywhere.

Blair had sidled towards her.

'Babe! I am bored out of my mind. Can we shake this hellhole?'

Carmen looked at him.

Even though it had only been a week, he seemed smaller somehow, a little pouting around the mouth.

'Come on – let's just go.'

'It's my party!' said Carmen stiffly. 'I can't go.'

'Sure you can! Let's ditch this joint and go and hang out, just the two of us.'

She frowned at him.

'What about Skylar?'

'What about her?' He shrugged. 'Come on. Let's go and have fun.'

'This is fun.'

Carmen was amazed at herself. For so long, it had been her dearest wish for someone to take her away from all of this, to do some wild and crazy things, to take her away from her life – it had been her dream. All she wanted.

But now, suddenly, all she could do was think of how lovely the bookshop was looking, and worry about Mr McCredie, and wonder where . . . just where was Oke?

She couldn't get his face out of her head, and his take on all the things that she normally accepted day to day, challenging her way of looking at life – he saw everything with fresh eyes. In a way that didn't make him a rube, or unsophisticated, or any of those other things she judged him on because of his shoes. Because he was just himself, at all times. His life was simpler, because he was never trying to be anything – a celebrity, like Blair, or some kind of Instagram yoga bunny like Skylar, or a have-it-all type like Sofia. Or even her, Carmen, just trying to pretend she was getting on all right. When she knew she wasn't.

She blinked, as Skylar spotted her there and dashed up and grabbed Blair possessively by the arm. He barely glanced at her.

'Hi, Carmen,' she said loudly.

'Hello, Skylar,' said Carmen. It was the weirdest thing: seeing

Skylar's face, she suddenly felt a burden lifted. It was fine. It was okay.

'Have you seen Oke?' she asked Skylar politely. Skylar shrugged.

'Oh, no,' she said, casually. 'Why, were you *really hoping* he'd come?'

Carmen looked straight at her.

'Yes,' she said.

She escaped into the quiet street for a breath of fresh air. The party was thinning out. Well. He hadn't come. That was okay. Maybe parties weren't really his thing. But then he'd been at Bronagh's party.

She had missed him. Dahlia wasn't here either: maybe he was out with her. The thought grabbed at her heart with far more force than she had expected.

As if she'd summoned her, she saw Dahlia trudging up the street from the coffee shop.

'Hello!' she said. Dahlia sniffed.

'What's up?' Carmen said. 'Are you going to see Oke?'

The girl turned red again.

'No!' she said. 'He's all yours!'

She looked tearful again.

'What do you mean?'

'I really, really liked him!' said Dahlia, choking. 'But he said he couldn't ever date me. Because ... he's a lecturer. And *he can't date students.*'

She burst into tears again.

Carmen blinked. She couldn't believe it.

'Really?'

'You're not a student, are you?'

Dahlia sniffed again, her nose red. Carmen shook her head.

'For once I'm delighted to say, I'm not,' she said. 'I'm ... I'm sorry.'

Dahlia sniffed.

'Aren't you dating Blair Pfenning?'

'I am not!' said Carmen. Then she smiled suddenly.

'But, you know ... it's the bookshop party.'

'I wasn't going to go. In case Oke was there.'

'He isn't. But I'll tell you who is.'

Dahlia looked up, eyes wide.

'He isn't!'

'He is.'

'Seriously?'

'Don't get mixed up with him!' said Carmen. 'But ... but do enjoy the party.'

Dahlia was already tugging out her braids, her face miraculously transformed as she almost ran up the rest of Victoria Street.

Carmen stood, irresolute, at the bottom of the stairs.

He was only in the student halls. She could just go.

Oh God. Although of course he hadn't turned up to the party ... but ...

Buzzing with nerves, she climbed the steps and walked into Patrick Geddes Hall, the ridiculously high building

301

opposite the steps, a grey stone courtyard next to the National Assembly Hall.

She knocked on the huge ancient studded wooden door and a porter opened it with a serious look.

'Hi! I'm looking for Oke . . . '

No. She couldn't remember his last name. Had he told her? Skylar had mentioned it surely. She hadn't . . . Goddammit. She hadn't put him in her phone; she hadn't googled him; she knew nothing about him. His bloody phone number was written down in the order book, she realised suddenly . . . that she'd got rid of when she'd brought an old laptop of Sofia's in to start transforming the admin.

'Oh *God*,' she said to herself.

'Who?' he said. 'Are you on the list?'

'I wouldn't think so,' said Carmen. 'This is a bit of a spur of the moment . . . It's . . . You'll know him. Tall. Brazilian. Ties his hair up? Bounces. A lot. Quite bouncy. Serious, but bouncy. Gorgeous. I mean. Amazing. I mean, just a brilliant guy.'

The porter was completely unimpressed.

'Can you call him?' he said.

'I don't have his number,' said Carmen through gritted teeth. 'But you must have seen him around.'

'There's four hundred students here, miss.'

Carmen sighed.

'Oke? Oke? Doesn't ring a bell?'

'Is that his first name?'

Carmen realised of course that he'd told her it was a nickname. She didn't even know his real name.

'Oh, never mind,' she said, turning round, her exuberance forgotten. What had she been planning on doing anyway? Throwing herself into his arms?

Maybe.

Stop fretting, she told herself, as she trudged against the snow-turning-to-dirty-old-ice of the courtyard, freezing.

She could see him again. She would. She'd track him down. Skylar would know what his surname was. She could find him again at the university. Oh God, Mrs Marsh could probably do it.

Maybe. And then see. If he was ... if he was interested. Or, if it was entirely possible – and at this she sighed – Oke was one of these people who was interested in everything, who found something to like in everyone.

She went outside and up the hill. The castle forecourt was blazing, lit up with footlights so the huge edifice beamed against the snowy sky, and looked out, tiptoeing like a little girl to see over the wall, to stare out at this city, its Christmas lights glowing, its huge Christmas tree shining, stars and snow and joyous people, even now the scent of someone roasting chestnuts, and sighed. She stayed there for a long time, even as her fingers grew numb and her breath was smoke in the air, thinking about everyone down below, so many people, and someone, somewhere in the teeming crowds, the only face she wanted to see; the only green eyes she wanted to look into ...

Eventually, she slowly descended the steps again, not even turning her head towards the Quaker meeting house where, if she had, she would have seen his bent head making sandwiches for the homeless with all his might, furiously trying to get rid of some of his pent-up energy and disappointment.

Most of the party-goers – including, thankfully, Blair and Skylar – had gone by the time she re-entered the bookshop, and Mr McCredie was counting up the cash box with an aura of disbelief. Carmen started picking up discarded glasses. Ramsay and Zoe passed her on the way out, Ramsay easily carrying a fast asleep six-year-old in each arm, Zoe waggling the sleepy baby's hand at her in farewell.

She cleared up. It had been an amazing, sensational evening for the shop as well as a lovely party. She had one thing to thank Blair for at least.

'How are you doing?' she said to Mr McCredie. She was amazed he'd managed to stay standing the entire night. As she looked closer, she realised he was extremely drunk and could actually barely stand.

'Oh goodness,' she said. In her own drama, she had almost forgotten his.

'Come on, you,' she said, taking him in her arms like a child – he was so frail – and, locking the door, walked him up to the flat, made him drink a pint of water, took off his shoes and his jacket and carefully put him to bed with a couple of aspirin and a fresh pint of water next to him.

'Ssh,' she said, as he muttered something incomprehensible. His hand was screwed tight shut, gripping something. She carefully unfurled his fingers and extracted the picture. She smoothed it out and placed it carefully underneath the Cherry-Garrard book by his bed, to keep it safe for the morning.

Then she slipped out of the tiny alleyway front door, and once more joined the huge wave of Christmas revellers sweeping down to the Grassmarket, dodging in and out among them, anonymous in the crowd, just like anyone else under the cold-starred sky.

Chapter Thirty-three

Carmen was dog-tired as she stopped dead on reaching the front door of the house. It was half-open.

'Um, hello?' she said, poking her head around. The house was quiet, the children in bed. No sign of Skylar. There wouldn't be, thought Carmen. She prodded her heart. No. She was cured.

'Sis? Sofia?'

There came a noise from the kitchen.

'Oh, you *are* joking,' said Carmen. Sofia was sitting slumped over on the floor in a pool of water.

'Don't you start,' said Sofia. 'I've had Federico on the phone all evening.'

'Why didn't you call me?'

'I thought Skylar would come home, then I could just get a taxi to hospital.'

'Why didn't you . . . ?'

'*Please*, Carmen.'

'Okay,' said Carmen. 'I'll get one.'

Sofia sighed.

'Good luck in Christmas week.'

'Well, I'll drive. I've only had one glass.'

Sofia shook her head 'Are you kidding? You driving sober on icy roads is bad enough. No. You're home now; get me a cab. I'll get to hospital. Federico's at the airport.'

'Okay. Have you called Mum?'

'Christ no, I can't handle the entire panic stations.'

The sisters tentatively smiled at one another.

'Okay,' said Carmen. 'Come on, let's get you up.'

But before she had finished the sentence and pulled up Uber, Sofia was bending double.

'Ah, bugger.'

'It's okay though?' said Carmen. 'Babies take ages to come, right?'

'The first one does,' said Sofia. 'Number four just kind of strolls out.'

'Shit,' said Carmen. 'Are you going to make it?'

Sofia pulled herself up, breathing heavily, to collapse in the big chair.

'You know you call me a control freak?'

'I have never called you that,' said Carmen, inputting the info for the route on her phone. 'To your face.'

Sofia did several more panting breaths.

'Well. This is the time when it comes in useful. Get me a cab, then you stay here and babysit.'

'You can't be alone,' said Carmen.

'I can,' said Sofia. 'I promise, it's not a new experience, and it has poo in it. I'll get them to call you when I'm done, okay? Don't worry. I got this.' They were holding hands then, and Sofia suddenly squeezed Carmen's tight. 'Yeah?'

'Yeah,' said Carmen. 'Federico will come straightaway, won't he?'

'Well, if he has a quick trip to a gym and spa I'm going to be very ... ach ...'

She bent over and squeezed Carmen's hand again.

'You're right,' said Carmen. 'This *is* painful.'

'Just. Don't. Wake. The. Children.'

They would have got away with it too, if the cabbie hadn't turned up and immediately honked four times, loud enough to wake the street. Carmen had Sofia's immaculately packed hospital bag and was about to help her sister out to the cab, when there came the familiar banging feet from upstairs.

'Oh no,' said Sofia.

'Oh no,' said the cabbie as they opened the door and he saw what he was picking up.

'Come on,' said Carmen. 'It's a booking for the hospital in the middle of the night – what did you think it was going to be?'

He scratched his head.

'Is she going to have it in the cab?'

'No,' said Carmen, then, quieter to her sister: 'Are you?'

'No!' said Sofia.

'But if she does, we'll pay for the cleaning and you'll be in the papers.'

'Mummy, where are you going?' It was Phoebe's voice.

'Just nipping out,' said Sofia.

'*Just nipping out?*' Carmen said.

'The thing is,' said the cabbie, 'I just got it cleaned and ...'

'Can we come?'

'Mummy's just going to hospital,' said Carmen.

'HOSPITAL?' said Jack.

'Jack!' said Pippa crossly. 'You never listen! It's for the baby.'

'I forgot about the baby,' said Jack. 'Oh. Bye then.'

'I WANT TO COME TOO,' said Phoebe.

'I won't be long. And Carmen will stay.'

'Can we watch a 12 film?'

'You can watch *The Driller Killer*,' said Carmen. 'Let's just get your mum to the ...'

But the cab had already taken off down the icy road without them.

'It was two hours ago,' said Carmen firmly. 'And it was one glass of wine and I didn't finish it.'

'Drinking and driving is very dangerous,' said Pippa disapprovingly.

'Surely this is why you bought that ridiculous Range Rover?' said Carmen. 'A car so oversized and stupid-looking, the only possible reason to buy it would be to keep your sister safe if she ever had to drive you to hospital. It will destroy everything in its path.'

'Oh God. Okay. All right then,' panted Sofia.

'Come on, munchkins. Put your dressing gowns on.'

They looked, Carmen mused, like the children in *Peter Pan* in their old-fashioned nighties and long striped dressing gowns and, excited by the entire experience, were skidding their way to the car, not even fighting about who had to sit in the middle as they usually did.

She helped Sofia into the passenger seat – why, wondered Carmen, had she bought a car that necessitated an escalator to get you up into it? – and belted her in, then skidded round to her side of the car.

She'd only driven her own little Fiat before, which was ten years old and had the heating stuck on full blast all the time. She'd never driven an automatic. She didn't know where the hospital was. She suddenly wasn't sure this was a good idea.

'Press—'

But another contraction came over Sofia and she couldn't finish.

Jack leaned over from the back.

'It's D,' he said. 'D for drive, see?'

Carmen put her foot down on the clutch, then realised there wasn't a clutch.

'No, that's the brake,' said Pippa.

'You're very useful, thank you,' said Carmen, trying to take deep breaths. She could feel herself getting a little panicky. She shut her eyes and thought of calm things.

'Okay,' she said. 'Let's go.'

The huge car rumbled into action. It was like a tank. Fortunately, it had absolutely no concern for the icy roads; it was as if they didn't exist.

'How do I get to the hospital?'

'Just point it downhill,' said Sofia. 'And head for the water. Oh shit, no. They moved it. Bugger. Take the bypass.'

Confused, Carmen spun out into Haymarket and followed the signs out to the ring road.

The bypass was quiet this time of night, or as quiet as it ever got, but they seemed to have to drive for a long, long time, far further than Carmen had suspected in the small city.

Sofia leaned her head against the cool window, tensing, attempting not to make too much noise.

'FINALLY,' Jack was saying. 'A boy in the family. I am going to start him on football straightaway.'

'Well, that's just silly,' Pippa said. 'Babies are small. For AGES.'

'Well, by next Christmas,' Jack said.

'He won't even be able to walk by next Christmas,' said Pippa.

'Seriously?' said Jack. 'That sucks. I mean that's, like, FOR EVER.'

'You'll be too old to want to play football by the time he's old enough.'

'I don't believe that,' said Jack stoutly, and Carmen thought that was probably true.

Phoebe was being uncharacteristically quiet as a large sign came up indicating the turn-off for the hospital. Carmen, hands gripping the wheel, was now terrified of stopping and parking. Fortunately, the maternity unit allowed you to drop off right at the door, and Pippa went and found someone to bring a wheelchair.

'Thanks,' said Sofia weakly then, quietly to Carmen: 'Thank goodness I'll have Pippa for when I kill Federico.'

Carmen smiled. 'When's his plane?'

'He's probably on his second glass of Champagne and watching a movie right over the Russian steppes,' said Sofia as she managed, with some difficulty, to transfer from the car to the wheelchair.

'See you inside!' And with that, Carmen took the children with her to park the car. Out here, beyond the city without its protective heated offices and walls, the cold was much more stark, surprising and fierce. The Pentland hills were right above them, thick with snow. There were marks where people had evidently been skiing. Goodness.

She unbuckled the children, and they jumped out, enjoying their night-time adventure.

'I am going to have a LOT to talk about in news tomorrow,' said Pippa happily. Carmen suspected she generally did.

'I'm not sure there's going to be school tomorrow,' she said, expecting happy cries all round.

'BUT! It's the concert!' said Phoebe, eyes round. 'We have to be there!'

'We do,' said Jack. 'We can't miss it.'

'But the baby might take a while to come ...'

Phoebe and Jack had taken a hand each, not even asking for her permission, just doing it. She felt incredibly privileged, like they had bestowed a gift on her.

'... you might be too tired.'

'No way,' said Jack. 'I've stayed up all night before.'

'You did not,' said Phoebe. 'It was a sleepover at Zack's house and he said he did but he totally didn't.'

'Did!'

'Shut up!'

'Come on,' said Carmen. 'They won't let you in the hospital if you're fighting.'

She hadn't been expecting that to work but as they reached the silent automatic doors, they fell quiet. It did, thought Carmen, have a similar feel to school when you thought about it.

The maternity unit was quiet at that time of night, as if most people had somehow managed to decide not to have their babies at such an inconvenient time of year, and there were certainly no other children there. It struck Carmen forcibly how her extremely organised sister had, for the first time in her life, managed to do something completely disorganised.

The nurse on reception nodded.

'She's gone straight to delivery suite six,' she said. 'We can't let you all in . . . but she shouldn't be by herself.'

'I can watch the others,' said Pippa.

'Hmm. Maybe not,' said the nurse. 'But let me show you the waiting room.'

To the children's absolute delight – it was a very new and shiny hospital – there was a waiting room with children's toys piled up and a television tuned to a cartoon channel. There was also a vending machine selling an array of absolute crap. They looked at Carmen wide-eyed. This was clearly heaven itself.

Carmen looked at them all. Even Pippa seemed to be relaxing her stance as commander-in-chief to examine a pony you could bounce up and down on. She stood at the door. She was agonisingly close to the delivery suites; she could even hear the unpleasant noises.

It was so odd. Every time Sofia had had a baby, she hadn't even thought about it, not really. Just a sense of 'oh God, here we go, now Sofia is going to get all the attention again'.

Then the baby would arrive and once again her parents would go mad for it and the looks at Carmen would start and people would try and make nice remarks about her career and it had built up and built up and driven her mad over the years, made her turn against her own family, through jealousy and defensiveness of her own choices, which often hadn't felt like choices at all.

But now her sister was in one of those rooms, all by herself, in pain, with nobody there to hold her hand.

'Okay, guys,' she said to the children. 'I am nipping across to see your mum for five seconds. Can you all manage to sit here and not get kidnapped or spontaneously stabbed and not stick your fingers in the plug socket?'

The nurse from reception was walking past. She halted.

'Okay,' she said. 'I'm on my break. I'll sit here for a bit.'

'Oh, I can't,' said Carmen. 'Not your break.'

'Yeah yeah yeah. On you go. Five minutes, okay?'

'Okay!' said Carmen. 'Guys. Don't bother the nice nurse, okay?'

'Well, I have some questions,' said Pippa, moving closer to the nice nurse, but Carmen had already disappeared.

The little room was full of monitors and beeping machines. There was nobody else there. Sofia lifted up her head as Carmen entered.

'You're by yourself?' said Carmen.

'They come and check you,' said Sofia. 'They have the machines on centralised—'

But it was no good. She couldn't keep it up. She burst into floods of tears. Carmen was there, and Sofia grabbed her hand once more as another set of contractions racked her.

'It's too late for the epidural,' she sobbed. 'I always have an epidural. That stops you feeling anything.'

'Can't they give you anything else?'

Sofia shook her head.

'I'm too far along. I've never done this before. Not without . . . all the drugs.'

She cried in fear and pain, and Carmen leaned over and hugged her fiercely.

'It's too early!' said Sofia. 'I had *everything planned*! Federico gets extra leave when he finishes this long trip so he could come home at the last minute and . . .'

'You are the fiercest, bravest, most amazing person I know,' she whispered into her sister's ear. 'You are going to kick the arse out of this. And the nurses are going to kick the arse out of Federico so you should probably tell them it was your idea.'

Sofia smiled weakly as a nurse came in to check on her.

'You are just about ready to go,' the nurse said, reading the printout, then, to Carmen's surprise although she knew it really shouldn't have been, sticking her arm up her sister.

'I've never . . . I've never done this without an epidural before. Is it too late for a section?' said Sofia.

'Are you kidding?' said the nurse. 'Squeeze it out now and you'll be home for breakfast. Have us chop you open and you'll be laid up for a fortnight. Also it's Christmas. Are you a hundred per cent certain your late-night surgeon won't have been at the sherry?'

'I am 99.999 per cent legally certain,' said Sofia through gritted teeth.

'Well, up to you.'

'Come on,' said Carmen. 'You can do it.'

'Are those your kids in the waiting room? Are you guys married?'

'Sisters,' said the girls at the same moment, squeezing hands.

'Are they killing each other?' said Carmen. 'I'll be back.'

'But I'm not having this baby without an epidural,' Sofia was saying in a wobbly version of her stern in-court voice. 'I can't. I'm telling you I can't . . . *aaaaargh!*'

Carmen kissed Sofia's sweating face briefly and dived back into the waiting room. Jack was fast asleep in a corner. Pippa was reading a book about reptiles and amphibians and taking notes. Phoebe was curled up on a chair. Carmen thanked the nurse and took over. As she sat next to the little girl, whose hair clumped frowsily all round her face, with the buttons on her nightgown done up wrongly, she saw she was crying.

'Phoebs,' whispered Carmen. 'What's the matter?'

They both shot a glance at Pippa, but she was across the room in front of the television, engrossed in what she was doing.

'The new baby is coming,' said Phoebe.

'It is.'

Carmen took her onto her lap. She was a comfortable weighty feeling, and Carmen cradled her quite naturally. It was nice.

'Everyone is going to love the new baby.'

'They are,' said Carmen. 'But they won't stop loving you.'

'How do you know?'

Carmen thought about it.

'Well,' she said. 'I'm the littlest too. And when I came along, do you think Grandma and Grandpa stopped loving Sofia? Your mum?'

Phoebe considered it.

'No. But . . .'

'But what?'

'But Mummy was nice.'

'You're very nice. I like you very much.'

Phoebe sniffed.

'But . . .' she said. Her voice went very quiet and her face went very red. 'Skylar said I was going to be fat.'

'WHAT?' said Carmen, louder than she'd meant to.

'She said I was going to be fat and ugly and nobody would love me.'

'When?'

'After Halloween. When we had sweeties.' She sniffed. 'We were given sweeties! Everyone gets sweeties at Halloween.'

Carmen was so angry she could barely sit still.

'She told you that at Halloween? And you've been carrying it around for *months*?'

'I think everyone will love the new baby instead. The new baby won't be fat.'

Carmen straightened Phoebe up until the child was sitting upright on her knee, and turned her round to face her. She looked her straight in the eye.

'You,' she said, 'are beautiful. And perfect. And funny and smart and completely loveable. And do you know how I know that's true?'

Phoebe stared straight into her eyes.

'Because,' said Carmen, 'I don't even *like* children. I never did.'

'Is that why you never sent us presents or came to our birthdays?'

'Absolutely. Couldn't be doing with children at all.' She paused and leaned in close. 'But, Phoebe d'Angelo. My *goodness*, I like you. In fact, I love you, which is very annoying because it is going to cost me a fortune in presents.'

And she gave the child a huge hug. And whispered in her ear for good measure: 'You will never be fat. And even if you were, that is *also fine* because you are *beautiful* to me.'

And Phoebe leaned in and said, 'Are you going to buy presents for all the years you missed?'

And Carmen asked if it was okay if some of the presents were books and Phoebe said that would be fine.

Carmen cuddled and held the child until she fell asleep and soon afterwards Carmen's parents arrived, and her mother's heart nearly broke open seeing her wayward girl love her granddaughter, and there were hugs and imprecations all round, and Carmen's dad found the beanbag in the corner of the room, took Phoebe and Jack under each arm and happily dozed off himself.

In the birthing suite, the midwife was not happy with Sofia, and was practically shouting at her.

'Come on,' she said. 'You really have to push now. This baby wants out, Mum. You have to get on it. Come on.'

Sofia was still wobbling, tearful and wretched. Their mother was standing in a corner, not sure what to do, keeping out of the way. It wasn't like Sofia to lose it, not at all.

'But this isn't how . . . ' Sofia was wailing. 'Federico isn't here! And it's too early! And I didn't get an epidural! And it hurts and I'm *so* tired . . . '

'You have to,' said the midwife. She turned to Carmen. 'Can you get her a bit more motivated?' she said in a low voice. 'The heart rate is dropping a little on the monitor. I'd really like this baby out of here before we have to go full blues on everyone.'

Carmen didn't know what this meant but it sounded bad. She had a plan.

'Sofia,' she said.

Sofia was writhing around.

'Just . . . I'm too tired,' she said, her voice fading away.

'Well, here's a thing,' said Carmen. 'I've just soothed Phoebe

317

to sleep but she really needs you back, and pretty quickly. Because Skylar called her . . . *fat.*'

Sofia frowned.

'She *what?*'

'Way back in October. The little thing has been worrying herself sick about it all this time.'

'*She what?!*'

'I knew she was awful all along.'

'GET ME OFF THIS BED!' said Sofia furiously.

Filled with the energy of molten fury, Sofia channelled her rage, grabbed the bars of the bed, squatted down with her yoga-honed limbs and New Boy Baby D'Angelo was born at 2.15 a.m., surrounded by his loving grandmother and aunt, straight down onto the floor, accompanied by his mother screaming colourful epithets at the ceiling.

Chapter Thirty-four

The hospital weren't kidding about being home for breakfast. As soon as they'd cleaned Sofia up a bit and waited for the placenta, they basically wanted the bed back.

'I'm not driving the baby home,' said Carmen immediately. 'No way. I only just didn't kill you lot.'

Fortunately Federico had charged in at about 7 a.m., his immaculate suit creased, and while Carmen was initially about to give him a sniffy look, surrounded as she was by his slumbering children, she couldn't help but melt a little at his face as he went in to Sofia.

What passed between them Carmen was never a party to, but by the time she brought some fresh tea and the amazing nurse had somehow conjured up some toast for Sofia – the best food, Sofia insisted, she'd ever tasted – and gently knocked on the door of the recovery room, they were both sitting on the bed, buried in one another and staring, hypnotised, at the rather plump, red, screwed-up features of their new baby.

There was a commotion behind her as, roused from their sleep and pursued by their grandmother, Phoebe, Jack and Pippa were standing outside the door, not sure whether or not they could enter.

'Come on in then, you lot!' said Sofia, and Carmen stood back as the door opened widely and the children flooded in. Sofia made a special gesture to Phoebe, beckoning her towards her and, when she got the child within hugging distance, pulled her close and whispered in her ear. Phoebe immediately perked up in surprised happiness and Carmen saw her whisper 'Really?' to her mother, who nodded emphatically. Phoebe beamed in a way Carmen hadn't seen before. Sofia nodded towards Carmen. 'She told me,' she said quite loudly, and Phoebe came over and flung her arms round her aunt.

'You,' said Carmen, bending down, 'are going to be the greatest big sister ever. Do you want to meet him?'

'John!' Jack was shouting. 'James! Jacob! Joseph!'

'Well, I haven't decided,' said Sofia. 'I'm not sure it should be a J name. We're always getting the Ps mixed up.'

'But I thought you liked things nice and symmetrical,' said Carmen, smiling.

Sofia smiled down at the newborn.

'Well, sometimes you can mix things up a bit too,' she said, and Sofia and Carmen smiled at one another.

'Wow,' said Phoebe. 'He looks like a tomato.'

'Phoebe, that is Very Rude,' started Pippa.

'No,' said Sofia firmly. 'He does. Doesn't he?'

'Well, call him Tom then,' said Carmen.

'I'm not calling him Tomato d'Angelo,' said Sofia. 'Mind you ...'

They were still amicably bickering as the nurse came to shoo

320

them all out and make way for the wan-faced women lumbering up and down the corridor, waiting for their own babies as the day shift arrived and new life appeared in the world, and everyone acted as if this was perfectly normal.

'Goodness,' said Carmen, yawning as her father drove them back to the house. 'I am going to be terrible at work today.'

'Auntie Carmen, you're not going to work today!' announced Pippa. 'You have to come to our school concert because Mummy can't.'

'Well, we can come to that,' said their grandmother. 'Once Sofia's settled.'

'But we want Auntie Carmen to come,' said Phoebe in a small voice.

Irene looked at her younger daughter, and for a moment couldn't speak. She squeezed her arm instead.

'Oh, I'll phone Mr McCredie,' said Carmen. 'He can do without me for a half day. I think I've got everything pretty much set up.'

Mr McCredie didn't know what hit him when he woke up with a hangover and had to open the shop entirely by himself. A week to Christmas and there was a steady stream of punters from the very instant he opened the door while fiddling with his coffee cup.

Everything – the Paddington pop-up book, the skiing anthology – all went as the final shopping day loomed and people started to get anxious. He received several offers on the train set, each of which made him lapse into gloom, which customers often took for silence as if he was mulling it over, and generally they upped their offers to no avail.

He was quiet, but thoughtful. Carmen's reaction to his news – sympathy, coupled with amazement that anyone could still worry about it in this day and age – had struck home.

He had been so terrified of letting people know, letting them in after the cruelty he had grown up with at home and at school. The shame, the shame of decades, which had dogged him through relationships, through the death of his parents. His mother had said nothing, ever; left nothing. He had been nothing but a crashing disappointment to his father. The world of books, vast landscapes to play in and hide in, had become his home, and he had hidden in here until almost everything – years, money, life – had gone.

But now, as he saw the happy faces, as his fingers flew while wrapping up brown paper packages with string for excited children and other cheerful customers, and observing the excited tourists taking photographs of the window, he wondered why he had turned away from this for so long.

Carmen had phoned in a gush, so happy that her sister had had her baby and that she now had to take care of the children that day, apologising profusely, and her happiness had bubbled over the telephone. She definitely made him feel more cheerful when she was around.

And they would have a good Christmas. The shop had never made so much money. So. Someone probably would want the business.

He would sell the house. And buy somewhere small, he supposed, as retired people do. One bedroom. Maybe a new flat with triple glazing so it was always warm, somewhere out in the suburbs where there were no steps to get everywhere so he wouldn't risk tripping on the ice. Maybe two bedrooms, one for him and one for his books. Just him. On his own.

'Are you all right?' said the nice lady who was watching him slow down and stop wrapping *The Snow Queen*, which was annoying as it was her last bit of shopping and she was very much looking forward to sitting down and having a coffee at the café Dahlia worked at and if he didn't hurry up it would be eleven o'clock and full of people who had planned to meet there then and she'd miss it and wouldn't get a seat.

'Yes, yes,' said Mr McCredie absently. 'Merry Christmas.'

The woman stopped short on her way out as a handsome, recognisable man held the door open for her. Oh no! How she regretted rushing to make her pre-11 a.m. deadline. She considered pretending she'd forgotten something but the shop was not large and Blair Pfenning – *Blair Pfenning!* – was holding the door for her.

'I'll just sign the rest of the stock,' he said loudly to Mr McCredie, who nodded gratefully.

In behind him slipped Oke, head down. It was the last time, he'd decided. He was fed up with making a fool of himself. It was ridiculous. She didn't want him. He was going home.

He had just thought . . . maybe one last time. Before he caught his flight. Just to say goodbye. To somehow explain, in a way that did not come easily to him, that he did not usually travel expecting to meet people; quite the opposite, in fact.

But he had liked meeting her. Very much.

'Ah,' he said. 'Where's Carmen?' He peered through the back.

'She's not here,' said Mr McCredie, about to explain, direct him the right way, but his head was pounding, and he felt very sick.

'So, yeah, these should do you,' interrupted Blair, brandishing a pile. He'd really also come to see Carmen, and was annoyed she

323

wasn't there. Whatever. There were plenty of women who were very happy to have him. He wasn't going to let her hurt his ego, just because she made him laugh.

'God, I can't believe I made it down. Bit of an exhausting night, know what I mean, lads?'

Blair could not have found two less laddish people to attempt having laddish banter with. Both men stared at him suspiciously.

'The weather up here is freezing but the girls are pretty hot, right? Right?'

Oke's face fell as he cottoned on. He remembered Carmen's expression the night before, deep in intense conversation with Blair, just as Skylar had said. And now Blair was bragging about . . .

No. It was over. He had to forget about it. It was time to go home.

'Goodbye,' he said to Mr McCredie, but he was a world away. 'I suppose I should say Merry—'

'You off, man?' said Blair.

'Yes,' said Oke. 'Back to Brazil.'

Mr McCredie looked up, his face terribly sad for Carmen. Oh, what a rotten shame.

'Wow. They have super-hot babes there too, don't they?' said Blair.

Oke shrugged. 'Well . . . '

Blair beamed at him.

'Well, you have caught me in a good mood – what's your name?'

Oke gave it, and Blair signed a book with a flourish, even though it wasn't technically his and Oke really hadn't wanted to buy it.

'Here,' he said, handing it over. The title of the book was *Love Every Day.*

Chapter Thirty-five

Carmen was worried about turning up to the school not knowing anyone, and having to loiter awkwardly around the school gates looking like a total weirdo, but Phoebe had point-blank refused to go into class on her own and was hanging on to Carmen with all her might and actually there were lots of mothers she recognised from the shop, who nodded and waved to her.

Pippa had marched in, hauling her bassoon and absolutely full of her amazing little brother news, prepared to be queen of the playground, but Phoebe had held back, and Carmen had remembered hearing about the disastrous last time when she'd frozen in front of the whole school.

'Are you doing a solo today?' she said, squeezing her hand.

Phoebe shook her head.

'I'm in the back row,' she said. 'Calintha McGuire is doing it.'

'She sounds *awful*,' said Carmen, and was rewarded with a half-smile. 'There she is.' Phoebe nudged her attention towards a girl in bright blonde immaculate plaits, over-enunciating to a group of acolytes.

'Bloody hell, she *looks* awful,' said Carmen, and Phoebe sniggered. It was lovely to hear the child laugh. 'Well, I've heard you in the bath,' Carmen continued. 'And I have to tell you, I think you're *tremendous*. I can't sing at all. Promise me you'll just perform to me and not all these other people, every single one of whom is stupid. Sing your song just for me. And for the new baby. It can be his song.'

'It *is* about a baby,' said Phoebe thoughtfully.

'Well, there you go. Make it his song. I've heard you singing with the record. Just do that.'

To her disappointment, Skylar hadn't been in when they'd all got home. Carmen wanted to be there when Sofia fired her. Then she wanted to call her back and tell her she was rehired, then fire her herself. It was astonishing how much the fire burned in her. She could handle Skylar making snide remarks to her, and for taking the chap she liked, or thought she'd liked. But as soon as she came for one of her family? No way, matey.

The other mums came up and gathered round, asking about the baby and names, and were full of praise and attention for Phoebe as the newly minted big sister, and Carmen had to wonder really what she had spent all those years sneering at Sofia's friends for.

She found, too, how desperate she was to tell Oke. He had, she knew, a lot of strong opinions about babies. She had spent a good twenty minutes that morning just staring at baby Tom/Finn/James/Albert/Captain America (they weren't quite there yet on names), contemplating his starfish toes and his eyes, a mystical colour between the sky and the sea, and thinking that he was quite impossible to name, and that Oke had quite possibly been right – not about most babies, but *this* baby – that this baby

326

knew every secret of the universe, and was love, uncomplicated, clear as crystal, under every frosted star. How strange that he understood already something she hadn't.

She shook her head and went forward to meet Phoebe's nice teacher, then was ushered into the primary school concert hall, a room that, she couldn't help but notice, was nicer than the school she and Sofia had attended. She took out her phone as she had been informed she had to tape all three classes of the children whether it was forbidden or not.

The children marched in in total silence and perfectly regimented lines; it was partly impressive and partly quite frightening. The parents sat up attentively, but only Carmen, not realising the etiquette, waved frantically to Phoebe as she passed. Phoebe didn't dare lift her hand, but smiled to herself nonetheless.

There were then the adorable nativity antics of the smaller classes, during which, it being rather warm and cosy in the hall, Carmen, who had had almost no sleep, started to drift off. She sat up with a start when the primary fours were announced, fumbling for her phone. There was a little skit about dancing babies which she didn't quite get, then the blonde girl stepped forward and looked anxiously at the music teacher at the piano, who nodded her cue.

'*Little Jesus sweetly sleep,*' she started. '*Do not stir. We will lend a coat of fur.*'

And then the rest of the class joined in, their sweet high voices soft and in unison:

'*We will rock you ... rock you ... rock you ...*'

To Carmen's amazement – she wasn't quite sure she was hearing right – there was one voice which soared above the others, strong and rich, singing loudly and sweetly over the top of the other children. She glanced towards Phoebe, who was staring straight out into the audience, so that she could hopefully spot her aunt across the lights. Clear as day, it was Phoebe singing. Carmen didn't even know if she knew she was doing it; she was simply immersed in making music.

The music teacher was gesticulating wildly and at first Carmen thought she was trying to stop Phoebe, but then she realised she wanted her niece to come forwards to join Calintha for the next verse. Timidly, Phoebe stepped forwards as Calintha started:

'Mary's little baby sleep, sweetly sleep ... sleep in comfort, slumber deep.'

Calintha's voice sounded like she was trying to play Annie in the West End, the result of many expensive singing lessons. Phoebe's came across straight, sweet and true, right from the heart. The hall was silent as the rest of the children joined in again.

'We will rock you, rock you, rock you ...'

And once again, Phoebe's voice, soaring over the rest in counterpoint. Carmen was thinking it was because of how tired she was, and her love for her niece, that there were tears running down her face. But when she glanced around, she saw that she wasn't alone; not even nearly.

Of course Pippa's bassoon solo was very nice, and Jack performed Jack things with his natural energy. But it was undoubtedly Phoebe's day and the smile she beamed at Carmen told her everything, who opened her arms wide to greet her afterwards.

It was still relatively early when she got back to Mr McCredie's, and Carmen quickly joined clearing the queues of people with a smile, telling Mr McCredie about the new baby. He was delighted and she vowed to bring him in as soon as possible.

'Oh, and your chap popped in,' he said.

'Who?' she said, glancing at him nervously.

'Oh, a man came in to sign some books . . .'

'Blair?'

'Yes.'

'Oh,' she said, completely crestfallen. For a moment, just a moment, she had thought he meant Oke, the only person she wanted to see. 'Yeah, he's off to London. Or LA or something, who cares?'

Mr McCredie smiled.

'Oh, and the dendrologist too.'

She stopped serving as a man in a kilt with a large beard patiently waited his turn – it was warmer on his knees in the shop than it was out.

'Oke came here?'

'He did.'

'*He* was in here . . . Did he buy a book?'

'He did.'

'And did he say anything about me? Did he ask about me?'

Mr McCredie looked sad.

'Well . . . he did actually.'

Her head shot up.

'He asked where you were and I told him you weren't here.'

'AND THAT WAS ALL?!'

'I'm so sorry, Carmen! When he didn't show up the other night, I confess I thought that I'd made a mistake with you two, and I shouldn't be interfering anyway.'

Carmen's heart was pounding dangerously.

'But he still came in?'

'Well, he needed a book ...'

Carmen grinned.

'This is Edinburgh. There are more bookshops per head than any city in the world. He can get a book anywhere. I am taking this as a *sign*.'

Mr McCredie sighed.

'Oh lord, we are going down the path of the dreaded lunch-break again, I see.'

Carmen blew him a kiss. Then she glanced at the till.

'I'll make it up to you with Burns Night sales,' she said cheekily.

'Ooh, I say,' said Mr McCredie, as what she'd intimated suddenly made sense to him. No horrible bungalow in the suburbs ... no two rooms ... was it possible?

Then he said, just to make sure, 'What?'

Thinking about Oke hadn't been the only thing that had occupied Carmen the night she had stared over the battlements of Edinburgh Castle. She had meant to find a better time to mention it, but it had just slipped out. If possible, she didn't want to leave this beautiful city. She didn't want to leave Phoebe, and the other two (well, three now) if she could possibly help it. And Victoria Street. This lovely shop.

She wanted to build a life here. They had done well so far. Why not have a shot?

'Um, you know your house upstairs?' she said. 'Just out of interest, how many bedrooms does it have?'

Mr McCredie looked puzzled.

'Well, a few, I suppose.'

Carmen looked at him.

'Okay. Well. Now I have to go because my boss failed to tie the man I love up in the stacks until I got back. But can we discuss this when I get back? Maybe ... prolonging things?'

Mr McCredie nodded, surprised.

Carmen apologised to the man in the kilt, who said that was absolutely fine, he'd just take a seat if that was okay, and banged out of the shop. Then banged in again.

'Where's the biology department?'

'King's Buildings!'

She'd just ask him for Christmas, she told herself, a mass of febrile agitation.

God, Christmas. With a sudden sense of shame, she realised she'd left it – as she always did, every year – for her mum and Sofia to work out between them. Even more shamefully, she thought, her heart starting to pound, she'd moaned at them when they'd asked her what she was doing for Christmas – whether she was coming home (or, latterly, to Sofia's) and she had resented being expected to spend money on the brats, couldn't see the appeal of watching them open their presents – for God's sake, didn't they have enough junk? – didn't want to wear matching bloody sweaters. It used to be a busy time at Dounston's; she usually went out and got drunk with her friends and normally turned up hungover . . .

That wasn't . . . that wasn't what she wanted this year. Not at all. She wanted to be part of all of it. All of it.

She looked at her phone in dismay. She thought the university was in the centre of the city but it turned out half of it was absolutely miles away, on the south side. In her rush, she hailed a cab, jiggling anxiously all the way down town, wincing at every traffic light, until the cabbie turned round.

'You need the bog, hen?'

Carmen frowned. This wasn't exactly what she'd been hoping for from a love dash across the city. She frowned as around her new flakes started to fall from the sky.

'No,' she said. 'I'm fine.'

'Oh bollocks. More bloody snow.'

'It's nice,' said Carmen.

'It's a bloody nonsense,' said the cabbie. 'Cannae get anywhere. Naebady's gawn anywhere. Hate the bloody stuff.'

'Okay,' said Carmen, biting her lip. She hadn't expected there to be so much small talk in her dash.

She thought of Oke though, and felt a thrill go through her. He had come into the shop. Surely there was a chance? Surely?

She sighed happily and glanced at her phone. And God, she would get his bloody number.

She WhatsApped the concert videos off to Sofia with an eye-heart emoji and got a quick thumbs up message back, together with a tiny pic of the baby captioned:

'What do you think about Jesus for a name? Too much?'

She laughed and sent it to her mother too, who to Carmen's slight embarrassment, typed back:

'Darling, just checking. Are you going to be around on Christmas Day?'

Carmen typed back, 'Can I do anything?'

'Oh, no, don't tell anyone but it's just a big roast,' came the response.

'It will be so nice to have us all together.'

'It will.'

Carmen felt a bit guilty typing it, as if she were tempting fate, but even so she did it anyway:

'Can I maybe bring someone?'

The three dots lasted a little while.

'Is it that *ghastly* man from the television?'

It was a proper blizzard by the time she got out of the cab, tipping the driver hugely, who sniffed, 'Only bloody students doon here, no bloody fares, eh?' and turned and took off again.

The King's Buildings campus was large and business-like. Tall buildings erupted from everywhere; students were passing through, chattering, probably heading home for Christmas. Some were wearing tinsel and there was mistletoe everywhere.

They didn't, Carmen thought, look snotty or entitled as she'd always joked about students being with Idra. They didn't look like they thought they were better than anyone else. They just looked normal; some were international, chatting in different languages, shouting and saying hi to each other, but normal.

Well.

'Excuse me,' she said. 'Can you tell me where biology is?'

'Sure,' said the first person she stopped. 'Biological sciences is the big grey building.'

'They're all big grey buildings!'

'One, two ... third on the left. Over there.'

Nobody was checking ID at the door of the low unattractive building, but Carmen was still daunted. It was quiet; lectures must be over for the term.

Oh God. Maybe she should have stayed in town after all and just sat outside the halls of residence, hoping she saw him before she froze to death. This was maybe an even stupider idea than that would have been.

She followed a sign that said 'PhD offices', hoping a nice member of staff would take pity on her once she finally got there. She was beginning to feel very tired and slightly spacey.

There was nobody in the offices either. It must be their Christmas lunch or something. She nearly cried. There were, however, doors leading down a large corridor, with names on each one. Surnames, which wasn't helpful. But many of them had little jokes on them – cartoons, or signs. And on one of them was a Gary Larson cartoon of his usual pointy-headed men examining the rings of an old tree and saying something that made no sense to Carmen whatsoever but was presumably hilarious if you knew a lot about trees.

Dr Benezet, it said. So. Dr Benezet was his name. Carmen rubbed her mouth. How strange – to come so far, and not remember his name.

She ran her fingers through her hair, blotted on some lipstick – God, she must look knackered.

Well. She couldn't think about that now. She couldn't. All she could think about was him. She steeled herself – and knocked.

There was no answer. Nothing. The entire building really did feel empty, as if there had been a fire alarm; she was sure she could sense nobody there. She turned the handle of the door and found it swinging open.

With a guilty sense of trespassing, she walked in. The window faced over the town; you could just see a snow-topped Arthur's Seat. The snowfall outside was thickening by the minute.

But in the room itself there was nothing. A whiteboard left

with a beautifully intricate sketch of some deep roots on it. Blu-Tack on the walls where perhaps pictures had been.

No computer; an empty desk, a lamp, an office chair and a sitting chair, with several other stacked chairs for seminars. Nothing else. A long bookshelf, with nothing but a thin line of dust on it. No books.

Carmen swallowed, a mounting dread growing in her. No. It wasn't possible. He hadn't gone. He was staying. He'd *told* her. That he ... that he might stay.

She heard footsteps and turned round, panicked, looking back up the corridor.

The figure advanced slowly, carrying a large paper box and as it gradually revealed itself, Carmen felt her heart pound.

'Skylar,' she said.

Skylar stared at her.

'Oh. You. Are you looking for Oke?'

Carmen felt a tiny prick of hope.

'Yes ...'

'He's gone.'

'Gone where?'

'Gone home. He decided not to extend. Why did you want to see him?'

Carmen couldn't answer that.

'Have you spoken to Sofia?' she said instead.

Skylar let out a hollow laugh.

'Oh yes. Don't worry about me. I don't need to work with those damaged kids for a second longer.'

'They're great kids!'

Skylar shrugged.

'None of you are in the least bit spiritual. None of you. It's so damaging.'

'No,' said Carmen, finding it in herself to smile. 'Well. Maybe not.'

She frowned.

'Where will you go?'

'Oh, don't worry about me,' said Skylar. 'I'm going to London for Christmas with Blair. Oh sorry, is that a sore spot?'

Carmen looked at her.

'Nope,' she said.

In fact, Blair had not invited Skylar at all and was making increasingly strenuous excuses to stop her coming, but Skylar had a gleam of persistence about her and couldn't bear to go back to her parents' new-build tiny little house on an executive estate just outside Slough where they called her by her birth name – Janet – and lived off Iceland lasagne which they ate in front of *Come Dine With Me* while talking about the Neighbourhood Watch scheme. A fate worse than death. She'd take her chances with Blair, even if he was spending a lot of time asking her to leave the hotel as he had work to do.

'But I did want to see Oke.'

'Well, you're too late,' said Skylar gleefully. 'He's flying out. I saw him at ...'

She realised her mistake and stopped.

'At what?'

'Uh, at your party,' she said quickly.

'But you said he wasn't there,' said Carmen, tears springing to her eyes.

'Um, yeah. Well, maybe I missed him then ... anyway. You know, you look upset. You should really try meditating? And chilling? And your diet can't help—'

'You. Are. *Vile*,' said Carmen. And she turned and fled.

Chapter Thirty-six

Outside, the snow was thicker than ever. There wasn't a cab to be seen anywhere. Blinded by the flakes and her tears, Carmen saw a bus coming and jumped on, waving her phone at the ticket point.

It was nearly empty, and she found a seat in the back upstairs where, as the bus trundled on, she could let the tears fall and drip down.

She thought of Mr McCredie, living his life tied up in shame, missing opportunities because he had spurned them. She thought of herself, turning away from opportunities, from education and work and all that life had to offer, in case she failed, in case it went wrong. It had taken the combined efforts of her entire family just to get her to take a new job, which had ended up changing her life.

She had been so scared to try. She had been too timid. And look, she was too late. She sighed, tears from the weather dribbling down the window in sympathy. She looked out into the fading light. The buildings were disappearing behind her, rather than approaching; she was moving away from the centre of the city, and home and at least the consolation of a family who loved her. Now they had crossed the bypass and were out in the countryside.

Oh God. She realised in her confusion she must have come out of a different exit, and taken a bus going the wrong way. Oh God. Where even was she?

She wobbled downstairs and jumped off the bus in a panic before she got even further away from home. She was standing in the freezing cold, with a rapidly decreasing phone battery, alongside a housing estate. She followed it, trying to pull up a map on her phone – and gradually she recognised where she was.

Ormiston. Why did she recognise that name? Ormiston. She sniffed.

Of course. His favourite tree. And now he was gone, all the way to the other side of the earth, unimaginably far.

She stumbled forwards. Where was it? She could shelter under it and call a cab, surely. There must be one somewhere but her hands were too cold to press on the phone and the battery was running out.

Increasingly chilled and starting to get frightened in the dark, as the street lights popped on above her, she couldn't figure out what to do. Federico could drive out and get her but he needed to be there with the children. Her thin woollen gloves were not helpful, especially as she kept having to take them off to try her phone. Her hair was covered in white flakes; her cheeks streaked with tears.

She stumbled down the track, remembering the instructions: keep left. The snow was higher than her boots; she was starting to shiver. It was so dark, just the lights from remote houses leading her on through a wooded lane, deeper and deeper.

Finally, in the fading light, she turned her head round to a path stretching to the right – and she saw it.

There was the tree – huge, broad, all-encompassing – ahead of her. It was beautiful, extraordinary.

She would sit inside, she told herself sensibly, even though it was not at all a sensible thing to do and, sleep-deprived and chilled she was not thinking remotely sensibly, get out of the snow and the wind, use her phone properly and figure out how to get home. She could go home and head into her little bedroom and maybe take the baby for a cuddle and cry a lot. If the baby was crying at the same time, well, all to the good. Then she would make some hot chocolate and pretend it was for the children. Another run on *The Muppet Christmas Carol* might not go amiss.

She felt, absurdly, like the little match girl, but without a match to light.

The smell of the deep ancient green made her think, and pause, and take in several deep breaths as she crawled through the narrow alleyway to the tree, a space cleared in the huge overhanging boughs. She was deeply, deeply cold, she realised. But here the wind was stilled; the snow could not penetrate the huge ancient branches, the heavy canopy of leaves. It was a cathedral of high green struts; stained green glass, brown-timbered pews. It was a place of worship. She slumped against the thickest of the multi-stranded trunks.

A noise came, a quiet rustle. A bird? A fox perhaps? There it came again. She froze. A rustling noise. She couldn't see a thing; it was pitch-dark beneath the tree. She fumbled with her phone, but she couldn't use the battery life up on the torch: she was miles from home and would never get back without it.

'He— Hello?' she called out.

'Hello?' came the voice back, slow, steady, assured.

It couldn't be. Her fevered consciousness was imagining things. Maybe she was becoming hypothermic. Her heart raced. Oh God. She was dreaming. This was awful.

'Carmen? Is that you?'

It wasn't possible. She stood, stock-still, frozen, then thinking that she could back away – run, stop any car, grab any bus, just get out of there and her stupid, over-fevered imagination. She managed to take one step backwards.

'Carmen?'

He put on his torch. She couldn't see a thing, completely dazzled by the light. She wanted to shout and run, but was stuck to the spot against the ancient trunk.

'It is you! No way! What are you doing here?!'

Her voice stuck in her throat; she was completely hoarse.

'Oke?'

'Of course!' She blinked as he came into focus. 'Who else?'

'But ... but you've gone home! You've gone!'

He glanced at his phone, turning the torch over.

'In three hours,' he said. 'I was about to start making for the airport. I came ... I came to say goodbye. To the tree,' he added hastily. 'It's odd – I kept ... I kept dreaming about it.'

Carmen didn't hear this.

'I ... I wanted to say goodbye,' she said, her voice low and hoarse. 'I wanted to say goodbye to you.'

'I came to the party at the bookshop,' frowned Oke. 'Did Skylar not tell you? I came to see you at the shop but she said you had a thing with Blair.'

340

'What? *Blair?*'

'Uh, yes? Then I saw Blair and he said he'd been with you . . .'

'Did he say that? Did he say those actual words?'

Carmen no longer felt cold, but boiling with molten fury. She saw Oke's face frown in the torchlight.

'Well, not exactly—'

'No, because it wasn't me! It's Skylar who was with Blair! I don't like him at all.'

'But I saw you speaking to him!'

'Yes. He texted me,' said Carmen. And she forced herself to do what he was doing: to be honest.

'I liked him to begin with. Then I saw what he was really like. And . . . and I got to know you.'

He looked at her, hope leaping in his heart.

'Are you sure?'

She shook her head and took the tiniest, most tentative step forwards, and realised she was trembling.

'Oh no,' she said. 'Oh. No.'

'You're frozen,' he said, examining her closely. 'Come here. Come here.'

And before she had the chance to think about it, he had her hands in his larger ones, soft and strong, and was holding them together.

'You are *freezing.*'

He drew her closer and she found herself still terrified, heart still racing, but in such a different way and for such a different reason.

'Can you . . . can you warm them up for me?' she found herself saying. He grinned, and took them and buried them under his four layers of clothing and her eyes popped wide open as she felt his bare back, his flat muscular stomach, his hairless chest.

'Oh!' she said.

'Better?' he said.

'So much,' she said, even though they stung as warmth drew back into them.

'Oh God, are you really going? Now?!' she added. She looked up at him.

'Oh, my mother would be disappointed if I don't. My sisters will think it is funny.'

'Yes, but it's not like you're going home for Christmas, is it?' she said, inching closer, her hands warming and unable, it turned out, to stop themselves from running up and down the smooth brown skin of his muscular back. Jesus, she found herself muttering under her breath.

'Is this very Quakery?' she said as she touched him.

'Do I have to keep explaining?' he said, smiling.

'No,' she said. 'I see it.'

'What do you see?'

She looked up.

'A religion. Without a church.'

The rustle of the leaves in the wind, the quieting sounds of the birds, the deep muffling of the snow.

'This is your church.'

He nodded.

'This is my church.'

'There are things you shouldn't do in church,' she said, suddenly mischievous. He looked at her, eyes glinting.

'Well,' he said. 'This is my church, nobody else's.'

'That's true. So you can make your own rules.'

He smiled.

342

'I should tell you my name,' he said.

'Oh, you should!' said Carmen.

'It is not a very good name for me.'

'I'll be the judge of that.'

'It's Obedience.'

'Obedience is your name?'

'It is. My sisters called me Obi and I thought they were saying Okay and, well, here we are.' He grinned. 'So I have left my family, travelled across the world, studied nature, and ...' He stroked her face very gently. 'Well. It turns out I am not a very obedient person.'

Carmen smiled.

'Oh, me neither.'

'Is your mouth cold?' he asked softly.

'Yes,' said Carmen.

And under a tree that was centuries old when Mary Queen of Scots was a child, that had seen plotting and murder and history pass beneath its boughs, that was so old Pontius Pilate's father could have known it, one more event in time was added: the best of many, many, many kisses that tree had seen.

They stumbled back up the muddy track, completely wrapped up in one another, Oke pulling his suitcase.

'What was your plan for getting to the airport?' said Carmen.

'There has to be a railway station,' he said. 'Look.'

They followed the map, but Carmen didn't feel optimistic. This wasn't a road to a brightly lit station; this was yet another muddy track up the side of the pretty village.

But somehow, wrapped up in this man, she no longer felt cold and she no longer cared, despite their dying phones' flashing warnings of transport disruptions and yellow and red warnings for snow and ice; cancellations and delays.

There was no station, no sign. There was a double rail track which was overgrown with moss and weeds, and a neglected little platform, cracked and overgrown too.

'I don't think this is going to work,' whispered Carmen in a dreamy voice. 'But I don't want you to go to the airport so I don't even care.'

The little train station, when they eventually found it, looked deserted. Warnings on their phones indicated all transportation had stopped, all journeys were finished, and people were being urged to stay indoors. They were going to figure something out – they had to. Oke had already managed to postpone his flight – and it was a good fifteen miles back into town, which was simply unmanageable. They walked down the little overgrown platform anyway.

Just as Carmen was about to suggest they give up, a light appeared down the track, and an answering green signal came on overhead, signalling go.

The train appeared; it was old rolling stock with a flat red nose. It stopped, but nobody got off; no conductor looked out to see if there was anyone there. Oke tried a door when they did not open automatically, and the handle opened to his grip and they climbed on, slightly giggling.

Inside, the train was completely empty; everyone must have obeyed the warnings on the radio as the snow streaked across the glass. The carriages were so old they still had sliding glass doors and separate compartments.

They walked up and down the corridors, hand in hand.

'I think it's just us,' whispered Carmen. She wasn't sure why she was whispering. There wasn't a guard, or anyone blowing a whistle; just the train surging into the swirling winter darkness.

They found a compartment, dimly lit with a small orange lamp at the window. They sat opposite one another; he was looking at her with a challenging eye and she held it as the strange little train racketed on through the dark countryside, the ancient lamps dimming and lighting again with every chuntering surge of motion and the old wheels clattered down the track.

Suddenly, Carmen couldn't take it any more. She stood up. And moved over. So there could be no mistaking what she meant. She did not break eye contact and he smiled easily and lifted her into his arms.

The lights of the trains stuttered and blinked on and off as they entered a long tunnel. When they emerged, Carmen was sitting on his lap. Another flash and he was kissing her deeply; another flicker and their heads were pressed close together. The train sped up and a whistle blew.

Chapter Thirty-seven

'Don't make me do it!' said Carmen at breakfast, not long before Christmas. Federico was taking the children to school; Sofia was staying in bed with the as-still-unnamed baby (Obedience had been briefly mooted, and speedily discarded), happily eating toast and accepting the many gifts the amazing Edinburgh witch ladies had somehow had the time before Christmas to find and tactfully choose and beautifully wrap and send to the house. They were amazing.

Sofia was also getting used to Federico and Carmen being the most irritating double act in history: Federico would say, 'Darling, I told you you had to slow down,' and Carmen would chime in, 'That's *exactly* what I have been saying,' and Federico would say, 'You don't need to organise everything,' and Carmen was like, '*Right!*' She liked them ganging up on her. Although she already had big plans for throwing the most impressive Burns' supper Edinburgh had ever seen, and it had seen a few. She was also looking forward to Federico being at home for a whole month – he had pretty much just resigned himself to lying on the floor while the children jumped on him, and playing nine solid hours of football a day with Jack – as well as the fairly monster Christmas present she was planning on reminding him she wanted. Things, she thought, really could not be better.

'But you have to do a story!' said Phoebe, cheerfully spooning up the cornflakes Carmen thought would probably do as a post-oatmeal compromise. 'That's what you do now!'

'It is not what I do now! It's always a disaster!'

'You should pick a good book?' said Pippa, helpful as ever. 'You know all those terrible books you are always picking? I suggest that instead you should pick a good one, Auntie Carmen.'

'Thank you for that,' said Carmen. 'Have you got one you would recommend?'

'Yes,' said Pippa. 'It's about a girl band saving Christmas on their magic unicorn. All the unicorns have different kindness skills.'

Oke looked up from the other side of the sofa.

'Yes! You have to do a story!'

'Yeah, all right, Christmas expert,' said Carmen, giggling. Oke was staying at Mr McCredie's shop. Mr McCredie, as it turned out, had never wanted lodgers before, but was finding it wasn't necessarily the worst thing in the world. He had rather taken to having a roommate who could talk about Neolithic forests with him all day and night so everyone was happy, Carmen in particular.

Oke came to pick Carmen up every morning to walk her to work. She had explained to the children that she might have a sleepover at her friend's soon, but she liked to be at the house for now to let Sofia lie in in the morning.

And she was finding it extremely exciting to think of Oke as a present she could not quite yet unwrap.

'Okay, okay,' she said.

'Now remind me,' said Sofia, looking tired but happy as she headed downstairs. 'Remind me how many are we on the day?'

'Isn't Mum doing this?'

'Just let me over-organise, please, sis; helps my stress levels.'

'But if I do it, we get to watch Christmas *Top of the Pops*.'

The children looked at her, their faces confused.

'Pop music. You're going to love it.'

'Carmen!'

'And Frosties. Come on. Let's have Frosties on Christmas Day. In fact, let's stay in our pyjamas *all day*. And *no bassoon*.'

'Go! To! Work!' said Sofia, but she was smiling really.

There was an even larger crowd than usual now the school holidays had started, and Carmen opened an old book, the most expensive they had to sell, and told them the story of the animals turning silent on the stroke of midnight on Christmas Eve, and the children's eyes were wide, and there was silence, and at the end everyone got a very small chocolate Santa and went home happy.

As the families dispersed, there were two tall people still standing at the door.

'We go tomorrow,' said the German woman. 'We just thought we should try. One more time . . . '

Carmen gripped Mr McCredie's hand tight and, nodding numbly, he turned the shop sign to closed, and took them upstairs.

'I'll leave you to it,' she said. 'Would you like tea?'

'Oh Carmen,' said Mr McCredie in a quavery voice. 'Please stay.'

So she did.

They had found the papers clearing out their grandfather's house – letters from the POW camp, from his youngest brother Erich, describing the conditions – and a nurse, Marian, who worked there. Mr McCredie's mother.

'I will show you the letters, of course,' said the woman. 'Although there are some parts you may not want to read.'

Mr McCredie sat there, listening.

'I think,' she added, 'I think they were very much in love. He was very young.'

'How young?'

'Seventeen.'

Mr McCredie took a sharp intake of breath.

'Goodness.'

'He was on a U-boat, patrolling the North Sea. Just a boy. He was conscripted, late in the war . . . '

Mr McCredie looked numb, his pale eyes staring out of the window.

'What happened to him?' said Carmen, when it was clear Mr McCredie didn't know how to ask.

'Oh,' said the woman. 'He was returned by the British, and shot as a spy.'

'You're kidding.'

She shook her head.

'It was . . . It was a hard time all round.'

Mr McCredie nodded, tears in his eyes.

'Did he . . . did he know about me?'

'I don't think so,' said the woman. 'When is your birthday?'

349

They matched the days. Mr McCredie nodded. 'He would have gone before my mother even knew.'

Silence fell. Carmen took Mr McCredie's shaking hand and squeezed it.

'You don't have to be ashamed,' she said. The visitors shook their heads.

'She gave me his name,' he said. 'I always, always hated it.'

Carmen looked at him in surprise. She had never even asked his first name. Goodness, she didn't know anyone's name.

'What, Erich?'

'Eric,' he said. 'Common enough in Edinburgh, of course. My father didn't suspect, or he didn't let on. But the other boys ...'

He shook his head.

'It's a nice name,' said Carmen again, squeezing his hand.

'It *is* a nice name,' said Sofia, as Carmen related the whole story over dinner.

They looked at each other, and over at the bassinet.

'No way,' said Carmen. 'No. He hates his name, never uses it.'

'That's before he found out his father was only a boy. A poor, frightened boy, by the sound of things.'

'I believe Sofia has her "mind made up" face on,' came Federico from the floor.

'Do you like it?' demanded Carmen.

'I do, as it happens,' said Federico. 'But I would have said I did even if I didn't.'

'*How* are you such a successful lawyer?'

'This will be a clean slate for him,' said Sofia decisively. 'And it's about him, not his father. Eric. Yes.'

She picked up the beautiful baby. 'We'll tell him when he comes for Christmas lunch.'

'Oh!' said Carmen. 'I forgot. He's not coming.'

'You're kidding?'

'I'm sorry!'

'What's he doing? Spending it with his new family?'

'No, although now *apparently* I have to make lots of money for the shop because he wants to visit them.' Carmen rolled her eyes. 'Then he wants to take a trip to the Antarctic. Apparently cruise ships go there.'

'So why isn't he coming for Christmas?'

Carmen covered her face.

'Oh my God. He's going to Mrs Marsh's.'

'Your old boss?!'

'Don't. Make. Me. Think. About. It.'

Sofia laughed.

'I think that's lovely!'

'She only has *one bosom.*'

'What's a bosom?' said Phoebe.

'Who wants to hang stockings?' said Carmen.

There was a family pile of stockings, each with a name embroidered on it. Typical Sofia overkill.

As she leafed through them though, she pulled out two more, one with 'Carmen' and one with 'Oke' on it.

'What?!' she said. 'When did you do these?!'

Sofia smiled an irritating smile.

'Oh, want something done, ask a busy person.'

'You are just *showing off*!'

They were a happy band round the Christmas Day table, introducing Oke to everything new which was hilarious to the children, particularly when he tried to pull a cracker by himself.

The turkey was perfect, the roast potatoes plentiful, and as they sat down at the table, the children pulled away from their lovely new wooden doll's houses (Santa) and plastic light sabre electronic game kit (Carmen). Sofia and Carmen's mother gestured to the newest place set at the table, whom she approved of, very much.

'Oke, would you like to say grace?'

He smiled.

'Ah sorry … we don't say grace in my culture. We take a moment of silence, to listen to the still, small voice within all of us. Not just on this … I suppose, this "special day". All days are special days. Every day we should feel, I hope, a little grace. And we can use it to bring peace in everything we do, to reconcile and bear quiet witness to our common humanity. Sorry. I don't really have anything special to say …'

'Actually,' said their mother, 'that was perfect.'

Epilogue

The adults were dozing or talking about boring things down-stairs, and Pippa and Phoebe had scrambled away to find something else to do. There was a tiny glass vial of something sitting on Carmen's dressing table.

'Don't grab that,' said Pippa. 'It's not yours.'

'I just want to smell it,' said Phoebe, opening the little swirly stopper. Instantly some spilled out onto the floor.

'Oh no!' she said, looking at her sister in terror.

'It's all right,' whispered Pippa, after a long pause.

'Let's not bother them; they'll just get cross with both of us. Let's clean it up together.'

'Okay,' said Phoebe, and they went and grabbed the most expensive towels from the bathroom to do so.

'What do you think it is?' said Phoebe as they scrubbed.

'It's from the magic shop,' said Pippa, reading the label. 'Wow! Maybe it's a love potion for Uncle Oke.'

'Hahaha,' said Phoebe. 'You can't call him that!'

'I'm just saying. Maybe.'

'Maybe it is,' said Phoebe. 'Hang on – if we fill it up with water, she won't know we spilt it.'

'Okay,' said Pippa. 'But that means we'll never know what the magic potion was.'

'Yeah, well,' said Phoebe. 'Still. Don't mention it. Okay? Sister pinky-swear?'

'Sister pinky-swear.'

Acknowledgements

Huge thanks to Jo Unwin, Lucy Malagoni, Rosanna Forte, Milly Reilly, Donna Greaves, Joanna Kramer, Charlie King, David Shelley, Stephanie Melrose, Gemma Shelley and all at Little, Brown; Deborah Schneider, Rachel Kahan, Rhina Garcia and all at William Morrow; Felicitas von Lovenburg, Jennifer Lindstrom, Lina Sjogren, Vivian Leandro, Kjersti Herland Johnsen, Nana Vaz de Castro, Ambre Rouvière, Alexander Cochran, Jake Smith-Bosanquet, and Kate Burton.

Special thanks to: Andrew Johnson of Camera Obscura for showing me round that magnificent establishment, Ian Rankin for walking me back from King's Buildings, Lit Mix, Weegies and a special thank you and huge love to Mr B who took on every single bit of cooking, housework and homeschooling during lockdown 3 so I could write this little extra bonus book I was so desperate to write. I can't express how lucky and grateful I am.

Don't miss Jenny's new heart-warming novel ...

Read on for an exclusive extract

OUT JUNE 2023

My great-grandfather, Captain Ranald Murdo MacIntyre of the RAF City of Aberdeen Auxiliary Squadron 612, was not a tall man. That was possibly, most people agreed, what made him so damn feisty in the first place.

He was stocky, though, with a bullet head and an expression that almost dared you to tell him not to defy him and then face the consequences. He was one of those for whom the war was a great time; a huge adventure that broke open his small view of the world from a small town on the north coast of Scotland.

He joined up right away – RAF, back when the life expectancy of those boys was about six months. From the second he took off in a spitfire, he loved it. He flew fearlessly and into anything, defending the Firth of Forth, and almost entirely buzzing their arch enemies –not the Luftwaffe, as it happened, but 602, the Glasgow Auxiliary Squadron, their west-coast rivals – more than was strictly necessary.

Finally, before his six months were up and the law of averages took him – not that Ranald MacIntyre had any truck with those – the RAF grounded him at Leuchars, and got him to train the next cohort, and the next, which he did with the same exuberant vehemence with which he had tackled the skies. And when the war was over, the chances of him going back to tend the family croft had dwindled to nothing.

He found a little plane, a Cessna from somewhere – it was

entirely possible, word went, that the RAF had given it to him simply to make him go away, as teaching pilots suicidal combat bravery wasn't quite as popular a requirement in the post-war period as it had been before – and immediately started a service flying the archipelago, the majestic chain of islands that run off the north coast of Scotland , which up until then had been connected with only intermittent ferries or, just as often, sail- and rowboats.

The islands thought they had been doing fine on their own, thank you very much, and didn't need this ungodly noisy oily interference in the rhythms of their year, until they started to find it more and more useful to get hold of a paper that was only a day old, or being able to visit a doctor or even spend a day visiting the huge big tempting cities and bright lights of Oban and Inverness. The kirk wasn't pleased, but not much pleased them anyway.

And the tiny air taxi service, which would stop and pick up more or less anyone anywhere, thrived. First for the novelty value, secondly for the convenience of the thing and thirdly for Ranald's complete inability to be put off or phased by all but the very worst of the weather, and if you are familiar with the north coast of Scotland at all, you will know that that is a formidable talent.

Everyone thought Ranald MacIntyre was married to that plane, so almost everyone was as surprised as he was when at the age of fifty he married pretty Margaret Wise from Thurso and had baby Murdo the next year.

Young Murdo soon became a regular sight sitting up in the cockpit with his dad, and Ranald's old mate Jimmy Convery, who was from the slums of Glasgow, so rough you could barely understand a word he said, and the best and most faithful co-pilot Ranald ever had. Ranald knew that Jimmy had never had a home to go back to after the war, and only the barest bones of one afore it, so when they were demobbed, Ranald brought Jimmy back and they rented the old draughty house not even the curate wanted, and Jimmy never left.

Murdo grew up and went to flying school at sixteen, which you could in those days. Very little can unsettle the pilot who has grown up landing in Scottish weather conditions: frequent fog, sideways rain, snow, hail, all on tiny runways. Inchborn, an island in the archipelago chain without a runway at all, simply had a long beach, so Ranald landed on that at low tide.

At twenty-one, Murdo borrowed the money to buy a new plane – *Dolly*, a brand-new Twin Otter which was his pride and joy – and tried to professionalise the operation a little with schedules, regular deliveries and touring schedules for people's new disposable incomes. But they were never above taking an extra parcel as a favour if they had the weight allowance, or picking up mums and babbies for a very small charge if they needed to get to the mainland for their check-ups, or helping out the air ambulance if need be.

Murdo married young, anxious to get raising the next generations of MacIntyre Air, and young Iain was just as devoted to flying as his dad and his granddad had been.

He was the light and joy of their days, as like Murdo as Murdo had been like Ranald, and excited plans were made to expand the fleet one day – until Iain, told to bring a punnet of red apples from the market, returned with a punnet of green, and the terrible truth emerged: not only was he severely colour-blind but his eyesight in general was also shocking, and the optician in Wick had quite a lot to say about why they hadn't brought the lad in earlier.

For Iain, it was a blow akin to being an injured professional footballer. A maudlin teenager, he took his new, huge NHS glasses off to accountancy school, studied hard and got a job in the finance department of a large commercial airline company based out of Aberdeen, where he got to spend his days in the company of pilots, dealing with the finances of aeroplanes, handling invoices and billing for planes and fuel and cargo, but never ever flying one. It was hard to tell if it were more consolation or torture for the boy who only ever dreamed of being able to fly.

But there was always the next generation. It's not that Iain MacIntyre asked very pointed questions about the eyesight of every woman he dated, but when he met Katherine Trawley, bonny, red-haired and better than twenty-twenty, it was pretty much a foregone conclusion, and when Jamie came along, the scene was set.

Whereupon Jamie cried and wailed whenever he was put to the skies on those long summer days up in Wick, and couldn't understand why people were constantly trying to strap him into a terrifying and noisy metal tin can when there was an entire beach outside with sand and sea and crabs and birds and shrimping nets and wildlife and all the beauties of nature that happen at the glorious top end of Scotland. He made such an infernal fuss that eventually the family gave up and turned reluctantly to their next best hope, babby Morag.

And, well, that was me.

My great-grandfather Ranald's medals lined the shelf of the big old draughty house in Carso, the northernmost town in Sutherland at the very top of the Scottish Highlands, with its tiny airfield and old grey stone houses, the wind blowing all the time, where the North and the Irish Seas met. I remembered him, just, as a crusty presence, firm in demeanour, given to occasional bursts of hearty laughter at jokes I didn't get and a fondness for launching into very long stories that most people had heard before.

Margaret died young of breast cancer, when Murdo was twenty – one of the reasons he wanted to get married so young, my mother thought – and Ranald had carried on, living with his best mate Jimmy Convery all his life. Jimmy didn't say much, but punctuated the anecdotes with throaty laughter fuelled by Woodbines. I remembered him dimly as a whiskery, slightly unnerving presence, but Murdo – Gramps – worshipped him, and I worshipped Gramps, so I figured he must have been okay.

The joy in that house – we lived outside Aberdeen but spent many weekends and all our summers up in Carso – when I showed an interest in flying was extraordinary to me. Ranald passed away the same year, Jimmy not long after, and there was a family superstition that he was somehow reincarnated in me.

I was used to Jamie being the centre of attention as he was an unusually pretty child, red-haired and grey-eyed. I had wild curly black hair that apparently Margaret had shared, but gave me, personally, nothing but grief, as I grew up at the height of GHDs and pencil-thin brows. At school, they called me Morag Grobag, because it looked like I'd been planted in one.

Jamie was clever, sensitive and a wonderful artist. I was quiet, terribly shy and, as the first girl in three generations, felt more or less inadequate. Until I clambered up in the cockpit of the Twin Otter.

It was immediate: the entire family's pride, and what felt suspiciously like relief. Everywhere we went, every summer, I was their little lady pilot, Morag, saviour of McIntyre Air. People would stop us on the street, talk about flying to me, while Jamie stood sullenly to the side, clutching the sketch pad that was never far out of reach, waiting to vanish at the first opportunity to the nearest burn or tree.

I remember taking my options at school but not as if I had much choice in the matter – maths for reckoning; physics, geography, obviously. Raising money for flight school felt like a full family operation – it's *really*, really expensive, even if you do have a guaranteed job at the end of it. So expensive. Everyone made sacrifices, and I felt that, very much. But I did learn to fly, and there was no stopping me. This sounds terrible, but as soon as I realised it got me more attention than my lovely, popular brother, I was in absolutely full bore.

I was such a shy, nervous child. My mother had to peel me off her when I went to nursery or primary school. I had precisely one friend, Nalitha Khan, who was the opposite of shy, and let me scurry along in her wake. But then, when the family hit upon me following into the family business – well, then everything changed. The chatty gossipy town where my grandfather lived – which normally intimidated me as the old ladies chivvied me to "speak up then, yon wee Morag, och, you're so peely-wally; it's a shame, with Jamie so bonny" – became somewhat easier to handle.

I kind of thought that it would all get even easier when I started flight school. In fact, the first thing ninety per cent of people said to me was "oooh, you're surrounded by those handsome pilots all the time, lucky you" which is obviously, you know, durr, very, very sexist and also rather disappointingly not at all the case. It was mostly men, but they saw me and the other couple of women in the class as mates, honorary lads practically. They were all off chasing the beautiful blonde drama students next door just like everyone else. Which is good, you know. I like being treated as a professional. Of course I did. They were just very, very, possibly too professional.

It was fine, being one of the guys. I was a good student, and good at what I did, and I was never excluded from anything. And I did like discussing engines and windspeed over a couple of pints of lager, of course I did. And talking about cars.

Then Jai and Abdul and Connor would all get into their very fancy cars and drive off and pick up other less technical girls for nights out, and I would just go home to the little newbuild flat I had rented because it was near the airport and not too expensive, no other reason. It was just a place to lay my head between shifts.

I dated a couple of engineers and that was fine, but once I graduated from flight school and moved into a proper job, well, I was just away all the time. So basically, I was a bit too square for the people who were used to people being away all the time, but a bit too exotic for people who weren't. For example, with men, either they were a bit intimidated by my job and never mentioned it ever, but talked a lot about how good they were at fixing cars, or they would ask me loads about crashes and terrifying things which, up until extremely recently, had never happened to me or anyone I know – it's really, *really* rare. Or they'd kind of pretend to feel sorry for me, asking me if it wasn't incredibly boring, mixing the reality of their bad travelling experiences with my wonderful job.

And I didn't know how to explain, not exactly, the feeling when you are just, *just* on the very tip of lifting a huge bird off the face of the earth; the exact second when you go from trundling along the ground, earthbound, to lifting up, up, then suddenly bursting free the chains of gravity; soaring up through the clouds, bursting through, even on the greyed and dullest of days, the poor commuters left far below, endlessly beetling through traffic in the rain while you join the great route of kings, the blue sky stretching ahead of you, the darker curve beyond all yours, laid out in front of you, the clouds soft cushions you wave past and even the snow-topped mountains cowering beneath your dominion.

Which is my way of saying that normally I really, really love my job. Or at least I used to.

But when it comes to dating, I won't lie, it's a conundrum.

Escape with
JENNY COLGAN

Escape to a remote little Scottish island and meet the
charmingly eccentric residents of Mure...

**'Charming, made me long to
escape to Mure. Total joy'**
SOPHIE KINSELLA

Escape with
JENNY COLGAN

In a quaint seaside resort, where the air is rich with the smell of fresh buns and bread, a charming bakery holds the key to another world…

'Deliciously warm and sweet'
SOPHIE KINSELLA

Escape with
JENNY COLGAN

In a delightful little sweet shop, pocket money jangles, paper bags rustle and, behind the many rows of jars, secret dreams lie in wait...

'An evocative sweet treat'
JOJO MOYES

~ DREAM WITH ~
# JENNY COLGAN

Keep in touch with Jenny and her readers:

f JennyColganBooks **🐦** @jennycolgan

📷 JennyColganBooks

Check out Jenny's website and sign up to her newsletter for all the latest book news plus mouth-watering recipes.

www.jennycolgan.com

LOVE TO READ?

Join **The Little Book Café** for competitions,
sneak peeks and more.

f TheLittleBookCafe **🐦** @littlebookcafe